LET
THE
SKY
FALL

Also by Shannon Messenger

Let the Storm Break

Keeper of the Lost Cities

Keeper of the Lost Cities, Book 2:
Exile

LET THE SKY FALL

BOOK ONE IN THE SKY FALL SERIES

SHANNON MESSENGER

Simon Pulse

New York   London   Toronto   Sydney   New Delhi

SIMON PULSE

An imprint of Simon & Schuster Children's Publishing Division
1230 Avenue of the Americas, New York, NY 10020
First Simon Pulse paperback edition December 2013
Text copyright © 2013 by Shannon Messenger
Cover photograph copyright © 2013 by Brian Oldham Photography
Cover design by Angela Goddard
All rights reserved, including the right of reproduction
in whole or in part in any form.
SIMON PULSE and colophon are registered trademarks
of Simon & Schuster, Inc.
Also available in a Simon Pulse hardcover edition.
For information about special discounts for bulk purchases,
please contact Simon & Schuster Special Sales at 1-866-506-1949 or business@simonandschuster.com.
The Simon & Schuster Speakers Bureau can bring authors to your live event. For more information
or to book an event contact the Simon & Schuster Speakers Bureau at 1-866-248-3049
or visit our website at www.simonspeakers.com.
Interior design by Mike Rosamilia
The text of this book was set in Adobe Caslon Pro.
Manufactured in the United States of America
2 4 6 8 10 9 7 5 3
The Library of Congress has cataloged the hardcover edition as follows:
Messenger, Shannon.
Let the sky fall / by Shannon Messenger. —
1st Simon Pulse hardcover ed.
p. cm.
Summary: Ten years after surviving the tornado that killed his parents, Vane Weston, now seventeen,
has no memory of that fateful day but dreams of a beautiful girl who, he now learns, is not only real, she
is his guardian sylph, who harnesses the power of the wind.
[1. Supernatural—Fiction. 2. Winds—Fiction.
3. Spirits—Fiction. 4. Amnesia—Fiction. 5. Tornadoes—Fiction.
6. Orphans—Fiction.] I. Title.
PZ7.M5494Let 2013   [Fic]—dc23   2012006109
ISBN 978-1-4424-5041-7 (hc)
ISBN 978-1-4424-5042-4 (pbk)
ISBN 978-1-4424-5043-1 (eBook)

For my husband, Miles

I never could have written a love story
(or channeled my inner snarky boy) without you

CHAPTER 1

VANE

'm lucky to be alive.

At least, that's what everybody keeps telling me.

The reporter from the local newspaper even had the nerve to call it a miracle. I was "Vane Weston: The Miracle Child." Like the police finding me unconscious in a pile of rubble was part of some grand universal plan.

"Family Survives Tornado"—now, *that* would've been a miracle. But trust me, there's nothing "miraculous" about being orphaned at seven years old.

It's not that I'm not grateful to be alive. I am. I get that I shouldn't have survived. But that's the worst part about being "The Miracle Child."

The question.

The same inescapable question, plaguing me for the last ten years of my life.

How?

How could I get sucked in by a category-five tornado—nature's equivalent of a giant blender—get carried over four miles before the massive funnel spit me back out, and only have a few cuts and bruises to show for it? How was that possible, when my parents' bodies were found almost unrecognizable?

The police don't know.

Scientists don't know.

So they all turn to me for the answer.

But I have no freaking idea.

I can't remember it. That day. My past. Anything.

Well, I can't remember anything useful.

I remember fear.

I remember wind.

And then . . . a giant, blank space. Like all my memories were knocked out of my head when I hit the ground.

Except one.

One isolated memory—and I'm not even sure if it *is* a memory, or if it's some strange hallucination my traumatized brain cooked up.

A face, watching me through the chaos of the storm.

A girl. Dark hair. Darker eyes. A single tear streaks down her cheek. Then a chilly breeze whisks her away.

She's haunted my dreams ever since.

CHAPTER 2

AUDRA

I t was my fault.

I knew the rules.

I knew how dangerous it was to call the wind.

But I couldn't let Gavin die.

Back then, guarding the Westons consumed every second of my family's lives. Constant worry. Constant running. Constantly looking over our shoulders for the coming storm. We'd holed up in two tiny houses in the middle of nowhere. Waiting. Watching. Holding our breath. The fear hung over us thicker than the clouds.

I survived the hardest days by seeking shelter in the sprawling cottonwood trees at the edge of the property. Balanced high in their branches, with the breeze sliding across my skin, I could let the world fall away and open my mind to the whispers of the wind.

To my heritage.

I never spoke to the wind. Just listened and learned.

But the songs of the wind weren't enough to fill the lonely days. So I turned to the birds.

Gavin's nest was hidden in the thin limbs at the top of the tallest tree, tucked safely out of reach of predators. But I was a wispy thing, and my nimble legs had no problem scaling the fragile trunk to reach it. Inside were three balls of fluff. Goshawks—proud and noble, even with their downy gray feathers and open beaks, waiting for their mother to return.

I'd never fully connected with a bird on my own before. I always needed my mother's guidance to make them understand me, respond to me, trust me. But she was too busy with the Westons. And Gavin was different.

He never screamed or flinched the way his siblings did when I came to inspect the nest. He just watched me with his wide, unblinking eyes, and I knew he was daring me to reach out and grab him. I visited him every day after that, as soon as his mother left to hunt.

I'd been counting down the days until his first flight, torn between excitement and dread. Longing to witness the moment he drank in the freedom of riding the wind, but crushed by the idea of losing my only company. My only friend.

Brave Gavin was the first to leap.

My heart stood still as he propelled himself out of the nest, his red-orange eyes staring at the horizon. Focused. Determined.

For one second his wings caught the draft, and he screeched in triumph from the rush of flight. Then a gust of wind knocked him off balance and sent him crashing toward the ground.

I'd love to say that I didn't think. That instinct took over, clouding out all reason. But I knew the risk.

Our eyes met as he fell, and I *chose* to save him.

I called the wind—the first time I'd ever done so—wrapping a swift gust around Gavin's tiny body and floating him to my waiting hands. He nuzzled against my fingers, like he knew. He knew I'd saved him.

I brought him home and showed my father, never telling him how Gavin came to be mine. I had plenty of chances. My mother asked lots of questions. All I had to do was tell the truth.

If I had, my father would still be alive.

Instead, I kept quiet—until one of Raiden's Stormers found us the next evening and swirled the three most powerful winds into an unstoppable funnel.

Then it was too late.

CHAPTER 3

VANE

For three months during winter it doesn't totally suck to live in the Coachella Valley. Then the heat comes and half the population hops into their fancy cars or private jets and escapes to their second, third, or fourth homes, leaving behind a bunch of old people, a few crazies, and the rest of us—trapped outside the country clubs in the "non-rich" areas.

My family's one and only house is unfortunately stuck in the middle of an unruly date grove in Bermuda Dunes, California, a.k.a. the hottest freaking place on the planet. Today it's 109°F. The kind of day where the locals sit around and talk about the nice "break in the heat," because two days ago it was 126°F. I can't feel the difference. But I'm not a local.

I moved to California just after my eighth birthday, when my adoption became final. So to this Nebraska native—even after nine years living here—pretty much anything over 100°F feels like sticking my body inside an oven. People keep telling me I'll get used to it, but I swear every year it gets worse, like the sun's melting me from the inside out and I'll eventually be nothing more than a Vane puddle on the ground.

On hot summer days like today, I do everything in my power to avoid leaving the dark cave I call a bedroom. Which is the main reason I refuse to let Isaac drag me out tonight for another one of his disastrous fix-ups.

There's another reason I don't like to date—but I'm trying not to think about *her*.

"Come on, man," Isaac whines. It's the third time he's called me in twenty minutes. "I promise it won't be like last time."

By "last time" he means when he hooked me up with Stacey Perkins. Apparently she's a vegan—which is cool. Her choice. But nobody told me that until *after* I brought her to Outback Steakhouse. Then she asked the waitress if they had any "cruelty free" items on their menu.

Things only went downhill from there. Especially when I still ordered a steak. There are few things worse than an irritated vegan.

"Not interested," I tell him, pulling my blinds closed and flopping on my bed. I spread out my arms so I can get maximum fan exposure. The breeze feels better than AC, better than jumping headfirst into a swimming pool. Almost like my body craves the rushing air.

"Come on, Hannah is Shelby's cousin and they've been joined

at the hip since she got to town. It's been three weeks. I'm going out of my mind."

"Pawn her off on someone else. I'm not getting stuck on another crappy blind date just so you can make out with your girlfriend."

"You know I'd do the same for you—if you ever *had* a girlfriend."

"Don't go there."

"But, I mean, dude—you're seventeen and you've never even kissed a girl. What is *up* with that?"

I don't say anything because he's right. I have no problem asking girls out—or even getting them to say yes when I do. But I officially have the worst luck with girls. If I don't screw things up on my own, something always happens. Drinks spill on their clothes. Birds poop in their hair. I swear I'm cursed.

"Come on, Vane—don't make me beg," Isaac finally says.

I want to hang up on him. The last thing I need is another dating humiliation. But he's my best friend.

So I throw on a slightly less wrinkled T-shirt, run water through my short, dark brown hair, and an hour later I'm stuck with Hannah from Canada, who didn't even crack a smile when I pointed out the rhyme. She's also complained about the heat at least ten quadrillion times. And we're only fifteen minutes into the date.

"Cheesecake Factory or Yard House?" I ask, pointing to the massive restaurants overlooking the shallow, man-made river we're walking along.

Tourist traps like The River are pretty much the only things open this time of year—though I'll never understand why any tourist gets excited about a fake river and some chain restaurants. Especially when it's too hot for any sane person to be outside. My T-shirt is stuck to my back like the sweat formed a vacuum, and all we've done is walk from the parking lot to the mall. Not even the tiniest breeze to help cool us off.

Hannah wipes a bead of sweat off her brow and turns to me. "I don't really like cheesecake, so maybe the other one, eh?"

I bite my lip. They do serve food *besides* cheesecake—but I'm not in the mood to argue. "Yard House it is."

The AC blasts us as we enter the crowded restaurant, and Hannah releases a sigh at the same time I do.

The tension between us evaporates. Whoever invented air conditioning should win the Nobel Prize. I bet they could bring peace to the Middle East if they gave everyone an AC unit and let them cool the freak down once in a while. I should e-mail the UN the suggestion.

The hostess leads us to a booth big enough to seat six people. Not that any other table would be more romantic. Between the loud music, sports games, and the guys at the bar drinking beer by the half yard and cheering for their teams, it isn't much of a date spot. Which is exactly why I suggested it. Maybe if I don't treat tonight like a date, I won't run into any problems this time.

"Looks like you've got some fans," Hannah says, pointing to three girls sitting a few tables away. All three blush and start whispering when I look at them.

I shrug.

Hannah smiles, flashing straight, white teeth. Her dentist must be proud. "Isaac said you were modest. Now I see what he was going on about."

"Is that what he went on aboot?" I ask, mimicking her pronunciation.

"Ah, I was wondering when we were going to get to the accent jabs."

"Hey, I think I've shown tremendous restraint. I let at least three or four 'ehs' pass without comment."

She tosses a sugar packet at my head.

I tell Canadian jokes until the waiter takes our order, relieved when Hannah orders a cheeseburger. I hate girls who refuse to eat around guys, like they're afraid we'll think they're fat because we actually see them putting food in their mouths.

Hannah isn't like that. She's confident. She isn't the prettiest girl in the room, but she's cute. Peachy skin, pink lips, and a mass of wavy blond hair. I'm sure more than a few guys would gladly trade places with me right now.

The problem is, I have a "type." Isaac says I'm too picky, but he doesn't get it. Honestly, I don't understand it either. I just automatically compare every girl I meet to someone else. It's dumb and crazy, but I can't help it.

But as we eat our burgers and drink sodas packed with more ice than soda—desert style, I explain to Hannah—I'm stunned to realize I'm enjoying myself. I like Hannah's laugh as much as her smile, and the way she brushes her hair behind her ears when she blushes.

And then, I see *her*.

Dark hair.

Dark eyes.

Dark jacket.

Leaning against the bar in the center of the restaurant, with only a sliver of her face pointed in my direction. I have to blink to make sure my eyes aren't playing tricks on me.

They aren't. Her hair is twisted into a tight, intricate braid, but it's definitely her.

She turns another inch my way and our eyes meet. My heart pounds so loudly it drowns out everything else. It's just me, and her. Locked in a stare.

Her eyes narrow and she shakes her head—like she's trying to tell me something. But I have no idea what it is.

"Vane?" Hannah asks, and I jump so hard I nearly fall out of the booth. "You okay? You look like you just saw a ghost."

She laughs, but I don't smile. She isn't that far off the mark.

Hannah follows my gaze, frowning. "Do you . . . know her?"

So Hannah can see her too.

She's real.

"Excuse me," I say, on my feet before she can say anything else.

The hostess is leading a large party past our table, blocking my path to the bar, and it takes every ounce of my self-control not to shove them out of my way. I rush forward as soon as the aisle clears, but the girl's gone.

I race for the door, ignoring Hannah as she calls after me, ignoring the way everyone stares at me, ignoring the blast of heat as I burst through the doors. And I find . . . nothing.

No sign of anyone anywhere—and certainly no gorgeous, dark-haired girl in a jacket. Just a face full of scorching desert wind and an empty courtyard.

My hands curl into fists.

She was *there*.

But how is that possible?

And how did she get away so fast?

I squeeze the bridge of my nose, trying to sort through the ten million things racing through my mind. I still haven't made any sense of them when I hear quiet footsteps approach behind me.

"I had to pay the check so they wouldn't think we're skipping out—that's what took me so long." Hannah won't meet my eyes. "I wasn't even sure if you'd be out here."

The thick June air sticks in my throat, closing off my voice. The sun has set, but that only makes the temperature drop a few degrees. I stand there, listening to the cicadas in the trees and searching for some way to explain—or apologize for—my behavior. "I'll pay you back," is the best I can do.

She turns toward the parking lot. "I guess we should probably go, eh?"

The silence buzzes with the things neither of us says.

Seriously, why does something *always* screw up my dates?

I still haven't come up with a way to salvage the evening when we reach my faded white car. It isn't much to look at, but it has a working AC, which was pretty much my only requirement. I open the door for Hannah, hoping it will prove I'm not a total psycho. She doesn't seem impressed. Not that I blame her.

The drive back is torture. I've never noticed how many noises my car makes—but I've never had such a quiet passenger. I've also never noticed how many lights Highway 111 has. It's the main road that connects all the desert cities together, so there's a signal. At every. Freaking. Block. And, of course, tonight they're all red.

Thanks a lot, universe.

We're about halfway home, just entering the string of "affordable cities" in the valley, when Hannah finally speaks.

"You gonna tell me what happened?"

I drag out a sigh, stalling for time. "I . . . thought I saw someone I knew." It sounds lame even to me.

"Did you used to date her?"

Ha—I wish.

Fortunately, I stop myself from saying that out loud. I can hear the hurt in Hannah's voice.

But it's nice to know that Hannah really *did* see her—even though I have no idea what that means.

I stare at the dark, empty road. "It's not what you're thinking. It's not like . . ."

"Like what?" she asks when I don't finish.

I take my eyes off the street long enough to look at her. "I would never chase after some hot girl when I'm with someone else—not that the girl's hot. I mean, okay, she *is*—but . . . that isn't why I cared."

"Why did you care?"

I wish I knew.

"She's just . . . someone from my past."

It isn't a lie, but it isn't the truth, either. She isn't just someone. She's *the girl.* The one I've been dreaming about since the day I woke up in that pile of rubble and found my whole world torn apart. The only clue to my past. The only thing I see when I close my eyes.

13

She's aged in my dreams. Grown up along with me. Which is the most confusing part. What kind of dream does that? And what kind of dream girl walks into Yard House?

The dreams are insanely vivid, too. Every night it's like she's in my room, leaning over me, watching me with eyes so dark blue, they're almost black. Her long, dark hair tickling my skin. Her lips whispering sounds I can't understand as they float through my mind. But when I wake up, I'm alone. Nothing but silence, and a faint breeze swirling through the air even though my window's locked tight.

It all sounds so crazy.

But I'm *not* crazy.

I don't know how to explain it—but one of these days I'll figure it out.

I turn down Shelby's street, searching the row of single-story houses for the gray pueblo-style one Shelby's parents own. The rounded architecture might look cool, if normal, flat-roofed houses didn't surround it. La Quinta's random like that, like no one could make up their minds what to build here.

Isaac's beat-up truck is out front, so I switch my phone off. He won't be happy with me when I drop Hannah off so early.

Hannah gathers her purse as I slow to a stop, but I don't unlock her door. I can't let the night end like this.

"I'm really sorry," I say, realizing I never apologized. "I was actually having a nice time, before I ruined everything."

"Me too." She tucks her hair behind her ears.

She looks so shy. So vulnerable. So different from the girl haunting me.

Maybe Hannah will make *her* go away.

I have to get over my obsession before she ruins my life.

A couple of June bugs—dumbest bugs on the planet—knock into the windshield, shattering the silence between us. I come to a decision.

"Can I . . . maybe have a chance to redeem myself?" I ask, ignoring the voice in my head begging me to let it go.

A half smile spreads across her lips. "Maybe—but only if you promise no Canadian jokes."

"Aw, come on, you have to give me at least one, eh?"

She laughs. Even though it sounds forced, I can tell things are on the mend. I'll have to be on absolute perfect behavior, but if I can pull that off things might be okay. And it surprises me how much I want them to be okay.

I don't want to be the crazy guy chasing a mystery girl. I want to be a normal guy who hangs out with his friends and has a summer fling with the cute girl from Canada.

So I get out of the car and walk her to the door, the sticky air smothering us as we stand under the porch light. Moths fly at our heads and crickets chirp in the bushes and our eyes meet. I have no idea what the look on my face says—but her expression seems to say, *Why not?*

I can't agree more. It's time to take control of my life.

My stomach does back flips as I step toward her, and I try to tell myself the sourness rising in my throat is nerves. I refuse to feel guilty for cheating on a girl I've never met. A girl I'm still not sure is real.

My hand cradles Hannah's cheek, which is slightly cool from the car's AC. She closes her eyes, and I close mine and lean in, hardly able to believe I'm finally doing this.

But in the split second before our lips touch, I hear a loud hiss, and a blast of arctic wind rushes between us.

Hannah staggers back as the fierce gust whips around her hair, tangling the blond waves. I try to reach for her, but the wind pushes and pulls at me with such force it feels like it's trying to shove and drag me away. I lean into it, fighting to resist, but it sweeps against my legs, nearly knocking my feet out from under me. It's like the wind has come alive—and only right here, around Hannah and me. The palms in the yard next door don't move.

Just when I think it can't get any weirder, a familiar voice blows straight into my brain.

Go home, Vane.

I look around, trying to see through the darkness and the swirling sand to find where she's hiding. But the street's empty. Just me and Hannah—who's still battling the crazy wind yanking her away from me.

"I'm going inside," Hannah shouts, swiping sand out of her eyes.

"Okay," I yell, watching helplessly as she turns away from me. "I'll call you."

She doesn't turn back. Doesn't acknowledge me at all.

The wind sweeps my words away before they reach her. And then she's gone.

CHAPTER 4

AUDRA

I've sacrificed ten years of my life for this assignment.

Trained physically. Mentally. Emotionally.

I've given up food and sleep. Suffered hour after hour under the relentless weight of the desert sun. Lived in total isolation. Relegated myself to demeaning tasks like playing chaperone while the stubborn, ignorant boy rebels against everything that matters.

And now he may have gotten us both killed.

But it's my fault as much as his.

Once again, I've called the wind too loudly. And once again I've given us away.

The Northerly wind was too far beyond my reach to command with a whisper. I had to shout. Which means my call is branded to the draft now—and it carries Vane's trace as well. There's no way the

Stormers won't check the cold wind coming from the warm valley. And when they investigate, they'll finally have their prize.

The world starts to spin and I suck in a breath.

I won't let it happen again.

I can stall them. Confuse their search.

Then I'll deal with Vane.

He drives away in his white smog machine, and my legs shake as I step from the shadows, scanning the street for the dark shape I know will be roosting on a roof nearby. I hold my left arm out and he swoops down, gripping the sleeve of my jacket with his talons. Gavin knows not to screech. Our role is to be invisible.

It's Vane's fault we're exposed. He's lucky I went gentle on him. He has no idea who he's messing with. But he'll soon find out.

I stroke the soft gray feathers around Gavin's neck, trying to calm the panic seizing my chest, making it hurt to breathe. "Go home, boy," I whisper. "I'll join you as soon as I can."

Gavin's sharp, red-orange eyes lock with mine and I know he understands the command. Then he spreads his wings and, with a powerful flap, takes to the skies. I envy his easy flight. Mine requires significantly more effort.

I retreat to the shadows, my fingers searching the air for an existing breeze to hide my trail.

Nothing. I have to wait.

The sporadic stillness of this place is like a drain, drying up my energy, my options, and my sanity. If the air hadn't turned stagnant earlier, I could've put a damper on Vane's "date" sooner. I wouldn't have been forced to walk among the groundlings to try to scare him off. I wouldn't have had to let him see me. And I wouldn't have had to call the Northerly to stop him from bonding to that girl.

We'd still be safe.

Of course, if he didn't insist on breaking rules, we wouldn't be in this mess either.

I hug myself, squeezing my shoulders to calm my trembling. He's *never* come that close before. Another second and . . .

My eyes blur as my mind flashes to the memory of him on the porch. His hand on her face. Leaning in. Their lips coming so close.

If I hadn't stopped him—I can't even think about the consequences.

An ache in my jaw warns me that I'm grinding my teeth. I force myself to relax. A guardian must be calm and clear-headed at all times—the Gale Force drilled that into me. Suppressing emotion is the key to our success. The only way to endure the life of sacrifice we're sworn to.

Plus . . . it isn't *technically* Vane's fault. He doesn't know about the ordinances he almost violated, or how big a commitment a single kiss is—though I've given him enough warnings over the years. He should've caught on.

But it's pointless to dwell on things I can't change. I know better than anyone that the past can't be undone. Moving forward is the only option.

A wispy wind tickles my fingers. An Easterly—finally, a stroke of luck.

Soft, untraceable murmurs bend the draft to my will, wrapping it around me. When I'm completely entangled in the feathery breeze,

I breathe one final command in the Easterly language and surrender to the force of its power.

"Rise."

The word sounds like a hiss, and the wind races away, pulling me along with it.

Riding a draft is the closest to freedom I ever come. Rushing higher and deeper into the sky brings clarity to my life. Meaning. I can never fully control the wind. I can coax it, cajole it, ask it to obey—but it's still a force of its own, free to do what it wills. The trick is to listen as it speaks and adjust as needed.

Most Windwalkers are twice my age before they reach my level of control. I can hear even the softest whisper of change or dissent, translate any turbulence or unease, and adjust. It was my father's gift. He passed it to me the day he returned to the sky.

Not a second goes by that I don't wish I could give it back.

Dark peaks appear on the horizon and I whisper, "Dive." The gust drops low enough for my toes to skim the ground. My legs speed to a run, and once I have my bearings, I release my hold. The wind unravels, racing away as I screech to a halt, my feet firmly planted on the cool, rocky ground of the San Bernardino Mountains.

The air is so much purer up high—the gusts so much stronger. I allow myself one minute to let the surging winds restore me. They ripple across my skin, filling me with strength and confidence that can only come from being in my natural element. Part of me could stand there all night, drinking it up.

But I have a job to do.

It feels wrong to command the wind at full volume—just like it felt wrong earlier. But that's the point. One mistake to hide another.

Still, my voice shakes as I send Northerly squalls on all sides of the mountains and order them to surge through the desert basin. Sandstorms streak across the empty dunes, leaving dusty footprints in their wake. Scattering my trace in every direction.

The Stormers won't be able to pinpoint our location—but they'll know we're here. And they won't leave until they find Vane, tearing the valley apart in the process.

The telltale flurry will reach the Stormers' fortress by nightfall tomorrow, and it'll take another day of swift flight for them to arrive in the region. I've bought us an extra day with the false trails they'll have to rule out.

Which means we have three days. Then people will start to die.

Vane has to have his first breakthrough tonight. Three days will be enough to train him in the basics, and I'm at my peak strength, thanks to my years of sacrifice. We should be able to fight them off together.

But there's only one way to be sure the breakthrough happens.

My mouth coats with bile at the thought.

I reach for another Easterly, focusing on the way the edge of my palm tingles as I call the swift gust and wrap it around me. The cool tendrils wash away my fears as they brush my skin.

"Return." I say the word so softly, the wind's roar washes it away. It sweeps me in its force, carrying me gently down the mountain, across the parched, empty sand, to my house.

It isn't much of a home, but I don't have time to stay anyway. I have work to do.

Tonight will be a very long night.

CHAPTER 5

VANE

My parents are still awake when I come home. Of course they are. It's barely ten o'clock. I'm probably the only teenager in the valley who never breaks curfew.

Course, I bet other guys don't have icy drafts attacking them out of nowhere or hear their name on the wind. Goose bumps erupt across my arms just thinking about it.

Deal with it later.

I find my mom in our cluttered pink family room, reading on the mottled brown couch. The salty scent of meatloaf still fills the air, and when I glance over her shoulder I can see plates piled in the kitchen sink. Great, I'm home before she even did the dishes. *Fail.*

My dad waves from the living room, but he doesn't get up from his worn leather recliner. He's too engrossed in some Discovery

Channel special—I have no idea how he watches those things—to want to hear about his son's latest dating disaster.

My mom, on the other hand, closes her thick book, sweeps her long blond hair out of her face, and motions for me to take a seat.

I'm not in the mood for one of her "chats," but I know she'll read too much into it if I flee to my room. My mom's a gold medal worrier. Part of her is probably glad I'm not out impregnating some poor teenage girl right now. But I know another part always worries I'm not having a normal life.

She has no idea how abnormal it is.

No way have I told my parents about my dream-girl stalker. I'd rather not spend endless afternoons sprawled on a couch while some shrink spouts useless psychobabble and drains my parents' limited savings account. I had quite enough of that when I was "The Miracle Child."

"How was the date?" she asks as I cross the brown shaggy carpet and plop down beside her.

I answer with a shrug—my best weapon against my mom's never-ending questions. It's always fun to see how long I can get away with it.

"Was Hannah nice?"

Shrug.

"What did you guys do?"

Another shrug.

"Vane! That's not an actual answer."

Dang—only three. Usually she lets at least four or five go. She

23

must be especially interested. Or especially worried. Can she tell how freaked out I am?

Her pale blue eyes don't blink as they watch me. They're the only feature we have in common, the only thing that makes people think maybe, *maybe* there's a family resemblance between the tall, dark-haired boy and his short, blond mother.

I try distraction. "Hannah was great. In fact, we drove to Vegas and got married 'cause she needs an American visa and I figured, why not? She's hot. She's packing her stuff right now. Hope you don't mind sharing a roof with a honeymooning couple."

My mom sighs, but I can tell by the way her lips twitch that she *wants* to smile. I let her off the hook.

"Hannah was nice. We went to dinner. Then I took her home. It was all very exciting."

"How come you're home so early?" she asks.

"We . . . didn't really hit it off."

It's sort of true.

"But you're okay?" The lines deepen across her forehead.

"Of course." I smile to sell it. "Just tired. I think I'm gonna play a few games and hit the sack early."

My mom relaxes. If I'm okay enough to play video games, there's no reason to worry—Mom's parenting rule number fifty-three. It comes right after *As long as the principal isn't calling, there's no reason to worry about his grades*, and right before *If his eyes aren't bloodshot, he's just hungry—it's not the munchies.*

That's why I love her. She knows when to keep me in line, and when to let me be—both my parents do. I totally scored in the adoptive family department. Even if they don't look like me and live in a town where the weather can be considered cruel and unusual punishment. They even let me keep my last name—which is awesome because Weston is way better than Brasier. It rhymes with Frasier, but I know I'd have been Vane Brassiere to every kid in school.

Plus, it leaves me something from my "other life."

My past is this giant void that makes me want to bang my head against the wall until I knock the memories loose. I don't care how many doctors tell me it's normal for trauma to repress painful experiences—I don't buy it. How can it be normal to completely forget your entire childhood?

And what kind of selfish jerk erases his family just because it hurts to think about them?

I feel my smile start to fade, so I head down the hall before my mom can notice. Once I close my bedroom door, I switch on the old tube TV I inherited when my parents finally invested in a flat-screen and log online, cringing when one of Isaac's war games starts up.

Isaac doesn't understand why I hate playing the first person shooters. I don't really get it either. The blood turns my stomach for some reason—not that I've told him that. Like I need to give him another thing to bug me about.

But I'm not playing anyway. I join the first match I find, crouch my guy in a corner and crank the volume up so my mom can hear the explosions in the family room. Hopefully that'll keep her from checking on me.

Gunfire blasts, and I sink to the pile of blankets I kicked off my bed last night—is my mom insane? Blankets? In the summer?—

and close my eyes. Cool air from my ceiling fan brushes across my face and my shoulders relax. The breeze always makes my head clear. Which is good, 'cause I have some serious crap to figure out.

Sure, I've caught quick glimpses of the girl before—but I was never sure I'd really seen *her*, and not some dark-haired girl who looked like her. Those times were nothing like this—with full eye contact and everything.

And I've heard whispers on the wind outside my dreams. But they've never been words I could understand or a voice I could recognize—and they've never used my name.

Not to mention I've never had the wind attack me before. Sudden breezes flaring up at odd times—sure. Winds that seem drawn to me—occasionally. But those never freaked me out. I know it sounds weird, but the wind doesn't scare me. Even after what happened to my parents. Even after what happened tonight. The wind calms me somehow. I've never understood why.

So the crazy, cold wind isn't the reason my hands are shaking.

It's because I know the girl called that wind to me. Controlled it somehow. Attacked me with it. The strange hiss I heard before the wind overpowered us was *her* voice.

Which means what?

She's magical? Some sort of wind god? An angel?

I laugh at myself, even though the last word makes my stomach squirm.

She was there the day I survived the tornado. A tiny part of me has always wondered if she somehow saved me. How else could I have lived?

Is she my . . . guardian angel?

Nah. I don't believe in that crap. Plus, she wasn't trying to protect me from anything tonight. I was on a freaking first date—where's the danger in that?

So, what?

Is she jealous?

A jealous guardian angel—that'd be just my luck.

And I'm officially creeping myself out. Not because I think any of this is true, but because my brain even went there. I'm definitely losing it.

I need to put this insanity behind me. My instinct with Hannah was right. I can't keep chasing dream girls or thinking about magical wind powers or angels—not unless I want to end up the star patient in the local loony bin.

Time to sleep it off and wake up tomorrow like nothing happened.

Except, she'll be waiting for me. Sneaking into my dreams. Refusing to be forgotten.

Life would be so much simpler if I could just sink into a drugged, dreamless sleep. But the doctors gave me sleeping pills after I survived the tornado and my body broke out in sweat and hives until I threw them up and passed out. Same thing happens with any meds I take. Good thing I never get sick.

Still, the medicine cabinet tempts me as I brush my teeth before bed. Maybe half of one pill could knock me out without triggering an allergic reaction.

It's not worth the risk. I'll have to learn to ignore her until she leaves me alone—whatever she is.

Or maybe I just won't sleep tonight. . . .

No.

Let her come. Then I can finally tell her to leave me alone.

I crawl into bed and flick off the light, pulling the sheet tight around me and squeezing my pillow as hard as I can.

Bring it on, dream girl. I'm ready this time.

CHAPTER 6

AUDRA

I thought he'd never fall asleep.

Crouching in the shadows below Vane's window, waiting for the sound of his breathing to slow, always makes my legs cramp, no matter how many nights I've done it. And tonight I have the added pleasure of sharp thorns from the pyracantha bushes pricking through the thin fabric of the barely there dress I had to change into.

The pain is nothing compared to what I'm about to endure. But the wind has to break through Vane's mind tonight and make a connection. This is the only way I can make sure that happens.

I've tried to awaken his mind every night for the last nine years, whispering on the gentle breeze I send to his room while he sleeps. It's the most natural way to learn the language of the wind, like a child learning to speak by listening to his parents talk. But I've never fully gotten through to him, and any progress I make always vanishes when he wakes, like the strands of a dream slipping away with the morning light.

Time and patience, the Gale Force told me.

I don't have the luxury of either anymore.

A date roach skitters across my bare foot and I bite back a scream. I've trained to face all manner of foe, but nothing is as horrible as the fist-sized, brown vermin that swarm the grounds of this awful place. They're almost impossible to kill—I've had many scurry away after I smacked them with my blade. And they can fly. It isn't fair that something so useless and ugly has greater skills than Vane.

The thought would be amusing if it weren't so terrifying. Vane can be crushed far too easily, and I know better than anyone what we'll face when the Stormers arrive.

A wave of pain rocks me as the memories I try so hard to ignore batter my mental barriers.

Vane's parents. My parents. The unfathomable force of the cyclone tossing them around like dry leaves in a storm. The vindictive smirk on the Stormer's lips.

I close my eyes, just like I did that day—but I can't close out the roar of the winds tearing at me, or the echoes of the Westons' screams. Or the sound of my father's voice, before he surrendered himself to save us, ordering me to take care of Vane.

Sounds that will haunt me until I draw my last breath, and probably beyond.

Four of them fought one Stormer, and only my mother survived.

Raiden always sends his Stormers in pairs now. What chance do Vane and I have?

My legs itch to run—to grab Vane and flee this suffocating place. Keep him hidden. Protected.

I fight the urge.

The Stormers will destroy the entire valley in their search to find us. As a guardian, I can't allow that to happen. Plus, they'd follow our trace. Overtake us eventually.

Forcing Vane's first breakthrough is the best option.

Our only option.

Besides, I'm strong, and prepared. I haven't tied myself to the earth with a bite of food or a drop of liquid since the day my father died ten years ago. None of the other Gales have kept the sacrifice so long. But I learned from my father's mistake. It's about to serve me well.

I have time to teach Vane to fight. Maybe even trigger his other breakthroughs. And if he can live up to even a fraction of his potential, we'll be more than enough to take them on. Assuming I succeed tonight . . .

I've joined the wind only once before during my training—and I could only bear the pain a few seconds. It will take Vane's mind a few minutes to have the breakthrough.

I'll hold on as long as it takes. This is my only chance.

I rise to open his window. It's time.

Usually I slip a breeze through the crack at the bottom to let the wind's songs stir his senses while I listen outside. Tonight I'll make direct contact with his mind. If that doesn't awaken him, nothing will. I reach for the Northerly I can feel prickling my fingers and send it under the sill, thrusting the gust against the lock until it clicks. An extra swell of wind pushes the window silently open.

Vane lies stretched out on his bed—asleep, but not peaceful. He's tangled in the sheets and strangling his pillow.

I almost feel sorry for him. He has no idea what he's in for.

Of course, neither do I.

Deep breath.

I'm stalling—and I don't have time for weakness.

I close my eyes.

Joining the wind requires absolute concentration. Even then, it will be easy to lose myself.

The Northerlies I sent from the mountains fill the air, but for this I need Easterlies. The winds of my heritage. Like the blood in my veins, their drafts flow through me. And if I surrender myself to them, they'll release me from my earthly form.

I murmur the call I've memorized, commanding every eastern wind to find me. Fortunately, there are some nearby, so the movement won't be detected.

I step into the open, blinking as the drafts whip my hair against my face. Usually I keep it bound in the Gale's regulation braid, but the intricate twists and folds can't be replicated in the transformation. Shifting requires letting go.

I stretch out my arms and let the cool air streak across my bare skin. The Gale Force designed my dark sleeveless dress specifically for this task, cutting it short and low to leave most of me uncovered. The smooth, sleek fabric is woven from tiny fibers that cling to each other in a mesh but can quickly break apart. Like dandelion fluff when the wind sets it free. It will dissolve and re-form as needed.

If only my body could make the switch so easily.

I wonder what the Gales would say if they could see me now. What my mother would say.

Would she be worried?

Would she care at all?

No. She would see this as fitting punishment for the crime I can never redeem.

Maybe it is.

I fight off a shiver caused only partially by letting the chilly drafts seep through my skin. They sink into the deepest recesses of my body, swirling and thrashing for freedom.

I have to let them out.

I can't explain the moment of surrender. It happens on an instinctive level, deep within my core. I just have to trust my gut. And withstand the pain.

With a final breath, I silence my resistance and let the winds rip me apart.

Icy needles and shredding teeth tear through me, breaking my body down cell by cell. It takes only a second to transform, but every fiber of my being will forever remember the agony.

Mixed with the pain is an unimaginable freedom.

No boundaries. No limits.

I *am* the wind.

My years of training vanish as an uncontrollable urge pulls at me. I yearn to take off, to follow the wind's teasing song to the ends of the earth and beyond. The farther away, the less the pain will be, until it's gone and I'm free.

Free.

The idea is so tempting. . . .

No!

I focus on the one thing that keeps me grounded: my father's face.

His lips are stretched wide with a smile. A faint dimple peeks out of his left cheek, and his sky-blue eyes have crinkles at the corners. He looks happy. Proud. I have to believe he would be.

Under control now, I flow swiftly through the open window, thrilling at the rushing motion as I swirl around Vane.

Time to wake up.

My thoughts fill the whispers in the air, speaking for the wind in the secret Easterly language. But the words aren't enough to break through. He needs more than the tendrils of my breezes wrapping around him, grazing his cheeks and tousling his hair.

He has to breathe me in.

I sweep across his face, waiting for him to inhale. When he does, I follow the pull in the air. Once I streak past his lips, I break free from the rest of his breath and press deep into his consciousness. To his very being.

It's dark and confined inside his mind. I thrash to escape, longing to push free when he exhales. The pain amplifies the tighter I'm contained, and my winds rage. I'm a tempest, battering his thoughts, trying to tear them loose.

Wake. Up.

Something stirs around me, a warm tingle of energy building to a hum—but no breakthrough. Not yet.

The urge to fly away tears and pulls at me like cold, clawed fingers. But I focus on my father. He was always calm, always confident. So full of life and love. What would he do?

He would be gentle. He would care.

So I ignore the pain and lessen the force of my drafts, letting only the soft threadlike breezes weave through the strands of Vane's consciousness.

Please, Vane. Wake up.

His body moves.

I'm reaching him.

Your people need you, Vane.

I almost add that I need him. But I can't bring myself to say those words. I don't want them to be true.

He doesn't need to hear them.

He wakes with a gasp and I retreat from his mind with the rest of his startled breath in a frenzied rush.

Finally.

My drafts stretch and spin, relishing the freedom as I watch him look around, his eyes wild. Feral.

There's only one way to know if the Easterlies have truly broken through.

I gather the winds—my winds. Me. All the parts of myself that float on the breeze—and hover in front of him. If he's had the breakthrough, he'll be able to see my true form. Otherwise, I'll be as invisible as the wind.

Please see me.

His eyes widen and he scrambles to his feet, shouting something I can't understand over the roaring rush.

But he *sees* me.

Vane Weston is ready.

With the last of my strength I pull myself in tighter. When I have a firm hold, I send the winds away.

Burning hot pokers and battering rams and a million other pains I can't begin to explain. The particles of my dress cool me where they cling, but there aren't enough of them to extinguish the fire in my skin as my body re-forms.

I stagger as I meet Vane's eyes. His mouth hangs open from something he must have said when I was blind and deaf from the pain.

"It's about time," I mumble.

Then I collapse.

CHAPTER 7

VANE

Ten million questions squish together and burst out my mouth—along with a healthy mix of words my mom would kill me for using. But I don't care about her conservative language rules at the moment.

I have a freaking ghost girl passed out on the floor of my room.

I suck in a huge gulp of air and let that process. She's *here*. If I want, I can reach out and touch her.

I take half a step toward her, then shudder and back as far away as my small, cluttered room allows. She may be real, but that doesn't explain what she is, or what just happened to me. It felt like she was actually *in* my head, an eerie presence inside of me.

Not to mention the wispy ghost thing I saw floating near the ceiling. A swirling cloud of dark and light and color and wind—with a face. Her face. Then somehow all the chaos mashed together and *bam!*—passed-out phantom girl on my bedroom floor. If I didn't feel my heart thumping against my chest, I'd be convinced this is a horrible dream.

"Vane, you okay in there?" my mom calls through my door.

I jump so hard I crash into my desk and knock off some books and video game cases.

If my mom comes in and finds a gorgeous girl in a skimpy dress passed out on my worn gray rug, I'll be grounded for the rest of eternity. Especially since all I have on at the moment are my Batman boxers. Pretty sure she won't buy my ghost/guardian angel/freak-of-nature theories either.

I stumble toward the door, prepared to barricade it with my dresser if I have to. "I'm fine, Mom," I say as I grab the first T-shirt I see off my floor and throw it on, along with my gym shorts.

"Then what's all that banging?"

Come on, Vane. Think!

Inspiration strikes. "I found a date roach in my bed."

"Did you kill it?" My mom sounds farther away, like she jumped back.

"I tried to, but now I can't find it." I don't need to worry about my mom offering to help. She's a big believer in the whole *boys should kill all the bugs* philosophy.

"Well, I won't distract you, then," she says, and I can't help smiling. "But make sure you kill it before you go back to sleep. I don't want it getting loose in the house."

"On it," I promise, my body relaxing as her footsteps retreat down the hall.

One crisis solved. Now I just have to deal with the passed-out, scantily clad girl on the floor of my room who's most likely a supernatural creature.

Riiiiiiiiiiiiight.

No clue what to do about that one.

I switch on my lamp and creep toward her, craning my neck to get a better look. Her eyes are closed, but her chest rises and falls in slow, heavy breaths.

It occurs to me that she might be hurt. I don't know if ghosts can get injured—or if she even is a ghost. She looks real enough right now. Pale, though—and her face looks like she's in pain.

Is she sick?

What am I supposed to do if she is? Pretty sure the hospital won't be able to help her. Do magical creatures have the same anatomy as humans?

My eyes scan her body.

Wow.

And . . . I'm checking out a girl who might be something other than human. Not to mention she's currently *unconscious*.

Awesome timing, man.

She clearly needs help. She's been out cold for at least five minutes. I have to do something.

But what?

Water.

On TV they're always giving it to people like it's a cure-all.

It can't hurt. I even have a half-finished water bottle by my bed.

I grab it, then tiptoe to the girl. She doesn't stir—even when I crouch beside her.

I hold my breath as I lift her head, gently propping her neck against my knee. Her skin is cool and smooth and I worry she's shaking—but then I realize it's me who's trembling.

She's *real*.

I didn't really believe it until that moment. All the dreams. All the fleeting half glimpses. Even seeing her so clearly tonight. All of that could've been a mistake somehow. But now I have her—in my room. *In my arms.* And despite anything my eyes just saw, she feels human.

She feels like me.

A tiny thrill jolts me as my fingers part her lips. They're even softer than I imagined. Yeah—I imagined them. I dare anyone to try being haunted by a hot girl for ten years and not think about kissing her.

I place the bottle against her lips. Will she be able to swallow if I pour it into her mouth? Or will she choke?

I pour just enough to wet her tongue, not breathing until I see her swallow. It's surreal watching her lips close and the muscles in her throat contract. Little, normal things in such an impossible situation.

I still can't believe I'm actually holding her. My fingers tangle in her hair—the same dark, wavy strands that always swirl around her face in the dreams. I'm glad it's not in the tight braid she was wearing earlier. She looks softer with it loose. Gentler. She still has a strong jaw, but it balances her wide eyes and full lips.

Back to her lips. I can't stop staring at them.

Dude—not now!

I pour more water in her mouth, and this time she drinks faster. She downs the rest of the bottle, but she still hasn't fully woken.

I scan the room for more water, freezing when she moans.

I set her head down and back against the farthest wall. I have no idea what will happen when she wakes up, but having some distance between us seems like a good idea. She may look gentle when she's sleeping, but there was something in the way she carried herself earlier that I definitely don't want to get on the wrong side of.

She moans again and rolls to her side. I glance at my door, hoping my parents haven't heard. But I don't have time to worry about it because the next second she jumps to her feet.

She wobbles, taking deep breaths as she squints at her hands. I can't tell if she knows I'm there.

I clear my throat.

She tenses, then turns toward me, her face a mixture of fear and pain and uncertainty.

"What did you do to me?" she whispers.

"Wait—what? I didn't do anything."

She moves forward, wincing with each step. I try to back out of the way, but she's quick—way too fast for someone who was just unconscious. She corners me. "What. Did. You. Do. To. Me?"

"I swear, I didn't do anything."

She grabs my shoulders, insanely strong for a girl her size. "I can feel it, Vane. What did you give me?"

Her voice is louder now—loud enough that my parents might

be able to hear. But I'm not sure that's a bad thing. I'm almost ready to call for help. Her nails cut through my shirt, digging into my skin.

I grab her wrists and try to pull her hands away, but she fights me. "Relax, okay? I gave you some water—that's it."

"Water?" Her arms go limp.

"Yeah." I point to the empty bottle near her feet. "Just water. Nothing else."

"Water," she repeats, sinking to the floor.

I glance at the door, wondering if I should take my chance and run, get as far away from whatever she is as I can. But I can't leave. Not after ten years of wondering about her, dreaming about her.

She lowers her head, letting her hair fall across her face. "Do you have any idea what you've done?"

"Uh, yeah—I helped you."

"Helped me." An oddly hysterical laugh slips out of her lips as she looks up, peering at me between the wild, wavy strands.

I stare into the same dark eyes I've seen every night. Every time I close my eyes. I always thought they were beautiful. Almost hyp-notic. Powerful, even.

Now they look defeated.

As if confirming my thoughts, she curls her knees into her chest, hugging them with her arms and rocking back and forth.

"You didn't help me," she whispers. "You just killed everyone."

CHAPTER 8

AUDRA

My eyes burn in a way I don't understand. Then something wet streaks down my cheek.

A tear.

Everything inside me knots with a mix of fear and rage.

I shouldn't be crying. Not because I have to be brave or strong or maintain any of the other aspects of my oath. I physically shouldn't be able to shed tears.

The fact that I can means it really is too late. My body's absorbed the water. I'll be weakened for months.

Just like my father was the day he died.

My shoulders shake as a tremendous sob overcomes me. I want to tear at my skin, scratch deep and hard, like that could somehow scrape away the water inside me. But it doesn't work that way. I've suffered so much to avoid my father's mistake, gone to such lengths not to tie myself to the earth. But I never planned for this. Never considered that joining the wind would make me faint, or that Vane would give me water to revive me.

Vane.

My head snaps up, and I smear the traitorous tears away with my hands. He's balanced on the balls of his feet, ready to jump back.

I can't blame him. My behavior is far from the composed, commanding presence I was trained to present when his mind finally had a breakthrough.

I have to get it together. This is another . . . complication. I'll find the solution.

I clear my throat, brushing my hair out of my face as I rise. I wish I had time to rebraid it—and change back into my uniform—but I have to settle for tucking it behind my ears and smoothing the fabric of my dress.

"I'm sorry," I say, proud that I sound strong and steady. "We need to talk."

"You think?" His pitch is an octave higher than I'm used to. "Who are you—and what the hell do you mean, *I just killed everyone?*"

"Keep your voice down." I step toward him, but he jerks away.

"Don't come any closer—and don't tell me what to freaking do. You're in my house."

"I know. And if you don't want your parents to find me, you need to be quiet."

He glares at me, clearly not happy I've made a valid point. "Who are you?"

"My name is Audra. I have all the answers you're looking for, Vane. But we need to have this conversation somewhere private. Will you come with me?"

Rebellion wars in his eyes. And after the way I acted, I can't blame him. Which only makes it more frustrating.

My head throbs from the strain I put my body through. I rub my temples and take a deep, slow breath as I study the lines of his face—a face I know so well I can recall every detail from memory. Fear is etched in every feature, making him look older. Pained.

I've been ordered to make him trust me, but in that moment I'm surprised to realize I *want* him to trust me.

"Please, Vane. I need you to come with me." My eyes hold his as I take a cautious step toward him. I reach out and let my fingers brush down his arm. He flinches but doesn't pull away—even when I take his hand.

His skin feels smooth and warm, and my fingers tingle as they absorb his heat.

Strange.

It's been years since I've touched anyone. My body must not know how to respond.

Vane stares at our hands, the fear in his face fading into uncertainty. "Is it safe?"

"Completely."

"Is it far away?"

"We can walk there."

"And you promise you'll explain everything?"

"Everything."

His eyes challenge me. Dare me to break my promise. He doesn't understand it's part of my job to tell him everything. But he will soon enough.

I pull him toward the window.

"Wait—we're going out that way?"

"I can't exactly walk out the front door—especially in this." I point to my tiny blue-black dress. It seemed revealing earlier, when I was alone. Now, in the light of his room, with his eyes trailing over me, I feel almost naked.

Especially when he grins and says, "Yeah, my mom definitely wouldn't approve."

I drop his hand and fold my arms across my chest. I'd almost forgotten how obnoxious he can be. "Let's go."

I leap through the window without looking back. It isn't a far fall—the house only has one story—but there's an unfamiliar ache in my joints when my feet hit the ground.

The water.

I bite my lip, taking deep breaths to remain calm as Vane heaves himself out the window. He yelps as his arm catches the thorns of the pyracantha. I roll my eyes.

"My home is this way," I say, dashing across the open lawn. It's the only part of the yard where the moonlight's bright enough for us to be seen, so we have to move quickly until we reach the towering date palms of the grove that borders the house on all sides.

A soft Southerly revives me as I run. Caressing my face. Drying the last of my tears. The wind can't lighten the extra weight I carry from the water, but it eases my headache. Vane matches my pace stride for stride. Whether that means he's stronger than I thought or I'm weaker than I feared, I can't tell.

Deeper and deeper we head into the trees. The air is sweet with the aroma of their sticky fruit, and I can feel fallen dates squishing between my bare toes. At least, I hope they're dates. The night is anything but silent, and all manner of giant insects chirp and skitter around us. This place is infested—*not* the kind of location I would've chosen for a home. But my options were limited.

A few minutes more and the pale walls of my shelter come into view.

Vane snorts. "Unbelievable."

"What?"

"You live there?" He points to the house ahead—or rather, what's left of it.

A fire condemned it long before I stumbled across it. But the two and a half remaining walls—one of which still has a cracked glass window—along with the scorched support beams from the former roof give me enough space to hide. I draped fallen palm fronds across the beams to provide shade from the heat, and piled more on the ground to form a place to sleep. They aren't nearly as soft as I'd like, but they're good enough for nesting birds. I demand no better.

"Why? What's wrong with that?" I ask, trying to understand his incredulous expression.

"I just should've guessed. I came here a couple times when I was a kid—but then I stopped because I was afraid it . . ."

He stops dead in his tracks.

I turn to face him, surprised at how pale he looks in the moonlight.

"I was afraid it's haunted," he says. "I heard whispers in the air, and sometimes the way the trees rustled, it seemed like there was a ghost." He hesitates, like he's trying to find the courage to ask his next question. "That was you, wasn't it?"

I nod.

He backs away from me. "What are you?"

"I'm the same as you," I say, treading lightly.

He laughs and the harsh sound slices the quiet night. "Please. I saw the way you floated in the air like that, and formed out of nothing and—"

"So you really did see me?" I ask, needing to hear him say it. I've waited so long for him to have the breakthrough, it's still hard to believe it finally happened.

"Yeah. So don't feed me that crap about you being human, because I know what I saw, and humans can't do that."

"Vane." I wait for him to meet my eyes. "I never said anything about being human."

He sucks in a breath. "So . . . you're not human."

"No."

His face is a kaleidoscope of emotions. Relief. Doubt. Fear. Vindication.

I don't say anything, waiting for him to make the last, most important connection.

I can almost hear the pieces click together in his brain.

His voice is barely audible when he finally speaks. "But you said you're the same as me."

I open my mouth to utter the words that will twist his world inside out and upside down, but my voice vanishes.

I'd give anything to forget who and what I am. To wake each morning not having to face what I must do. Or what I've done. Vane's been living that kind of blissful ignorance for ten years. Oblivious to his responsibilities. Unaware of his role. Innocent to the overwhelming challenges he'll face.

Now I'm about to strip that freedom away from him.

The guilt and regret nearly choke me.

But he needs to hear the truth. And I swore an oath that I'd tell him. So I square my shoulders and yank his universe out from under him.

"That's right, Vane. I'm not human. And neither are you."

CHAPTER 9

VANE

I can't stop laughing.

I laugh so hard I scare bats out of the trees. My sides ache and I have to gasp for air and tears stream from the corners of my eyes. But what else am I supposed to do?

This is officially entering new realms of crazy, and I refuse to be dragged there. I may not understand a few things about my life or my past, but I'm absolutely positive that I'm a *human being*. I mean, I look like everyone else. I feel like everyone else.

So does Audra.

Right—because she's human too, I tell myself.

Psycho. But human.

I must've dreamed what I saw in my room. I've had plenty of other crazy dreams about Audra—why not one more?

That's a good enough explanation for me.

"I'm out of here," I say as I head back toward my house. "Get off our property—and stay away from me, or I'll smack you with a restraining order so fast you won't know what hit you."

"I can't do that, Vane."

I ignore the chills I get when she says my name. "Yes, you can."

She isn't my dream girl. She's a problem I'm getting rid of.

She doesn't follow me. Instead, I hear her start whispering.

I don't want to listen—fight to ignore her—but it feels like her voice bores into my skull. The sounds are mush, but after a second they sink in and become words.

"Come to me swiftly, carry no trace. Lift me softly, then flow and race."

The words fill me with warmth and ache and I want to run to them and away from them at the same time. But I can't move. I'm frozen—enchanted by the whispers swirling in my consciousness.

Enchanted.

"Are you putting a spell on me?" I yell, shaking my head, trying to break whatever voodoo she's using.

She doesn't answer.

Instead, a blast of wind tangles around me, and I learn what a fly feels as a spider binds it with a web. Among the chaos and torrential gusts I feel her arms wrap across my shoulders and an explosion of heat as her body presses against mine. Then we're airborne.

I swear my stomach stays behind as we climb up and up and up. I have to keep popping my ears as we shift altitudes.

But I'm not afraid.

I know I should be. My life is literally hanging on a gust of wind that Audra's somehow controlling—and she's clearly some sort of witch or goddess or other impossible creature.

I don't care.

It feels *right* up in the dark sky. Natural. Like scratching an itch I didn't feel until the burning relief rushes through me. Up high, with the wind whipping around me and Audra's warmth mingling with mine, everything else washes away.

I close my eyes and listen to the wind—and I don't hear the thundering, whipping sound I expect. I hear the ancient language that belongs to the wind and the wind alone. It whispers of the places it's been.

Of change.

Of power.

Of freedom.

I want to listen forever. And that's when I know.

I'm *not* human.

I have no idea what I am, or what I'm supposed to do with that revelation. But it doesn't stop it from being true.

A lurch in my stomach rips me back to reality and I open my eyes. We're falling, fast and hard. I can't be sure—but I have a feeling the girly scream comes from me.

"Hit the ground running," Audra shouts in my ear as the dark earth races toward us.

Right. 'Cause moving my feet will stop me from turning into a Vane-splat.

But my options are limited, so when she shoves me away from

her and whispers, "Release," at the same second the wind cocoon unravels, I follow her lead, pumping my legs as my toes graze the hard earth.

I laugh as we both run across the rocky ground as fast as our feet will carry us.

I'm not dead. In fact, I've never felt more alive.

I force my legs to a stop and take in the scenery. We're high in the foothills, with the lights of the desert cities twinkling in the distance and the freeway snaking below. Stark, pointed poles shoot out of the ground in neat rows, with tri-pointed blades spinning at the top.

Windmills.

The San Gorgonio Pass Wind Farm.

I've driven through it on my rare escapes from this suffocating valley, but I've never walked among the enormous turbines. The night rings with the sound of their massive blades slicing the air as the wind shoves against them. Red lights at the top of each tower glow like evil eyes. I let my vision go out of focus as the windmills spin round and round.

Footsteps crunch behind me, reminding me I'm not alone.

"So what am I?" I ask without turning around. I'm afraid to look at her when she says the words that will change my life forever.

"We're sylphs."

"Sylphs?" That isn't the answer I expected. I mean, if I have to be a mythical creature, it could at least be one I've heard of. "What the hell is a *sylph*?"

"That's what humans call an air elemental."

"An air elemental?"

"Are you going to keep repeating everything I say as a question?"

I spin to face her. "Uh . . . I'll stop when you say something that actually makes sense."

"How's this? You're a Windwalker. We control the wind. We're part of the wind."

"We're *part* of the wind?"

She grits her teeth and I realize I repeated her again. I don't care. "How can we be part of the wind?"

"The same way humans are part of the earth. When they die, they turn back to dust."

"So—what?—when we die, we go back to being wind?"

A shadow passes across her face, even in the dim moonlight. "Yes."

I shake my head, ready to tell her how ridiculous that sounds. But a memory knocks the words out of me: two tangled forms—a little bit like bodies, but mostly they're just hollow, twisted masses. I don't remember seeing them in person, but when I was ten I finally got brave enough to Google the grainy photos, hoping it would spark a few repressed memories.

"That's what happened to my parents—why their bodies were unrecognizable when they found them, isn't it?" I whisper.

She looks away. "Yes. It can be a slow process sometimes, but eventually there's nothing left but air."

So my real parents weren't human either.

It makes sense—if I'm a sylph, they had to be too.

Would've been nice if they'd clued me in on that one. *Hey, son—*

heads up, you're a Windwalker. Though, maybe they did and I just don't remember.

I swallow and force my lips to ask the question that's plagued me for the last ten years. Now that the answer's finally in my reach, I'm a little afraid to hear it. "What happened to my parents that day, in the storm?"

Audra takes a slow, deep breath before she speaks. "They were murdered."

Murdered.

The word feels cold and foreign. I always thought their deaths were a fluke.

My hands clench into fists. "By who?"

Her voice is ice when she answers. "His name is Raiden."

I memorize the name of the man who killed my family. Almost killed me. "Why did he kill them?"

"It's . . . hard to explain. It involves things your mind is not yet ready to understand. I'll tell you when the time is right."

I open my mouth to argue, but my brain is already twisting in a thousand different directions. I'm not sure I can handle a long, complicated explanation—especially about such a painful subject.

I sink to the ground, leaning against one of the windmill bases. The soft vibration seeps through my thin blue T-shirt, and I can't help wishing I could rewind the last few hours and go back to being the regular guy with the weird dream stalker and the blank past.

How am I supposed to go home or see my friends, knowing what I know now? How am I ever supposed to be normal again?

I've crossed a line. I feel maxed out. But there's one thing I have to know. "Why am I still alive?"

"What?"

"The day my family died. How did I survive?"

"My—" She stops, like she can't push the words out. "My father saved you."

"Your father? But . . ."

"What?"

"I always thought you saved me."

Her eyes drop to the ground. "I was there. But I wasn't strong enough."

Her voice catches, and it occurs to me that this is a painful memory for her, too. I clear my throat, struggling to find a sensitive way of wording my next question. "And your father. He's . . ."

"Dead," she whispers. "He sacrificed himself to save you."

I don't know what to say as she turns her back to me and walks off. Only a tiny sliver of moon lights the sky, and she vanishes into the darkness. I fight off a wave of panic. She wouldn't leave me here, would she?

No. I've never had any reason to believe she means me any harm. Except tonight.

"What did you mean earlier?" I ask quietly.

"Earlier?" Her voice is a faceless sound in the darkness. Like she really is a ghost.

"When you woke up in my room. You said I killed everyone."

A long stretch of silence passes before she speaks. "Water weakens us. Same with food. It ties us to the ground, which limits our capabilities—"

"Whoa—you're saying I can't eat?" That definitely falls into the *not cool* category.

"Your body's not ready for that kind of sacrifice yet. The starvation would actually make you weaker right now, since you're so reliant on earthly foods. But soon you'll have to start working your way toward it, if you want to reach your full potential. The closer to the wind we are, the more powerful we can be. I've been denying myself for years to be at my peak strength. Now the water's weakened me."

That makes about as much sense as the quadratic functions we studied last year. "It was half a bottle of water. It'll be out of your system by tomorrow."

"Our bodies don't work that way. Anything physically of this earth is at odds with the wind. Even the tiniest bit of something as small as water will severely limit what I can do—for months. And it couldn't have happened at a more crucial time."

I hear a scraping sound, like she kicked the ground.

"Why is now so crucial?"

"Because Raiden knows we're here. He's the most powerful Windwalker alive, and he's been trying to find you for years. I did everything I could to shield you, but now his Stormers—his warriors—are coming to capture you, and if we run, they'll tear the whole valley apart looking for you. Thousands of people could die. And the Stormers will find our trail and hunt us down. Our only option is to fight, and if I'm not at my full strength, our chances . . . aren't good."

Somehow I'm on my feet, though I don't remember deciding to stand. "All of that over me? Why—why am I so important? I'm no one."

"That's where you're wrong, Vane. You're our only hope."

I have to laugh. It sounds so Princess Leia. *Help me, Obi-Wan Kenobi.*

"I think you have the wrong guy."

"Believe me, I don't. You're probably the most important person alive at the moment."

And . . . my brain pretty much shuts down.

In one night I find out I'm not human, that my parents were murdered, and that the same evil punk who killed them is sending warriors to get me because I'm supposed to be some big important person—even though I'm *no one*. Oh, and we can't run, can't hide, and can't win in a fight. It kinda makes me want to do something lame like pinch my arm and hope I wake up.

But I'm not dreaming. I can feel the breezes streaking across my face. And I'm definitely not imagining the songs floating on the wind. The melodies satisfy a craving I've always felt but never knew how to understand.

Audra moves close enough that I can make her out through the dim light. The fabric of her skimpy dress looks like it's come to life in the wind, rippling over the curves of her body. I have to force myself to focus on her face—which looks just like it does in my dreams, the way her eyes are watching me and her hair's swirling around her cheeks. Her lips part and I expect her to whisper the same floaty sounds I'm used to hearing every night.

Instead, she says, "None of this matters. Right now you need to focus on your training."

"Training?"

"You need to learn to fight. To defend yourself when the Stormers come for you. It's why I'm here. To teach you what you need to fulfill your role."

"My role?"

"We're back to you repeating everything I say."

"Well, what do you expect me to do? Nothing you say makes any freaking sense!"

I can tell by the way her jaw locks that she wants to yell at me. "You're right," she says instead. "But you've had more revelations in one hour than anyone can handle—and I have to figure out what to do about the Stormers coming."

A hint of defeat returns to her eyes.

"Are people really going to die?" I ask, giving her the cue to tell me this is all a big, elaborate prank.

"I hope not."

Not the reassurance I'm looking for.

But then she squares her shoulders. "I won't let anything happen. I'm one of the strongest fighters—even with some water in my system. And I'll get help."

"Help? Like . . . other sylphs? What, you call them up and say, 'Hey, Windwalkers, we need you to come fight some bad guys,' and they just blow into town and save the day?"

One side of her lips twists into a smile. "It's not that simple." The smile fades. "It's not simple at all. But I'll take care of it. As soon as I take you home."

My mouth opens with a new question—but I freeze when she puts her finger on my lips.

"I know you want more answers, but if I'm going to call for backup, I need to do that as soon as possible. Please, just give me a few hours and I'll explain more in the morning."

I want to argue—there's a boatload of crap she hasn't explained—but I'm too distracted by the electric warmth radiating from her fingertip, tingling through my whole face. I've never felt anything like it, and it's a tremendous accomplishment to give even the slightest nod.

Her eyes lower, focusing on her finger on my mouth, and some sort of indecipherable emotion flickers across her face. "Thank you."

The words sound almost choked as she drops her hand to her side and shakes it. Then she turns away and whispers the same incantation she used before.

"Come to me swiftly, carry no trace. Lift me softly, then flow and race."

This time I know what she's doing. She's controlling the wind. And the wind obeys her command, streaming around us.

She steps toward me, standing only inches away. Close enough that I can feel her body heat radiating through the air. Close enough that I become even more aware of her lips. The winds tangle tighter, separating us from the rest of the world. A safe, private space for just the two of us.

"Hold on to me," she orders, and it takes me a second to realize I didn't imagine it. I was thinking of doing just that.

My hands circle her tiny waist, so small my fingers almost touch. Everything about her is fragile and delicate. But she surges with strength and warmth and power.

And I want her.

She's all I've wanted for years. No matter how much I've tried to fight or ignore it.

Does she want me?

Would she stand so close if she doesn't?

I wet my lips, searching for the courage to make my move. I lean a tiny bit forward and . . .

Almost throw up on her when the wind yanks us off the mountain.

The free fall makes any roller coaster I've ever been on feel like a merry-go-round, and I cling to her, hating myself for yelping again.

Way to be cool, man. I'm sure she's really impressed.

I can't tell if she heard me scream. Her eyes are closed, and her mind seems a million miles away—which would be a relief if we weren't on a collision course with the valley floor.

"Uh—Audra," I shout, my pounding heart drowning out the wind.

She doesn't blink.

I shake her, but she still doesn't flinch, like she's decided that plummeting from a mountain is the perfect time for a nap. "Seriously, Audra, this isn't funny!"

Still she doesn't respond. So I shut my eyes as the ground races toward us, preparing to experience what a bug feels when it hits a car windshield. But at the last second she whispers, "Steady," and the winds pull up, moving parallel to the ground.

"Don't do that again!" I yell between gasping breaths.

"Did I scare you?"

"Uh—yeah." I damn near wet myself—not that I'd tell her that.

"Let that be lesson number one. The things I'm going to teach you will seem impossible, but I know what I'm doing. You have to trust me."

I snort. "I'm still trying to convince myself the mushrooms on my burger weren't the psychedelic kind and I'm gonna wake up tomorrow and find out this was all a hallucination."

She doesn't smile. Her eyes narrow.

"Fine, I trust you." Sheesh.

We fly in silence for a few seconds before she whispers, "Release," and shoves me away from her again.

We hit the ground running as the winds unravel, setting us down in the soft grass of my front yard. The house is dark—except for my bedroom, which glows with the lamp I flicked on after she collapsed on my floor.

Seems like years ago, not hours.

My window is still open. Great. My room's probably swarming with moths.

"I'll be back to start your training tomorrow," she says, turning toward the date grove.

"That's it? I'm just supposed to sleep now?"

"You need rest. Tomorrow will be a long day."

"What about you?" My skin itches just thinking about that pile of palm leaves she's been sleeping on. "You could stay in my room if you want."

She raises an eyebrow.

I feel my cheeks heat up. "I didn't mean *that*. I'd take the floor."

Half a grin stretches across her lips. I wonder if she knows how to give a full smile.

"I won't be sleeping," she says. "I need to see about getting help."

"Oh. Right." To fight the psychos coming to capture me, for a reason I still don't understand. Yeah—sleep will definitely be a lost cause.

"Rest well, Vane," she whispers, then races toward the palms.

I wait until she disappears into the grove before I climb through my window—cursing my parents for putting thornbushes in the planter underneath. I pull the window closed and lock it.

The clock on my nightstand says 1:03 a.m.

I stare at the empty water bottle on the ground. At the place on the rug where Audra passed out. At the thrashed pillows and sheets from when I startled awake.

I don't know what to do with anything I've seen or felt or anything Audra told me. So I do what she ordered. I get into bed, wondering if this will be the first night I don't dream about her.

I'll miss her.

A soft breeze brushes through my room, singing some sort of ancient lullaby.

I close my eyes and let the whispers carry me away to dreams of my heritage.

Dreams of Audra.

CHAPTER 10

AUDRA

pace the length of my tiny shelter so many times it's a wonder my feet don't wear a groove in the floor. Finally I collapse to the hard, dirty ground. Stalling, like a coward.

My eyes start to close and I rip them open. I haven't slept more than two hours a night for ten years. The Gales warned me not to exhaust myself, but guarding Vane is a round-the-clock job. I can't give in to self-indulgence and risk letting them down.

Letting my father down.

At least Vane gets to rest. The Easterly I sent will sing his overwhelmed mind to sleep. It's a trick my father used, twisting a breeze into a whirl of lullabies. He sent one to my room every night after he'd tucked me in—adding his warm, rich voice to the mix.

My father couldn't speak to the birds like my mother and I,

but he sang like one. It wasn't truly a *gift*, but something we shared nonetheless. Every time we flew together we'd sing duets.

But I didn't add my song to the wind I sent Vane. My melodies were silenced the day my father died.

It felt like a piece of my heart crumbled away just weaving together the lullabies, but Vane deserves a last night of peace. He has a heavy burden resting on his shoulders—far heavier than the tasks resting on mine. The next few days will be the hardest of his life.

It surprises me how easy it is to empathize with him. Over the years I've had a hard time not resenting him. Hating that his life is more important than my father's. More important than mine. I worried it would be hard to be civil once we were forced to interact.

And he is . . . *challenging*—but not always in the ways I expected. Some of my reactions tonight are a mystery to me. Like my hesitation to tell him the truth—one of the most fundamental aspects of my assignment. Or the times I was moved to touch him.

His arm.

His lips.

Why did I do that? I never intended to do that.

Had it been pity?

I want that to be the answer—but it doesn't explain why my skin still simmers everywhere we touched. Why even now, just remembering the way he held me, or the look in his eyes, leaves my chest strangely empty. Almost like . . .

I stamp out the thought before it can finish.

Whatever those feelings are, I'll squelch them immediately. I don't need Vane Weston complicating things any more than he already has.

Gavin nips at my hand and his talons dig into my wrist, his not-so-gentle way of reminding me that I've stopped stroking the silky gray feathers along his back. He can be a demanding creature, but he's my best friend. And he's the only one who doesn't hate me for what happened. He also ignores his instinct to migrate north, just to stay with me. So I tolerate his difficulties. Even when he leaves a half-eaten rabbit on the floor.

My stomach rumbles at the sight, shooting needles through my abdomen.

Another side effect of the water.

The longer we go without eating, the more our stomachs shrink. It's a painful process—and why most guardians end up giving in at least once a year to stop the hunger pains.

Not me. And after ten years, my stomach had all but shrunk away.

Now the water's revived my appetite, and the craving burns so intense, even the gruesome carcass or the rotting dates on the floor tempt me.

A flame of anger sparks, but I snuff it out. I deserve every hardship, every discomfort, and then some. My life doesn't matter. It might as well have ended that day in the storm.

But I *did* survive. And earned my father's gift—though I'll always feel like I stole it.

I can still feel my mother's fingers digging into my skin as she rocked my shoulders. Screaming that I took the only part of him she had left. That he shouldn't have chosen me over her.

I still don't know why he did.

The whispered message he sent with it left me no clue. Just, *I know you will use this well, my darling Audra.*

He'd wanted me to have it. So I'd breathed in, letting the wisdom and energy flood my mind as the tears streamed down my face and the last wisps of my father drifted away with the squalls.

I vowed then and there that I'd finish what he started. Become a guardian. Prepare Vane. Make him stronger than anyone ever thought he could be, so he can end Raiden's reign of terror.

And now I'll protect the innocent people in these arid cities from the Stormers.

Which means calling for help is my duty.

But . . . I can't seem to make myself do it.

I don't have a safe way to contact the Gale Force on my own. They divide the information guardians are allowed to have—and since I know everything there is to know about Vane Weston, they tell me nothing further.

It's a safety measure that saved us four years ago, when Raiden captured two of our best. None of us know the full horrors he put them through—but he broke them. And learned the Gale's deepest secret. That Vane survived the attack that killed his parents all those years ago.

But he didn't learn where we'd hidden him.

And so Raiden's relentless search began.

That's when I finally became a guardian. Before, I was merely "in training," and had to report to my trainer daily with my progress. Even then, the Gales worried the pressure was too much for my age and tried to force me to take breaks from my duties. But I always snuck back to watch Vane. I couldn't risk that something would happen in the time I was away. And once Raiden knew Vane was alive, the Gales could stall my appointment no longer. Vane needed constant protection, and I was the best Gale available. I'm the youngest guardian by far, but no one can match my skill and determination. The decision was almost unanimous. Only one vote against.

My mother's.

Not because she worried for my safety. She didn't think me capable.

Now I have to go to her and explain what a mess we're in. Beg for help.

All I've endured and survived tonight will be nothing compared to that.

Which is why I sit frozen, stroking Gavin and searching for some reserve of strength to do what needs to be done. I finally find it in the stuffy black jacket now buttoned across my chest. In the slight pull from my braid.

I rewove my hair and changed back into my uniform the second I came home. I can't let myself forget my role.

So I give myself to the count of five to wallow in fear and pity. Then I send Gavin to his perch on the windowsill, order him to carry away his mutilated carcass before I return, and push myself off the floor.

I call two of the Northerlies I sent from the mountains and

wrap them around me with barely a breath. Their song of power and endurance fills my mind as they float me away.

I haven't flown this path since the day I left four years ago, but the way is scarred into my brain. Over the hills, past the forest of spiky, twisted Joshua trees to the small, square house hidden in a stretch of desert so vast and empty I'm not sure the groundlings have any idea it exists. Which is why the Gales chose it.

The house is dark, but she's home. I can feel her presence in the chill in the air. In the tightness in my chest.

I send the winds away, touching my feet to the soft sand quieter than a cat stalking its prey. Still, a slight movement near the window tells me she knows I'm here. Nothing can sneak up on her. It's another of her *gifts*, and it only failed her once.

But that was my fault.

Birds of all shapes and sizes watch me from their rooftop perches as I cross the sparse yard, their glassy eyes glowing in the moonlight. They're drawn to her, abandoning their instincts in order to stay within her reach. Years ago they would've greeted me like their kin. Filled the air with their ringing songs as they swooped and swirled, brushing my skin with their silky feathers.

Now only their judgment surrounds me. They've rejected me as much as she has.

Once a month my mother sends one gloomy crow to check my progress. He claws me with his razor-sharp talons as he delivers her message—the same message every time. My only contact with my mother, or the Windwalker world.

Has he had the Westerly breakthrough?

An update on Vane. The only thing that matters.

I ignore the birds' mocking stares and focus on the lone, gnarled oak—a testimony to survival and endurance in the arid desert landscape. I kneeled in the shade of its leaves when I swore my oath to the Gales. My mother didn't even bother to come outside.

I left that day and never came back. Never planned to return.

This is necessary, I remind myself as I force my feet up the steps.

The house is small, plain, and beige—the kind of place your eyes might skip entirely unless you tell them to pay attention. My mother despises it.

If she had her way, she'd return to our old estate in the east. Surround herself with the soothing tradewinds of our heritage and escape the turbulent desert storms.

But that's not an option now.

An icy wind blasts the door open, and I'm proud of myself for not jumping. I'm prepared for her games. But I can't stop my legs from shaking as I cross the threshold into the sparsely furnished, unlit room.

Leave it to my mother to keep our first meeting in four years in the dark.

"Well," she says in her deep, throaty voice as she rises from a plush armchair by the only window. Moonlight streaks down the delicate lines of her perfect figure and face. Even darkness—or the scowl on her lips—can't dull her beauty. "Given your dejected demeanor, and the shifting Northerlies I've been feeling all night"—she shudders, rubbing the skin on her arms like it itches—"I'm assuming you're here to ask for help."

"It's nice to see you too, Mother." I can't keep the bitterness out of my voice. I don't blame her for the way she's treated me since my father died. That doesn't make it hurt any less.

She doesn't respond. Instead, she rubs the skin on her arms harder—like the itch has grown into pain—and waits for me to speak again.

I clear my throat. "I need you to call the Gale Force for aid."

One perfectly arched eyebrow rises in my direction and I fight back my sigh. She'll require every last detail before she extends even the smallest bread crumb of assistance. So I give her the full story: how I used the Northerly to stop Vane from bonding to a groundling. How I joined the wind to force Vane's Easterly breakthrough. And how Vane gave me water while I was unconscious. I don't explain the predicament that leaves us in. She knows as well as I do.

My mother makes dramatic pauses a work of art, but I refuse to so much as blink until she finally tosses her long, raven-black hair and turns away. As a fellow guardian, she should be wearing the regulation braid. But my mother's like a wildwind. She follows her own flow. It's what my father loved most about her.

She swishes down the hall, flicking on the light so I can see her silky green dress shimmer with each movement. My mother's never worn a true guardian uniform, needing her skin exposed to the wind in order to use her gift. The slightest ripple in the air speaks to her as clearly as the words of the wind's song. A secret language only she understands. A constant push and pull. An ebb and flow of power and drain, stillness and motion.

A rare gift *and* burden none of us have ever understood. But my father tried harder than anyone. He was awed that her strength caused weakness, and he did all he could to steady the turbulence so she could rise above it.

It's what *she* loved most about *him*.

She scrapes a chair across the floor and sits at the narrow, empty table. She doesn't invite me to join her. I wouldn't anyway.

Against my will, my focus is drawn to the place it hurts most to look. To the wind chimes hanging over the table, where a chandelier would be.

A blackbird—carved in exquisite detail—soars with spread wings over a series of gleaming silver chimes. My father made it for her the day she chose to bond to him and it has hung from the breeziest eaves of every house we stayed in, filling the air with its tinkling song. It's the only thing from her past that survived the Stormer's tornado—not counting me.

Given the perfect shine on the chimes and the way they're kept away from the elements—safe, protected—it's obvious which means more.

My eyes burn, but the snub isn't what upsets me. It's seeing the chimes trapped inside. Never to sing again.

My mother clears her throat and I force myself to look at her, hating that she caught me staring.

"What was he doing with another girl in the first place?" she asks. "Vane should be so madly in love with you he'd never so much as think of wasting time on anyone else—especially a groundling."

"How? I wasn't allowed to talk to him until his mind broke through, and I tried not to let him see me."

My mother sighs. "And that was your mistake. You're a beautiful girl, Audra. You should be able to turn boys to mush with a simple smile, and use that to your advantage."

Easy for her to say. My mother can melt the heart of any man—sylph or groundling—with one toss of her shiny hair or a single wink of her sapphire-blue eyes.

"I don't know how to make Vane feel that way," I admit, shaking my hand as my fingers tingle again. Remembering Vane's warmth. "I'm not like you. I can't have any guy I want."

"Neither can I." Her right hand darts to her chest, clutching the silver feather hanging from a black cord at the nape of her neck.

My father's guardian pendant.

I have a similar necklace tucked under my jacket, though my cord is blue. My life force still flows through mine.

I nearly gag on the emotions as I swallow them.

I study my mother. Shadows under her eyes. Thin frown lines at the corners of her mouth. They appeared the day we lost my father—instant aging. And they've only deepened with time. My mother's bond should've broken with my father's death. But somehow it seems stronger. Like she's clinging to it, fierce and white-knuckled, refusing to let go. Much like her refusal to remove their *link*.

The wide gold cuff has covered her left wrist since my father clamped it there when they made their official vows. But the jeweled rings in the center have lost their shine. And the intricate black-bird mounted across them looks worn and tarnished. Like it's been rubbed dull by nervous fingers.

I clear the thickness from my throat. "It's better if Vane doesn't care for me. That would only complicate things when he learns about Solana."

My mother nods, conceding my point. The Gales have big plans for Vane. Nothing can or should get in the way.

"Still—calling a Northerly? You couldn't think of any safer way to prevent the bond?"

I stare at the floor, tracing trails in the wood grain with the toe of my polished boot. She's right again. I panicked. I saw Vane lean toward that girl and I just . . . *reacted*.

But what was I supposed to do? A Northerly was the only wind strong enough to shove him away, and there hadn't been any nearby.

Though . . . I suppose I *could* have had Gavin swoop between them. The thought didn't occur to me. Some guardian I'm turning out to be.

"I guess I shouldn't be surprised," my mother says quietly. "You're good at calling the wind when you're not supposed to."

If she punched me in the stomach it would hurt less.

"What's done is done, and I can't undo it," I whisper, reminding myself as much as her. "I've hidden the trail as much as I can and I'll train Vane to fight. But we need help. Will you call the Gales?"

Her slender fingers stroke my father's pendant, and she stares at the still, silent wind chimes when she answers. "No."

"What?" Surely she won't deny a request *this* important just to spite me.

My mother shakes her head, like she knows what I'm thinking. "Raiden's launched an all-out attack against the Gale Force, determined to extinguish our resistance. They can't afford to spare anyone—especially for such an easily resolved problem."

It takes me a second to find my voice, and another after that to choke back my anger. "I know you'll never forgive me for what happened to Dad—but this isn't about me."

"Of course it isn't. You have no idea what we've been up against these last few years. You live, breathe, and sleep Vane Weston. You don't hear how many bases Raiden found. How many Gales have been slaughtered. Raiden learned all of our secret workings from those guardians he tortured. Our depleted force is under constant attack. Calls for aid have to be restricted to absolute emergencies."

"But this *is* an emergency. Vane's too important to put at risk. Plus, the groundlings in the valley could be killed."

"Then it's up to you to train him and defend them."

"How? What can I teach him in three days?"

"Three days," my mother murmurs. She raises her arm, letting her fingers dance like they're playing an invisible instrument. Feeling the mood of the air. "I can buy you more time."

"I already stalled them every—"

"I do not share your limitations." She turns toward me, her arm a blur as she sweeps it upward, twisting her wrist and gripping the air in one fluid motion. I jump as a loud crack shatters the silent night, followed by a thunderous crash outside.

I don't need to look through the window to know she's used the wind to tear a branch from the oak and then hammered it against the ground. Controlling the wind without words, manipulating it entirely through touch. Another artful trick I've seen my mother perform dozens of times. Another skill only she understands.

"I know you're powerful—"

"Power is not the point." Her hand returns to her lap, and her fingers rub the blackbird on her golden cuff. "The wind tells me things—secrets that will save you from this mess you've made. The same secrets that would've saved your father's life ten years ago, if you hadn't lied to me."

Her face blurs to a smear of colors as my eyes well with tears. She waits for me to say something. But I don't have the words.

Eventually, she sighs. "I will buy you five more days."

"*Five* days? How can you possibly be so precise?"

"If you could feel what I feel, you'd know."

My nails prick my skin as my hands curl into fists.

She's been using that same vague answer my entire life, demanding that everyone trust her blindly. This is too important for mysteries and secrets—regardless of how powerful she's proven herself in the past.

But I know she won't tell me anything more. It's another game she plays. Always keeping the upper hand. So I say, "That still only gives me eight days. It won't be enough."

"It'll have to be."

"Vane has no skill. He's only had one breakthrough—not even the important one. I'm not strong enough to fight two Stormers by myself anymore. If you won't call the Gales, I'll need your help." I swallow, needing a second to choke down my pride. "Will you fight with me?"

The words are no louder than a breath.

Her fingers rub harder against the etched blackbird as she simply says, "No."

She knows I wouldn't ask unless I'm desperate. And still she denies me.

"The Gales need me to keep watch more than ever," she explains, meeting my eyes. "I'll be risking too much as it is by stalling them. Remember, Raiden's been desperate to find me, ever since he learned I survived. That's why I'm stuck in this hovel, cut off from the world."

I laugh—but there's no humor to it. "And you think the Gales value your life over Vane's?"

"Of course not. But Vane has you as his guardian."

"And I'm not strong enough to protect him—not with the water in my system. There's no way I can do it alone."

"I can think of a way."

Her voice is hushed, but everything inside me still twists into knots. "Is that what you're hoping for?"

"I'm *hoping* you'll trigger his Westerly breakthrough before the Stormers arrive. That's what you were supposed to do, years ago. The Gale Force chose you because they knew no one would push him harder in his training. They knew how much you had to prove. Or redeem."

Redeem.

It's the closest she's come to admitting that she blames me for my father's death, and a rebellious tear sneaks down my face before I can smear the others away.

"The Gales have been incredibly frustrated with how slow

Vane's progress has been," she adds quietly. "So take this for what it is—proper motivation to show them that you *are* a guardian and can get Vane to live up to his potential. Prove them right for trusting you. But . . . if you should fail . . . there is another option."

She doesn't look at me when she says the last part, so I can't study her face—not that it would tell me how to respond.

None of my training taught me what to say if my mother tells me to end my life. Especially since she sounds more like she's warning me I might break a nail. Not *die*.

I fight back the flurry of anger and pain that swells inside me. Hadn't I sworn—and planned for—this possibility when I accepted the role as Vane's guardian?

I knew the risks. *Better than anyone.*

"I'm prepared to make the sacrifice if it's necessary," I whisper, surprised at how true the words feel.

Every breath I take is stolen from my father, so if it comes to that I'll follow his lead and make the ultimate sacrifice.

If it comes to that.

If Vane can master all four languages in the next eight days, he'll be undefeatable.

It's a big if, but it's still a possibility.

Otherwise, I'll do what has to be done.

My mother clears her throat, almost like she's battling back emotions of her own. But her face is the same unreadable mask she's worn since the day my father left the earth. "I'll send warning when I feel the Stormers arrive in the region," she tells me.

I nod.

Trusting her goes against every instinct I have—but I'm out of options. All I can do is dive straight into Vane's training and hope she delivers on her promise. I turn toward the door.

"I'll need your windsong before you go," she calls after me.

I freeze.

Every Windwalker is born with a song on their lips—a melody only they know. When we die, the tune becomes part of the wind. A small piece of us that carries on. Our mark on the world.

They don't have to stay secret, but most of us never share them. Hearing someone's windsong is like peering inside their heart. The last person I would ever want to reveal mine to is my mother.

"Nothing leaves a more powerful trace," she explains when I stay silent. "Nothing will confuse the Stormers more."

I'd rather strip bare and expose myself to the whole of the Gales. But this isn't about me.

I can't look at her as I sing the simple verse:

A wandering breeze, swaying restlessly.
Swept up by flurries. Lost and led astray.
Storms rage and roar, and threaten all that remains.
But the breeze drifts ever onward. Finding its own way.

Each word pulls a tiny part of me with it and swirls in the air around us. My mother calls the verses toward her, tangling them together, like my breath has become the wind.

"You sing like your father," she whispers.

I risk a glance at her, but find no warmth in her eyes. They're colder and harder than I've ever seen. Like it's a crime for me to remind her of him.

Part of me wants her to follow me down the hall, even though I know she won't. She won't care that this could be the last time she sees me alive. She'll be relieved when I'm gone.

So I almost don't hear her whisper as I open the door to leave. "You're stronger than you think, Audra."

I take a shaky breath. "Goodbye, Mother."

I leave without turning around. She doesn't say goodbye.

CHAPTER 11

VANE

Wake up, Vane," a familiar voice whispers. I try to cling to the dream I'd been having—something about flying and wind—but the voice speaks again, breaking my concentration. "It's time to start training."

I force my eyes open, annoyed to find my room dim and gray. The sun's only begun to rise—*way* too early for me to be awake.

My vision clears and I focus on a dark-haired girl standing at the foot of my bed.

I jerk upright, pulling the sheet up to my neck before I realize I slept in last night's clothes. "Audra?"

She nods. "You remember?"

"Sort of." It's too dang early for me to think coherently. "And don't watch me sleep—it's creepy," I add, frustrated she saw me lose my cool.

She ignores my complaint. "How much do you remember about last night?"

I do a quick mental inventory.

Hot dream girl is real—check.

Though her hair is back in a tight braid like it was at Yard House and she has her stuffy jacket and pants on again—all of which makes her look a lot less hot and a lot more intimidating. I much prefer that tiny dress she wore last night.

My fingertips prickle, remembering the feel of her lips when I parted them. The way she looked at me when we were alone. The way she wrapped her arms around me . . .

Wait—what am I doing?

Right, mental inventory of last night.

The morning breeze sweeps through my now open window, and it whispers a song about the morning dew and sunrise and the coming heat. It's more than a little trippy. Especially since it means I didn't imagine the part about being a sylph-Windwalker-whatever-you-call-it.

Not human—check.

Weird revelations I don't know what to do with—check.

But there's something else I'm forgetting.

I notice the shadows under Audra's eyes. She looks tired. *Worried.*

More memories slam through the mental fog. Warriors are coming—which sounds so surreal, like my life has officially turned into a video game. I mean . . . *warriors!* Who has those besides evil warlords in RPGs?

Then again, I'm apparently a mythical creature. A fake-sounding one I've never heard of, but still—*mythical.*

Note to self: Google "sylphs" later.

"Is help on the way?" I ask, trying to stay focused.

She doesn't look at me as she answers. "I've come up with a different plan. It's time to train. Get dressed."

She jumps out the window before I can ask any follow-up questions, like: *What the hell does that mean?* And the *dragging me out of bed before five a.m. and telling me what to do without explanation* thing is going to stop—immediately.

Part of me wants to slam the window, lock it tight, and crawl back under the covers. Maybe I'll even put up a sign that says *Don't come back unless you're wearing the sexy dress.*

That might be worth getting up early for.

But the other part of me is too curious what Audra means by "train" to put up much of a fight. Especially since I also need to know what this new "plan" is, and make sure I don't need to get my family out of town and hidden somewhere safe.

So I seethe at the wall for a few seconds, then kick the sheet off my bed and grab a T-shirt from the stack on the floor by my dresser. The cargo shorts I wore yesterday are crumpled from a night on the floor—but at five a.m., after only four hours of sleep, I don't give a crap what I look like. I snatch them and creep down the hall to change in the bathroom.

Audra doesn't seem like the Peeping Tom type—and I'm not

sure I mind if she is. But I'm not going out there without brushing my teeth. No way I want her to get a whiff of my wicked morning breath.

Two minutes later I hop out my window minty fresh and with a scowl that hopefully says *You'd better have a darn good reason for waking me up this early.* If she catches my meaning, she doesn't seem to care. She just shushes me as I start to ask what the plan is and motions for me to follow her deep into the date grove.

We stop walking when we reach the burned-down house she's been squatting in. "What time do your parents wake up?" she asks.

"I don't know. Seven or eight." I wave a swarm of gnats away from my eyes, mentally cursing the stupid desert. It's already hot enough to make my back sweat. "But they know I'm never up before nine."

I emphasize the word "never," hoping she'll get the hint.

"Good. We can get four hours of training in every morning. Though it'd be better if you can give your parents some excuse for where you are, preferably something that will explain where you go at night, so we don't have to worry about them catching you sneaking out."

"Whoa whoa whoa. There's no way I'm waking up at five every morning—especially if you'll also be keeping me out at night. I need my beauty sleep."

Not only is it my summer vacation, but I need at least eight hours of sleep to function, and no way I'm going to walk around like a zombie just because her "new plan" doesn't involve calling for backup. What if I want her to call for backup?

Audra cocks her head. "You'll train when I tell you to train, whether it's early in the morning or the middle of the night."

I cross my arms and give her the same *Are you serious?* look I perfected when Mr. Gunter used to lecture me on how I'll be using advanced algebra in everyday life.

Yeah, right.

She's lucky I'm willing to train at all. I could just as easily hop in my car and head out of town, leave her to deal with whatever's coming on her own. I still haven't ruled that out as a possibility.

Clearly, it's time to lay down the ground rules and let her know she can't order me around. This is *my* life, and *I'm* going to be in control of it.

"I can train with you in the afternoons, as long as we go somewhere with air-conditioning. But before we do that, you're explaining *everything*. Got it?"

Personally I'm pretty proud of the line I just drew in the sand.

But Audra's eyes narrow and her jaw sets, turning her face into a series of hard lines. "You seem to be under the misimpression that you're in charge here, so let me correct that right now." She whips her arms in front of her and whispers, "Rush."

A blast of wind slams against my chest and sends me flying backward. I grunt as my back crashes into one of the remaining walls of the fire-scarred house. The wind pins me to the scratchy stucco and my eyes water from the racing air.

Audra steps toward me, the glare in her eyes leaving no doubt that she can end me right here, right now.

"Let's get a few things straight," she says, her voice deadly serious. "We're in a *tremendous* amount of danger, and I am responsible for keeping everyone in this valley alive—including you. No one will be making greater sacrifices than I will, so you will do what I say when I say it—and you will do it without complaint. Is. That. Understood?"

"I thought you said you'd answer my questions today," I shout over the roaring winds. I *distinctly* remember her promising that last night. Right around the time she promised to get help. What brought on the change of plans?

"I will, Vane. But we have to train when no one's around to see us, so you'll have to wait a few more hours. I'll answer your questions this evening, and then you'll understand how serious the situation is. Deal?"

I don't want to cooperate—she slammed me into the wall hard enough to leave the mother of all bruises. But I can tell she's more than willing to continue to beat the crap out of me with her voodoo wind control, and I'm not in the mood for any further humiliation.

"Fine."

"Good." Her hands return to her sides and she whispers, "Release."

The winds whisk away. I slump to the ground, hacking and coughing from all the dust she stirred.

She looks a little guilty as I rub my throbbing shoulders. "Did I hurt you?"

I shrug and stand, swiping the sand off my shorts and legs. I'm not about to admit I got beat up by a skinny girl.

She stalks inside her dilapidated house and I follow, intentionally dragging my feet to take as long as possible.

She may think she can push me around—but one of these days I'll be strong enough to take her on. And as soon as I am, wind girl is going down.

CHAPTER 12

AUDRA

Vane doesn't seem to be grasping the gravity of our situation. Either that or he truly is the most annoying boy on the planet.

Probably both.

At least my fingers aren't tingling from touching him anymore. If anything, they itch to strangle him. And if he weren't so crucial, I'd do just that. Too bad he has to be a *Weston*.

I stomp through my house, releasing bits of my built-up frustration with each pound of my boots. *This* is what my father died for? What I'm supposed to surrender my life for? This bratty, ungrateful boy I can hear trudging through the sand, taking his sweet time to frustrate me?

I'm done playing nice.

I move to the room's only corner and sweep the palm leaves away from the wall, unearthing the handle of my blade. Calm settles over me as I reach for the hilt, each finger finding its perfect place in the grip. The sword wasn't made for me, but I've practiced with it so much the metal has conformed to every curve of my palm—tangible proof of my mastery.

The smallest flick of my wrist sweeps the blade from the slit I carved in the ground, and with a single motion, I swish and spin, stopping my rotation with the pointed tip of the weapon aimed directly between Vane's eyes.

"What the crap?" he shouts, backing up.

I smile at his sudden lack of bravado. Windslicers make quite an impression.

Thousands of razor-sharp, unbreakable needles line a steel vein in the center—a deadly feather that can slice through flesh as easily as it can shred the strongest gust or flurry. I slash a couple of times, letting the tearing air echo off the walls like a breathy scream.

Vane backs farther away, stumbling over his feet.

"Are you ready to start taking this seriously?" I ask, thrusting the point closer, practically grazing the skin of his nose.

"I already said I was—put that thing down before someone gets hurt."

"Lots of people are going to get hurt if you don't start listening to me. The Stormers have blades just like these. Do you think they'll hesitate to use them? Can you imagine the level of damage they can inflict?"

I tilt the blade to let the orangey sunlight trace across the needles' points. Vane's wide eyes follow the glinting trail, and I can almost see his mind picturing how it'd feel to be wounded with such a weapon.

I don't have to imagine. My forearm caught the tail end of a blow during my training, and I can still remember the agony as my skin was pierced, shredded, and smashed at the same time. The only pain worse is joining the wind.

"And weapons are nothing compared to the power of three," I add, waiting for Vane to meet my gaze. He looks ashen. "Raiden requires his Stormers to *master* the languages of the three most powerful winds, making them virtually unstoppable. They'll show no mercy. Think about what happened to your parents. To my father."

He struggles to swallow, and his eyes stay glued to the sword I keep trained between his eyes. "So why don't we run, then? Why stay here and face them?"

"Stormers are expert trackers."

"Yeah, well, I can be an expert hider. I can stay so far off the grid they'll think I vanished for good."

"It doesn't work that way. And even if you could get away, what about your family? Could you convince them to abandon everything and flee with you? What about your friends? What about the innocent people living here? Would you let them die for you? Could you live with that?"

He doesn't have an answer.

"Believe me, Vane. If there were any other option, I would take it. This is it. You and me against them. And it isn't a game. No amount of snarky jokes will spare you in a wind battle. I can teach you to defend yourself, but only if you let me. Otherwise, you might as well hand yourself over to Raiden now. See if he appreciates your sense of humor more than I do."

His eyes dart between my face and the blade.

Back and forth.

Back and forth.

I have no idea what he's thinking, but he looks as scared as he should be.

I breathe a sigh of relief when he *finally* asks the right question.

"So where do we start?"

I lower the windslicer. "Take a seat."

He drops to the dusty ground, scooting to the far edge of the floor, against one of the walls. Keeping a safe distance from me.

Good.

I sink to my knees in front of him, placing the windslicer between us. "Rule number one—the most important rule for our training sessions: Never speak to the wind in anything other than a whisper—is that clear?"

"What does that even mean?"

"You don't have to understand. You just have to agree. Until the Stormers find us, you cannot do *anything* other than whisper to the wind. We don't need the breezes telling them more than they already know."

I wait for him to agree.

"Yeah, fine. Whatever."

I roll my eyes. He *has* to be difficult. "Hold out your right hand, palm facing me, and spread your fingers like mine." I stretch my fingers wide, curling the tips like I'm gripping an invisible sphere.

"Memorize that position. It's the easiest way to feel for the nearby drafts."

He copies my position. "Okay. Am I supposed to be feeling something?"

"You tell me. What do you feel?"

"Besides feeling like an idiot for sitting in a burned-down house at five-freaking-a.m., holding out my hand like it's some sort of deformed claw . . . not a whole lot."

I grit my teeth, but I refuse to let him get to me again. "Then maybe you should try actually paying attention. Close your eyes."

He heaves a heavy sigh but does as I ask.

"You should be able to detect any movement in the wind within at least a twenty-mile radius—and be able to tell where it's coming from. Focus on the way the air hits your skin. You'll feel something like an itch wherever the wind stirs."

He opens his mouth—probably to complain again. But then his hand twitches and his jaw falls slack. "My thumb itches. Like . . . something moving across my nerves, tugging at me."

I release a breath I didn't realize I was holding. His senses are strong. Really strong. That draft barely tickles the base of my thumb-nail, and it's at least thirty miles away.

Maybe this task won't be as impossible as I thought.

"There's a weak Easterly stirring over there," I explain. "That's what your thumb is telling you."

He drops his hand, shaking his fingers hard. "That's really freaky. I don't like it."

"Well, get used to it. It's part of who you are. And it's an amazing thing. Groundlings would kill to do the things we can do. Maybe you should try being grateful for your gifts."

"Groundlings?"

"Humans. We can have a vocabulary lesson another time. Right now I'm trying to teach you how to call the wind—another one of those 'freaky' things Windwalkers do, so brace yourself. We'll start with the most basic call. It's one you heard me use yesterday, and it will be the one you use most often. Repeat after me. 'Come to me swiftly.'"

He shakes his head like he doesn't understand, and I know he's struggling with the language shift. I switched to the Easterly tongue. I repeat the phrase, waiting for his mind to translate.

"Come to me swiftly," he finally says, his tongue fumbling with the swirling intonations of the words.

I grab the windslicer and point it at his throat. "I told you to *whisper*—it's a good thing the wind needs a complete command to respond, otherwise you could've just given away our exact location."

"Hey—you didn't whisper!"

"I was testing you to see how well you were paying attention earlier. You failed."

"Because you set me up for it." His hands clench into fists and he looks like he wants to pummel me. But his gaze settles on the windslicer. I have him right where I want him—and he knows it.

"Try it again. Focus on the draft you're feeling—and whisper this time," I order, setting the blade back on the ground between us. "Come to me swiftly."

"Come to me swiftly."

It's actually quite impressive the amount of disdain he slipped into his whisper.

I smile at his pettiness. "Carry no trace."

"Carry no trace."

"Lift me softly."

"Lift me softly."

"Then flow and race."

"Then flow and race."

The Easterly rushes through the half room, stirring the leaves and cooling the sweat pooling at my hairline before it whisks away.

Vane's eyes widen. "Cool."

"Memorize those four phrases. They will save your life a thousand times over."

He doesn't say anything, too busy staring at the giant grasshopper that jumped onto the flat edge of the windslicer.

I snatch the disgusting insect and toss it at his head. "Pay attention, Vane. What did I just tell you?"

He shrieks, waving the now flying creature away from his face. "Memorize the spell. Got it—no need to get psycho with the bugs."

The grasshopper lands on his shoulder and he flails to shoo it away, fixing me with a glare that would've been evil if he weren't blushing so bright red. It distracts me from what he said, but only for a second.

"Wait, did you say 'spell'?"

"Spell. Command. Whatever you want to call this crap."

My mind spins with the implications of his words.

"I'll ignore for a second that you just referred to the single most valuable element of our heritage as 'crap'—though you can bet we'll get back to that. Do you think I'm teaching you . . . magic?"

I feel crazy even saying the word.

"You control the wind. What else am I supposed to think?"

He has a point—from a human standpoint, at least. But he's still wrong.

"We control the wind through words, Vane. We ask the gust to do what we want and convince it to obey. It's a simple communication— no different from what you and I are doing right now."

"We *talk* to the wind? Like it's alive?"

"In a way. Each of the four winds has a language. Only sylphs can understand and speak the languages because we're part of the wind ourselves. But there's no magic or spells. Just a simple dialogue between wind and Windwalker."

I should've realized he was confused. It explains why he isn't taking this as seriously as he needs to. "I can't believe how little you know about your heritage. I know your mind was wiped, but I thought some things were just . . . instinctive."

I realize my slip a second too late.

"What do you mean my mind was *wiped*?"

"Nothing."

"Like hell it's nothing." He scoots closer, the windslicer no longer intimidating him. "Tell me what happened to me. Now."

I want to be angry with him for once again interrupting this very important lesson—and as his trainer I should demand he pay attention, and whip him around with some winds if he refuses.

But I can't.

I feel sorry for him.

Sorry for what I know.

Sorry for what I've done.

"You have to understand," I tell him, trying to sound calmer than I feel. "When the Stormer attacked it was like the world ended. Everything gone, destroyed, sucked up, or broken and left in splinters. My mother found us huddled on the ground, sobbing. She didn't have any choice."

"There's always a choice."

"No one can hide from Raiden—not for long. We had to make him think we were dead. My mother and I could disappear easily enough, but you were too important. The only place we knew Raiden would never look for you was with the groundlings, and the only way to hide you there was if you didn't know who or what you are. Humans don't know we exist—and we couldn't risk that you would tell them."

"So she *wiped my mind*?" His hands tear through his hair, like he's trying to feel for a wound or injury. "What the hell did she do to my brain?"

"She called a Southerly and sent it deep into your subconscious. The wind did the rest."

I can still remember the way his skinny, bruised body collapsed to the ground as she wrapped the draft around him and sent it into his mind. My mother didn't explain what was happening. So he turned his wide, terrified eyes to me, silently begging me to help him.

Vane watches me now, looking so much like the little boy that day it nearly takes my breath away. I owe him the truth. As much as I'm willing to tell, at least.

"You said it felt like a million butterflies were flapping around in your brain," I whisper. "I held your hand and told you to close your eyes. When you woke a few hours later, you didn't remember much of anything. The wind wiped all your memories away."

Vane doesn't speak—doesn't move. I take his hand, stunned at the overwhelming urge I feel to reach him. Comfort him. Try to make it right.

He jerks away. "How do I get them back?"

I can't blame him for asking. But I need him to forget. One memory at least.

"You can't, Vane. They're gone. Forever."

He closes his eyes, looking fragile. Crushed.

Hopeless.

I close my eyes too.

Wishing on every star out there that the words I just said were true.

Hoping even harder I'll never have to tell Vane they aren't.

CHAPTER 13

VANE

'm speechless—probably for the first time in my life.

My memories were stolen.

Not repressed.

Stolen.

I've lived the last ten years with a black hole for a past—not the easiest way to grow up. And apparently that's all I'll ever have.

I want to throw something. Or maybe pick up that crazy needle-sword thing and see what kind of damage I can do to the walls with it.

But another piece of me—a tiny, much quieter piece—is relieved that I didn't forget my parents.

I'm not the horrible, selfish jerk who erased his family because it hurt to remember them. It wasn't my fault. Audra's mother stole my memories while Audra held my hand and promised I would be okay.

Which at least explains the only memory I have. Audra leaning over me, staring at me with those dark, haunted eyes, until a breeze whisks her away. That was *real*. I just don't remember the rest because the memory was swept out of my mind by the wind.

How does it even work? How does a gust of wind steal my memories?

"I know this is hard to understand," she says quietly. "But we had to keep the fact that you survived top secret so Raiden wouldn't come searching for you. That's why we let the human authorities run you through their adoption system. We kept watch, to make sure you were okay, but we needed you to disappear, stay off the grid—as you call it. And that wouldn't happen if you were running around talking about sylphs and Stormers and the four languages of the wind. I'm not sure which would've been worse: what the humans would've done to you or what would've happened when Raiden found you. And he *would* have found you."

"He found me anyway, didn't he?" I'm surprised at the growl in my voice. "And how is that, by the way? I'm guessing he didn't just wake up and think, 'Hey, I bet Vane's in the crappy Coachella Valley.'"

Her shoulders sag. "No. I . . . made a mistake."

"So it's your fault."

She shrinks even more, like she's trying to hide from the words. But she doesn't deny them.

It's strange to see her so deflated, like her guilt's drained all the fire inside her.

I bite back my apology.

She deserves to feel guilty. How many different ways has she screwed up my life?

She reaches for my arm, her warm fingers stroking my skin. "Please. Let's not waste our training time on this."

I shake off her hand, shoving my body back to put some space between us.

"Why is he looking for me, Audra? Why me? Why my family?"

She looks away, like she doesn't want to answer. But she does. "It's because you're a Weston."

"What, my family's important?"

"Yes. No. Well, yes and no. And I guess the proper term is 'Westerly.' Weston is just your family name."

"Gonna have to be clearer than that."

She straightens, a little of the fight returning to her eyes. "This isn't going to make a whole lot of sense, but fine. If it will make you take your training seriously, so be it." Her hands twist around each other and she stares at the space between us.

"I told you earlier—there are four languages for the wind. There are also four kinds of Windwalkers: Northerlies, Southerlies, Easterlies, and Westerlies. Everyone's born with what's called their 'native tongue.' The language of their heritage. For most of our history no one bothered learning any of the other languages. There wasn't any point. We lived in separate corners of the earth. We rarely mixed company. Why mix languages? It wasn't until the Gale Force that things changed."

"The Gale Force?"

"A force we created for peace and safety, in both our society and the groundlings'. The winds have been shifting—becoming more wild. More reckless. And it's our responsibility to calm the storms, stop them from destroying human cities like they do now. Not for glory or power or respect, but because it's right."

She points to a small blue patch on the sleeve of her jacket, just below her right shoulder. Four wavy lines twisted together in the middle, like a knot. That explains the crazy outfit. And probably the freakishly tight hair.

"So, you're a soldier in the army?"

"A guardian. But yes. At first, all the guardians were Northerlies, because the northern wind is the strongest. But it's also the coldest and the most unstable, as are its people, so—"

"I take it you're a Northerly?"

"Why would you think that?"

I almost laugh. Does she not realize how cold and scary she can be? Or is it normal to threaten people with evil swords of doom in sylph-land? "Never mind."

"My family name is Eastend. Easterlies were the next to join the Gales, to be a softening influence. But they were commanded to learn the Northerly language, to increase their strength. And when they did, they discovered something unexpected."

She scoots back and whispers the call she taught me. A small breeze swirls in the air between us. I cough as sand and bits of dead palm leaves catch in my throat.

"A single draft of wind has power of its own. But mix it with another wind and it changes."

She whispers something I don't understand and another draft rushes from behind me. A colder wind. Louder. I can't make out its words as it whips around Audra.

She whispers again and the gusts swirl together to form a dust devil.

I jump to my feet, away from the tiny cyclone growing larger by the second. Audra stands too, hovering over the mini-tornado.

"When you combine the different winds, they play off each other, becoming stronger and more flexible. And if you know how to control them, they can do anything you want them to."

She mumbles something unintelligible and the winds race harder. Faster and faster they spin, until the dust devil's strong enough to suck up the needle-sword thing and shoot it out the top of the funnel. Audra catches it with a graceful sweep of her right arm as she whispers, "Break free, be free." The winds sweep away, leaving a dusty trail in their wake.

Okay, *that's* pretty cool.

"The possibilities that knowledge opened up were endless. But they discovered something else—something that changed everything. When you combine the winds, their powers increase exponentially with each wind you add. So if someone were to combine all four winds and command them perfectly, they would be unstoppable. Raiden became determined to be the first to learn all four."

My stomach sours at the name.

"He's a Northerly—but he's mastered the other languages so completely he uses them more fluently than those native to the tongue. He joined the Gales when he was young, but after a few years of service, he decided we were wasting our power on protecting the groundlings from storms. He thought we should embrace the wilder gusts—not tame them. Claimed they were the wind's way of telling us it's *our* time to be the dominant race on the planet, and that we should focus on building our own strength and skill while we let the winds wipe away the weaker groundlings. His promise of power appealed to a number of other guardians—especially the conquering Northerlies—and he began amassing a following. Before the Gales discovered his mutiny, Raiden attacked the Westerlies."

I feel like I should sit down for this part of the story, so I sink to the ground. She sits next to me, staring at the floor.

"No one had bothered learning the Westerly tongue. The west wind is a weak wind. A peaceful wind. And the Westerlies were outsiders. Kept to themselves. Most were nomadic. Everyone thought they were crazy. They probably were."

I have a feeling I should be insulted by that, but I'm too interested in the word "were." Past tense.

"Raiden was determined to master the fourth language. Determined to become all-powerful. So he tracked down a Westerly family and tried to force them to teach him their language. When they refused, he slaughtered them in retribution—and to send a message to the other Westerlies. Make it clear he would not take no for an answer. It was the bloodiest crime our world had ever seen."

Her voice cracks, and she swallows several times, like she's fighting for control. "It all happened before I was born, but my Gale trainer showed me pictures so I would understand my enemy. A family of five—including three children—torn apart like rag dolls. Like he'd bound their limbs to tornados and sent the winds in opposite directions. There was barely anything left to recognize."

It isn't until a fly almost zips into my mouth that I realize my jaw's hanging open. To murder kids over a language? Over wind?

"Things spiraled out of control after that," she whispers, like the words are too horrible to say at full volume. "What remained of the Gales rallied against Raiden. But he was too powerful and had too many guardians who fought at his side, either because they believed in his cause—or feared him. The loss was devastating. Only a few escaped with their lives. And without the Gales' protection, our world—as we knew it—crumbled. Windwalkers have always been a small, scattered race, but the Gales had established one main city, high in the mountains, where the clouds meet the earth. Raiden and his warriors blasted it with everything they had. When it fell, he murdered the king and took the crown. Anyone who didn't swear fealty to him was killed, and he rebuilt the city as a private fortress for his army of Stormers. The strong mountain winds fuel their power, and he's been able to spread his reign of terror to the rest of the earth."

She turns to hold my stare. "Any who oppose his rule are annihilated. The remaining Gales fled underground, organizing their resistance away from Raiden's ever-watching winds, trying to build a force strong enough to defeat him. But they need the same thing he does. Raiden's still determined to master the Westerly tongue, to complete his power and dominance. To ensure that no one will ever rise against him. Can you see where this is going?"

I can—but it all sounds so absurd. Since when does one person have the ability to rip apart an entire society like that?

"Why not screw the whole secrecy thing and turn to humans for help?" I ask. "Have the president call in an air strike and blast the crap out of Raiden and his Stormers? Problem solved."

"Do you honestly think human weapons are stronger than the full force of the wind? Have you seen a hurricane in action?"

I suppose she might be right—but it's still hard to believe. "That doesn't explain why my family mattered so much. I mean, so what if we're Westerlies? What makes us more important than the others . . . ?"

My voice trails off as Audra shakes her head.

"Raiden's spent the last few decades tracking the Westerlies down one by one. If they refused to teach their language, he ended them, hoping to scare the others into submission. But it turns out your kind are surprisingly brave. None were willing to compromise, and none would share their language—even with the Gales. They didn't want the knowledge to fall into the wrong hands, and didn't trust anyone to protect it besides themselves. They'd rather let the language die than have it be used for destruction. On it went, until, as far as everyone knew, your parents were the last living Westerly family."

I can't think of anything to say to that. Audra keeps going anyway.

"Protecting your family became the Gale Force's highest priority, so they assigned my parents—their top guardians—to watch them full-time. But a Stormer found them, and somewhere in the struggle to capture them they were accidentally killed. Leaving only you. The last Westerly. And up until four years ago Raiden didn't even know you were alive. Now that he knows, he's been tearing the world apart to find you, and you can bet if he gets his hands on you, he'll show no mercy. Sure, he'll be careful to keep you alive. But you're the only thing standing between him and ultimate power. The only chance he has at satisfying his obsession. Do you think he'll take no for an answer when he demands that you teach him?"

"But . . . I don't know any secret language of the west wind. I didn't even know there was a west wind until a few minutes ago—I thought there was just *wind*."

Seriously, there's no way I belong to any part of that crazy story. It has to be ripped out of some cheesy fantasy movie with a bunch of scrawny actors running around in tights, shooting arrows at each other because of some evil man trying to rule the world. That stuff doesn't happen in real life—and it certainly doesn't happen to me.

I'm just an average guy.

Well, okay, fine—apparently I'm a sylph, so I'm not exactly average—but still. I'm not some ultra-powerful answer to all their problems either. I'm not Superman. I don't even like that comic.

"You're right," Audra says as my mind fills with horrifying images of me in tights and a stupid cape being asked to save the world like it's no big deal. "You don't know the Westerly tongue. Your parents chose not to teach you, thinking it would keep you safe from Raiden. But you are a Westerly. So we're hoping the language is instinctive."

"Hoping?" I need to move, to think this through on my feet. I stand and pace. "You're *hoping* I'll speak the language that gets everyone killed?"

"We're hoping you'll be the first to master the four languages. Then you'll be powerful enough to defeat Raiden."

I laugh, too loud and too hard, feeling the threads of my sanity stretching dangerously thin. "Oh, good, because I was afraid you were going to put pressure on me."

It's all too much. I can't breathe. The choking heat beating down is nothing compared to this heavy, crushing weight Audra just dumped on me.

"Vane," Audra says, standing and blocking me as I try to walk away.

I'm not sure where I'm going—I just have to get out of here, and I'm not above shoving her out of my way if I have to. "I can't do this, Audra. I'm not a warrior and I can't . . ."

I freeze when she grabs my shoulders. "I know what it's like to have huge responsibility dropped on your back and to feel like you can't bear it. But you have to remember, Raiden murdered your family."

There's that word again. *Murdered.* It shakes everything inside me, making it twist and thrash with hate.

"*You* have the power to stop him," she says. "That's why my father gave his life to save you. You had to live."

She looks at me then, like she thinks I'm some sort of savior—or miracle.

The Miracle Child.

Apparently, that stupid newspaper article wasn't that far off. Didn't see that one coming.

"Wait—Raiden didn't know I was alive until a few years ago, right?" Hope calms the shaky, dizzy feeling. "They ran an article about me surviving the tornado. It was just in the local paper in a Podunk town, but Raiden would've seen that, wouldn't he? So he must've investigated me already and realized I'm not anyone special."

That sounds *much* more likely than me being some sort of hero.

"Raiden had no reason to investigate. Not once the echoes reached him." She looks at the sky. "When we pass on, the winds carry an echo of who we used to be—for a time, at least. My mother knew we'd need to hide from Raiden, so she made echoes for you, me, and her, and sent them along with the ones for your parents, my father, and the Stormer. Raiden had no reason to doubt the wind's report. The wind doesn't lie."

"If the wind doesn't lie, how did your mom pull that one off?"

"She used our losses. When someone you love dies, part of you dies with them. It's why you're never the same after losing someone. And the winds that touch you carry the loss with them. It's not exactly like an echo, but she tweaked them somehow, bent them and changed them with her gift until they were close enough to convince Raiden of our demise."

Just when I think my weirdness meter is maxed out, she finds a way to push me further.

"My mother commanded the shifted losses to flow to Raiden's city, and not long after, the Gales heard reports that Raiden had declared us dead. A mistake on his part, sure—but we're fortunate he made it. We might not have been able to hide you this long, otherwise."

"Lucky me," I grumble, hating her for convincing me again that I'm Vane Weston: Most Wanted Boy Alive.

"You *are* lucky."

"Ugh—I'm so sick of people telling me that."

"You have the potential to stop Raiden, Vane. Make him pay for what he's done. I would kill for that kind of opportunity. You have no idea."

I know I should be hungry for revenge—and I am. But the thought of *me* attacking Raiden makes the world spin and my spit taste sour. "How? How am I supposed to be strong enough to take him down? I don't even know the slightest thing about any of this crap—"

"That's what you have me for." Her grip tightens on my shoulders. "I'm here to teach you everything you need to know. That's my job."

"Oh, good. I'm a *job*."

I try to twist away, but she locks her arms and pulls me back. "It's not just a job. It's—I . . ." She stops, like she can't find the words she needs.

I meet her gaze then, and the look I find makes me suck in a breath.

She cares.

About this job-mission-whatever-it's-called—yes.

But beyond that—and beneath the uniform and the tight braid and the cold, hard exterior that makes her slam me into walls and wave swords in my face and seem ready to strangle me half the time—I can see the deeper truth.

She cares about me.

And that's enough to make me put aside my fears, my worries about what they expect from me, my anger at my memories being stolen. Enough to make whatever sacrifices it takes to train for the battle that lies ahead worth it.

I probably don't have a choice anyway, but that doesn't matter. She cares.

I'll do this for her. And for the family we've both lost.

"I guess we need to train, then," I say, stepping back into the charred room and peeling off my shirt—already soaked in sweat from the morning sun. I toss it in the corner and turn to face her. "Let's get started."

CHAPTER 14

AUDRA

I have no idea what convinced Vane to put his anger and fear and bratty, sarcastic attitude behind him, but I'm not complaining. When he stepped back into my shelter and stripped off his shirt, he became a completely different guy. Like the Vane I know was kidnapped and replaced with a serious, hardworking fighter—with incredible abs.

Not that I notice.

I try not to, at least.

It isn't easy. Westerlies were known for being the most physically beautiful of our kind. Maybe it's the warm, peaceful winds that nurtured them. Or something in their genes. Whatever it is, Vane's *definitely* a Westerly. Nothing but sculpted, tanned muscle and long, graceful limbs. Not to mention a face with chiseled, symmetrical features and the most stunning blue eyes I've ever seen.

Solana's a lucky girl.

He's remarkable. In more than just looks.

Before the sky is bright blue with daylight, Vane masters our prime call and bends his first draft around the room. And by the time the day's heat weighs on our shoulders like a thick, suffocating blanket, he's learned to feel drafts over fifty miles away. Still a long way to go—when he tried to wrap the draft around his body, he didn't hear the wind rebel and knocked himself flat on his back—but considering he had his first breakthrough yesterday, he's amazing.

Well, until Gavin returns from his morning hunt. Then Vane's a blur of flailing arms, shouted curses, and high-pitched screams as Gavin swoops and flaps around his head.

"What are you doing?" I shout over the commotion.

"That crazy bird is trying to kill me." Vane grabs one of the palm fronds from my makeshift bed and runs through the room, scattering dust and broken bits of leaf as he waves the branch in wild, erratic patterns.

I race to his side and grab his wrist, freezing his arm midswipe. "Stop it, both of you. Gavin, quit dive-bombing Vane. And you!" I yank the branch from his hand.

Only then do I realize I'm practically pressed against his chest.

His *bare* chest.

It's suddenly hard to breathe.

I drop his wrist and step back, letting the space between us calm my racing pulse. I toss the branch back into the pile and clear my throat. "Can you please refrain from injuring my pet?"

Gavin screeches. He doesn't like when I call him that.

"And put your shirt back on before he scratches you," I add, grateful for an excuse to get Vane clothed again.

He covers his head as Gavin dives. "That creepy bird is your *pet*?"

"Yes. So I'd appreciate it if you didn't try to kill him." I lock eyes with Gavin and hold my left arm straight out from my side. "Land."

Gavin releases an earsplitting shriek and changes course to land on my arm, digging in his talons hard enough to prick through the thick fabric of my uniform. His silent protest.

Great. Now I have two difficult boys in my life.

I stroke Gavin's cheeks, trying to calm him.

"Ugh—how can you touch that thing?"

"Please tell me you're not afraid of birds. You do realize how absurd that would be, considering we share the sky with them?"

He grabs his T-shirt from where he flung it earlier, shakes off the sand and bugs, and throws it over his head, rushing to shove his arms through the sleeves like he doesn't want to take his eyes off Gavin for a second. "Hey, I used to get attacked by a crazy hawk when I played in this grove as a kid . . ." His voice trails off. "Oh, God, it was that—that thing attacking me, wasn't it?"

I try not to smile, but the corners of my mouth tilt up anyway. "It's possible. Gavin knows to keep anyone from discovering my hiding place when I take a short nap. Maybe you wandered too close for his liking."

"Or maybe he's demented and likes to tear hair off kids' heads for his own sadistic pleasure." Vane wipes the sweat off his brow and dries it on his shorts. "So you've attacked me with wind, convinced me this place is haunted, and sent your killer bird after me. Any other ways you've made my life difficult? Is it your fault medicine gives me hives?"

"What?"

"The few times I've tried to take any pills I broke out in hives and threw up like crazy. That got anything to do with you?"

"No. Your body must've rejected the medicine because it's designed for humans."

"Right. And I'm not human. Still getting used to that, by the way. Kind of a big, life-changing thing, just so you know."

There's nothing I can say to that.

He shakes his head. "So does that happen very often?"

"The hives? No. None of us have had any reason to try groundling medicine. In case you haven't noticed, we aren't affected by the same viruses or ills as they are. It's amazing they're so much more prolific than we are. By all counts, we're the superior creatures— that's why it's our responsibility to protect them. But what they lack in durability, they make up for in volume. It's shocking how many children they produce. And the way they choose to crowd together in giant cities."

I shiver at the thought of being packed in like that. People around all the time. Breathing my air. Stealing my wind. Makes my skin scream for a cool breeze.

But the morning drafts have stilled. And judging by the way the sun's hammering us even at this early hour, it'll be a stifling day.

Honestly, I don't know how Vane's borne it all this time. He's fortunate to live in a fairly sparse area, as far as human cities go— the heat keeps the huge crowds away most of the year. Still—*the heat*. I steal away to the mountains for fresh air and space whenever I can. I don't know how he doesn't wither, trapped in this valley all these years, with no real release. Maybe he's tougher than I think.

Vane ducks when I send Gavin to his perch on the windowsill.

Maybe not.

A loud gurgling rumbles around the half room.

Vane's cheeks tinge with pink. "I haven't eaten since the burger last night."

The mention of food makes my mouth salivate and I clutch my waist, willing my stomach not to make a similar sound. The water has fully invaded my body. Every muscle aches from fighting the extra pull toward the earth, and everything inside me feels hollow and drained.

Much as I hate to surrender to the vulnerability—I need a break. "You should get back to your room so your parents won't notice you were gone."

"And what am I supposed to tell them if they have?"

I consider that. "What if you tell them you've started a new exercise program, early in the morning to beat the heat?"

"That doesn't sound like me. I'm pretty lazy."

"I've noticed."

He grins and steps closer, blocking the sun as his shadow falls over me. "How about I tell them there's this gorgeous girl who's invited me to work out with her every morning, and I'm suffering through so I can be with her? *That* they'd believe."

My face flames, and I know if I meet his eyes he'll be looking at me the same way he did last night by the windmills, right before I had the winds rip us away. That deep, intense stare with those wide blue eyes that are so clear they remind me of ice, except they're anything but cold when they look at me.

He moves even closer, leaving us only inches apart. His breath feels smooth and warm on my skin—like a slow Southerly breeze.

I take a step away, jumping when my back meets solid stone. Honestly, this tiny structure only has pieces of walls; how did I let myself get trapped against one of them?

"That's fine," I say when I recover. "If you're more comfortable with it."

"I am," he says. "Because it's true."

He puts his arms on either side of me, caging me between them. My heart slams against my chest so hard it feels like it will bruise me from the inside out.

All I have to do is shove him away and I'll be free. But I'm afraid to touch him, to feel that strange heat spread through me. That would be more dangerous than meeting his eyes.

But I have to stop this.

I crinkle my nose. "Someone needs to hit the showers."

He laughs. "I call that Eau de Vane. It's my signature fragrance."

"Well, it smells like something died."

I duck under his arm and slip away, relieved when he doesn't try to stop me. I'm not sure what to do about his . . . advances.

He's *finally* cooperating. I can't afford to have that change if he feels rejected.

But I can't give him what he wants. Even if I want to—which I don't.

I don't.

I rub my temples, trying to calm the headache flaring behind my eyes. I'm used to the pain—my regulation braid often pulls too tight. But this time my skull feels ready to crack from the strain.

"You should let your hair down," Vane says, clearly watching me closer than I want him to.

"I never let my hair down."

"You did yesterday."

"Not by choice." I turn away from his scrutiny, heading toward his house. "We can get back to training later. After you've had a chance to cool off."

He laughs. "I'm not the one who looked hot and bothered earlier."

I'm not current with groundling slang, but I'm fairly certain what he's implying—and he's *wrong*.

"Anyway," I say, changing the subject—quickly. "I recommend taking a nap. We'll be putting in a long night tonight."

"Sounds good to me," he says, his smile stretching wider.

I roll my eyes. "For *training*, Vane. We'll tackle some of the harder skills tonight, when it's dark and the winds pick up."

"Looking forward to it."

That makes one of us. Just when I start to enjoy his company, his annoying side returns.

Then again, being annoyed is far better than that fluttery, breathless feeling I keep getting. I need to cling to the irritation, store it away, in case any of those other emotions resurface.

His stomach growls again.

"Better eat something too."

"What about you?"

"Me?"

"Yeah, want to grab breakfast or something?"

"What? No—I can't eat."

One muffled growl erupts from my stomach before I can stop it.

"But I thought you said the water already weakened you. And it'll take months to get out of your system, right? So why starve yourself if the damage has already been done?"

I can't believe he'd even suggest such a thing. Clearly, he's a long way from understanding the type of self-discipline I adhere to.

He does have a *tiny* point, though—and I hate him for it. Hate myself for seeing it. Hate my stomach even more for growling again.

"Eating or drinking will only extend my days of weakness, something I cannot allow."

"Suit yourself. But your stomach agrees with me," he adds when a third growl erupts from my gut.

If I could rip the noisy organ from my body, I would. "That will pass."

"I hope so. Otherwise, it'll be like training with a growling kitten all night."

I ignore him, and we walk in silence until we reach the edge of the date grove.

"We should both grab a few hours' rest while we can. I'll be back when the sun sets."

"You don't want to come in? Cool off for a bit?"

"Your family's not supposed to see me."

"Come on, you can't hide forever."

"I've hidden for ten years. Pretty sure I can manage a few more days."

"Days?"

My hunger fades to nausea as I nod. "The Stormers will be here in eight days."

His smile vanishes. "That's, um . . . soon."

Yes, it is. "We'll be ready."

He looks as skeptical as I feel. The Stormers will pick up our traces by this evening. Will my mother really be able to stall them as long as she claimed?

I glance at the sky, half-expecting to see dark clouds creeping over the mountains. But vivid blue stretches as far as I can see.

We're safe. For now.

"And what happens after that?" he asks. "I mean . . . assuming we win and stuff, then what? 'Cause I'm guessing Raiden has more Stormers to send after me, right?"

Honestly, I don't know. All the Gales' plans centered around Vane having the Westerly breakthrough long before Raiden found us. I'm the one who screwed things up by giving away our location.

But I can salvage this. I have eight days to force the breakthrough. I'll find a way.

I force my voice to sound more confident than I feel as I say,

"Assuming everything goes according to plan, you'll pose a far greater threat to Raiden than he'll ever prove to you."

"And if things don't go according to plan?"

"Then the winds will tell the Gales what happened. They'll come get you."

My mother will know I made the sacrifice almost the second I surrender myself. My heart picks up speed, imagining scattered pieces of me spreading far and wide.

I push the thought away.

My mother will collect Vane. Take him to the Gales for protection. Tell them I failed.

"What about you?" he asks.

I look away, afraid he'll see more on my face than I want him to. "All you need to know is that you'll be safe. The Gales will take you to their fortress and train you to be ready to fight."

"Whoa—hang on. So basically my options are: prisoner of Raiden or prisoner of your army? Please tell me there's a secret option number three, because—no offense—those options suck."

"No one is a *prisoner* of our army. And certainly not you. You're our future king."

He stops walking. "*King?* As in, a crown and a scepter and everyone calling me Your Majesty?"

"Not exactly. But yes, king. After you defeat Raiden, you'll be given the throne."

For a second he just stares at me. Then he laughs. "The throne? You guys have a throne?"

"Of course. We're a scattered race, but we still have order. We still have laws and a ruler—or, we did, before Raiden usurped the kingship. But when we take our capital city back, you'll be the one to restore the royal line. Everything's already been arranged. We just need your help to overthrow the tyrant."

He runs his hands through his hair. "That's . . . crazy. I don't know what to do with that. I don't *want* to know what to do with that."

"I know it's a lot to take in, but this is the life you were meant to live."

"I already have a life. What's the plan for that, by the way? I just disappear in the middle of the night and my parents never see me again? What about school? What about my friends?"

"Those are . . . human things, Vane. They've only been a part of your life because we needed to keep you hidden. But the secret's out. No matter what, you need to come back to your own kind. Put all the rest of this stuff behind you."

"*Stuff?* You're talking about everything I care about—you can't expect me to just walk away from it all."

I do expect that. Everyone expects that.

But there's no point in saying that. He isn't ready to hear it.

So I stand beside him, watching the heat waves swirl from the ground and listening to the dry desert breeze creak through the palms. It's a Southerly, singing a slow, melancholy song. Vane can't understand it, which is better. Southerlies are the sad winds, speaking of loss and unwanted change. Of the fleeting summer they're always chasing.

The Gales worried that Vane would have a hard time adjusting when the time came to separate him from his "other life"—even with the bright future they've planned for him. But worry doesn't change anything. Vane's caught between two worlds, and the only way to fix that is to rip one away.

I know how much it will hurt him, though, when the time comes. I know how it feels to lose a parent.

Vane has already lost two. Now he'll lose two more.

"Is there any other way?" he whispers.

There isn't.

But he's asking for a lifeline. And I know he needs it to get through the next few days. So I take his hand, touching him only to convince him—not because I want to—and say, "Maybe."

Another lie shoved between us.

But it works. He squeezes my hand harder and looks at me with those striking eyes of his. "Let's hope."

Hope.

Such a funny, fickle thing. We need a lot of it right now.

"Yes, Vane," I whisper. "Let's hope."

CHAPTER 15

VANE

My room is exactly the way I left it—no sign my parents noticed I was gone—and I can hear my mom watching some lame infotainment talk show thing in the living room, like she does every morning after my dad leaves for work. I sneak down the hall to the bathroom and turn on the shower to buy myself a few minutes before I have to see her.

I haven't figured out what I'm going to say. It feels too weird. *I* feel too weird.

I knew they weren't my biological family—and that never felt awkward before. But knowing I'm not even their *species* forms this, like, giant gap between us. I mean, what would they say if they knew their son's a mythical creature?

Pretty sure they'd freak. And I can't blame them.

I strip off my filthy clothes, coughing when I get a whiff of them. Audra's right, my pits are hummin'.

My back aches from where she smashed me into the wall, and I feel the tender spot, where there'll be a bruise later. More proof all of this is real.

It really is, isn't it?

I'm not Vane, the unmotivated student who's cursed around girls anymore.

I'm Vane Weston: The Last Westerly.

Great—it sounds like something out of an anime cartoon.

I jump in the shower and let the streams of hot water beat against my skin, calming the shiver that creeps up my spine as I think about the stories Audra shared. Or the evil-looking weapons the warriors will use when they come. Or what'll happen if we lose.

I want to wash my fears away, let them swirl down the drain like the gritty sand the shampoo knocks loose from my hair. But it isn't that simple.

The threat is coming whether I want it to or not. I have to face it head-on and hope Audra guides me through. Then I'll find out if her army's planning to take me away, expecting me to be their king.

I squeeze the soap so hard my fingers leave dents.

I'm not going to let this Gale Force control my life. I'll stay and train and fight whatever these Stormer things are—but only because I have quite a few people in this valley who are worth protecting.

After that, I'm done. I have no interest in being a soldier or a ruler for a world I don't even know. My life's *here*. I won't let anyone tear it apart, and there's nothing Audra—or any of her little army friends—can do to stop me.

Shoot, if I'm as strong as she says I am—or will be with training—then there's definitely no way they can tell me what to do. I'll fight them all if I have to, and win.

But maybe it won't come to that.

Audra said there's hope. I'll try to believe her. Even if it felt like a lie.

She's holding something back—I can see it in the careful way she chooses her words before she speaks. In the way she sometimes won't meet my eyes. I have no idea what it is, but there has to be a way to wear her down, find out what she's hiding.

While I'm at it, maybe I can get another glimpse of what she's hiding under that crazy-thick jacket, too.

My mind wanders back to her skimpy dress, remembering the way it clung in all the right places. It should be a crime to cover a body like hers with that thick, bulky uniform she had on today.

In fact, if I ever become king Windwalker, my first act as ruler will be to institute a new wardrobe for the guardians and make Audra's dress even tinier. That might be worth the life-changing responsibility.

Honestly, being with Audra makes the whole living-in-sylph-land-forever idea sound not so bad. I might be able to deal with it if I finally get to taste those full lips of hers. Undo that tight braid and run my hand through her silky hair as I move closer. Pressing every inch of her body against mine as she tangles her arms around me and slides her hands down my back, pulling me even closer . . .

I shove the handle of the faucet all the way to cold.

But even with the icy streams trickling down my skin, I can't block the fantasy that never goes away—no matter how many times I've tried to resist it: That Audra's out there right now. Wanting me as much as I want her.

CHAPTER 16

AUDRA

Air. I need air.

If I can't satiate my hunger or quench my thirst, I need to give my skin the wind it begs for. Draw extra strength where I can.

The water sits too heavily in my weary, sleep-deprived body for me to fly to the mountains. So I weave my way to the unruly, overgrown center of the grove, where the trees are taller, with thicker leaves to provide better camouflage.

The air is still. I ignore Gavin's taunting gaze as I choose the tallest tree and climb its slender trunk, careful not to cling too tightly to the crumbling bark. It's a precarious job, and watching Gavin swoop to my intended location with a quick flutter of wings only makes it more arduous. But I eventually make my way to the top and nestle myself among the prickly leaves.

I close my eyes and feel for the winds. They're whisking across the foothills, but still within my reach.

Soft whispers bring them closer and I swirl them around me. It's tempting to strip off my jacket and let my hair down, but I refuse to remove any part of my uniform. It doesn't matter how much the desert sun weighs on the dark, rough fabric or how much the braid pulls. It's part of being a guardian. Part of who I am.

Bits of wind slip through the coarse fibers of my clothes, sweeping away the dirt and sweat and leaving me refreshed and clean. Nothing rivals the intoxicating relief of a gentle breeze. Not groundling foods or ice-cold water. Not even the thrill of skin meeting skin. The wind is part of who I am, and when I expose my heart to it, I feel it calling me home.

The wind is all I need.

Over the years, those words have become my mantra, making everything I've endured more bearable.

But they're not the only thing lightening my heart.

Vane shows more promise than I expected—when he commits to his training, at least. And if he has the fourth breakthrough before the Stormers arrive, we can beat them despite being bound to the earth.

I wouldn't have to sacrifice myself.

Which means there might be life for me after this assignment.

Maybe.

I squint through the blinding light, searching for any sign of the coming storm. All I find is the oppressive desert sun blazing down. For once I'm grateful to see it.

I'm trying to believe my mother's out there, somehow buying us five extra days, like she can pluck the time from the sky.

What if she isn't?

She's cared so little for my safety the last ten years, treating me like a splinter in her skin. A stone in her shoe. What if she's taking her chance to flick me away? Be rid of me for good?

I fling the doubts to the scattering breezes, let them wash far away.

It's Vane's safety she's concerned with—and she would never hesitate to protect *him*.

Resentment rises in my chest and I choke it down.

Vane's safety is my only concern as well. I can't let myself forget that.

I settle deeper into the palm leaves, leaning my head against a nearby branch and focusing my mind on the solitary Easterly in the air. Its song is one I seek out whenever I can find it, telling of the shifting waves of change that affect us all, and the fortitude to keep going despite them. Mostly it's a promise. A promise that things won't always be so turbulent.

A promise of calm.

Sometimes I let myself believe it's my father's windsong, and that it seeks me out. Like a tiny part of him still watches over me, just like he did when he was alive.

Cling to the rock until the storm sweeps past, the wind sings through the air.

My father was my rock. My shelter. Warm arms that wrapped

around me, shielding me from the tempests of my mother's ever-shifting moods. The only place I felt truly safe.

Please keep me safe now, Dad.

I don't dare say the wish out loud—but I think it all the same. And the silly fantasy feels more real than any promise my mother made for my protection.

But he's not here.

She is.

I have to trust her.

I have to trust myself.

So I surrender to sleep, ready to recharge. Ready for the sweet dreams the song always brings, filled with memories of my father.

Instead, I dream of Vane. And the dream is anything but sweet.

CHAPTER 17

VANE

I emerge from the bathroom to the aroma of eggs and salty breakfast meat, and a burrito the size of a football waits for me at the kitchen table. Before I can stop myself, I rush to the couch and wrap my arms around my mom from behind.

"Whoa, what's that for?" she asks, laughing.

"Breakfast." It isn't just because of that—but she doesn't need to know I might only have eight days left with her.

Maybe eight days left to live.

I pull away before she can feel that I'm shaking.

"Well, it's nearly lunchtime. I was half an hour from dragging your lazy butt out of bed when I heard the shower start."

"I know. Guess I was tired."

She must catch my hesitation because she spins around to study my face. I can almost feel her noticing my dark circles, wondering why I don't look more rested. "You okay?"

I'm . . . not sure.

"Yeah, just *starving*." My stomach growls for emphasis and my mom laughs.

"Better eat while it's hot, then."

She doesn't have to tell me twice. I run across the room, practically drooling when I get a closer look at the burrito-y goodness. Bacon, eggs, avocado, and Tater Tots all smothered in pepperjack cheese and doused with hot sauce before getting wrapped in a gigantic tortilla and grilled on the stove. My dad calls it "the torpedo."

They're life-changingly good, and after a hard morning of training on an empty stomach, the first bite is pretty much the best thing I've ever put in my mouth. Isaac used to claim his mom's homemade chorizo and egg burrito was better, but then he had a torpedo and was forever converted. Nothing tops it.

I finish the whole thing in five minutes flat, and even though it probably contained enough food to feed a small country, I want another. But hey, who knows how many more I'll get to have?

My appetite dies with the depressing thought.

I have to get a grip.

I thank my mom for breakfast and duck back to my room, glad she doesn't ask any more questions. I check the lock on my window—not that it seems capable of keeping Audra out—close the drapes, and collapse on my bed.

Next thing I know, the clock on my nightstand says it's after four and my mom's pounding on my door.

"Vane, phone."

My door opens, and I squint through a triangle of sunlight that creeps across my face.

"You were sleeping?" my mom asks, her face falling into a frown. "I thought you were in here playing games or something."

I pull myself up, still trying to gather my bearings. "I was tired."

She scans my room as she hands me the phone, like she's searching for the drugs I must be taking to cause my fatigue—not that I've ever messed with that stuff. I can't even take a freaking aspirin.

"It's Isaac," she tells me.

I run my hand over my wild bed hair, trying to smooth it down before I press the phone to my ear. "Hey."

"What the hell, man?" Isaac practically shouts on the other end. "First you crap out on Hannah hours before curfew, then you shut your phone off and ignore my calls all day? Don't tell me the date was *that* bad."

"Sorry, I forgot I turned my phone off. The date was fine."

"Uh-huh. That's not what I hear."

"Why? What did Hannah say?" I hear the worry in my voice at the same time I realize my mom's conveniently forgotten to leave me alone. I give her my *Do you mind?* look and she reluctantly closes my door behind her.

Isaac laughs. "Nothing, man. She just said she'd be in her room and left us alone. But it sounds like something happened. What'd you do this time? Don't tell me you laid one in the middle of the date again."

"No! And I told you that wasn't me."

"That's not what Lauren told Shels. She said you guys were at the Date Festival and you must've eaten too many tamales or something 'cause you ripped one so loud it turned heads. Which usually I'd applaud you for, but, dude—not when you're trying to make your move. She said it was right after you tried to hold her hand. Not the best timing, man."

Freaking girls have to tell each other everything. "Lauren was just lying to cover up the fact that she farted."

"Yeah, 'cause girls do that. Dude, I've been dating Shels for almost a year and she still hasn't farted around me—even when my mom stuffs her full of beans and molé. But just take some Pepto before we leave tonight and you'll be fine."

I rack my brain for a brilliant insult to shut him up when I realize what he said. "Tonight? What's tonight?"

"A movie with you, me, Hannah, and Shels."

"I can't."

"Come on—it was Hannah's idea, so whatever you did couldn't have been that big of a turnoff."

"I didn't do anything!"

And that reminds me. Audra still has to explain why she ruined my date.

Maybe she was jealous.

Hmm. I like that idea. A lot.

"Dude, are you even listening to me?" Isaac asks.

"Uh, what?"

"I said we'll pick you up at seven thirty."

"I told you, I can't. Sorry."

I'm not sorry, though. Hannah's a nice girl—and last night I thought she was what I wanted. I don't anymore. Not when I have a shot with my dream girl.

Isaac half growls, half sighs. "Fine. But you better be spending the night with a hot girl, and she better be worth abandoning your best friend for. Otherwise, you owe me big-time."

He's so spot-on that all I can do is mumble something along the lines of, "Call—talk—later, haveagoodnightbye," and hang up the phone.

Isaac's right.

She better be worth all this hassle.

But Audra is.

Even though I know she'll probably throw more bugs at my head and threaten my life and attack me with winds, I'm looking forward to whatever she has in store for me.

So I throw on fresh clothes, splash some water on my hair, and tell my mom I'm going out. I'm not waiting until sunset to see Audra again.

CHAPTER 18

AUDRA

Screams. Horrible, bone-chilling screams whip around me in an unintelligible blur of noise as rocks, dirt, branches, and so many other things I can't begin to identify pummel my body.

I stumble, fighting to keep my feet on the ground, refusing to let the gusts carry me away. We can't fight this storm—it's already destroyed too much. But I won't leave without my father.

Something tugs at my wrist, yanking me back a step. I spin around, squinting through the pebbles and dirt and blurry wall of wind to find the outline of a boy's face. Takes me a second to piece together that I know him.

"We have to go back," Vane yells.

Before I can answer, a bloodcurdling screech pierces the air.

"Mom?" Vane drops my wrist and races deeper into the storm.

I chase after him, arriving at his side in time to see a woman in a blue dress streak across the sky. She thrashes against the winds that wrap around her like bonds, but she can't break free.

"Mom!" he screams again, jumping, trying to reach her.

She's too high.

"Vane?" She thrashes harder. "Run. You have to—"

Her words are carried away by a shifting gust. The sudden flurry alters course, rushes past an uprooted tree, and whips it toward her. I close my eyes, but I can't block the sickening crunch as one of the jagged branches slams into her, and when I look up her body's bent at an unnatural angle. Her head lolls to the side. Bloodred rain showers around us.

Vane screams, an unearthly yelp of agony and rage and terror.

I do nothing.

I cannot move.

Cannot think.

Cannot do anything except stare at the broken body in the blue dress, trailing blood through the sky as it whisks into the darkness.

"Audra?" my dad shouts, yanking me out of my daze. "Audra!"

His calls get more frantic when I don't respond, so I turn, searching the sky until I spot him, fighting his way through the drafts high above me.

"You have to get out of here, Audra. Take Vane and get outside the storm's path."

"Not without you." I start to jump the same way Vane did. There has to be a way to reach my father. Bring him back to me.

Everything in me aches to fly up to him. But I'm not strong enough yet.

"Go, Audra!"

Never, in all my life, have I heard my father so deadly serious. It knocks the fight out of me, lulling me almost into a trance as I turn and do as he ordered. I grab Vane's hand and drag him away, my feet moving faster with each step I take away from my father, like the winds are spurring me along.

"Keep going," my father urges. "Don't come back."

Somehow we make it to the edge of the storm without being hit by any of the debris raining around us. I shove Vane through the wall of wind to the calmer ground, watching him tumble along the safe, steady earth. I know I'm supposed to follow him, but I can't leave, can't abandon my family. I turn to head back, but my father's voice stops me.

"No, Audra."

He hovers lower. Still out of reach, but close enough that I can see his tear-filled eyes.

"Go, my darling. And take care of Vane."

He sends a powerful Easterly to yank me away. I kick and scream and battle the force with everything I have, but I can't defeat it. It whips me out of the funnel, a few feet from where Vane lies, sobbing. Before I can rise to my feet, the storm explodes.

"Daddy!" I scream, so loud it feels like my throat rips.

The funnel unravels before my eyes, and the threads of winds scatter in every direction. I search the sky for some sign of him, strain my ears for the sound of his voice. But I know I won't find him. I can feel him in the air all around me, and I know he's made the sacrifice. Let the winds tear him apart so he can fight them from the inside.

I reach for the drafts, try to hold them in my grasp.

They slip through my fingers.

He's gone.

Debris claps like thunder as it collides with the ground. It bruises me. Pummels my limbs.

I don't run. I collapse in a sobbing heap, shaking uncontrollably.

He didn't say goodbye.

He didn't say he loved me.

All he said was, "Take care of Vane."

A pair of arms wraps around me and I jump, the relief like a warm blast of sunshine as I turn to hug my father.

But it's not him.

I stare into Vane's watery eyes, feel his arms shaking as he strangles me in a hug, clinging to me like I'm the only thing holding him to the ground.

I want to shove him away. Pound him with my fists.

Why is he here and not my dad?

It's his fault.

His. Fault.

But even my rage won't sell me on the lie.

The truth slices through me, rips me apart, knocks me off my feet. I steady myself against Vane, sobbing onto his shoulder as hard as he cries onto mine. And I tell him the truth.

I tell him it's my fault. Scream it over the winds. I have to, before the weight of what I did crushes everything inside me.

I know he hears me because he stops crying. Still, he doesn't let go. Doesn't pull away.

He pulls me tighter.

The winds are cold and icy, and the world has never felt so lonely and dark. But I feel Vane's warmth through the fabric of his coat, and the longer we hold each other, the more the heat spreads through me, filling me with energy and life.

I never want to let go.

Take care of Vane. *My father's last wish.*

I promise whatever's left of my father that I will.

I can never make this right. But I'll do everything I can to try.

CHAPTER 19

VANE

Audra isn't in the burned-down shack, which seems ... strange. Not as strange as the soft whimpers echoing through the air, drowning out the buzzing, chirping, crackling sounds of the grove.

"Audra?" I call, trying to follow the sound. It seems like it's coming from above, but the sun's too bright, and even when I squint, all I can see in the fuzzy light are palm leaves.

My whole body shudders as an awful possibility occurs to me.

They're here. They've got her.

I race back to the burned-down house, scrambling to the corner where she stashed the sword. I rip it from the slit in the ground and hold it in front of me. It's heavier than I expected, and my stomach turns as I stare at the needled edges.

Tearing flesh.

Blood spilling from jagged wounds.

Dripping down the blade.

The mental images make my hands shake so hard I almost drop the sword.

But Audra needs me.

I race through the palms, following the sound of her sobs. Broken branches scratch my legs and the sharp bark scrapes my arms as I tear deeper into the grove.

"Audra!" I scream.

The crying stops.

A loud screech replaces it, and that evil hawk of hers dives out of the sky, aiming for my head. I barely duck in time.

"I'm trying to help her, you stupid bird!" I shout, swiping the sword, even though he's already flown out of my reach.

"Vane?"

Audra's voice bounces off the trees in so many different directions I can't tell where it came from. "Where the hell are you?"

"Up here."

I squint at the treetops and there—peeking out from the leaves of the tallest one—is Audra.

Alone.

Safe.

Nothing to worry about—except the glare in her eyes as she asks, "What do you think you're doing? Why do you have the windslicer?"

Windslicer?

Awesome name.

I move to the shade of her tree, trying to cool off. Running in the heat is not the best idea. Good thing I put on extra deodorant.

"I was . . . trying to save you," I admit, hating how cheesy it sounds. "I thought the Stormers were here."

"*You* were trying to save *me*?"

"Hey, I heard crying. I thought the warriors were torturing you or something."

Sheesh—ungrateful much?

She stares at me, her expression a little proud, but mostly sorry for me. Like a parent listening to their child's plan to capture the closet monster. "If the Stormers were here, the sky would be inky black and the winds would be picking up these trees and tossing them around like matchsticks."

"Oh, good. Something to look forward to."

We both glance at the sky, like we need to double-check that there's nothing there.

Not a cloud in sight. But her hawk dives at me again and I almost drop the windslicer as I flail to cover my head. "Seriously, call off your attack bird."

"Go to your perch, Gavin," she commands, and instantly the stupid creature obeys, screeching one last time as he flaps toward the house.

Freaking bird.

"Step back," she warns, moving to the edge of the leaves.

She's not going to jump, is sh—

My thought's cut short as she spreads her arms and steps off the branch. She whispers something I can't understand and a hot gust of wind rushes past me. The draft wraps around her, slows her descent, and sets her gently on the ground.

"Show-off," I grumble.

She holds out her hand for the sword and I readily hand it over. Holding it makes me queasy. She inspects the blade, probably making sure I haven't somehow damaged it in the five minutes I held it. "Why were you looking for me?"

"Why were you hiding up in a tree, crying?" I counter.

For a second she looks thrown. Then she says, "I needed the wind to restore me," and cuts through the grove, heading back to her house.

I follow, waiting until she's put the deadly weapon away and turned to face me before I press for an answer that isn't a total load of crap. "Okay, that explains why you were in the tree. What about the crying?"

I stare her down, daring her to deny it.

"That's none of your business."

She tries to move past me but I block her path.

"You can trust me, you know," I tell her, my voice a little heavier on the emotion than I mean it to be. "I know you're used to doing everything on your own. But we're in this together now."

She doesn't say anything. Just stares at the ground, like the ants scurrying across the dirt are the most fascinating things in the world.

I move closer and take her hands—thrilling to the strange zings that shoot through me the second we touch. "Let me help you."

The air feels charged between us as she considers my offer, and for a second it looks like she might take me up on it. Then she shakes her head and slips her hands out of my grip. "I just had a bad dream. That's all."

"About what?"

She turns away. "About the day my father died."

Her voice is barely a whisper, but the words hit me like a stone.

Her father died saving me.

"I'm so sorry," I tell her, hoping she knows how much I mean it.

She turns back, and when our eyes meet, I see a slight shift. Like a tiny piece of her iron guard just cracked. "It wasn't your fault."

I shrug, wondering if that's really true. "Either way, I'm still sorry it happened."

"Me too."

She leans against the wall, into the tiny patch of shade it creates. From her pained expression I can tell she's reliving every moment of the storm in perfect detail.

I want to crawl inside her head, watch the replay—even if it'll hurt.

"What was it like?" I whisper.

"The storm?"

"Yeah. How did it all . . . go down?" I can't think of a gentler way of saying it.

She stares at me like I've just massacred half a dozen kittens. "You want me to tell you the gruesome details of your parents' murders?"

"No. Yes. I don't know." I swipe my hands through my hair, trying to find the words to explain it. "For the last ten years of my life I've had hundreds of people ask me what happened—and do you know how they look at me when I say 'I don't know'? Like I'm brain damaged. 'Cause wouldn't I have to be, to not remember the single most defining moment of my life?"

"You're lucky you don't remember."

"Lucky?"

If I have to hear that *one more time* . . .

"So I'm *lucky* your mom stole my memories? Erased the first seven years of my life?"

"In some ways, yes."

She doesn't get it—nobody ever has.

"All I'm asking is for you to help me fill in the blanks. If I can't get my memories back, you can at least share yours."

I lose track of how many seconds pass in silence. Her voice is cold when she says, "My memories are my own."

She stalks over to the cracked window and strokes her demented hawk. The one place she knows I won't go near her. Not that I want to, at that moment.

I know her memories are painful, but with all I've been through she could throw me a freaking bone.

Everything goes back to that day of the storm.

I need to know what happened.

CHAPTER 20

AUDRA

t was only a dream, I tell myself. *Only a dream.*

But I know it's more than that.

It's a memory.

The memory. The one I can't let Vane recover.

Where I told him I killed his family.

It was a foolish, impulsive decision, and the only reason he didn't unleash any of his rage was because he was too shocked by what happened. I'm lucky my mother had to erase his memories, so I never had to live with the consequences of my confession.

I won't make the same mistake again.

I won't tell him. No matter how much he pushes.

My fingers curl into fists and I squeeze, trying to stop the tingling I still feel in my palms from when Vane took my hands.

I finally know what the feeling means.

It's the same feeling I had when we clung to each other in the rubble of the storm. I forgot that detail, but I remember now—the way the warmth passed between us, radiating through my body.

Guilt.

That's the only thing I felt as I leaned on the boy whose life I'd ruined. Let him support me. Deluded myself into believing he could forgive me for what I'd done.

White-hot, burning, stinging guilt.

My body's way of punishing me for my crime.

"So," Vane says, reminding me I'm not alone. "What are we going to do now?"

I'm honestly not sure. I'd always planned to make him master each language on its own, hoping his increased familiarity with the wind would trigger his Westerly breakthrough.

Now we have eight days—assuming my mother delivers on her promise. Less than eight days, since today is mostly over. We don't have time for him to master anything.

The smartest tactic would be to trigger his Northerly and Southerly breakthroughs now, and train him in the power of three. Even the most rudimentary knowledge of combined drafts will be more powerful in a wind battle than competency with only one.

But can he really handle three breakthroughs in less than a day?

My mind was nearly overwhelmed when I chose to have my Gale trainer trigger two at once—and I'd been speaking the Easterly tongue for almost my entire life.

Vane's mind is already taxed with all he's learned and felt since last night. To add the strain of two more breakthroughs would be a tremendous temptation on his senses—one even experienced sylphs would find hard to resist.

"Uh, you want to clue me in to what you're thinking about?" Vane asks. "'Cause standing in a date grove in the hundred-and-twenty-degree heat getting attacked by flies isn't really what I had in mind for the rest of the evening."

I stall for a long breath, forcing myself to admit this is our only option. "The best way to train you is to force your mind to have two more breakthroughs. That's what we call it when the wind shoves its way into your consciousness and makes a connection, so you can understand its language. I triggered your Easterly breakthrough last night, when I joined the wind and entered your mind. That's why you could see me in my wind form—and why you can understand the Easterly tongue now."

"So . . . pretending any of that makes sense—which, by the way, it totally doesn't," Vane says, jumping in, "one question: Why do you say that like you're telling me we need to chop off both my arms, make them into a stew, and feed them to me for dinner?"

I sigh. "Because triggering three breakthroughs so close together is going to be very . . . unpleasant."

"Unpleasant?"

"Dangerous."

"Okay, I'm not a fan of that word."

"If there were any other way—"

"There is. You could call for backup, like you promised last night. What happened to that plan? I liked that plan much better."

"I did ask for backup." My eyes drop to my feet. "My request was denied."

"Denied?"

"Yes." His tendency to repeat everything as a question will definitely push me over the edge by the end of this.

"But I thought I was the last Westerly. Future king. All that jazz. Doesn't that make protecting me kind of a high priority?"

"It does. They're stalling the Stormers as long as they can. And they know I'm one of the best guardians in the Gales."

"Yeah—and you said last night you're too weak to fight them on your own—even with my help."

"Not . . . necessarily. There's something I can do that will definitely defeat the Stormers."

"Uh—if it will *definitely* defeat them, why don't we just do that?"

"We don't 'just do that,' because it's the *ultimate sacrifice.*"

The words slip out before I can stop them.

I feel him watching me, but I refuse to look at him—refuse to face whatever emotions he has written across his face. I don't know what I want him to feel.

I don't know how *I* feel.

"So if I'm understanding this right," he says after a minute, "these Gales you worship so much—they've sent you on a death mission instead of providing reinforcements?"

"It's not like that."

"Really. Then what is it like, Audra? 'Cause it seems pretty clear to me. And it's wrong. They can't make you—expect you . . ."

His voice trails off, and I can't help stealing a glimpse of his face.

My heart skips when I see the look in his ice-blue eyes. It's been so long since anyone looked at me that way, I almost don't recognize the sentiment.

He cares.

Vane Weston cares about me.

I blink the tears away before they can form.

It doesn't change anything. "I've sworn an oath to protect you with my life, and I intend to keep it. No matter what."

It's a simple statement, but the effect it has on Vane is profound.

He steps closer. Close enough that I feel his warmth in the air. Closer than I should let him stand. "It's not going to come to that," he says, his voice more serious than I've ever heard it. "Trigger the breakthroughs. Whatever it takes."

I swallow to find my voice. "You understand that the process is going to be very difficult."

"Yes."

"Painful, even."

"I'll . . . deal with it."

Who is this boy and what did he do with Vane?

"You're sure?"

He takes my hands, gently locking our fingers together. "I'm not going to let anything happen to you, Audra."

I look away, battling back the explosion of emotions erupting inside me.

My palms tingle so hard from his touch, they practically throb. My burning, scorching guilt, punishing me for my newest crime.

I deserve it. I'm letting Vane risk everything to save me—and he has no idea I'm the one who destroyed his life.

I'll never tell him, either. It would break his commitment to the mission. Get him captured and me killed, along with thousands of innocent people.

But that's not the only reason.

Vane's the first person since my father died to care whether I live and breathe. I can't give that up.

The guilt burns hotter as I own up to my selfishness, but I bear the pain. It hurts less than the aching loneliness I've endured for the last ten years.

So I take a deep breath to clear my head. "You should probably sit down. This is going to be . . . intense."

CHAPTER 21

VANE

Audra has me sit cross-legged on the pile of palm leaves on the floor, and they're just as scratchy as they look. I can't believe she sleeps on these things. She rattles off a long list of instructions I should probably be paying attention to—but I can't focus. My brain's stuck on auto repeat.

Intense. Intense. Intense.

I'm pretty sure what she means is intense *pain*—and I'm not exactly known for having a high tolerance for that.

At least Audra seems pretty impressed that I'm willing to do this to help her—which is crazy. Does she really think I want her to die to save me?

"Hug yourself tighter, Vane. Northerlies are incredibly aggressive winds."

It's hard not to groan. "Aggressive" is almost as bad as "dangerous."

She adjusts my hands and arms, bending me into a Vane pretzel.

"You okay?" she asks when I jump at her touch.

"Yeah, sorry. Just jittery, I guess."

Doesn't she feel the way the sparks jolt between us? Now, *that's* intense.

The waves of heat make their way to my heart, settling in like that's where they belong. I know how cheesy that sounds—Isaac would hurl if he knew I was thinking it. But I like it. It feels like she's becoming a part of me, more and more with every touch.

Makes me want to grab her, pull her against me, feel the warm rush spread as I run my hands down—

"Are you ready?" she asks, ripping me out of my fantasies.

"Yes." I hate my voice for shaking.

"Okay. Let's get the most painful part over with first."

"Sounds awesome."

Her lips twist into that small half smile she's becoming famous for. "The only advice I can give you is to not fight back. I'll command the winds to slip into your consciousness, but you have to breathe them in. Once the gusts are in there, you have to force yourself to concentrate. They'll feel foreign and unwelcome and your head will probably throb. Just remember that your mind does know how to do this."

"You kind of lost me at 'throb,' but I'll do my best. Let's just . . . get this over with."

She nods. Then she closes her eyes and whispers something that sounds like a snake singing. The winds kick up around her.

A chill settles over us—which actually isn't so bad after baking in the heat. The gusts wrap around me, crackling the palm branches as they lift me off the ground. The pressure's much stronger than I expected, and my twisted limbs uncoil until I'm sprawled out flat, rolling with the storm.

"Breathe them in, Vane. Then concentrate on what you hear," Audra shouts before the roaring air drowns her out. Leaving me alone, shivering in my icy wind cocoon as the drafts hammer my face.

I want to block them, close off everything and hope they go away. But I lock my jaw to stop my teeth from chattering, and the next time a gust comes full force at my face I take a long, deep breath. Instead of flowing into my lungs, the air pushes into my mind. It burns like when water goes up my nose—only a thousand times more painful.

The winds streak inside my head, forming a vortex and slamming me with the most intense migraine ever, like my brain's being kicked and punched and stabbed and ripped apart. I want to tear off my scalp to let the gusts out.

Concentrate, Audra told me.

How the hell am I supposed to concentrate with a wind tunnel in my head? It's like standing by a waterfall as a jet engine blows past and a million claps of thunder rumble at the same time.

But mixed with all that chaos is a simple, solitary note.

It rings with a long, low whine—nothing I can understand. But the more I strain to hear it, the closer and clearer it becomes, like it's shoving its way to the front of my focus, demanding my attention.

It reminds me of when Isaac turns on the subwoofer in his truck.

All the music and lyrics get drowned out by the throbbing, pulsing bass, making his truck vibrate and his old, grumpy neighbors glare at us as we *thump thump thump* by their houses.

The pain in my head amplifies as I concentrate on the sound, and the wind feels like it's freezing me into a Vane-cicle.

Come on, you stupid wind, break through before I seriously lose it here.

This is hopeless. I'm never going to feel or hear whatever freaking thing I'm supposed to hear or feel. I'm a failure as a Windwalker, and Audra's going to die because of me.

The realization smacks me back to my senses—and that's when I catch it.

A single word. Over and over.

Strength.

The instant I separate the word, the wind seeps into my consciousness. It feels like draining a tall glass of water all in one gulp—only my brain's doing the drinking.

My limbs fall still and I focus on the lyrics behind the melody, which I now understand. The north wind sings of power. Of invincibility. Of balance.

"Vane, can you hear me?" Audra calls from very far away. "Open your eyes."

I want to obey, but I don't know how to make my body function at the moment. The winds have coiled around my mind. Teasing. Tugging. Begging me to come with them. And I want to. The Northerlies sound so brave and strong.

They'll protect me.

"Vane, listen to me!" Audra yells. "You can't believe everything the winds tell you. I know it sounds like wisdom, but you have to resist. They're pulling you away, and if you let that happen, you won't come back."

I don't want to listen to her, but a blast of warmth shoots through both my arms like an electric shock.

My body jerks and my eyes shoot open. The blinding sunlight makes my head pound, and a loud moan slips through my lips. Then my vision clears and I get a glimpse of Audra leaning over me, clasping my wrists with her slender hands.

"Breathe," she orders.

Why would she have to tell me to . . .

Burning pain in my chest wakes me up to the fact that it's been a while since I've taken a breath. I suck in a huge gulp of air, hacking and coughing as it enters my oxygen-starved body.

Audra pulls me into a sitting position, pounding on my back. "You okay?"

"I've been better." I hug myself, needing to feel my body again. I forgot about it for a second. "What happened?"

"The wind started to carry your consciousness away."

I rub my throbbing head. "How about in English this time?"

She flashes a small, sad smile. "I don't fully understand it myself. My father used to tell me Windwalkers are caught between two worlds. Neither purely of the earth nor the sky, and when we allow ourselves too much contact with either, it starts to lead us astray. In the earth's case, food and water ground us, bind us to the land. Limit our abilities. And the wind's call tries to take us with it, like an old friend begging us to come along for the journey."

That I understand. Part of me still wants to follow.

"But if we let it lead us away, we leave our earthly forms behind, never to return," she warns.

"How come it didn't feel like that last night?" I was asleep for most of it, but I don't remember having a hard time waking up.

"When I triggered your Easterly breakthrough it was me inside your head, and I could control the drafts and build the connections you needed to make without exposing you to the full force of the winds."

"So . . . you were literally *inside* my mind—like how the wind just was?" I shudder, remembering the weird swishy, spinning feeling.

"Yes. When we shift into our true forms, we are the wind. We move and work and feel exactly the same way, only with more control."

"That might be the freakiest thing you've told me yet."

She rewards me with another partial smile. Then she looks down, watching her fingers as she twists them together. "I'm not sure if I should trigger the Southerly breakthrough. It might be too much for you to handle right now."

I can't begin to explain how much I don't want to go through that again—ever. But this isn't about me. "I need to learn the three languages, right? As soon as possible?"

A few seconds pass before she says, "Time is running out."

"Then we have to do it."

I can't believe the words are coming out of my mouth.

But I can't wimp out now. People might die. *Audra* might die. "I know what to expect now. I'll be fine."

"If the lure was that strong from the harsh, cold Northerlies, it'll be ten times worse from the warm, welcoming Southerlies."

"I'll come back."

"How can you be so sure?"

I take her hands. She tries to pull away, but I hold tight. "When you touched me, it yanked me back. So just do that again, and I'll come back. For you."

The last words I kinda mumble, but I'm pretty sure she caught them, because a hint of pink colors her cheeks.

She stares at our hands for a second, taking slow, deep breaths. "Okay. Let's get this over with."

CHAPTER 22

AUDRA

Vane has no idea how irresistible the Southerlies' pull will be. Their warm rush is intoxicating. The comfort they promise so alluring. Tempting you to slip away forever in their soft, wandering drag.

I'd been ready to follow their whispers anywhere they led, and I very nearly had. The vow I made my father was the only thing that pulled me back.

But all I can do is stick with the plan and hope Vane really will come back for me.

To me, I correct. And not even *me*—specifically. Come back to the world, to continue with his training. Live up to his potential. Step into his role as king. Those are my primary—my only—concerns.

I repeat the reminder in my head as I reach for the winds. The nearest Southerlies are several miles away, ambling through a stretch of empty dunes. They shift toward me when I whisper their call.

I hold Vane's gaze as the winds form the first tendrils of his cocoon. "You must come back," I order.

"Hold on to me and I will."

His honest trust, his willingness to face such a challenge for me—not to mention the intensity in his eyes—makes my guilt burn hot in my hands. In my heart.

I stuff the pain as deep as I can shove it. Then I whisper the last command, close the cocoon, and Vane's gone, tangled in the silky strands of Southerlies.

I catch myself holding my breath and force air into my lungs. I have to keep my head clear. Be prepared for anything.

Vane's limbs stay locked in place as his body lifts off the ground. No thrashing or flailing like the Northerlies caused. It's hard to make out his form through the sandy gusts, but I can see his face and he looks peaceful. Happy.

I remember that feeling. The Southerlies carry pure bliss.

My nails press into my palms as I count the passing seconds, watching for the breakthrough to occur. The longer he's at the wind's mercy, the more he relinquishes control.

Ten seconds.

Twenty.

Thirty.

Forty.

I live an eternity in each moment. I could have destroyed our only hope with this hasty decision.

Fifty seconds.

A minute.

"Come on, Vane—you can do this!" I shout over the gusts.

Sixteen more seconds pass. Then the winds unravel, fleeing to freedom.

He had the breakthrough.

His body collapses on the bed of palm leaves, and I call his name over and over. He doesn't stir, but I take his hands the way I did when he was fighting the Northerlies, ignoring the guilt searing my skin as I do.

His eyes remain closed. He doesn't so much as twitch.

"Breathe, Vane," I order, squeezing his hands harder. "You promised."

No reaction.

I shake his arms, trying to rock him awake. *"Breathe!"*

Nothing. Even when I pound on his chest with my fists.

My heart jumps into my throat as I watch his lips tinge with blue. I have to do something—anything.

I've seen groundlings blow air into each other's mouths, trying to jump-start the lungs. But I can't risk forming a bond to Vane. And that might not even work. His lungs aren't the problem. It's his mind whisking away, following the alluring call of the winds. Wandering too far from his rightful place.

The blue spreads from his lips, painting his face with a gray pallor.

I grab his shoulders and shake as hard as I can. His head lolls and falls limp.

I can't just sit here and watch him suffocate. Even if his lungs aren't the problem—putting air into his body has to help.

I refuse to let myself think about what I'm doing as I lift his chin with shaky hands.

"It's not a kiss," I whisper, saying it out loud to stand as testimony. "This is a lifesaving measure. Not a kiss. No bond will form."

No bond. No bond. No bond.

I will not bond myself to Vane Weston.

No. Bond.

I take a trembling breath—barely able to believe what I'm about to do as I place one hand on each of his cheeks.

"Vane!" I yell. "Vane, wake up."

Nothing.

Tears burn my eyes as I stare at his blue-gray lips.

Now or never, Audra.

I lean closer, whispering in his ear. "Please don't leave me, Vane."

I didn't plan to say that—but I don't have time to analyze my word choice. I suck in a huge gulp of air, holding it in my lungs as I part his lips with trembling hands and lean in.

No-bond-no-bond-no-bond-no-bond.

Before I make contact, Vane's body thrashes with a hacking cough. His forehead crashes against my chin, knocking me backward as he rolls to his side, gasping for breath.

I rub my smarting jaw with one hand and wrap my other arm around myself, trying to calm my shaking. I can't make sense of any of the emotions washing over me. All I know is: Vane's alive.

He wheezes and struggles for a minute before he catches his breath. I sit to the side, feeling too much like I've had the world yanked out from under me then shoved back into place to do anything except watch.

I want to tell him how much he scared me. How close he came to leaving me behind—to leaving everyone and everything behind.

How much I'd been ready to risk to save him.

But he doesn't need to know any of that.

When his color returns and his coughing calms, he sits up, smooths his hair, and meets my eyes. "Told you I'd come back for you."

CHAPTER 23

VANE

My legs move like two soggy noodles as Audra drags me through the grove toward my house. I've been tired before. Been beaten up before. Shoot, I survived a tornado—and even though I don't remember what happened, I remember every ache and pain in the days that followed. But I've never experienced anything like this.

I feel empty. Like everything that makes me *me* oozed out my ears, leaving just a shell of Vane.

Nothing could've prepared me for the pull of the Southerlies. It felt like I was a kid again and my mom was promising everything would be all right if I just did what she said. Her voice sounded different, higher and softer than usual, but the words still coiled around my mind and heart—and the more I tried to shove them away, the harder they latched on.

I was a goner.

Until Audra's desperate voice whispered through the wind, begging me not to leave.

I wouldn't leave her.

In that determination, I found the strength to break free, my head spinning and my body screaming with a thousand different pains as I forced myself back to reality.

But I swear the wind took part of me with it. It definitely stole my warmth. I can't stop shivering—even though I'm sure it has to be at least a hundred degrees. The noodle legs aren't cool either. And my head feels like the soccer team used it for practice.

The worst part is the hollowness. I know what Audra meant by "caught between two worlds" now. The wind made parts of me feel freer, fuller, happier than I've ever been. Without them I feel lost and empty. I'm glad to be back, though. The sky may call to me, but I want my feet firmly on the ground. Preferably without the Jell-O legs.

Speaking of which—*how* am I going to explain my current condition to my parents? Knowing my mom, she'll probably worry I'm drunk or high or both. She watches too many news reports on troubled teens.

And it looks like they'll get to meet Audra, because unless I slither into the house, there's no way I'm walking in there on my own. Audra's basically carrying all my weight right now—which is pretty impressive, considering how slender she is.

The sun-bleached walls of my house come into view, and my

stomach tightens. Audra tenses too, so I have a feeling she's thinking the same thing I am: *What the hell are we going to do now?*

She slows to a stop at the edge of the tree line. "I need you to lean on a palm for a second," she says, already wrapping my arm around a rough trunk. I shift my weight, leaning at an awkward angle, but I manage to stay upright as Audra starts unbuttoning her jacket.

Man, I hope whatever she has under there is thin and lacy.

When she undoes the last of the shiny gold buttons—her jacket reminds me of something an eighties pop star would wear—she slips the heavy coat off her shoulders, revealing a plain black tank and a whole lot of creamy skin. Not the sexy bra I'd been hoping for, but at least it's tight and cut low. A blue necklace with a silver feather hangs just below the lines of her collarbone, drawing my eyes right where they probably shouldn't go.

She tosses the jacket in the general direction of her house. "Hopefully this looks close enough to a workout outfit to fool your parents. We'll tell them we were training and you ran too hard and got leg cramps. That should sufficiently explain your condition."

I can't think of anything better, and I'm getting pretty tired from holding myself up, so I let her wrap my arm back around her shoulders. A million lightning bolts zing as my skin meets hers. My shivering vanishes. Without her thick uniform-coat thing, her touch is a thousand times more electric. Not to mention how smooth and soft her bare skin feels against mine.

Note to self: Steal and destroy her jacket as soon as possible.

I try not to trip as we start moving again, but my useless legs refuse to cooperate, and I nearly knock us over. She shifts her weight in front of me and pulls me back to my feet. Leaving us face to face, her body pressed so tightly against mine I can feel her heartbeat through her thin shirt.

I swear the air around us is seconds away from catching fire.

Audra shuffles me back to her side. "Once we get inside, I'll lay you down in your room and see myself out. Try not to get up. Eat something. Eat a lot, actually. Your body could use a few more ties to the earth. And stay away from the wind. Close your window tight—turn off your fan. You're too vulnerable right now."

"Vulnerable how? Like . . . I could get swept away again if I stand too close to an AC vent?"

"Probably not. But I'm trying to be cautious. I've never heard of anyone being as tempted by the wind as you were. Maybe it's a Westerly thing. Or maybe you've been so wind-deprived these last ten years your body doesn't know how to handle it. Either way, you need to stay grounded, so it's safer to stay away from temptation."

The only temptation I'm feeling is to run my hands along the sliver of midriff peeking from the bottom of her tank top. Now, *that* would motivate me to stay grounded.

I'm ready to tell her that, but we've reached my house's ugly blue front door.

"Should I . . . knock?" Audra asks.

I've never heard her voice crack before. "Nervous to meet the parents?"

"I just haven't had a lot of contact with groundlings."

"You realize they're going to think you're my girlfriend, right?"

She pales. "Whatever it takes to protect the truth."

Does she have to sound like having me for a boyfriend is some exhausting assignment she wants to get rid of?

"It should be unlocked," I tell her.

She takes a deep breath, squares her shoulders, and pulls the door open.

"I'm home," I call, loud enough to be heard over the TV. "And don't freak out—but I kinda wore out my legs, so I needed help inside."

Before I even finish my sentence, my mom shrieks, "What?" and both her and my dad stampede down the hall. So much for not freaking out. They stop dead when they spot Audra.

Audra turns rigid and stares at the ground.

The awkwardness would be awesome if I weren't suddenly overwhelmed by nerves of my own.

"What happened?" my dad asks, gesturing to my rather pathetic, slumped position.

"I got shin splints pretty bad, so Audra had to help me in. I must have pushed myself too hard while we ran."

My dad laughs—one of those huge belly laughs you'd expect to come from some six-foot-five guy with a beer gut, not a five-foot-nine skinny guy who wears preppy golf shirts every day. "That's what you get for showing off."

"Thanks, Dad."

My mom snaps out of her Audra-staring stupor. "I'm sorry, I don't think we've really been introduced. I'm Carrie."

She extends a hand for Audra to shake. Audra trips over my feet as she moves to take it.

"We should probably let him lie down," she says when she recovers. Her cheeks are bright pink. "Which way to his room?"

I have to give her credit. Acting like she doesn't know exactly which room is mine is a nice touch.

"Oh, um, I don't know—Jack, maybe you should take him," my mom says, biting her lip like she's worried we might feel the uncontrollable urge to rip each other's clothes off the second we get near a bed.

My dad laughs, runs a hand over the shiny part of his head—he proudly rocks the cul-de-sac of hair curving around his bald spot—and says, "Relax, Carrie." He points down the hall. "It's that way."

"Thank you." Audra flashes her half smile and drags me away.

"It's the door on the left," my mom adds, hot on our heels, determined to play chaperone every step of the way.

"I can lead her to my own bedroom," I mutter.

Audra ignores us, kicking my half-closed door open and leading me to the unmade bed. She plops me down—not as gently as I'd like—and helps me lift my legs up, all while my mom "supervises" from the doorway.

Sheesh, one hot girl walks into the house and all trust vanishes.

"You okay?" Audra asks as I attempt to scoot into a more comfortable position. Mostly I just flail.

"Yeah."

I want to say more, but my dad's joined my mom at my bedroom door, and while he doesn't have her look of nervous terror, he looks like when he's watching the Discovery Channel.

Aren't the mating habits of teenagers fascinating, honey?

I sigh.

"So, tell me again how this happened," my mom says, adding to the awkwardness.

Her tone's light—but I know she's really saying, "I don't believe your story. Let me pick holes in it."

Audra answers before I can send her any sort of warning about the dangerous ground we're on. "I'm teaching Vane to run faster. But I guess I pushed him too hard in the heat, because his legs cramped and he passed out."

I think that sounds reasonable enough. It doesn't satisfy my mom, though.

"Are you on the cross-country team?" She smiles when Audra nods. "Me too—when I was your age. What's your best event?"

Uh-oh.

I try to think of something so I can jump in and answer for Audra, but for the life of me I can't think of a single track event. Aren't they all just . . . running?

But Audra doesn't even blink as she says, "I'm equally good at them all."

"She is," I say. "She's amazing."

That comes out a bit gooier than I mean it to, and my cheeks burn. My whole head practically bursts into flames when I notice my parents. My mom's grinning her *my little boy is growing up* smile and my dad looks like he wants to pat me on the back and call me "slugger."

Parents: perfecting ways to humiliate their children since the dawn of time.

"Well, it's very nice to meet you," my mom whispers, her voice thick.

If she starts crying, I'm going to smother myself with my pillow.

Audra steps forward, offering a sturdy hand to shake. "It's nice to meet you, too. Vane talks about you guys all the time."

My parents beam and I can't help grinning. She sure knows how to charm the parental units.

"I wish I could say the same," my mom says, shooting me a glare. "He told us he had a date, but you're the first girl he's brought home. He must really like you."

"Mom," I complain, ready to bean her with my pillow. Or maybe the bedside lamp. Especially when Audra blushes bright red.

"Well," my dad jumps in, "thank you for bringing him home. And thank you for getting him outside. The only exercise Vane gets these days is with his thumbs on those video game controllers."

"Dad," I whine.

"I have no doubt you'll whip him into shape in no time," he adds, ignoring me.

"I certainly hope so," Audra says quietly.

I'm sure my parents don't catch the way her shoulders slump, or the hint of doubt that snuck into her tone. My eyes dart to the window. Watching for the storm.

The sky's bright red and orange. A vivid desert sunset. But after all I've learned, I can't help thinking it looks violent.

"Well, come on, I'll show you out," my dad says, draping his arm across Audra's shoulders like she's already part of the family.

Audra accepts his lead but glances at me before she leaves. "Get some rest."

I nod, not missing the way she flicks off my fan on her way out.

The air goes still and my body calms. I hadn't noticed the way my skin was straining toward the breeze.

Audra's right. I *am* vulnerable. In more ways than I can count.

And I'm sick of it.

Tomorrow I take control.

Time to find out how strong I am. Before it's too late.

CHAPTER 24

AUDRA

My legs barely manage to carry me from Vane's house to my hideout. I sink to the floor and lean against the rough wall, wondering how I'll find the strength to get up again.

I don't have much left to give. Not to mention an overpowering hunger churns inside me. The air in Vane's house was laced with the scent of whatever dinner he'll be enjoying tonight. I can still taste the rich, salty aroma on my tongue.

What would it be like to take an actual bite, let the flavors explode in my mouth, let my body be full for the first time in years?

That isn't why I feel so overwhelmingly empty, though.

The way Vane's father wrapped his arm around my shoulders—for a second I thought I'd turn my head and see my dad's dimpled smile beaming back at me. Then he'd laugh and twirl me and it would be like the last ten years never happened.

But he wasn't there when I glanced over.

Just Vane's perfect, happy family.

I punch the ground, releasing the rising resentment before it can choke me.

I don't need food or family.

I don't need anything. Except to stay focused.

I concentrate on a nearby Easterly's song, listening for any sign of the Stormers' approach. The lyrics hold no clue to their presence. It should be a relief. But the song carries no note of anything out of the ordinary. Not even my mother's trace.

I know she'll be careful, hide any glimmer of her trail. Still, I wish I had some sign that she's really out there stalling them. Keeping us safe.

If she isn't, the Stormers could arrive any second. And even if she is, can I really push Vane to be ready for the fight? I almost lost him today.

But if I don't . . .

My hand clutches the pendant resting against my chest, and I can't help wondering how much longer my cord will stay turquoise blue, vibrant with the energy I breathed into it before the Gales clasped it around my neck. When I stop breathing, it will turn black like my father's.

I can't imagine him wanting me to leave this earth the way he did. He didn't even want me to become a guardian. I still remember the look on his face when I told him.

He'd brought me to a meadow for my first lesson in windwalking, and when I'd finally lifted my feet off the ground—even though it was only for a second—I'd been so proud. I told him I was on my way to being just like him. My first step to becoming a Gale.

The crinkles around his eyes sank into ravines and his dimple vanished. Then he wrapped his arms around me and ran his fingers through my hair, untangling the knots caused by the afternoon breezes. And he said, "I want you to always be free."

He didn't want me to be bound by oath or duty. At least not then.

But something changed. Why else would he send me his gift and beg me to take care of Vane? He knew what that meant. And he knew how that journey would end for him.

Was it because what happened was my fault? Did he shove me toward a life of sacrifice as penance? Or did he choose me because he thought I could do what he couldn't? Protect Vane *and* live to breathe another day?

I want to believe I'm strong enough—and that Vane will have the fourth breakthrough and be powerful enough to protect himself. But we only have seven days until the Stormers arrive, and I can't force the final breakthrough. I don't know the language, so I can't call the Westerlies to him or send them into his mind. He'll have to reach them on his own—and if he doesn't . . . I only have seven days left to live.

I smear my tears away, pressing hard enough to hurt. I loathe the physical proof of my body's weakness almost as much as I loathe myself for giving in to self-pity.

I made this choice. And it isn't about protecting Vane or fulfilling my promise to my father. This is my one chance for redemption. My one chance to make up for the horrible mistake I've made.

I will do what needs to be done—and I will do it willingly.

No more pathetic weakness.

I need to be strong. And for that, I need pure, powerful wind.

I dust myself off as I rise and reach for my jacket, shoving my arms through the coarse sleeves. The heavy fabric makes me sweat, but I ignore the discomfort and fasten the buttons across my chest. Then I call every nearby draft—twice as many as I normally use—twisting them around me into a knot of wind. The extra gusts and the muted tones of twilight obscure my form in the sky.

I fly almost entirely on instinct, relying on my father's gift as I creep through the scattered clouds at more of a walk than a race. The drafts sing their scattered melodies, some promising life, others promising rest, and I drink in their words, even if I know they aren't meant for me.

When my feet touch down, I collapse in a heap. But I'm on San Gorgonio Peak—the highest in the range—and I already feel the fresh mountain air reviving me. The faster, stronger, richer winds skim across my face, cooling me to the core as they share their strength and energy.

I curl up and close my eyes, focusing on the gusts as I clear my mind. Surrendering my consciousness. Drifting with the wind. It's somewhat like sleep, but a deeper kind of rest. One that washes through every cell, leaving a clean slate.

I'm not sure how long I stay that way, but when I open my eyes the stars are out. Tiny pricks of light, warring with the darkness. They remind me of the few highs in my mostly black existence. Glints of happiness and good—that can't erase the bad and gloom, no matter how much I want them to. But they hold their place anyway.

Soon I will add another star to my constellation of highs. I'll get Vane through this, no matter what it takes. And with my death, I will finally give my life meaning.

In that, I find peace.

But I can't stop trying, either. Our world needs Vane Weston to have the fourth breakthrough as much as I do. There has to be a way.

If only his parents had taught him something of his heritage. *One tiny word.*

But they'd refused. They'd refused to teach anyone. Even my father, when he asked.

I spent many nights crouching in the shadows, watching my parents argue about that very thing. My mother's anger was a storm, her accusations like flurries slicing the air. She'd scream that the Westons didn't deserve our help if they wouldn't share their language. We could've used their power to protect them. Defeat Raiden. Save everyone. Return to our lives, our home, our native winds—winds that were gentler for her, because she belonged with them.

Why should we make sacrifices for people who would never do the same for us?

Why should we help them, if they selfishly refuse to share their knowledge and help us?

But my father would wrap his arms around her and shield her from the raging winds that always seemed to surge with her tempers. When she'd calmed, he'd whisper that the Westons had the right to protect their heritage however they wanted. If they didn't trust him with the responsibility, it was their choice.

I tried to agree with him then—and most of the time I still do.

Sometimes it's hard, though.

They couldn't have known for sure that they'd die for their language—that their son would be left alone and defenseless without it.

That doesn't change the fact that they condemned us with their decision.

If they'd taught my father Westerly, he'd still be alive.

If they'd taught Vane Westerly, I wouldn't have to sacrifice myself.

But . . . if I hadn't saved Gavin, none of this would have happened.

If.

If.

If.

Infinite possibilities. And none of them matter.

What matters is here and now.

The Stormers are coming.

Seven days left.

CHAPTER 25

VANE

I expect to sleep deeply, pretty dead to the world, after everything I've been through. But the wind did something to my head.

I went to the beach as a kid, and after hours of getting tossed by the waves, my body absorbed the rhythm of the ocean. That night I'd felt like I was still in the water, letting the tide toss me around.

The winds cause the same effect—but it's way more surreal. I float and fall through a world of shadow and light. Shapes blur together. Sounds overlap, and I can barely make them out over the roar of the wind as I swirl and spin and hover.

And as my mind flips with the gusts, something shakes loose.

Shattered bits of scenes flash through my mind. Shards of reality that don't fit, smash-cut together, like a montage in a movie.

CLOSE-UP: AN UPROOTED TREE

Its gnarled branches flail as it shoots through the sky, pulled by the wind. Then the drafts shift and the tree spins, revealing the jagged edge where a thick bough has been ripped away. The sharp splinters at the break are bright red. Like they've been painted.

Or coated with blood.

CUT TO: RIPPLES ON A GLASSY LAKE

Rocks skip across the surface, blurring the reflection of the mountains and puffy white clouds. It should be a peaceful scene, but I don't feel peaceful. More rocks break the water, splashing as waves of anger wash through me.

CUT TO: A YOUNG GIRL

Long, dark hair whips her face. Her bony legs and arms thrash. I squint through the storm and realize she's tangled in the drafts. Her scream rings in my ears as the winds pull her higher and higher. Then they let her go, flinging her in a death drop to the rocky ground. Our eyes meet as she falls. . . .

I jerk awake and kick off my sheets even though I'm shivering. Sweat glues my hair to my forehead.

The girl in the sky. The girl about to die. It was Audra.

But I have no memory of that moment, not unless . . .

I sit up, gripping the edge of my bed.

"Unless the memory came back." I say the words out loud, hoping it'll make them true.

Audra told me they were gone—permanently. But there was something in her eyes when she said it.

Fear.

I want to shake the thought away, refuse to let it rattle my trust in Audra. But she is hiding something from me. I already know that.

Could it have to do with my memories?

What could I have possibly seen or known when I was seven years old that would be important now?

"Vane, are you awake?" my mom asks, knocking on my door.

I lie back down, trying to look normal. "Yep."

She peeks her head through the doorway. "I thought I heard you moving around. I brought you some breakfast. The protein will help your muscles."

She holds out a plate filled with the biggest torpedo she's ever made. The growl my stomach makes echoes off the walls.

She sits on the edge of my bed, watching me eat. I do my best to ignore her, concentrating on the spicy, cheesy goodness, but I know she's hanging out for a reason.

"So, about yesterday," she finally says.

Aaaaaaaaaand, there it is.

I shoot her my best *I really don't want to talk about this* look. She doesn't take the hint.

"You ready to tell me the truth?" she asks.

I keep my eyes glued to my plate. Playing dumb doesn't usually work, but maybe this time I'll get lucky. "The truth?"

"What really happened with you and Audra? I know what shin splints look like, honey—and those weren't it. You couldn't even support your own weight. And I've never seen you so pale."

I try to shrug it off, but she shakes her head.

"I didn't say anything because I didn't want to embarrass you in front of Audra. But now I want to know. Why couldn't you walk? And don't tell me it was some sort of training injury."

"It was."

"You're really going to lie to me?"

"I'm not lying." It did happen during training. Not the kind of training she's thinking of, but still—*training*.

"You're not telling me everything, either—which is exactly the same."

I *really* hate when she makes a good point.

I concentrate on tearing remains of my torpedo into shreds.

"Are you in some sort of fight club?" she whispers.

I snort. "Seriously, that's your theory?"

My mom flushes. "I don't know. You looked pretty beat up yesterday—and Audra looked like a fairly tough girl, dressed all in black with her military-style boots. I just thought . . ."

"I'm not in a fight club. And neither is Audra."

She nods, relieved, and I hope we're done.

No such luck.

"Then what is it?"

I sigh.

I hate lying to my mom. So I toss her a bread crumb and hope it'll be enough. "Audra's kind of training me for something."

"Mind telling me what for?"

I can't tell her—but I won't lie, either.

I hold her gaze, knowing I need to look confident to pull this off. "How about I tell you once I know how it goes?"

She considers my offer. "Is it illegal?"

"No." I'm pretty sure there aren't any specific laws against battling sylph warriors.

"Is it dangerous?"

"It's not supposed to be." Not totally a lie. Audra keeps telling me we'll be fine. And if I ignore the worry in her eyes when she says it, I might believe her.

"You're making this really hard, Vane."

"I know." I take her hand, something I used to do all the time as a kid. Makes me wish I could go back to being ten, knowing my mom can fix whatever problem I'm having.

But she can't fix this.

"I promise, I'll tell you more when I can. For now, just know that I'm not involved with anything featured on one of those special news reports you love to watch." She's softening—I can tell. So I go for the gold. "Have I ever given you reason not to trust me?"

"No," she admits after a beat.

"Then can you please just believe me when I say I'm okay—and that if I need your help, I'll come to you?"

I can tell by the frown lines around her mouth that she doesn't want to agree. So I play my final card.

"I'm seventeen, Mom. You have to start letting me handle things on my own."

She shakes her head, and I expect her to argue. But instead she whispers, "Don't make me regret this."

"I won't. I promise."

She stands and takes my plate. "How are you feeling?"

"Better." I stretch my legs under the covers. They throb like I've just run ten thousand miles at top speed—but they're working. "Just tired."

"Then I guess it's a good thing you don't have anywhere to be."

My dad had tried to force me to get a summer job, but my mom talked him out of it. She knows how sick I get in the heat. But I know she's really telling me she doesn't want me going anywhere. She doesn't trust me.

I hate that.

I can't do anything about it, though, except force a smile and reach for the remote. "Yep. I'll be resting up all day."

Tonight will be another story—but she doesn't need to know that. I just have to keep the act up for seven more days. Then everything will go back to normal.

Or . . . I'll be a prisoner of an evil warlord. Or prisoner of a sylph army. Or dead.

Not a lot of good options in that mix. And not a lot I can do about it. Except train as hard as possible, and trust Audra.

Assuming I *can* trust Audra.

When my mom leaves, I close my eyes and try to force myself to sleep, hoping to trigger more flashbacks. I want my memories. *Need them.* And now that I know they're within my reach, I'll do whatever it takes to get them back.

Audra has her secrets. Now I have mine.

CHAPTER 26

AUDRA

Vane looks pale when I come to collect him for training, and the circles under his eyes are the color of storm clouds. Like he lost a fight with gloom.

"You okay?" I ask as I move closer to him.

He shrugs and focuses on tying his shoes. "Just tired."

He isn't the worst liar I've ever seen—but he's close. I sink on the bed next to him, careful to keep a wall of space between us. "Did you rest?"

"I tried to."

"But?" I prompt.

He shrugs again.

Does he think that counts as an answer?

Apparently. He says nothing further.

I don't have the energy for this.

"We can do this two ways," I tell him. "You can keep ignoring my questions, and I can keep pestering you with them until you finally come clean and tell me what's wrong. Or you can tell me now and save us a ton of time and frustration. I leave it up to you."

He lets out a long, slow sigh, slumps off the bed, and walks to the window, keeping his back to me. "Fine. I had a hard time sleeping after my mom called me out about the shin splints. She didn't buy our story."

"What did you say?" I keep my voice casual, despite the fact that my mind is racing in a million directions.

He wouldn't tell his family the truth—would he?

What will I do if he did? What will I tell the Gales?

Vane shrugs—so help me, if he shrugs one more time I'm going to shake him so hard his teeth will rattle—and turns to face me, not quite meeting my eyes. I hold my breath, bracing for the worst possible answer.

"I told her the truth. That I couldn't tell her what was going on, and that I needed her to trust me."

"Did she agree?"

"For now. But I know she's worrying—and I hate it. I can't keep this up forever, Audra."

I know I should sympathize with his struggle—but it's hard to feel sorry for him. Poor Vane has a mother who cares. I barely remember what that's like.

"You only have to keep it up for a few more days," I tell him, trying to keep the resentment out of my tone.

"Right—'cause after that I'll either be Raiden's prisoner or the Gale Force's new slave."

The venom in his voice slices into my brain. Instant headache.

I can't have this argument again. "Are you feeling well enough to train? We should probably get started."

"Do I even have a choice?"

"Not if you want me to live through this."

I don't realize I said that out loud until I see Vane's face. He looks like the scared little boy watching his broken mother float away.

"Vane, I . . ." I'm not sure I have the words to fix what I just did.

He shakes his head and turns his back on me.

Neither of us speaks as we sneak through his window and run to the darkest corner of the lawn. When we're safely in the shadows, I call the nearby Easterlies and wrap them around us.

"We're not training in the grove?" Vane asks as the winds coil tighter.

"It's time for you to practice the power of three. You'll need more space."

I move toward him and he steps back, meeting my eyes. His mouth opens and closes a few times before he finally says, "You know I'm trying, right? I mean—I—"

"Vane." I force myself to hold his gaze. "I don't expect you—"

"But I'm going to," he insists.

I don't deserve that promise—especially from him. I take it anyway.

The winds brush my face, reminding me why we're standing there. I clear my throat. "You remember how windwalking works?"

He nods, shifting his weight as I drape my arms around his shoulders. His hands wrap around my waist, and heat melts through me. He exhales right as I inhale and his breath is the sweetest thing I've ever tasted. I want to lean closer and drink it in. Instead, I let the winds launch us into the dark sky.

Maybe it's the chilly air up high, or the long, lonely day I've spent worrying, but his touch doesn't scald me with guilt this time. It feels safe. *He* feels safe. Strong. Warm.

"When do I get to fly alone?" Vane asks, his face flushed. Eyes bright with energy.

"Not for a long time. Windwalking is one of our most complicated skills. It requires an extremely fluent communication between you and the wind, and you barely know a few words."

"That sucks."

Something inside me sinks. "You don't like flying with me?"

I want to yank the words back in the second they leave my mouth. Especially when Vane's grin returns, carrying a decent helping of his trademark cockiness.

"Oh, I do." His hands trail to my hips, and I hope I haven't inspired him to make another move with my ridiculous behavior. But they freeze when they reach the windslicer belted to my side in its etched, silver scabbard.

"Seriously? You brought the sword?"

"Why?"

"Well, I mean, it's a cool weapon and all—but you guys have seen the gun, right? Don't you think it's time to upgrade to something a little more effective?"

"Please. Even a breeze can redirect a bullet. I'd like to see a gun stop a cyclone with a single slash."

His smile fades.

Good. He needs to understand the kind of danger we'll face in a wind battle.

Hundreds of glowing red dots appear on the horizon, and I angle the winds toward them, dropping us low when the narrow, spiked windmills come into focus. I can't help being impressed by the way Vane automatically pulls away from me. He remembers how to land.

We hit the ground running, screeching to a stop at the edge of one of the lower foothills.

Vane laughs. "The wind farm? You're joking, right?"

"What's wrong with it?"

"I guess I assumed we'd practice the power of three—or whatever you call it—in the middle of nowhere, so I couldn't do any damage to, oh, I don't know, huge wind turbines that probably cost more than my life." He waves his arms at the rows of windmills all around us. "Not to mention, they look like they'll slice me to Vane-bits if I get too close."

I can't help smiling. "Don't worry, I'll make sure nothing gets out of hand. But you need the windmills. They'll help you separate the different winds, since your senses aren't fine-tuned enough to determine that on their own. See how each windmill is turned differently? They're angled to pick up winds from every direction."

"Is that why there's always like, one or two random windmills spinning, even though none of the others around it are moving?"

"Exactly. So when we practice tonight, and I tell you to find an

Easterly, you would reach from there." I point to four windmills at the base of the lowest hill, lined up like soldiers, their pointed blades blurring in unison. "Watch for their speed. Easterlies are the stealthy winds. They also tend to cluster, so you want to look for a group. Let's see if you can spot a Northerly."

He squints through the darkness, examining the spinning blades.

"There." He points to a pair of windmills in the middle of our level.

I repress a sigh. I can't expect him to know these things—they're not something he'd learn in groundling schools. But it's still disappointing when he gets them wrong.

"Those are Southerlies. See how it looks like they don't have enough force to keep moving, but somehow still do? Southerlies are the steady, sluggish winds. Easterlies are the swift, tricky winds. And Northerlies"—I point to the edge of a hill, where the freeway carves its brightly lit path in the night. A line of windmills stands taller than the others, their enormous blades whirling at top speed—"are the strong, forceful winds."

"What about Westerlies?"

I swallow the lump that rises in my throat every time I think of Westerlies. They stand behind every pain, every sacrifice I've endured in my seventeen years in this world. "They're the soft, peaceful winds."

Vane snorts. "That's ironic."

Indeed, it is. The greatest war our world has faced is being waged over the language of peace. Makes me want to scream. Or punch something really, really hard.

Instead, my eyes search the rows of turbines, seeking out the one spinning to a rhythm all its own. I find it at the lower point of the highest hill, silhouetted against the starry sky. "There's a Westerly."

Vane hesitates before looking where I point.

"It's the only draft here I can't feel. I can see it, and if I were in its path I would feel it against my skin. But I can't feel it prickle my senses. Can't call it. And if I tried to listen to its song, all I would hear is a hiss of rushing air. Its language is completely lost to me."

I don't tell him to feel for it, but Vane closes his eyes, stretching his hands toward the lone Westerly powering the windmill. Reaching for his heritage.

Please let him feel it. Please let there be hope.

I send the silent plea into the night, wishing the winds could hear it and grant my request. But it isn't up to them.

It's up to Vane Weston.

Everything comes down to him.

CHAPTER 27

VANE

I want to feel that freaking Westerly so bad.

Not because I'm expected to. Not because I can hear Audra holding her breath beside me, hanging the weight of the world on my shoulders.

I need to know. If I really am a Westerly. If I have any chance of saving us—of stopping Audra from sacrificing herself to protect me. Of stepping into the role everyone expects me to fill.

So I concentrate on the windmill until it feels like the world disappears. All sound. All thought. It's just me and that draft, straining to make contact.

But I can't feel it. No itch in my palm. No pull in my fingers.

If it weren't for the spinning blades right in front of me, I'd have no clue the wind's even there.

Epic Vane fail.

I glance at Audra and watch the disappointment flicker across her face like shadows.

She forces a smile. "I didn't expect that to work."

"I wish—" I start, but she waves my apology away.

"Don't worry. I have a plan for how to trigger the breakthrough."

I turn back to the Westerly whipping the windmill at a brisk, steady speed.

I do feel . . . something. An ache deep, *deep* inside. Almost like hunger.

My body craves that wind—in a way I don't crave any of the others. Like it's a part of me, and I'll never be complete until I let it fill me, wrap around my mind, and sing its song, tell me the long history it carries.

Just like that first night in the sky with Audra, I know.

I'm a Westerly. A broken, defective one, but still a Westerly. And I need to have a breakthrough to my heritage, or I'll never be complete.

So I let myself hope Audra will find a way to make her fake promise come true.

Because seriously, she's not that great of a liar. I can see the hesitation in her eyes. The doubt. The fear. Like now. As we watch the elusive Westerly, I know what she's thinking. I feel the same way.

The draft is racing away, taking our safety with it.

Audra clears her throat. "We'll worry about the fourth breakthrough later. Tonight we're here to train you to protect yourself."

I can't tear my eyes away from the Westerly. It's so close. I just need one word. One tiny clue to its secret language. I can almost . . .

The sound of a roaring windstorm snaps me back to reality.

I turn to find Audra standing in front of a spout of swirling gusts soaring at least a hundred feet into the sky. The winds feed off each other as they spin, stretching the funnel higher with each passing second.

Audra makes sure I'm watching her, then steps through the winds.

My jaw drops as her shadowed form shoots up the wind spout and rockets out the top. She hovers in the sky, a dark angel at home with the stars. Then she's falling, fast and hard.

She barely blinks.

I hear her whisper, "Catch me gently, hear my call. Sweep me softly before I fall," and a Southerly uncoils from the funnel—at least, I think it's a Southerly. It feels warm, but it's hard to tell. The breeze wraps around her waist and sets her safely on the ground.

"Whoa."

Audra smiles her small half smile as she whips the windslicer from her scabbard and slices the funnel to shreds. The winds howl as they unravel and streak away, tearing at my clothes and hair. I cough as sand peppers my face.

Okay, maybe windslicers are more powerful than I realized.

She sheaths the blade, dusts off her hands, and turns to me. "Your turn."

"Good one."

"I'm serious."

"You expect me to fly up a giant funnel and hope I'm fast enough to call a draft to catch me—and avoid all these blades of doom all around us?"

She nods, and that kind of kills my laughter.

"Okay, you're starting to scare me, because I don't think you're kidding."

"I'm not."

I cough. "Need I remind you that the last time I 'practiced,' I knocked myself flat on my back—and all I was doing was standing there?"

"Do you ever pay attention?" She points to the shadowed space between us. "Do you see a funnel? Am I asking you to step into it and shoot into the air right now?"

"I . . . guess not."

"Exactly. First you have to create the funnel. And believe me, if you can master the skill to create it, you'll be able to catch yourself when you fall."

Somehow I find that hard to believe, but I'm willing to see where she's going with this.

"Okay. You need to learn how to make what we call wind melds—specific groups of drafts woven together in a specific order. Making them is like following a recipe. You have to do it precisely in order to get the right result."

I resist telling her that the few times my mom's tried to teach me how to follow a recipe, the only thing I made were inedible black lumps.

"The funnel I just showed you is called a pipeline. It's a rapid method of transport, and it's an important skill for you to master, because you can use it offensively, to hurl your enemy away from you, or defensively, to quickly escape a dangerous area. You can bend them in any direction you need to go. And it's a basic formula, so even you should be able to complete it."

I want to protest her whole "even you" thing. But I have a feeling I'm going to suck at this.

"Okay, the formula for a pipeline is three Northerlies blended with two Southerlies. Once they're combined, you add four Easterlies one by one, and when that's done you say the final command and jump back as the funnel expands. Memorize that."

Yeah—I'm going to need that written on my hand or something. *Mental note: Bring a Sharpie to training next time.*

"Start by calling the Northerlies and Southerlies to your side, so you can tell them what you want them to do. You'll have to call each draft on its own, so the faster you get at calling winds the better. And each type of wind has its own call. I've already taught you the one for Easterlies. To call a Northerly you say, 'Obey my command. Follow my voice. Race to my side and surrender your choice.'"

Her voice sounds like a sharp hiss—almost a snarl—and it takes a second for my brain to translate the words into the Northerly language. Making my mouth replicate the sounds is even harder. My tongue doesn't want to bend the right ways. But I reach toward the Northerlies she's shown me earlier and concentrate on the pins and needles in my palm as I whisper the call. After two tries I finally say it right, and a Northerly sweeps to my side, the cool air licking my skin.

"Coooooool."

"Not bad," Audra agrees as I call two more Northerlies to join the other. "Now you need two Southerlies. Their call is, '"Sweep to my side, please don't delay. Share your warmth as you swirl and sway.'"

The Southerly tongue is sleepy, and the words flow into each other, almost like the command is one long sigh. I get it right on my third try, and make two Southerlies streak toward me. They feel like a hair dryer blasting my face.

"How do I make them stay?" I ask as the Northerlies push forward, ready to break free.

"You don't want to make them stay. You want to make them merge."

"That's what I meant."

"The wind doesn't care what you meant. It's extremely specific, and very literal. It won't make assumptions, or read between the lines and figure out what you need. You have to be clear and precise. Give the exact command, or it won't cooperate."

"Fine, whatever." I wish she'd lecture me another time. The Northerlies have tangled around my legs, trying to knock me over.

"You want the drafts to merge, so you need to command the Northerlies. They're conquering winds. They want to dominate. They won't merge unless you force them to. You have to tell them, 'Yield.'"

I hiss the strange Northerly sound, and the drafts bend around each other into a small funnel.

"I did it." I bounce on the balls of my feet. I can't believe I made a tornado. A really tiny, wimpy one—but still. A *tornado*!

"You did it," she repeats, and the surprise in her voice makes me meet her eyes. There's a shine to them, a light that hasn't been there before.

"What?"

She shakes her head. "It's just . . . that's not an easy thing to do. I was lying earlier when I said it's a basic formula. I figured if you knew how hard it was, you wouldn't even try."

"Hey, I'm not *that* stubborn."

She raises an eyebrow.

"I'm not," I insist.

"It doesn't matter. What matters is you did it." She grins at me through the darkness. Not quite a full smile, but much, much closer than she normally gets. "You're very talented, Vane."

My cheeks get hot. That might be the first compliment she's ever given me. "What do I do now?"

"You need to add four Easterlies one by one. You already know how to call them. And to combine them, you say, 'Connect.' Make sure you count to five between each draft."

I do as she says, and with each draft I add, the funnel in front of me grows, until I have a narrow cylinder of force shooting into the sky almost as high as Audra's did.

So awesome.

"Now you concentrate on all the winds under your control. And you whisper 'Amplify' to the Northerlies. Then you jump back as far and fast as you can, or you'll be in for the ride of your life."

I jump back as the command is still leaving my lips, and the funnel triples, stretching wide enough to suck up a car, and soaring at least a hundred feet high.

"Holy crap, I can't believe I did that," I breathe.

"I can't either." But she doesn't say it meanly. She looks at me and laughs.

Laughs.

It's the best sound I've ever heard.

And then she has to kill the buzz and say, "Now step into the funnel."

My insides bunch up. "You're still serious about that?"

"You need to get used to keeping your bearings in a windstorm. And stopping yourself from falling is pretty much the most important skill you can master."

"Yeah, but isn't there a way to help me master it that doesn't involve a hundred-foot free fall from the top of a cyclone?"

"Nothing will motivate you more to get it right. Come on. You can do this, Vane. Do you remember the command I used to call the Southerly to catch me?"

I have a feeling it's only going to make her more gung ho with her *make Vane step into the giant vortex of death* plan, but I love seeing her so confident in my skills. So I tell her, "Catch me gently, hear my call. Sweep me softly before I fall."

"Perfect. Wait till you're actually falling before you whisper the command. But don't wait too long, or it won't have enough time to slow your landing."

I stare at the funnel.

"Want me to push you in?" she offers.

Stepping into a tornado screams *This is the dumbest thing you will ever do.* But I'm *finally* impressing her.

I close my eyes, take a deep breath, and kind of walk/fall into the funnel.

The roar of the winds drowns out my scream as the gusts shove me skyward so fast I'm certain I'll throw up. As soon as my stomach returns to its rightful place in my body, that is.

The winds tug at my skin, making it ripple from the force, and for one brilliant second, I'm weightless. Not flying. Not falling. Just floating above it all, nothing but me and the sky. Then I start to drop and can't—for the life of me—remember a single word of the command I need.

Think, Vane. Remember the freaking command or you will splatter on the ground into a million pieces.

But I can't. My mind is blank. Except for one sickening thought. *I'm going to die.*

CHAPTER 28

AUDRA

Watching Vane plummet from the sky rips me back to the past.

A man floats above me in the Stormer's trap. A tangle of dark clothes and thrashing limbs and wind.

For one horrifying second I think it's my father and my body shakes with sobs. Then I get a better look at his face.

Not my dad.

Vane's dad.

I hate myself for being relieved—but I can't help it.

His wide, terrified eyes meet mine and he tries to twist his arms free. But he's too tightly bound by the winds to move. He'll never escape on his own.

I have to help him. I have to fix this—make this right somehow.

Before I can decide what to do, a gust untangles from the wall of the storm, coils around the dark trunk of a dislodged tree, and whips it toward me like someone's controlling it. I drop to the ground, covering my head with my skinny arms, and wait to be shredded by the jagged branches. But the wind shifts again and I hear Vane's dad cry out.

Something red and wet drips on my arm.

It's too bright among the gray and black of the storm. I don't understand what it is or where it came from. Until another drop splatters my cheek.

I look back up and see crooked branches protruding from his arms, his neck, his chest. Streams of red trickle from the wounds.

I scream, harder and louder than I've ever screamed before.

Vane's scream snaps me out of it, and I command the draft I'd wrapped around me to "Rush!"

I don't breathe until I snag Vane by the waist and pull him into the nest of winds supporting me.

"Told you that was a bad idea," he mutters with a shaky voice.

He's right.

He's even more helpless than his parents were.

I can't let myself forget that—no matter how much promise he shows.

Our feet touch the ground and I realize I'm leaning on Vane more than he's leaning on me.

I can't let him end up the same way his parents did.

I can't.

I won't.

I pull away from him. "What happened up there?"

"I don't know. I guess I blanked."

"You *blanked*?" He's being too easy on himself. His parents didn't push themselves, and now they're both dead.

"Hey, I'm not exactly used to being shot through wind funnels like a Vane-bullet. I don't even like heights."

"You don't like *heights*?"

His cheeks flush. "I didn't say I'm afraid of them. I'm just not used to them."

"Well—you'd better get used to them."

"I know."

"Before the Stormers come."

"I said I know—I'm not an idiot, okay?"

I sigh, trying to get ahold of myself. "Look, Vane. I know I'm pushing you really hard. But I'm trying to protect you. I have to teach you as many basic lifesaving skills as I can. And stopping yourself from falling is essential. So we're going to have to practice this until you get it right."

He pales as I point to the wind funnel, still swirling away in the darkness.

"Try to relax this time," I suggest.

He runs his hands down his face as he stares at the funnel. "I can't."

"You have to."

Endless seconds pass as he watches the winds swirl. "Come with me, then," he finally whispers.

"What?"

"Come with me." He holds out his hand. "Maybe having you there will help me keep calm enough to remember the command."

"I'm not always going to be at your side during the fight. You need—"

"I know what I need. But right now, when I'm still trying to get the hang of all this, and still trying to make sense of the three crazy wind languages in my head, and still sore from almost dying yesterday, and still trying to wrap my head around all the impossible things you've told me. Maybe with all that, you could help me learn this very complicated—and, by the way, terrifying—new skill. I know you think you can teach me how to swim by just dropping me in the deep end and telling me to paddle, but sometimes people need floaties."

"Floaties?"

"Those dorky inflatable things that go on your arms, to keep you floating when you're first learning how to swim."

I have less than zero idea what he's talking about.

"Never mind." He kicks the ground. "I'm just saying that maybe I need help when I'm trying to do a skill that makes every single part of my brain scream, *This will be the death of me.*"

I can tell he hates admitting the weakness.

And I guess I can't blame him for being frustrated. I haven't been holding his hand through this process. I've told myself it's because no one needed to do that for me. But deep down I know it's more than that.

I don't want to get close to him. I can't let myself get close to him.

But I have to get him through this. No matter what it takes.

I reach for him. "You're right. I'll ride with you this time."

He stares at my hand for a second, like he can't believe his eyes. Then, slowly—tentatively, even—he twines our fingers together. The familiar jolt of heat shoots up my arm, and I hope he can't feel my racing pulse.

"Thank you," he whispers.

I nod. "You ready?"

He licks his lips and swallows, watching the winds spin and race.

I think he must need another minute. But then he squeezes my hand and meets my eyes. "With you, I am."

Goose bumps prickle my skin. Chills mixing with the warmth of his touch.

I pull him into the vortex, letting the winds launch us into the sky.

CHAPTER 29

VANE

I expect to dream of Audra that night.

Not because it took us at least a dozen trips up the wind funnel for me to figure out how to call the stupid Southerly and wrap it around us so Audra wouldn't have to step in.

And not because holding her hand that long left my skin humming with energy—though that does make me want to close my eyes and let a few of my favorite Audra fantasies play out.

It's because falling through the sky with her was so eerily like the memory I saw in my dream, I expected to drift off to sleep and pick up where I left off. And I wanted to. I want to know what happened next. How she survived the fall. Who saved her.

But I don't dream of young Audra, screaming and thrashing as she plummets through the sky. I see my father.

My *real* father.

I cling to the dream, committing it to memory before it slips out of my reach. I want to zoom in, adjust focus, and stare at his face forever.

For so long I've had absolutely no memories of what he looked like. Now I can see his dark, wavy hair, his pale blue eyes, and his square jaw.

He looked like me.

It shouldn't be a surprise, but it is.

My. Dad. Looked. Like. Me.

I don't want to let go of his face, but I can't forget the rest of the memory. I play the dream back, trying to find something to help me place it into the broken time line of my life.

I stand next to my dad at the edge of a glassy lake. My legs are skinny and my hair flops around my eyes, so I guess I'm about seven. Snowcapped mountains reflect off the water's surface. My dad has his hand on my shoulder, but I don't look at him—too busy skipping rocks over the water. Watching the tiny ripples distort the perfect reflection.

"It's time to go, Vane." His voice is clear and deep. Cutting through the tranquil silence around us.

I skip another rock. Harder this time. Breaking the water. "I don't want to."

"I know." He pulls me against his side. "But Arella can feel them coming. If we don't leave, they'll catch us."

More rocks splash into the water. I fling them hard this time. "How do they keep finding us?"

"I don't know," my dad whispers.

I turn to look at him.

He stares into the distance, frowning. "But we have to leave."

He reaches for my hand, and even though I want to jerk away—want to run so fast and so far he'll never catch me—I take it. He squeezes my fingers. Not hard. More to reassure. Then he whispers something that sounds like a dragged-out sigh.

I can't understand what he says, but I know what's coming. I hold on tight as the cool breeze closes us in, then lifts us into the sky and floats us away.

A wind bubble.

I remember calling them that—and the way my mom would laugh and tell me I was silly when I said it. I can't see her face, but her deep, rich laugh fills my mind.

Tears sting my eyes.

I love my adopted parents, and I always will. But to see the father I lost? Hear his voice in my mind? Hear my mom's laugh? It feels like I have them back—for a few minutes, anyway.

But the memory raises just as many questions as it answers, and the gaps feel almost painful. I need the missing pieces.

I lie back down, trying to clear my head.

Deep breaths. Think it through.

If I was seven, then the memory is from not that long before my parents were killed. Which makes sense. It seemed like we were on the run for our lives. But where were we? I saw the lake in the first dream too, but I don't recognize it. It could be anywhere. And who's Arella? The article said my mom's name was Lani, so it has to be someone else. Audra's mom, maybe? How did she know it was time to run?

It's tempting to ask Audra, but I can't think of a way to do it without giving away that my memories are coming back.

I'll have to solve the puzzle myself. The answers are in my mind. I just need time to let the memories resurface.

I glance at the clock: 3:24 a.m. Audra will be here at dawn, but I still have time to see what further memories sleep will give me.

Come on, dreams. Give me the missing pieces.

CHAPTER 30

AUDRA

Vane is already awake when I come get him for training.

And he's dressed.

And his hair is combed.

"You're up," I say, trying to recover from my surprise.

He laughs. "Thank you, Captain Obvious."

He's right. Stupid, idiotic thing to say. I just didn't expect him to be awake. Or to look so . . . good. His plain blue shirt is unrumpled—for once. And the color makes his eyes look like the sky on a warm, breezy day. The kind of sky that begs, *Fly with me*.

I smooth my braid. "Could you not sleep?"

He shrugs—those infernal shrugs of his—and stands. "I slept most of the night. Anyway, I left my parents a note telling them I'll be training with you all day, so we don't have to rush back. You ready to go?"

It throws me, the way he's taking charge of everything. But I follow his lead, climbing through the window and padding across the grass in the purple predawn light.

He waves away the gnats swarming our faces. "Where are we training today?"

"My place. We can only train by the windmills after dark. We'll be too conspicuous otherwise."

He nods, and we walk in silence. I fall back a step so I can study him unobserved.

He walks taller. Straighter. Shoulders set with confidence.

He's falling into his role. Owning it.

Finally.

The more seriously he takes his training, the better chance we have.

He hesitates outside my pathetic house, glancing around. "Where's that evil bird of yours?"

"On his morning hunt. Don't worry, the big scary birdie won't get you."

He whips around to face me. "Are you teasing me?"

I stop short.

I *am.*

I feel my lips stretch wider.

"Whoa," he says, stepping closer. "I think that's the first time I've seen you really smile."

Blood rushes to my face. Apparently, Vane isn't the only one changing.

Time to get back to business.

I march to the corner to retrieve the windslicer. "It's time to teach you some basic attacks. I'll be the main offensive fighter in the battle, but you still need to learn how to deal with the Stormers."

I strap the sword to my waist and call two Easterlies—grateful the air has plenty of breezes swirling through the trees before the day's heat chases them away. I order the winds to twist into a tight vortex, about the width of my leg. They spin so fast I see nothing more than a blur in the air in front of me. "This is called a wind spike," I tell Vane. "Or it will be in a second."

I call a Northerly and braid it through the Easterlies. When the winds are properly entwined, I switch to Easterly and say, "Concentrate," and the winds lock together, tightening into a narrow pole of whipping drafts the same height as me.

Vane leans in for a closer look. "Awesome."

"Grab it."

"You can't—" He stops himself. "Never mind. None of the stuff we do makes any sense. Why would this?"

He reaches out, his hand changing positions several times, like he can't figure out how to get a grip. Finally he just grabs it. "Whoa, it's squishy."

I can't help laughing at that. "Wind is never fully tangible, but if woven tight enough, there's something for us to take hold of."

"I guess." He tosses it back and forth between his hands. "Now what?"

"Line up your aim and launch it as hard as you can. Try to hit that tree." I point to an easy target—a stocky palm, branches heavy with unharvested dates.

Vane raises the wind spike over his shoulder. "This is so weird," he says as he makes a few practice thrusts. Then he lets the spike fly.

His throw is strong, but his aim isn't true, and the spike curves right, hitting a palm to the side of his target.

The tree explodes. Bark, sand, rocks, and bits of leaves rain on us, sticking to our sweaty faces as the thunderous crack echoes off the trees.

Vane stares at the destruction.

I wipe the filth from my cheeks. "We'll have to work on your aim, or you'll never be able to hit a moving target."

He starts to nod, then turns to face me. "What kinds of things am I supposed to hit?"

"Well, ideally you'll hit the Stormers. I doubt you'll be good enough to catch one, but maybe you'll get a lucky shot."

He recoils, his skin fading to a ghostly pallor. "I'm supposed to hit *people* with those things?"

"Only the Stormers. I'll try to make sure you don't hit anyone else."

He swallows, and his face twists as he does, like he's ill.

"What's wrong?"

"I never realized you'd expect me to kill people." He takes another step back, leaning against a tree for support.

I move toward him slowly, trying to understand his reaction. "It's a battle. What do you expect?"

"I don't know. I guess I was thinking, like, punching and stuff. Maybe a few wind tricks to knock them unconscious. I never thought I'd be *killing* them."

He starts to shake—hard. I reach for his shoulder to steady him, but he flinches at my touch.

"I don't understand what's wrong, Vane."

"Neither do I." He sinks to the ground. "It's just . . . the thought of killing people. Making them explode like that tree." He shudders, pulling his legs into his chest and leaning his head against them.

"They're hardly people," I mutter as I lower myself next to him. "*People* don't massacre hundreds of innocent Windwalkers. They don't tear innocent children limb from limb. They don't launch tornados and hurricanes into human cities because they suspect the Gales are hiding there—oh yeah, the Stormers do that," I add when he turns toward me. "Raiden will stop at nothing to wipe out the resistance. Not to mention they're coming here to capture you and force you to share your language. All so Raiden can be strong enough to control the world."

I glance at him, expecting him to look calmer. But he's paler than ever. I don't see what his problem is.

"Remember, Vane. We're at war."

We're at war.

My father said those exact words to Vane's father, pleading with him to take his training seriously.

A memory flashes back.

I hide in the shadows on the edge of the field, watching my parents train the Westons. The four adults stand in a circle and my father demonstrates how to make a crusher, a thick funnel that tightens on command, annihilating anything inside.

The Westons shake and turn away.

215

Vane's dad says they won't learn.

Not can't.

Won't.

Winds rage as my mother screams at them. Calls them selfish. How dare they expect others to risk their lives to protect them when they aren't even willing to learn basic self-defense?

Vane's parents just cling to each other in her storm, shake their heads, and say, "No."

I want to tear across the field and shout at the Westons like my mother. My life is miserable because of them—because my family has to protect them. How can they stand back and let us make all the sacrifices?

But I stay in the shadows.

I ask my father about it when he tucks me in that night. He stares into the night and says, "Westerlies are the peaceful winds." Nothing more.

I didn't understand what he meant. What the problem really was. Not until right now, looking at the green tinge to Vane's skin.

Westerlies are the peaceful winds.

Violence makes them physically ill.

Now I know why none of the Westerlies surrendered to Raiden's threats and taught him their language. Why they were willing to die to protect it. They aren't just brave or stubborn, like I thought. Violence goes against their very nature, triggering an actual physical reaction.

Honestly, it's quite noble. Except it renders them completely vulnerable. And useless.

My jaw locks as I work through the ramifications of this new development.

My only fighting companion is *incapable* of killing. Which means even if Vane has the fourth breakthrough, it won't matter. He won't use it to fight.

My anger kindles, deep and hot.

So *I* have to die because he refuses to harm a Stormer—the people there to kidnap him? The people who had no problem killing his parents?

Their lives are worth more than *mine*?

Maybe their lives aren't. But that doesn't change the oath I willingly swore. And with that thought, I'm able to snuff the fire out.

I've already accepted that I might not survive the fight. All this means is that my job of protecting Vane during the storm will be twice as hard. Five times as hard. As if the water hadn't complicated things enough.

Vane takes a deep, heaving breath and wipes away the sweat dripping down the sides of his face. "Sorry," he mumbles. "I don't know what's wrong with me."

"I do. You're a Westerly. Westerlies are peaceful. Violence is abhorrent to you. Your nature rejects it."

His fingers tear through his hair, mussing it into wild peaks. "That actually makes sense. But that probably makes me pretty useless in a battle, doesn't it?"

Yes.

I can't say that, though. "I just want you to be able to defend yourself in case you get into a bind. You don't have to hurt anyone— but I think you should at least know how. Do you think you can handle that?"

Several seconds pass. Then he nods.

I release the breath I'd been holding. At least he's willing to try—unlike his parents.

Bitterness rises in my throat, but I swallow it.

They were true Westerlies. They spoke the tongue. Rode the winds. Of course their instincts were stronger than Vane's. He can't even hear the Westerlies' call. I never thought that would be a good thing—but maybe it is.

"You ready?" I ask him, squinting at the sky. The sun blazes through the cloudless blue, and soon the last of the morning winds will flee to the mountains.

He stands. His legs are shaky, but his eyes are determined. "Yes."

I teach him how to meld wind spikes, and I make him practice his aim. He looks queasy with every toss, but I remind him that an accurate aim will be safer. Less chance of hitting an innocent bystander.

After that, his throws rarely miss their mark.

It gives me hope.

The world isn't black and white, like his parents treated it. Violence sometimes has its place—its purpose. Maybe if they'd accepted that, they could have survived the Stormer's attack. Lived to see their son grow up. Helped stop Raiden from destroying the world as we know it.

Instead, the responsibility rests on Vane. If I can get him to see the shades of gray, maybe he'll be the first Westerly to stand up to Raiden. The first Westerly to survive.

His shirt turns a midnight blue from the sweat, and I make him rest in what little shade the walls of my shelter provide. The last thing I need is him taking it off again—even if a small part of me wouldn't mind another glimpse of his sculpted muscles.

I sit next to him. Our legs touch, but I don't pull away. "How are you holding up?"

He gives a shaky shrug.

I place my hand on his arm. "Try to remember, if you don't stop the Stormers, they'll launch tornadoes into this valley. Hundreds— or thousands—of innocent people will die. People you know. People you love. You're doing this to save those innocent lives."

The silence seems to stretch.

"So you have no problem with . . . killing?" he asks.

"No. But I'm an Easterly."

"The swift, tricky winds," he recites. "What does that even mean?"

"Easterlies are survivors. They do whatever needs to be done."

"So you would kill?"

His stare is intense—but not judging.

"If I have to."

I focus on my fingers, surprised to realize they're tracing slow circles on his skin. The contact is soothing and thrilling at the same time. It makes me feel daring. Maybe too daring, because I can't stop myself from asking, "Do you think you could?"

"Kill?"

I lock eyes with him again. "If it saved a life? If it saved your life? If it saved . . ."

I stop myself. I can't ask him to save me. I'm supposed to save *him*.

Vane turns away as he considers my question, staring at what remains of the tree he destroyed. "I don't know."

He takes my hand, cradling it gently between his palms. Warmth travels up my arms, heading straight to my heart and making it flutter as he looks at me again, knocking my breath away with the tenderness in his haunting blue eyes. "I hope so."

Me too.

It's a miracle I don't say the thought aloud.

I have no right to hope. But if he's offering it freely, I can't help but take it.

So I don't pull away, even though I should. And I let myself believe he might be strong enough to save us all.

To save me.

He's the only one who can.

CHAPTER 31

VANE

t isn't until Audra's bird returns from his second hunt of the day that I notice how late it is. I trained through breakfast and lunch—but it's probably better. If I'd had anything in my stomach when I realized Audra was training me to kill, I would have heaved it all over myself.

It reminds me of the way my body reacted when the doctors gave me pills. Sweat, hives, spasms, puke, like my system will do anything—everything—to purge the medicine from my bloodstream. The idea of killing feels just as toxic.

Great—I'm allergic to violence. I'm sure Audra's *thrilled* with that news.

Maybe I can fight it. I mean, sure, I don't like violent movies or video games—but they don't make me wig out like that. Maybe the fight will be the same way.

But those are fake, I tell myself. *And this is horrifyingly real.*

My head spins and I suck in air to try to clear it.

I have to get over this. Lives are at stake.

The innocent people in this valley.

Me.

Audra.

I'll do whatever it takes to keep her alive. If that means taking out a Stormer or two, well . . . I'll have to deal with that. Even if just thinking about it makes me nauseous.

"How did my parents handle the training?" I ask, hoping they knew some trick to be able to fight without throwing up.

Audra bites her lip and looks away.

I guess that means they didn't do very well. I decide not to ask for the gory details. Especially since I've thought of a better question. "What were they like?"

"Your parents?"

"Yeah." She's been stubbornly secretive about my past, but she could at least tell me *that*. Maybe it would help trigger more memories tonight.

She sighs. "I wasn't around them much. When my parents weren't trying to train them, they kept all three of you inside, away from Raiden's searchwinds, which were always so close on our trail."

I have no idea what that means, but I guess it doesn't matter.

"Your mom was always sneaking outside with you, though," she adds, turning toward me. Her lips twist into a sad smile. "I used to watch you guys play together in the fields. She seemed like a great mom."

"I wish I remembered her." I'm surprised at how thick my voice sounds.

"I know," she whispers.

There really isn't anything else to say.

"Actually . . . ," Audra says, jumping to her feet and heading to the corner of the house where her crappy bed of palm leaves is.

"What are you doing?" I ask, joining her as she starts rummaging around.

"Looking for something."

My phone beeps and I pull it out of my pocket to check it. A text from Isaac, begging me to go out with him, Shelby, and Hannah tonight.

"Everything okay?" Audra asks as I text him back.

"Yeah. My friend's just trying to convince me to go on a double date with Hannah tonight. I'm telling him thanks, but no thanks."

"Good," Audra says quietly.

My head snaps up. "Good?"

I definitely want clarification on *that*.

"Of course," she says. "You need to train tonight."

"Is that really the *only* reason?" I press, stepping closer. My phone buzzes and I shove it in my pocket. I'm not letting anything interrupt this conversation.

"What do you mean?" She tries to back away, but she's standing in the only corner in her broken house and I'm blocking her escape.

Good. It's high time Audra and I come to an understanding about whatever's going on between us.

"I mean, are you sure there isn't another reason you don't want me going out with Hannah?" I lean closer, leaving only a foot of space between our faces.

She stares at the ground. "Actually, there is."

My heart does an extra jump.

I step toward her, gently grabbing her waist to pull her to me.

She pushes me back. "What are you doing?"

She might as well have slapped me.

She shoves past me and stalks to the opposite end of the room. Her hands pull at the ends of her braid as she paces. "There's something I haven't told you. I didn't know how you would react—and I didn't want anything to interfere with your training."

"And that would be?" I ask when she doesn't continue. My voice shakes with the anger I'm trying to hold back.

Her sigh feels like it lasts an eternity. "You're . . . not *free*, Vane."

That's . . . not what I was expecting. "What does that mean?"

"It means I can't let you go on a date tonight—or any night."

"What, there's some law in your world that says Vane Weston isn't allowed to date?"

"Sort of. Remember, Vane, you're the last Westerly. You're not like everyone else."

This is seriously giving me a headache. And I'm about to ask what the freaking law actually says when a horrible thought occurs to me.

"That's why you ruined my last date with Hannah, isn't it?"

"Yes. And if you'd just left the restaurant and gone home like I'd tried to tell you, I wouldn't have had to call the Northerly and brand it with our traces. We'd still be safe."

"So, you're telling me you *risked our lives* just to stop me from *dating*?"

She straightens, and her eyes blaze. "No. I called the flurry because I had to stop you from bonding to her—and I didn't have time to think. I just reacted."

There are so many things wrong with that, I don't know where to start.

Actually, I do. "Bonding? What the hell does that mean?"

She pinches the bridge of her nose. "Kissing is different for our kind than it is for the groundlings. They do it for fun, like it means nothing. For us, a kiss sparks an actual, physical change. It creates a connection between the pair who kiss, bonding them together until death parts them. That's why I've always stepped in to make sure you never got that far with any of the girls I found you with. I didn't know what would happen if you bonded with a groundling, but I couldn't risk letting any sort of attachment form."

I put aside the whole *a single kiss sealing your fate for the rest of your life* thing for a second, because it's way too weird and crazy to think about.

What does she mean she "stepped in" with the girls she found me with?

Oh. Crap.

"It was you. All my bad luck with girls. Drinks suddenly getting knocked over by the breeze and spilling on their clothes so they'd need to go home. Birds pooping on their heads."

Every single one of those disasters was caused by birds or wind or something in the sky. All except the Great Farting Debacle. Unless . . .

"Oh my God—you made the farting sound that day I was at the Date Festival, didn't you? You broke the wind somehow, made it sound like a fart, and framed me for it?"

She doesn't deny it.

I laugh.

How can I *not* laugh at the insanity of it all? "Do you have any idea how much you've jacked up my life over the last few years?"

"I know it's been hard, Vane. But I couldn't explain what was going on until your mind was ready to understand your heritage, and you just had a breakthrough a few days ago. In the meantime, I was under strict orders from the Gale Force to make sure you didn't bond to anyone."

"Why does your army give a crap about my love life?"

"Trust me when I say you won't mind once you meet Solana."

Solana?

I have a feeling I don't want to know the answer to this question, but I have to ask it anyway. "Who the hell is Solana?"

"Our former king's heir—all that's left of the royal line after Raiden destroyed it. She'll be crowned queen when Raiden falls."

"And what's she got to do with me?"

I can tell she doesn't want to answer just as much as I don't want to hear it. But we've come too far now. So she closes her eyes and whispers. "You two are betrothed."

The word hangs over us, practically casting a shadow.

LET THE SKY FALL

I'm betrothed.

To some spoiled princess I've never met.

Too. Many. Emotions bubble inside.

Anger. Annoyance. Confusion. Frustration. Fear. Rebellion. Rage.

But one feels stronger than the others, and it takes me a second to identify it.

Hurt.

Takes me another second to figure out why. "And . . . you're okay with that?"

She looks away. Refuses to meet my eyes. But she nods.

I know I probably should leave it at that, but I can't stop myself. "What about us?"

She doesn't say anything, and that spurs my courage. I move toward her, trapping her against the wall. "There's something between us, Audra." I grab her hand, letting the familiar sparks shoot through my skin. "Don't tell me you don't feel that."

I'm not sure if I'm fueled by fear or want or just sheer desperation. But it's cards-on-the-table time. I've dreamed of her for too long—wanted her for too long—to let her shove me away because her stupid army thinks they can arrange my life.

I know she feels something for me.

I know it.

"Stop thinking about what your army wants. They're not here right now. It's just you and me. And you want me," I whisper. "I have to believe that. Because I want you, too."

It's hard to push the last words out. But it feels good to say them.

I reach up, trying to slide my fingers into her hair, but her braid's too tightly woven. I settle for stroking her face.

She doesn't pull away, but she shakes her head. "I swore an oath, Vane."

"Screw the oath." I lean in until I feel her breath against my face, then stop. I don't want to rush her. "You've done enough for them. You're protecting me. Who cares about the rest?"

"I do." She closes her eyes, and her jaw quivers. "I swore to get you safely through this—and I will. And then you'll return with the Gales and meet your betrothed."

"They can take their betrothal and shove it. I want *you*."

I lean in more, until there's barely an inch separating us. I don't know if she's right about the bonding thing, but I actually wouldn't mind bonding myself to her. In some ways, I feel like I already have.

She sucks in a shaky breath and I know. She *wants* this.

"No," she shouts, shoving so hard I stumble halfway across the room. "My loyalty is to the Gales."

She draws the windslicer, pointing it at my heart. "I mean it, Vane. I can't do this. I *won't* do this."

"So, what, you're going to stab me?"

She presses the point of the blade into my chest. Not enough to break the skin, but enough to sting.

"Don't make me hurt you," she begs.

"You already are."

Her eyes turn glassy. But something about her posture—the strong set of her shoulders, the rigid line of her spine—tells me she won't back down.

She'll kick me aside. Pawn me off on some girl I've never met. All to please her stupid, useless army.

Her grip on the sword doesn't waver. Her eyes look through me, not at me.

I've already lost her.

So I do the only thing I can do.

I run.

CHAPTER 32

AUDRA

I can't breathe.

I feel like someone's pressing on my chest, crushing the life and air out of me as I watch Vane race away. All warmth fades from my body, leaving me shivering under the hot desert sun.

I've made a lot of sacrifices in my life, but none hurt as much as what I've just done.

As soon as Vane's out of sight, I collapse to the floor and curl into a ball.

Vane's right. I do care. More than I ever can or will admit.

But the realization makes everything inside me squirm with revulsion.

Who am I to care for Vane Weston?

When he learns what I've done, he'll loathe me as much as I loathe myself.

I cling to that harsh fact like a lifeline, pulling myself back into the hard, emotionless walls I've maintained for the last ten years.

Vane would never want me if he knew I'm the reason his parents are dead. I'm a selfish, callous creature who ruined everything because I chose to save Gavin's life—a bird Vane *hates*. Then I lied to him about his memories being permanently lost, because I can't bear the thought of him knowing I'm to blame.

And how would I have explained to the Gales if I bonded to Vane? Stole their king? With Vane's potential for power, they want to make sure he's bound to the royal line, so our people will have confidence in our world once again. Come out of hiding. Trust the Gales.

Plus, Solana's a Southerly, and her bond will be a softening influence—should the power of four go to his head.

If I interfered with that, I'd be banished for such treason. Permanently branded a traitor.

No, it has to be this way. Even if my treacherous heart still scalds the inside of my chest.

I've burned so many different ways for Vane.

Guilt.

Desire.

But this is the worst.

The scorching heat of loss.

I dive into the pain, let the fire consume me. It'll make me tougher. Stronger.

Water may have weakened my body—but it didn't weaken my resolve.

It's time to prove how strong I am.

I pull myself upright, squeezing my pendant with one hand. My other hand rubs my temples, easing the headache caused by my braid.

It took me months to master weaving the intricate style. The hair is divided into five equal sections, and the four outer strands are twisted and folded around the central strand, to represent the way our lives are inseparably bound to the four winds. Even the men wear a variation of the braid. It's a physical display to show that we live not for ourselves, but for the service of the winds. The service of the guardians.

I'm a guardian.

My plans have been turned inside out and ripped to shreds, but my purpose holds true. And I will honor that purpose. With everything I have.

But I have to figure out what to do about Vane. We still have to train together, and judging by how hurt and angry he looked as he left, that's going to be a challenge.

Spots flicker behind my eyes just thinking about being close to him again. Flying together. Holding on to each other . . .

I scrape together the last of my willpower and push those feelings away.

I can do this.

I just need to get used to it. And Vane clearly needs the night off. So tonight we'll take our space. Give ourselves time to come to terms with everything. No harm can come from that.

Unless . . .

Panic closes off my lungs.

Vane has a rebellious side. I've seen it flare against even my smallest attempts at control during our training—and this is much, *much* bigger. Who knows what he might do in response?

I can think of one thing that would be *very* bad.

Irreversible.

I curse my stupidity as I take off through the grove, leaping over fallen branches and pushing my legs harder than I've ever pushed them. But when I reach the main road, his car is long gone.

Quick and catlike, I scale the nearest palm, standing on the wobbly branches at the top. I don't care if anyone sees me. I have to feel as much air as I can.

Hands shaking from nerves and adrenaline and anger at myself for allowing yet another disaster, I undo the buttons of my jacket, slipping it off my shoulders and dropping it to the ground, exposing as much skin as possible. I close my eyes and concentrate on the air around me, feeling for Vane's trace with each cell of my skin.

Every sylph leaves their mark on the wind. A change in the draft's tune, as though the wind ran into a friend and added new notes to its song to carry away the memory of the meeting. We can brand the wind by commanding it too loudly—like I did when I called the Northerly I attacked Vane with—and have it carry our trace permanently. But even silent contact leaves a faint trail. The draft only carries it until it finds something else to chant about and drops the tune. Before that, anyone listening can pick up the trace and follow it to the source.

I read traces better on the winds of my heritage, so I focus on the Easterlies in the grove. Most carry no sign of having seen either of us. But when I listen near Vane's house, I find a soft breeze singing of the jarring blur of motion caused by someone on the run.

That has to be Vane.

I call the draft to me and inhale the trace.

A tingling rush knocks me back, and I lose my footing in the branches, toppling to the ground. A nearby Southerly saves me from a painful fall, but when I'm safely on my feet, I can't calm my tremors.

It's like I've taken in a small part of him, a fractured piece he left behind.

Almost like a *loss*.

I have no idea if that's possible—or what it means if it is—but I'll worry about it later. For now, all that matters is finding Vane. I have to track him down before he does something he'll regret. Something we'll both regret.

Already running, I call the nearest Northerly and spin the wind around me so fast I'll be nothing more than a blur in the sky.

"High," I whisper, catching my breath as the gust sweeps me away.

In seconds I'm over the main roadway, the setting sun making me squint as I concentrate on the air. The warm tingles of Vane's trace tell me which way to turn. An inner compass guiding me straight to him.

I just hope I reach him in time.

CHAPTER 33

VANE

I didn't plan to meet up with Isaac after I sped down my driveway. I just needed to put as much distance between myself and that crazy life Audra was trying to cage me in, before it was too late to escape. And I was too mad/hurt/disgusted to look at her anymore.

But then my phone vibrated and I realized the first step to taking back my life was right there, in my hands. Well, in my butt pocket—but still.

Which is how I ended up back at the River, this time at the noisy, crowded Cheesecake Factory. They really need to build some decent places to hang out in this crappy valley. I'm crammed into a booth next to Hannah, and Isaac and Shelby are across the table, watching us with the smug grins all long-term couples wear when they watch their friends on a double date.

Probably waiting to see how I'll blow it this time.

Shoot, knowing Isaac, they probably placed bets on it.

But I'm not screwing up tonight. I left Audra and her chaperone-from-hell skills in the dust at my house.

Which is good because I have big plans for me and Hannah, number one of which is kissing her and proving that (a) I don't need Audra, (b) I make my own decisions regarding my life, and (c) a kiss is just a *kiss*. I don't buy that bonding crap. And I'm determined to prove it.

The thought makes my palms sweat and my heart race and my stomach twist like I swallowed something alive. I tell myself those are nerves.

But I know it's mostly guilt.

I feel guilty for using Hannah. It's not that I don't like her—she's really nice. Cute, too. Especially tonight, in her tight pink halter top. More than a few guys have checked her out. But when she bumps my leg under the table or grazes my arm, I don't feel any warmth. If anything, I feel colder. Like my body's telling me I'm sitting next to the wrong girl.

And there's the other type of guilt too.

Guilt for betraying Audra. Cheating on her by simply being here with Hannah.

It's insane. She made it very clear that she doesn't want me—at least, not as much as she wants to please the losers in her army.

This is her choice. Not mine.

Hannah launches into some story about hockey—she's so Canadian it's hilarious—and I take the opportunity to study Isaac and

236

Shelby. He has his arm draped across her shoulders and his fingers are playing with the soft red curls that frame her face. She's pressed up against his side like she doesn't want a millimeter of space between them. The grin on Isaac's face says he doesn't mind that at all.

Everything about them screams "couple." And I have to hand it to them. They look happy. I mean, I know why Isaac's happy. Shels is way out of his league. He isn't bad-looking, or he wouldn't be if he shaved the ugly mustache he insists on sporting, which is surprisingly thin and scraggly considering he's full-blooded Mexican. All the other guys in his family—including his fourteen-year-old brother—have beards.

Shelby's *hot*, though. Long legs, despite being what girls would call petite, and enough curve to make the buttons pop on almost every shirt she wears—not that I look. Well, not now that she's with Isaac.

But Shelby looks even happier than Isaac. Like she belongs in the crook of his arm. And she's spent so many months in that exact spot I almost can't picture him without her there. Makes it kind of annoying when I want a night with my friend without his girlfriend joined at the hip. Right now, though, it makes the careful gap Hannah and I are keeping between us feel like the Grand Canyon.

Maybe I need to try harder. Hannah has her right hand resting on the table, and before I can change my mind I grab it.

Hannah flinches and I relax my grip, realizing my big move came across more like an attack than a romantic gesture.

Isaac and Shelby share a look.

Strike one for Vane.

But I'm not out yet. Hannah doesn't pull away, and she turns her hand over, twining our fingers together.

I smirk at Isaac. *How you like me now?*

This is good. I'm doing this. I'm on a normal date with normal friends on a perfectly normal night. No crazy winds. No talk of evil warriors or languages of the wind or arranged marriages. Just random chitchat about movies or music or school or whatever—exactly the way a date should be.

So what if everything about this moment screams, *This is wrong?*

The waitress delivers our food, and I smile when I see the giant bowl of pasta she sets in front of Hannah. A girl who *eats* when she's hungry. Score one for Hannah.

There's an awkward moment when I stare at our clasped hands and try to decide what to do—*strike two.* Then I let go of Hannah so I can dive into my gigantic sandwich and mountain of fries. I eat way past the point of fullness, like it's another form of protest.

Take that, you crazy sylphs with your not eating and controlling people's lives!

I scoot closer to Hannah, letting our legs touch—skin on skin, since we're both wearing shorts. Another point for Hannah: She's dressed appropriately for summer in the desert. Not buttoned up to her neck in some ridiculous uniform.

I still feel nothing when we touch, but her closeness brings a different kind of thrill. The thrill of success.

Hannah takes my hand again, lacing our fingers tight.

"Vane?" someone calls over the noisy restaurant.

My sandwich and fries threaten to come back up.

Isaac, Shelby, and Hannah turn to see who's calling me. I stare at my plate, wondering if I can stab myself to death with my butter knife.

"Vane," Audra says again, her voice louder now. Breathless.

A shadow falls over the table, but I don't look up. My plan is to pretend she's not there. It needs work, but it's all I have.

Isaac and Shelby are silent. Probably sitting back to watch the show.

Hannah shifts in her seat. "Vane, what's she doing here?" The edge to her voice tells me she's less than happy to see Audra again.

"I'm here," Audra answers for me, "because I'm his girlfriend. So I'd appreciate it if you'd take your hands off of him."

"Dude," Isaac half-laughs, half-mumbles.

He grunts, like Shelby elbowed him.

I say nothing. I'm in a crapload of trouble, but, God help me, all I can think is how good it sounds when Audra says "his girlfriend."

I risk a glance at her—and, oh man, she's hot. Lots of hair has escaped her braid, falling around her flushed face, and her jacket's gone, her black tank even tighter and tinier than I remember. I'm not sure "hot" is a strong enough word. "Smokin' hot" might be more accurate.

Hannah snaps me out of my staring when she yanks her hand away and scoots as far toward the wall of the booth as she can possibly go.

I know everyone's waiting for me to do something—say something—but my brain isn't equipped to deal with this situation.

Isaac clears his throat. "Dude, if you have a girlfriend you should've just told me."

"More importantly," Shelby interrupts, "he shouldn't be putting the moves on Hannah."

"No one was putting the moves on me," Hannah mumbles, like the very idea of me being interested in her is suddenly disgusting.

"Yes, he was. And he went out with you a few nights ago. Did you have the girlfriend then, too, Vane?"

"Hey, I—" I start, not sure where I'm going with this.

"It's a recent development," Audra interrupts. Then she leans forward and strokes my face with her fingers.

Not playfully.

Possessively.

I don't pull away. I might even lean into her hand as ten thousand sparks shoot through my skin at her touch. What can I say? I'm weak.

The difference between the way my body responds to Audra and to Hannah is night and day. Everything about them is night and day. Hannah's blond hair and blue eyes are the sun to Audra's dark-haired, dark-eyed night.

"I'd like to go home," Hannah announces. Her voice sounds choked, like she's seconds from crying.

She doesn't deserve this.

I owe her the mother of all apologies. I just can't figure out what to say.

She doesn't wait for me to try. She doesn't even wait for me let her out of the booth. She pulls her feet up on the bench and climbs onto the table. Plates and glasses rattle as she crosses to the edge and jumps, racing for the door as soon as she lands. Shelby shoves Isaac out of the booth and chases after her—shooting me a death glare on her way out.

Isaac laughs. "Well, I gotta hand it to you, man. You find the most unbelievable ways to ruin dates."

"I—"

He raises a hand. "I'm *dying* to hear what's up, but I'd better take the girls home. See what kind of damage control we need."

I nod and he turns to leave.

"By the way"—he turns back and points to Audra—"Niiiiiiiiiiiiiiiiiiiice."

I wonder which one of us blushes brighter, me or Audra.

When Isaac's out of sight, I force myself to meet Audra's eyes.

"You went on a date?" she snaps. "Have you lost your mind?"

"Me?" All my anger races back. "I love how you think you can just throw on the 'Vane's girlfriend' hat whenever it's convenient for you. Jerk me around, screw up my life, then stomp on my feelings as soon as we're alone. All to please your precious Gale Force."

"We can't have this conversation here."

She stalks toward the exit, and I dig my wallet out and toss all the money I have on the table before I follow.

I figure Audra will be miles above me, flying home so she can rip me a new one the second I get there. But she stands against my car, her arms crossed, her eyes trying to bore holes into my skull. I'm just as furious with her, but my heart still skips a beat when I think of the long ride home, just the two of us.

She doesn't look at me as I open the door for her. Just climbs in and slams it.

I know my car is small. But filled with me and Audra and the mountain of complicated emotions between us, it feels like a shoe box.

"Why aren't we leaving?" she asks.

"You need to put on your seat belt. Or do you only follow the Gale's laws?"

Her sigh is epic length. Then she fumbles with the seat belt for a hilarious amount of time, twisting it all kinds of wrong ways. "How does this infernal device work?" she finally asks.

I snort and lean across the seat.

She jerks away. "What are you doing?"

I lean closer, my eyes glued to hers as I take the seat belt from her hand and pull it across her body. My fingers brush her arm as I click it into place, and I hear her breath catch at my touch.

"Oh," she mumbles as I back off.

I throw the car in reverse.

She watches the strip malls blur by, her fingers resting on the glass. I hit the button and roll down her window, grinning when she jumps.

The night is hot and sticky, but wind streams through the window and Audra stretches out her hand, waving her fingers in the breeze.

"Do you have any idea what you could have done tonight?" She doesn't look at me, and her voice is hard to hear over the wind. But she doesn't sound *as* angry.

I sigh. "I don't buy the bonding thing."

"That's because you've never experienced it."

"Have you?"

"Of course not."

We stop at a red light and I turn to face her. "Then how do you know it's not some story they made up to keep kids in line? Like parents lying to their kids about Santa Claus to make them be good all year? How do you know it's true, if you've never kissed anyone?"

"Because I've seen the effect a bond has. My mother is still bonded to my father, even all these years after his death. She's never recovered from the loss. And I doubt she ever will."

Well, that's . . . sad. But it doesn't prove anything. "Human couples have that happen too—doesn't mean they were bonded or whatever. And besides, I thought you said the bond ends at death."

"It does."

"So then, your mom might not be bonded at all. Maybe she just loved him."

She doesn't say anything. Just stares at the stars.

I have no idea what she's thinking, but I've never seen her look so sad. I want to reach out and take her hand, but I know I can't.

The light turns green and we start moving again.

"You didn't answer my question. Do you have any idea what would've happened if you'd bonded yourself to that girl tonight?"

"No, but I'm guessing your army wouldn't be too happy with me."

"That's putting it mildly. And you wouldn't be the one they'd punish. I'd be the one dishonored."

"That doesn't sound so bad."

She lets out a slow sigh. "You don't understand."

"You're right—I don't."

More silence. Then she whispers, "Honor is all I have left. The Gales. My oath. Take that away and I have nothing."

She says it without any self-pity. But it makes me sorry for her anyway. I can't imagine how lonely the last ten years have been for her, squatting in that crumbling shack.

"And that would only be the beginning," she adds. "You're our future king. They could rule my act as treason. Lock me so far underground the wind would be nothing more than a memory."

"They would do that? Over a kiss?"

"Over a *bond*. Our betrothed king's bond—one which has been very carefully arranged. Your life has to be handled in the best way possible, to benefit everyone. Including you."

"Handled."

"You have tremendous power, Vane. They want to make sure you don't turn into another Raiden. Even as a Westerly, there's no telling how the power of four will affect your mind. There aren't any other Westerlies for them to pair you with, so they've chosen Solana. Her family was made up of the meekest, most humble of our kind—it's the reason they were our royals. We chose rulers who would put the good of the masses above themselves. Who would be generous, kind, and fair. And bonding to her will enhance those qualities in you. Make you a good king."

"But I don't want to be king!"

"That doesn't change who you are. And it won't change the fact that part of my job is to make sure you don't bond to anyone. So if you do, I'll be held responsible. Maybe you don't care what happens to me, but—"

"Of course I do." The light ahead turns yellow and I slow to a stop, grateful I can turn and face her again. "I care *a lot* about what happens to you."

It's more than I meant to say, and I have to look away.

She shifts in her seat. "Then promise me you'll stay away from that girl."

I laugh. "Pretty sure she'd kick me in the crotch if I showed up again. I'll pass on that."

"Other girls too, Vane. Even me."

The last words are a whisper. Almost a plea.

I focus on the road as we start moving again.

"You're meant to be with Solana," she presses. "When you meet her, you'll realize you've wasted all this precious time and energy trying to prevent the best thing that ever happened to you."

There's zero chance of that happening. But there's no point arguing with her. For now.

"Fine," I mumble.

She swallows several times before she speaks again. When she does, her voice sounds strained. "You won't regret it. I promise."

I'm not so sure about that.

But I am sure of one thing.

I've never felt *anything* like what I feel when I'm around Audra, and if I needed convincing, feeling the difference with Hannah tonight proved it.

Audra's *the one*. My head knows it. My heart knows it. Even my senses know it.

So if I can only bond myself to one girl in my lifetime, I know who it will be.

CHAPTER 34

AUDRA

I don't want to leave the car.

Tucked in the private space, with the wind streaming through the window and the night draped around us, Vane and I reached a strange sort of truce. I can't shake the feeling it will slip away as soon as I step outside.

Vane hesitates as he turns off the engine. Maybe he fears the same thing.

Then he opens his door and steps into the stuffy darkness.

I try to follow him, but I can't figure out how to unlatch the absurd seat restraint. Thankfully, I find the switch before Vane opens my door to assist me—the last thing I need is another jolt of his strange heat.

"Do we still have to train tonight?" he asks, staring at his parents' house instead of me.

He has so much left to learn. And we have so few days left. My eyes dart involuntarily to the sky, searching for traces of a storm.

The stars wink back at me, promising a calm night.

My mother must be keeping her promise. Otherwise, they'd have found us by now.

I need to make the best use of the extra time.

But I need to regroup. Figure out where we go from here.

"You haven't checked in with your family all day. You should probably stay in tonight. We'll get an early start tomorrow to make up for it."

He nods. "Well . . . good night."

I retreat to the grove before he can say anything further. On the way to my shelter I retrieve my jacket and windslicer from where I discarded them in my hasty flight. Both are covered in bugs and dirt. It's like this place overruns everything, tainting it, smothering it, trying to ruin it. I won't let it do that to me.

Gavin screeches from his perch on the windowsill when I stumble home. Poor bird has been severely neglected these last few days.

I stroke the feathers at the scruff of his neck and stare out the window. The moonlight's bright enough that I can see my reflection in the cracked, dirty glass. I look pale. Dark shadows rim my eyes, and strands of hair have broken free of my braid, sticking out in wild, erratic tufts. Hardly attractive.

My mind flashes to the girl Vane was with tonight.

Soft blond hair.

Soft blue eyes.

Soft fingers twined around Vane's hand.

He chose me.

The thought feels foreign.

But it's also true.

The thrill that gives me is wrong for more reasons than I can count—but I feel it nonetheless.

My head aches from my tight braid, and it's too much for my exhausted brain to handle tonight. I undo the careful knot at the end, letting my hair unweave, finally releasing the pressure. The dark, wavy strands settle around my face.

I will never be glamorous like my mother. I have too much of my father in me. His square jaw and narrow nose. The low arch of my brows.

Still, there's something dark and mysterious about my reflection in the window. Something striking and powerful.

Is that enough to count as beautiful?

What does Vane see when he looks at me?

I turn away, tempted to punch the glass. I'm in the greatest danger of my life, and I'm playing with my hair and wondering if the boy I can't have—and refuse to let myself want—thinks I'm pretty.

It's time to get ahold of myself—now.

I reweave my hair into the braid, pulling the strands tighter than ever. If only I could wrangle my feelings as easily.

I can't. So I'll do the next best thing.

I slip into my jacket, unsheathe the windslicer, and stomp outside to the widest clearing in the grove. The still night is thick with the sounds of skittering rodents and chirping insects, and the warm air makes my clothes cling to my skin. But I don't care.

I bend my knees, squatting into my starting posture. Two deep breaths bring me focus. Then I throw myself into my memorized exercises.

I slash and stab. Dip and spin. Race up the sides of trees and back-flip off. Dive toward the ground and somersault back up. Push my lithe muscles as hard as I can, ignoring the extra weight of the water, the extra burn in my limbs.

Sweat soaks my uniform and I pant for breath. Still I swipe and thrust, hacking leaves off the palms, slashing trunks, slicing the air with a surge of strength and speed.

This is who I am.

A fighter.

A guardian.

Stronger than Stormers.

Stronger than Vane.

Beyond all emotion.

I don't give in to fear or pity or love. I'm the one in control.

The reminder fuels my weary body with an extra burst of energy, and I swing the blade with a vengeance. My thoughts vanish. My brain steps back, letting my limbs remember the motions on their own. Running on instinct.

My muscles throb, but the pain is liberating. Helps me clarify my purpose.

Vane needs to have the fourth breakthrough.

I can't stand back and wait for it to happen. I have to trigger it myself.

But how?

My legs turn to rubber and I collapse to the sticky, date-covered ground. I reach for the nearest Easterly and pull it around me to help cool me down. And as I listen to its song I realize . . .

Wind.

Vane needs maximum Westerly exposure. The more winds bombarding him, the better chance there is he'll find a way to breathe one in and let it settle into his consciousness. To *hear* it.

I may not be able to call the Westerlies to him.

But I can bring him to the Westerlies.

Tonight.

Now.

It will work. I have to believe it will work.

And if it doesn't, I doubt anything else will.

CHAPTER 35

VANE

I yawn for the ten zillionth time, shaking my head as my eyes blur from staring at the endless, empty stretch of freeway. I point the AC vent at my face to let the cold air jolt me awake.

"You know, when you said you'd come get me a little earlier," I tell Audra, "I was thinking like four thirty—which is still ridiculously early, by the way. But two a.m.? Are you trying to kill me?"

"I need to know if this will work." She sounds way too alert for this time of night. Doesn't she ever get tired?

Her words hit me then. "*If?* I thought you said this *would* work."

She shifts in her seat. "Nothing is guaranteed. But this should work."

Should is a whole lot different than *will*. "And if it doesn't?"

Silence.

Guess that means there isn't a Plan B. Though, honestly, I'm surprised she found a Plan A.

We pass a sign that says LOS ANGELES 81 MILES.

I groan. "Remind me why we aren't flying there?"

"I wasn't sure I had the energy to get us there and back."

The change in her tone makes me turn toward her. She's fidgeting with the ends of her braid. She tends to do that when she's hiding something from me.

I'm tempted to call her on it, but I have better questions to ask. The way I see it, this drive is an hour and a half of uninterrupted "Ask Audra" time—and I *will* get some answers.

"So," I say, trying to figure out where to start, "assuming this works, and I have a Westerly breakthrough or whatever, where do we go from there?"

She considers that, like she hasn't thought it through. Which says wonders about how unsure she is. "I suppose I'll contact my mother so she can send word to the Gales."

"Your mother? Your *mother*'s the one you went to a few nights ago? Who denied your request for backup?"

"She's helping as much as she can."

I snort. "If that were true, we'd have a whole army at our side."

"She's a guardian too, Vane. She's bound by her oath to serve just as much as I am. Personal connections can't get in the way."

Her voice is calm. Detached.

But I don't buy that she doesn't care. I mean, dude, I'm not even related to my parents, and I still know they'll do *anything* to keep me safe. Even if it means breaking the law or oath or code or whatever. And that's how it should be.

So I can't stop myself from saying, "She sounds tough."

"She can be," she mumbles under her breath. "Especially since . . ."

I know what she means, even though she doesn't finish. "Was she better before that?"

"Sometimes."

She falls quiet, and I figure that's all she's going to say. But then she adds, "She used to love to watch me make the birds dance."

"Dance?" I can't help picturing a bunch of pigeons twitching their necks to the beat.

"If I've connected with a bird, I can command it to flutter and twirl and flip through the sky. My mother used to lie next to me on the grass, and we'd watch them sweep across the clouds. She said it was the one way I reminded her of herself."

Her voice sounds warmer, lighter with the memory.

"So, what does your mother do as a guardian—besides turn her daughter away in her time of need?"

Audra ignores my snipe. "She keeps watch on the winds. She can feel things in the gusts—traces and warnings and secrets—and she uses her birds to send that information to the Gales so they know of any possible dangers. Right now she's using her gift to stall the Stormers as long as she can and send warning when they draw close. I expect to hear from her any day."

Any day.

I know time is counting down quickly, but it gives me goose bumps to hear just how little we have left.

"So what's your mom's name?" I ask, partially to get my mind on something else, but mostly because I have to know if the name I heard in my dream is real.

"Arella."

"Arella." That explains why she's the one who told my father we had to move again. She must have caught the Stormer's trail early.

It also means Audra lied to me when she said my memories were gone forever. I figured as much. But now I know for sure.

I need to know why.

So far none of the fragments I've recovered give me any clue. And I'd barely begun a dream tonight when Audra ripped the sheets off me and dragged me out of bed. Which was actually pretty sexy. She can—

"Did you hear me?" Audra asks.

"Sorry. What did you say?"

"I said the Gales will send reinforcements if you have the fourth breakthrough tonight."

"Oh, sure. Send help *after* I have the breakthrough that makes me invincible or whatever. Why bother protecting me now, when I'm vulnerable? Idiots."

She sighs.

"It's true, and you know it. Do you really expect me to believe you don't mind that they'd rather let you sacrifice yourself to save me than send you some backup?"

"They just believe in me. Believe that I'm strong enough to handle this."

"Even if they do, they're still gambling with your life. And mine."

She can't argue with that.

"And how exactly does it help me if you sacrifice yourself? Even if you take out the Stormers, all that does is leave me here like a sitting duck, no way to contact the Gales, just waiting for Raiden to send someone else to come get me. Brilliant plan, guys."

"It wouldn't be like that. My mother would know what happened and send for the Gales immediately."

"So why not just do that in the first place? Why let her daughter *die* first?"

"You don't understand."

"You're right. What kind of people expect someone to sacrifice their life to save someone else, when they could send help?"

"Because the Gales are under constant attack from Raiden. They can't spare anyone right now just to save my insignificant life."

"You're *not* insignificant," I blurt out before I can stop myself.

She clears her throat. "Besides, you wouldn't be defenseless. I'd pass my gifts to you. Give you my knowledge and skills by letting you breathe me in."

"Why does that sound creepy?"

"I assure you, it's not. You just don't know how the ultimate sacrifice works."

She takes a breath before she continues. "We have two forms. Our earthly form and our wind form. Our wind form is infinitely more powerful. We're almost invulnerable to injury, and it gives us a whole other arsenal to fight with. If you have no ties to the earth, you can shift between the two. Like what I did in your room a few nights ago. It's rarely attempted and hard to achieve and quite painful. But possible."

"And if you have food or water in your system?"

"Then the parts of yourself that were bound to the earth will crumble and drop away in the shift, and you won't be able to reclaim them. That's why the water weakened me so much. I'm grounded until the last drop is gone."

It's way too late at night for my brain to understand crazy concepts like this. "But if that happened, you wouldn't really be dead. You'd just be wind, right?"

"Yes. But you've permanently sacrificed your earthly form. Life as you know it is over. And the ultimate sacrifice requires you to sacrifice your wind form as well. I don't know that much about it—it's only happened one other time, besides my father."

Her voice catches and she clears her throat before continuing. "As I understand it, you let the winds rip you apart and tackle the storm piece by piece in a unified, mass bombardment. Your consciousness stays with you long enough to let you whisper thousands of commands that shred the storm and destroy anyone inside it. But you scatter with the winds. And there's no way you can put yourself back together before your consciousness fades away."

My grip tightens on the steering wheel.

No way I'm letting her do that.

"But as you surrender yourself, you can send your gifts to someone else. So the talent isn't lost. My father—" Her voice catches again and she pauses for another breath. "My father sent me his gift when he sacrificed himself. It's why I can walk so easily on the winds. Why I'm a guardian so young. And if I have to sacrifice myself, I'll send it to you."

"I don't want it." My hands shake so hard we swerve toward the shoulder. "I don't want your *talent*. You're not doing that, Audra. I don't care how bad it gets. Promise me that."

"I'll only do it as a last resort. But I will make the sacrifice if need be. And there's nothing you can say or do to stop me."

My palms throb from squeezing the steering wheel so hard.

She's wrong. There is something I can do to stop her.

I can have the fourth breakthrough.

I press harder on the gas, breaking the speed limit and not caring.

The Westerlies and I have a date. And I have no intention of screwing this one up.

CHAPTER 36

AUDRA

The salty air hits me as soon as I open the car door, as does a strong ocean wind singing in a language I can't understand. A Westerly.

Vane parks near the beachfront, and we make our way across the empty parking lot toward the massive wooden structure stretching into the churning ocean. The Santa Monica Pier.

It's almost four a.m., and the night is clear, the heavy winds sweeping away any fog or clouds. The amusement park in the center of the pier is mostly dark, a tangled maze of twisting lines and shapes rimmed with flashing blue and red lights, set against the black, starry sky. All the shops and restaurants are closed. The only things lit are the streetlights lining the railings along the edge of the pier. This place was built for large crowds, but right now it's empty, save for a few fishermen sitting silently by their poles on the scattered benches.

The solitude is eerie. I feel exposed—vulnerable—as I struggle to keep up with Vane. He climbs the wooden stairway like a man on a mission.

As I step onto the pier the Westerlies pick up speed, filling my head with their unfamiliar song. It's unsettling to be surrounded by winds I can't understand. Like being mobbed by strangers.

But this place is familiar.

I've been here once before, a day I've buried deep in my memory with all the other things too painful to think about.

Crowds of people swarm around me, blocking my view of Vane and his brand-new family as they wander the pier.

My weary legs are tired of standing in the shadows as his parents buy him drippy swirls of ice cream and pink puffy candy and buckets of popcorn and put him on rides that make him flip and twist and spin.

Vane gets to have the perfect, happy life. I can only watch from a distance.

For the first time since I joined the Gales, I'm tempted to leave. Take a break from training to fight and kill. From mastering the winds. From shadowing Vane. Do something for me.

I stare at the seagulls gliding above the rippled water. They call to me, beg me to join them, and I can't help wondering how long I could fly on my own. Would it be far enough to forget? Far enough to be free?

I step toward the rails.

Vane's dad shouts for him to come along, and I obediently return to my duties. I follow them into the fancy building with the blue trim and the arched windows. The room echoes with music and conversation, and I watch Vane circle the carousel, selecting his favorite horse. He picks a gray stallion with a red saddle and a black mane.

I stop to stare at the familiar building, having to remind myself that it's not nine years ago. The doors are locked and the windows are dark, but when I squint through the glass I can see the painted ponies staring at me with their lifeless eyes. And I can see the fortune-telling machine I'd hidden beside. The place I heard a voice so familiar it made my heart freeze.

"Audra."

"Dad?" I scream, drawing far too much attention to myself and not caring in the slightest. I shove people out of my way, run up to every man I see, but none of them is him.

The carousel starts to spin and it feels like the rest of the world is spinning around me. The music plays louder, making it harder to hear. Harder to think. I can't separate the voices, much less find the one I need. Several of the groundlings ask me what's wrong, but I shove them away. I'll be in big trouble with the Gales for making such a spectacle, but I don't care. I have to find my dad. Tell him I'm sorry. Beg him to stay.

"Audra."

I spin toward the sound and lock eyes with Vane as he rides past me. We only hold each other's gaze for a few seconds, but it's clear: He knows me.

I gasp as someone grabs my shoulder.

"Hey, easy," Vane says, holding his hands palm out. Showing me he means no harm.

I clutch my chest, wishing I could reach inside and steady my hammering heart.

"What's wrong? One second you were behind me, and then I find you here, pressed up against the glass, white as a ghost."

"You saw me that day."

"What?"

After Vane saw me, my father's voice disappeared. I didn't know if part of him was really there or if it was all some big mistake, but I did remember that I'd promised him I would take care of Vane. I never let myself forget that again. And I never let myself think about that day or wonder what it meant. Which is probably why I missed the most important part of the memory.

"Nine years ago, you came here with your family," I remind him. "I followed you to keep an eye on you. And while you were riding the carousel, you saw me in the crowd, and you knew me."

He shouldn't have known me.

I was supposed to be erased.

He stares into space and a slow grin spreads across his lips. "I forgot about that. That was the first time I started to think you were real. I wanted to jump off the carousel and find you, but my mom had her arms wrapped around me. And by the time the ride was over, you were gone. I figured I must've imagined seeing you."

A few seconds of silence pass as I digest that.

"So, how does it work?" he asks. "How did you make me dream about you every night?"

"You dream about me?"

The idea stirs such a mix of hot and cold I don't know which sensation to settle on.

"That's how I recognized you." He keeps his voice low as a

fisherman passes us, whistling a tune that feels far too cheerful for the moment. "I've dreamed about you almost every night for as long as I can remember."

I never realized. I'd assumed he only recognized me from the few times I'd revealed myself. But if he's dreaming about me . . .

There's only one way that could be possible. His mind would have to separate my voice from the whisper of the wind. We can do that with the people we care about. Like how I'd dream about my father after he sent me his lullabies.

But . . . how could Vane care about me? Before his memories were erased, he barely knew me. And in order to find my voice on the wind and attach it to my memory—a memory he should have forgotten?

He'd have to *love* me.

"Are you sure it's me?" I ask, grasping for some other explanation.

"Trust me, it's you."

There are dozens of different ways to love somebody. But how could Vane Weston feel any of them for me—especially back then?

"Your hair's always loose," he adds quietly.

"Loose?"

"Yeah. It's not in the braid. It's free . . . and beautiful."

His voice is soft. Tender. Laced with the kind of emotions he needs to cast away.

I shouldn't meet his gaze—I know what I'll see. But it's like he draws me to him, and when our eyes lock I find the same intense stare I've seen too many times in my brief days with him.

I feel the air heat up as he takes a step closer, and I can't believe we're here again. I have to say something—do something to stop this. But my head is swirling too fast. I can't think.

"Why didn't we fly here, Audra?" he asks. "You must have flown here when you followed me as a kid. So why not tonight—when we were in such a hurry?"

"I couldn't." The words slip out before I can think them through.

"Couldn't do what?"

I look away, trying to recover. Trying not to imagine myself wrapped in his arms, surrounded by nothing but wind and darkness and stars. Our warmth blending into one as his hands slide down my waist . . .

"I was too tired." I finally answer.

"Is it because of the water?" he asks.

I don't want him to doubt my strength. But the lie is easier than the truth. So I nod.

He takes another step closer and cups my cheek, so soft. So gentle. "I'm sorry I gave it to you. I didn't realize—"

"I know," I whisper. I lean against his hand, closing my eyes and giving myself one second to let his warmth erase the chill that's settled inside me from the strange winds and the stranger memories. Then I turn my face away.

"We should get started. We're losing time."

He takes a step away. "Where do you want to do this?"

"Down at the end. The winds should be strongest there."

I expect him to turn and head that way, but he holds out his hand. When I don't reach for it, he sighs. "We're in this together, right?"

"Yes."

"Then walk with me."

I should protest. But after the emotional roller coaster I've just ridden, I'm not sure I can keep going on my own.

I take his hand.

Waves of heat rush up my arm as our fingers lace together, and I feel Vane shiver at the same time I do. Neither of us says a word as we walk toward the end of the pier. It feels like we're both holding our breath. Waiting.

For what, I'm not sure.

Hopefully, for a new beginning.

But deep down it feels like the beginning of the end.

CHAPTER 37

VANE

I wanted to lean in and kiss her so badly I thought my body might explode from the pent-up pressure—but I fought the urge.

Not because I think it's wrong. Not because I'm scared of her army. Shoot—if I'm their future king, then I'm the one with the power. No way I'll let them charge Audra with treason.

But Audra's too . . . broken.

It's like something shattered inside her years ago, and until she fixes it, she'll just keep shoving me away. I have to wait until she's ready.

Huh—I'm actually figuring her out.

Cool.

The winds pick up speed the farther the pier takes us out over the ocean. I try to listen to their songs, but all I hear is a loud hiss, like static. My nerves knot into a big ball in the pit of my stomach and by the time we make it to the pier's edge, I kinda want to hurl over the railing.

What if I can't do this?

What if I'm . . . defective?

Great—like I need more pressure. Now I really am going to hurl.

The end of the pier is empty, probably because the wind is so strong. I lean against the blue railing and try to look way more relaxed than I feel. "So, how do we do this?"

"I don't know," Audra admits. "I guess you have to sit back, close your eyes, and hope your instincts do the rest."

That really isn't much of a plan. I can't think of anything better, though, so I flop onto an empty bench. Audra tries to pull her hand away, but I tug her onto the bench next to me. Close enough for our legs to touch. "I need you with me for this. In case you have to bring me back when I have the breakthrough."

Her body radiates as much tension as it does heat, but she doesn't pull away.

Good.

I try to concentrate on the songs. It feels like fifty people are whisper-shouting at me in a foreign language.

"Just relax," Audra tells me. "Let your mind drift with the winds. Follow their lead and hope they accept you."

That falls into the category of advice that sounds helpful but actually makes no freaking sense. But I try to do as she says.

Yeah . . . it works as well as I figured.

Doesn't help that the bench is arguably the most uncomfortable seat ever invented. Cold wooden slats dig into my back. I slouch, and they dig in more. I try to lean my head back, but my neck throbs. I shift again and my butt goes numb.

"What are you doing?" Audra asks as I reposition again, this time lying across the bench on my back.

She's probably referring to the fact that I've rested my head in her lap. Hey, when I see an opportunity, I take it.

"Do you want me to be able to concentrate or not?"

Her eyes narrow, but she doesn't shove me away.

Awesome.

And actually . . . being this close to Audra makes everything else fade away. I focus on each Westerly as it slides across my face and feel the pull I felt at the wind farm.

My heritage is calling the winds.

But the winds don't respond.

Minutes pass. Or maybe hours. I lose track of reality. My whole world narrows to me and those drafts. And the more my mind reaches for them, the faster they pull away.

Isaac likes to tease his sister's cat with a laser pointer. I always thought it was hilarious—but as I lie here, grasping for something that insists on staying just out of my reach, I feel sorry for that dumb cat, chasing a red dot it will never catch.

The winds whip and swirl, and I feel my body move with the drafts. But no matter what I do, they won't reach deep enough inside me, to the part that craves them so strongly it actually aches.

Then . . . something shifts.

A small strand of wind lets me breathe it in, and it slips inside my mind. It darts around my consciousness, stirring feelings I can't understand because I have nothing to attach them to. I strain to focus, grasping for whatever piece of myself the wind needs to make a connection. But I can't find what it wants, and the longer it's in there, the harder it thrashes.

Sparks flash behind by eyes and my stomach cramps. I want to vomit, but I can't move, can't think. Can only lie there as a million different splinters rip apart my skull and slam into my brain.

I hear myself groan.

"What's wrong?"

It's Audra's voice. I know I should answer, but the throbbing has taken over my body. I'm not Vane anymore. I'm a lump of pain.

"Vane?" Audra calls. "Vane, wake up."

Her warm hands press against my face—or I assume they do, based on the electric shocks that jolt me.

But it's not enough to pull me back from the agony.

My brain fuzzes and I can't fight it anymore. Darkness swallows me whole.

CHAPTER 38

AUDRA

This isn't happening. There's no way this can possibly be happening again. My whole body trembles as I fumble to get a better hold on Vane's limp body.

I shake his shoulders, trying to jar him awake.

Useless.

His chest rises and falls, but they're slow, shallow breaths.

Why isn't he waking up?

I squeeze his hands. Whisper pleas in his ear. Hold him as tightly as I can. All the things that brought him back before.

No response.

So I smack his face. Shake him. Shout his name—not caring if anyone hears me. Try anything—everything—I can think of.

Still he lies there. Completely beyond my reach.

This isn't like the breakthroughs, when I could see his body shutting down, surrendering to the winds. It's like he's left his body entirely, and all I'm holding is a cold, empty shell.

I don't know how to bring him back.

I taste bile as an image of Vane spending the rest of his days in this useless half life flashes through my mind. Worthless. Hopeless.

My fault.

I pound my fists against his chest, and his breath echoes in his lungs. Like a death rattle.

Something inside me breaks.

Everything—the fear and stress and anger, the hurt and regret and sorrow, the doubt and longing and turmoil—bubbles over in a fit of heaving sobs.

He left me.

How could he leave me?

And what am I supposed to do now?

Nothing.

Nothing except hold his limp body and cry. For Vane. For me. For every mistake I've ever made.

And for the ten millionth time, I wish I'd died instead of my father.

He would've known what to do.

Maybe he still does.

I turn to the lone Easterly swirling over the ocean and call it to my side.

"Please," I whisper as the draft cocoons around us, "please, Dad—if there's any piece of you left, *please* tell me what to do.

I can't lose Vane. Not now. Not like this. Please help me wake him up."

The seconds race by in silence and I give up. I release my hold on the Easterly, let it float away with the last of my hope.

I close my eyes, cradling Vane in my arms and resting my head against his chest, soaking his shirt with my tears.

"I'm sorry, Vane. I don't know if you can hear me or if you're there anymore. But I'm sorry. Not just for this. For everything."

It's the closest I've ever come to a confession, and as the words leave my lips I feel a tiny bit of the burden I've borne so long slip away with them.

My head clears a little, and as it does I catch the faint whisper of a nearby Easterly—one I didn't notice before. Its song is similar to the typical Easterly melodies I've heard my whole life, singing of the constant fight for freedom. But four words stand out from the others.

Caged by the past.

The winds can be called and tamed and controlled. But they can *never* be caged.

It has to be a message.

But how is Vane caged by the past? He doesn't even remember his past.

Unless that's the problem.

My heart races as fast as my mind, making me dizzy.

What if his consciousness chased the Westerlies deep into the mental abyss my mother created to store his memories? Could he be trapped there?

I stretch out my hands, feeling for the slow tug of a Southerly. For a moment I don't find any. Then a soft itch stings my thumb, on the farthest edge of my reach.

My voice shakes as I call it to us.

The warm, sleepy breeze coils around me and I part my lips to command it into Vane's mind. But my voice betrays me.

The command will release Vane's hidden memories.

All of them.

I hug my shaking shoulders and take deep breaths.

This is bigger than my secret shame—or how it will change Vane once he knows. This is about saving his life.

If this even works, my selfish side reminds me.

I can't believe I'm sitting here arguing with myself when Vane could be slipping further away.

I grab Vane's hands and whisper the command, ignoring the fear that stabs me with each word.

"Slip with his breath, then fall free. Release what's been hidden and return to me."

Southerlies have a magnetic quality. Any part of us that touches them wants to follow. So when my mother erased his memory, she sent a Southerly into his mind and told it to bury itself deep. All his memories drifted along with the draft, sinking so far into his consciousness they'll never return without a trigger.

Now I'm drawing them back, hoping they bring Vane with them.

His neck jerks as the draft climbs into his mind and I squeeze his hands harder, hoping the energy between us will prevent him from getting caught by the pull of the Southerly. It's only one weak wind, not the dozens I used to trigger his breakthrough. But in his altered state there's no telling what effect the wind will have on his consciousness.

His arms twitch, and my breath catches.

"Vane," I whisper, leaning closer. "Please come back."

His shoulders rock.

"Vane," I call louder. "You need to come back. We need you."

I have more words on the tip of my tongue—words I know I shouldn't say. Before I let them slip, his eyes snap open and he takes a deep, shaky breath.

Tears stream down my face and I send a silent thanks to whatever part of the winds helped me figure out what to do. I won't let myself believe my father spoke from the great beyond. But I know my heritage saved me.

Saved us.

Vane twists in my arms and I pull him against me, burying my face in the nape of his neck.

"What happened to—" he starts to ask in a raspy, broken voice.

"Shhh." I breathe in the warm, sweet scent of his skin. "It's all going to be okay. Just rest."

He doesn't argue. Just wraps his arms around me and pulls me even closer.

I call the lone Easterly and swirl it around us, adding my whispers to its song. The bench is cold and hard and my heart is heavy from all the emotions I've forced through it. But tangled there in Vane's arms, I finally relax.

CHAPTER 39

VANE

cling to Audra, afraid to lose my grip on her. Afraid to lose my grip on reality.

But the rhythmic pattern of her breath on my skin calms me, and the whispers of the Easterly fill my mind, leading me to sleep.

The second I leave consciousness, a tidal wave of memories slams into my brain. An entire childhood sliced and diced. Smiles, hugs, laughter, tears. Faces I know. Faces I don't. Places I can't recognize. Places that feel like home. All laced with different emotions—love, joy, fear, anger, hurt, regret. And wind. Lots and lots of wind.

I want to make sense of it all, piece my past back together and finally feel whole. But it's too much to process all at once. My brain throbs so hard I want to tear it from my skull.

Then Audra's whispers wash away the chaos and her face fills my dreams for the first time in days. Her dark hair sweeps against my face, and her sad eyes watch me as her lips speak words I actually understand this time. A hushed apology.

What is she sorry for?

She doesn't say. Just repeats "I'm sorry" over and over and over. So softly it feels like she doesn't want me to hear it. But I do.

I yank myself from the dream.

"Try to relax," Audra murmurs. "Having your memories come back can be overwhelming."

I jerk away from her, sitting up. "You know about that?"

She frowns as she sits up next to me. "Were your memories coming back before?"

Crap.

"I've had a few resurface since the breakthroughs," I mumble.

She hisses something that sounds like a curse word. "I should have realized that might happen. The Southerlies during your breakthrough probably drew a few toward them on their way out of your mind."

I have no idea what that means. Though it does tell me one thing. "So . . . you knew the memories could come back. Funny, considering you told me that was impossible."

She scoots away, like she needs space from my accusation.

I take that as a yes.

"Why did you lie to me?"

Her hands find her braid, twisting the loose ends. "I thought I was sparing you. You have a lot of hard memories in your past. I honestly don't understand why you want them back."

My mind plays through some of the flashes from my dreams. I still can't make sense of them. But there's one that stands out.

My mom—my real mom.

I can finally remember her face.

I'm six, and we're in a wide-open field, our hands locked tight as she spins me so fast my feet lift off the ground, twirling me in the wind. It feels like flying.

Round and round we go until we're both so dizzy we collapse to the grass in a fit of giggles. She wraps her arms around me and I bury my face in her tangled red-brown hair as she kisses my cheek. Then she tilts my chin up and makes me look into her clear blue eyes. And she tells me she loves me. That she'll always be there for me. No matter what.

I've never felt so safe and happy.

"Because there are good memories too," I remind Audra. "Proof that my parents loved me—that I loved them. Do you know how much I worried that I erased my family because I didn't love them enough to remember them? How guilty I felt?"

My anger deflates when I catch the way she flinches at the word "guilt."

Bingo.

"So, my memories will keep coming back?" I press.

"I removed the barrier locking them away. I'm not exactly sure when and how they'll return, but they'll all resurface."

"Any in particular I should worry about?"

She hesitates before she answers. "You . . . have a lot of pain in your past."

"I can handle pain."

"I hope so." Her hands tug at the buttons of her coat and she swallows a few times. "There's something you should know. About the day your parents died. About what happened to them."

My stomach tightens and my mind flashes to the gnarled tree I dreamed about a few nights ago. Coated in blood.

Does Audra have something to do with my parents' death?

Will it matter if she did?

My heart launches into overtime as her lips part, ready to spill the secret she's been hiding so long.

What if it's something I can't forgive?

She closes her eyes and I hold my breath.

Everything hangs on her next words—and I'm not sure I'm ready to hear them.

CHAPTER 40

AUDRA

This is it. Time to strip away the layers and lies I've piled on top of my secret shame and show Vane the dark, ugly truth.

If only I can find the words.

I feel like my voice has dropped away, fallen into the pit of my stomach and tangled with the sourness filling me. If I try to drag it back up, it will reduce me to a crumbled, heaving mess.

I focus on the morning sun on my skin. The breezes in the air.

Calm. I need to stay calm.

All I have to do is say it: *It was my fault.*

Four simple words that have been the sum total of my existence for the last ten years. They flash before my eyes, making the world blur. Or maybe that's my tears.

Just say it.

Maybe he'll hate me.

I deserve it. But I don't know if I'll survive it.

I may be brave in training or in battle—but I'm a coward. I can't tell the truth to Vane Weston. *Especially* to Vane Weston.

Which is absurd. I already made my confession when I was seven.

Back then he just held me tighter and soaked my shoulder with his tears.

Will he react the same way today?

Or will he do what I deserve? Shove me away for betraying him? Destroying him?

Does it even matter?

Vane didn't have the fourth breakthrough—and I refuse to try again. His mind is too fragile, too overwhelmed by all I've put it through. The winds could push him too deep again. Or pull him away. Either way, I can't chance it. Won't chance it. Vane is too important.

To the Gales.

To our world.

To me—though I shouldn't let him be.

So if I only have a few days before I sacrifice myself, is it too much to hope that his memory of my confession doesn't resurface until after I'm gone? That I leave this world knowing Vane Weston cares?

It's the most abhorrent, selfish desire I've ever indulged. But staring down my death makes me allow it.

I force myself to meet his eyes. "You . . . need to know that you watched your mother die."

His mouth forms several different words before he speaks. "Why are you telling me that?"

"Because I don't want you to stumble blindly into the dream."

"It was a tree, wasn't it?" he whispers.

I shudder, remembering the way the tree shifted in the sky, aiming right for her heart. The crack of bone and branch mixed with the screams and the wailing wind. "Did you—?"

"Not yet. But I dreamed about a bloody tree floating through a storm. I figured . . ."

The silence that follows feels like a vacuum, expanding, closing off the world as Vane stares at the horizon, watching the white lines of waves streak toward the shore. An unstoppable force. Like the storm heading our way. Bearing down. Ready to crash any day.

"Was that really what you were going to tell me?" he asks.

My heart plummets, but I straighten up to sell the lie. "Of course. Why?"

"No reason." He turns on his phone. "We should probably get on the road. It's ten a.m. I'm sure my mom is freaking out." His phone beeps. "Yep. Three voice mails."

"Wow, she's really worried about you."

"I'm sure she's planning different ways to murder me. As soon as she finds out I'm okay, of course."

"That's because she loves you." I don't mean to sound bitter, but I do.

Vane scoots closer, resting a hand on my knee. "Your mother loves you."

She used to—I think. But not anymore.

I shrug my sadness away.

It doesn't matter.

Nothing matters anymore.

So I don't hesitate to take his hand when he offers it this time—and I don't try to pull away as we walk to his car.

Maybe it's everything I've been through. Maybe it's knowing my days are numbered. Or maybe I'm finally giving in.

Whatever it is, I'm just along for the ride. For as long as I have left.

CHAPTER 41

VANE

Winds sing through the open windows as we streak down the freeway and I watch Audra from the corner of my eye. The motion lulled her to sleep, and it's strange to see her so peaceful. The hard line of her jaw softened, turning her lips into a perfect heart.

Fantasies of kissing her flash through my mind, but I shove them away. Because I see something deeper, too. Something that forms a lump in my throat.

She's giving up.

We didn't talk about the whole *me not having the fourth breakthrough* thing—but we both know what it means. I won't be strong enough.

I'm not sure what I'll do with my power if I find it—if I can fight. Destroy. *Kill.*

But I'd kinda hoped that if I just found a way to understand the Westerlies, they'd have the answer.

I lean my head toward the open window and concentrate on the gusts I still can't translate.

"If I'm really part of you," I whisper, "tell me how to save her. How to save us."

No answer.

I'm officially losing it. What do I expect? Some magical voice to whisper the perfect solution?

I need a plan.

The white lines on the freeway blur into streaks as I think harder than I've ever thought before. The brain's a muscle, right? Maybe I just need to push it.

Fifteen minutes later all I have is a wicked headache.

I'm insanely grateful Audra slept through that little experiment. I probably looked constipated.

But there has to be a solution.

Has. To. Be.

I could always knock her out.

There's no way I could ever bring myself to hurt her—but it's too bad there's no other way to make that happen. She can't sacrifice herself if she's unconscious.

"You look like you're going to burst a vein in your forehead," Audra says, making me jump. "What are you thinking about?"

It's a strange question coming from her. She's rarely curious about me. So I decide to be honest. "I don't want you to sacrifice yourself for me."

She sighs. "We've been over this."

"Yeah, and I keep waiting for you to stop acting crazy. Face the facts, Audra. I may never have the fourth breakthrough. So everyone needs to stop hanging their hopes on me like I'm the miracle they've all been praying for."

"You're the last Westerly, Vane. Breakthrough or no breakthrough doesn't change that."

"Pretty sure it does."

"No, it doesn't. Right now you're an unknown variable. Raiden doesn't know how powerful you truly are. And as long as he doesn't, we can use that. Keep him worried and distracted, waiting to see what you can do."

"Great, so you'll give up your life to save a pawn."

"Not a pawn. A weapon."

Ice slices through my veins at the word. "I don't want to be a weapon."

"I know." I can barely hear her soft whisper over the wind. Not that I have any idea what to do with it.

We drive in silence as my car crests the mountains, and the San Gorgonio Pass Wind Farm comes into view. The gleaming windmills line the hills, stark white against the bright blue sky, their blades pumping from the force of the swirling winds.

In a few miles we'll be home.

I'm not ready to go back to reality. Not with so few days left until the Stormers arrive. Not with parents who will demand answers I don't have. Not without figuring out how to save Audra.

Golden arches appear on the horizon at the same moment her stomach rumbles.

Inspiration strikes.

I change lanes, heading toward the off-ramp.

If I can get her to live her life for herself in small ways and see how awesome it is, maybe that will convince her not to sacrifice herself.

"Where are we going?" Audra asks.

"We're stopping for lunch."

CHAPTER 42

AUDRA

The heavy scent of grease and salt clings to the inside of Vane's car, practically suffocating me. The late-morning sun hammers through the glass, but Vane keeps the windows closed tight, trapping me with the smell.

Sharp pains sear my stomach but I ignore them. Much like I ignore the soggy bag of untouched food he set on the dashboard in front of me. Or the seething Vane next to me, taking his frustration out on his poor, shredded hamburger.

"You won't even try a bite?" he asks again. He holds out a French fry to tempt me.

My mouth fills with saliva, but I shake my head and swallow, hating the sloshy thud I feel in my gut as I do.

Honestly, I don't know why he seems so surprised. This isn't exactly a new development.

"You *want* to eat," he says when my stomach growls. "You're just too stubborn to admit it."

I can't disagree with that. So I take a page from the Vane book of arguing and simply shrug.

He doesn't seem to like that, tossing the fry back into the bag with extra force. "You're starving yourself so you can be strong a few *months* from now—when you probably won't even need to be. Do you see the insanity there?"

My stomach growls again and I clamp my arms around my waist, trying to wring out the sound. The hollowness in my gut feels like it's swallowing me whole.

Vane snorts. "So what'd you do?"

"What?"

"You live in a piece of crap burned-down house in the middle of the freaking desert. You barely sleep. You aren't allowed to eat or drink. It's like someone's trying to punish you."

"No one is punishing me. I chose this life for myself because it's what I wanted."

It is, I remind myself. *And it's what my father asked me to do.*

"Then why do you want to punish yourself?"

Silence sits between us. An ugly, awkward thing I can practically feel staring at me. But I have no way to break it.

Vane grabs my hand again. His touch is soft, gentle—but firm, too. He isn't going to let me pull away.

"Why do you live like your life doesn't matter? You do matter. You matter to me—and not because you're this fierce warrior thing who's going to sacrifice yourself to save me. You matter because you're you."

He mumbles the last words, like he's embarrassed to say them.

I've been trying not to look at him, trying to keep this moment under control. But my head seems to turn on its own, and my eyes pull to his.

"You're the one constant thing I've had in my life. I lost my entire past—except you. You stayed with me. And kept coming back, every time I closed my eyes." His cheeks look flushed and he shifts in his seat. "I looked forward to seeing that girl with the long, dark hair whipping around her face. I looked forward to you. The *real* you. Not this buttoned-up soldier girl you pretend to be."

"I'm not pretending."

"Maybe not. But it's not who you are, either."

I flinch as he reaches for my braid, running his fingers along the intricate weaving.

"Doesn't this give you a headache?" he asks.

Yes. "No."

He doesn't look convinced as he drops my braid, trailing his hand across the sleeve of my jacket. "Doesn't this get suffocating in the desert heat?"

Yes. "No."

We both stare out the window as a group of teenagers walk by, laughing and joking while they jump into the car next to us. They crank up the volume on some pulsing dance song and zip off for a normal day of fun with friends.

I hate myself for being jealous. "Why does it matter if I wear a uniform or braid my hair?"

"I'm just trying to figure you out."

"It's easy. I'm a guardian. Everything I do is to fulfill the oath I've sworn. It's the life I chose. The life I'd choose again."

My voice sounds louder than I want. Defensive.

Vane stays calm and quiet as he replies. "Is it? Or is that what you're telling yourself, because otherwise you'd have to admit your life sucks? That you swore some oath a long time ago because you believed you deserved to be punished for something, and you've been torturing yourself ever since?"

Even if he's right, even if I am punishing myself, I deserve the punishment. And he'll know why soon. I should just tell him now. Get it over with.

"You deserve to be happy," he whispers. "No matter what you think or what you did. You *deserve* to be happy."

"I—"

"You *do*. And what better time than now—staring down a fight we might not even make it through—is there to start? Let your hair down. Throw that horrible jacket in the Dumpster. Give yourself a break."

"I can't, Vane."

"Yes, you can. You just have to let go."

My stomach growls again and he swears.

"Come on, this is insane."

He looks so earnest. So honest. And he *cares*.

No one cares about me—not even me.

He reaches into his bag and pulls out another fry, holding it out. "You can start small."

The whole world fades away, leaving just me, Vane, and that French fry. It looks almost as tempting as the boy holding it.

"Your body is hungry, Audra. Give it *one* thing it wants."

All my years of training scream at me to resist. To shove his hand away and refuse to prolong my days of weakness.

But deep, *deep* down, a tiny voice whispers something else. The same words Vane says next.

"What's it going to hurt?"

Only me, when I have to endure extra months of weakness.

But I probably won't live through the week. Why not give myself one tiny thing I want?

Before I can change my mind, I grab the fry and shove it in my mouth. My first bite of real food in ten years.

And it's the best thing I've ever tasted.

CHAPTER 43

VANE

I can't believe she did it.

I watch her close her eyes and chew, half-expecting her to spit it out any second. But she swallows. Then her hungry eyes meet mine. I've never seen her so shy. So timid. So . . . happy.

"Can I have another?" she whispers.

I reach into the bag and grab another fry. It's one of the soggy ones—the kind that feels more like a worm—and it isn't even hot.

"You know what? If we're gonna do this, we're gonna do it right," I say, dropping the bag in my lap and throwing the car in reverse. I can't believe I didn't think of this in the first place.

"Where are we going?" she asks, reaching for the bag. I pull it away from her.

"No way. I will *not* let your first meal be cold McDonald's fries. I'm taking you to In-N-Out."

I push the gas pedal to the floor, hoping she won't change her mind in the fifteen minutes it takes us to get there. But she doesn't. She doesn't even hesitate to take my hand as she climbs out of the car in the crowded parking lot.

The heat hits us like a wall, and she pushes up the sleeves of her jacket.

I stop walking. "Just take it off."

Resistance flares in her eyes, but I squeeze her hand. "Come on. What's it going to hurt?"

She sighs. Then pulls her hand away and starts undoing buttons.

My heart beats double-time. I know she has a skimpy black tank on under there—but that isn't what makes the action so sexy. Well, okay, it *helps*. But it's way hotter watching her do something she wants to do for a change.

I'm tempted to make her undo the braid, too, but I don't want to press my luck. So I toss her jacket in the car and take her hand again, leading her into In-N-Out.

"What's so great about this place?" Audra asks, looking a little intimidated by the crowd.

Her dark clothes stand out in the bright white, red, and yellow restaurant, and I catch several people staring at her. Though half of them are guys checking her out.

I squeeze her hand tighter. "You'll see."

I order two combo number twos. "Animal style," I specify.

Audra's brows shoot up.

"Just trust me," I tell her, taking our cups and filling them with soda.

Miraculously, we score a small table in the corner, and I have Audra take a seat while I grab ketchup and napkins. Five minutes later they call our number and I set two perfect cheeseburgers with fries on the table and sink into the seat across from her.

Audra eyes the food with a mix of hunger and intimidation.

"Eat as little as you want." I hand her a cheeseburger and sprinkle salt on her fries. "But you won't be able to stop once you taste it."

She holds the burger like it's a foreign object, like she's afraid to touch the bun beyond the paper wrapping.

I can't help laughing. "You're overthinking it. Just dive in."

She watches me take a huge bite—which is beyond amazing, by the way. In-N-Out has perfected the cheeseburger—but still she hesitates.

"I can't believe I'm doing this."

"You already ate the fry, remember? Might as well go for it now."

She looks like she might put the whole thing down and walk away. Then her eyes narrow and her back straightens and she dives in, her lips stretching thin so she can take the biggest bite possible.

"Oh. My. Goodness," she mumbles through her mouthful.

Sauce runs down one side of her chin and a tiny piece of grilled onion sticks to her lip, but she's never looked sexier. I want to jump across the table and kiss her face clean.

"Life-changing, right?"

She can only nod—her mouth already full with her next bite.

Within ten minutes she's devoured the entire burger and most of her fries. She leans back in her chair, clutching her stomach.

"You okay?" I hope I haven't just given her the mother of all stomachaches.

Audra nods. "I forgot what it feels like to be full." She shifts her weight, stretching out her legs. "I feel so warm."

"I still can't believe how long you deprived yourself."

"Ten years." Her smile fades. "I'll probably regret this later."

"Only if you let yourself."

She stares at the table, playing with part of a French fry left behind. "My father died because he ate—did I ever tell you that?"

"No." She's never told me anything about what happened to her father. Other than the fact that he sacrificed himself to save me.

Her fingers rip the fry into tiny crumbs. "My parents gave up eating when they started guarding your family, needing to be as strong as possible. They still fed me—I was too young to deprive myself that way—but they never touched the food themselves. My mother complained constantly about the hunger pains. The Gales had never required that kind of sacrifice from her before. They never required anything from her. She had the golden gift, and they were so grateful to have her on their side, they treated her like a queen."

Her eyes glaze over, lost in the memories.

"Then one day, my dad and I came home from training in the meadow and my mother was eating a dark purple plum she'd picked off the tree in our new front yard—our third house in as many months. My dad panicked, but she just took another bite, letting the juices stream down her chin. Then she offered it to him. He started to shake his head, but she told him the Stormers would never find us. That her gift would *always* allow her to feel them coming and we'd run. Then she told him, 'We have to live for ourselves, too.' He looked at me—almost like he wanted to say something, but I still don't know what it was—and then he took a giant, juicy bite. We spent the rest of the night feasting on plums."

A tear slides down her cheek and she wipes it away. When she speaks again, her voice is barely a whisper.

"A couple weeks later the Stormer found us. I don't know if my dad could've beaten the Stormer just by shifting to his wind form during the fight. But he didn't have the option. He was tied to the earth. All he could do was sacrifice himself. So that's what he did."

I take her hands and for a minute we just cling to each other in the crowded restaurant.

But there's something I need to say. I clear my throat. "I'm the one who gave you the water and weakened you. And I'm not going to teach Raiden what he wants—I can't, even if I wanted to. I haven't had the breakthrough. So just . . . let the Stormers take me, if it comes to that, and get the rest of the Gale Force and come rescue me."

The warm color that's filled her cheeks since her burger binge fades. "Do you have any idea what he'll do to you if he gets his hands on you?"

"No, and I'm trying not to think about it."

"He'll torture you, Vane." Her voice is too loud, and a couple heads turn our way.

I grab our trash and head toward the door. Neither of us speaks until we're safely in my car. I turn the key and crank up the AC. But we stay parked.

"He'll torture you," she repeats.

"I'm sure he will."

"I don't think you have any idea what that means." She shudders. "The things he's done are unspeakable. Pain and torment you can't even begin to imagine."

I have to remind myself to keep breathing. "I'd still rather live through that than watch you die. I—I can't imagine trying to live without you, Audra."

Oh God—here we go. Cards on the table time again.

I promised myself I'd go slow, try not to scare her off. But she's come so far in the last hour, and I can't help feeling like I might never get a chance to say this again. I just . . . have to.

I take her hands and stare into the face of the only girl I've ever really wanted.

"I love you." My voice cracks from nerves and I curse myself for sounding like I'm twelve. I clear my throat, trying to recover. "I know that's inconvenient for you. But it's true."

"I can't, Vane—"

"Yes, you can. If you can eat a cheeseburger—and enjoy it—you can let yourself love me. You can do anything you want. You just have to want to."

I hold my breath, waiting for her response.

She won't look at me. Not a good sign.

"I care for you, Vane," she whispers. "But you're not a cheeseburger—a single meal that will be out of my system in a few months, like it never happened. You're a permanent mistake."

Permanent. Mistake.

Talk about ouch.

She pulls her hands away, taking her sparks with her. "I'm sorry."

A couple tears streak down her cheeks.

Seeing them makes it hurt more. Makes it feel final.

I've done everything I can—said everything there is to say. And it isn't enough.

I shift into reverse without looking at her. She buckles her seat belt—getting it right in one try—and turns away.

She doesn't speak again until I pull into my driveway and park. "I have something I should've given to you a long time ago." She reaches into her pocket and pulls out some sort of copper-colored cord with something round and silver in the center. "Hold out your right hand."

I don't have the energy to argue, so I do as she asks and she wraps the braided strap around my wrist and latches it with the worn copper clasp.

I turn my wrist over, surprised to find that the silver piece in the center is actually a small compass. The arrow spins for a second, then comes to a stop on *West*.

Audra sucks in a breath. "It's never done that for me. But I'm not a Westerly." She sighs. "It was your father's, I believe—though both your parents had them. I found it in the rubble after the storm and kept it for you. I figured you'd want to have something that was theirs."

The copper band looks worn and weathered, and the glass on the compass is scratched and dulled. But it's perfect.

Audra buttons her jacket, becoming guardian Audra again. "We're going to need to come up with a battle plan tonight. The more prepared we are, the better our chances."

There are so many things I could—should—say.

But I don't know what the right move is anymore.

Audra decides for me. She exits the car.

As she steps outside she turns her face to the wind, closing her eyes. It should've been a peaceful gesture, but her brow creases. Her lips tighten.

"What's wrong?" I ask as she spins around, her wild eyes scanning the sky.

She doesn't answer. Just walks toward the grove, touching the trunks of the palms. She glances at the treetops, searching for something.

"You realize how much trouble you're in, don't you?" my mom calls from the front door.

Crap.

"I know, Mom. I'm sorry."

"If you're sorry, you'll tell me what the hell is going on." She steps outside, shaking her head as she moves down the path toward me. She folds her arms across her chest. "Where were you?"

"Santa Monica," I say, only half paying attention as I climb out of the car and head toward Audra.

Audra scoops up a small white dove and inspects the feathers of its wings. Her frown deepens with every feather she checks.

"Are you even listening to me?" my mom asks.

I turn back toward her.

My mom sighs. "I want to trust you, honey—but you're making it very hard. Ever since she came along, you haven't been the same. What's she doing over there, anyway?"

Audra fiddles with the dove's feathers, rearranging them some-how. Her hands shake.

"I don't know." But something is clearly wrong.

I run to her side, annoyed at my mom for following but knowing I can't stop her.

"What happened?" I ask Audra.

Her face looks pale as she stares into space, ignoring me. She tosses the dove into the sky, its wings flapping in my face as it flies away.

Freaking birds.

"Tell me what's wrong," I beg.

"We just ran out of time," she says, finally meeting my eyes. "The Stormers will be here tomorrow."

CHAPTER 44

AUDRA

I can barely believe the words as I speak them. It wasn't her usual crow, but the dove came from my mother. And I checked her message three times, counting and recounting each mark she made in the feathers to make sure I hadn't missed one.

There's no mistake.

But . . . it's only been four days since I gave away our location. *Four.*

How could we have lost so much time?

My mother said the Stormers are better trackers than she's ever seen. They saw through her confounded trails much quicker than they should have, and now they've locked onto ours.

They must be more powerful than I feared.

But why wouldn't they be? Raiden's been searching for Vane for years. He sent his best.

My heavy lunch churns in my stomach as the fear settles in and I wonder if I'm about to vomit.

"What do you mean they'll be here tomorrow?" Vane asks, his face ashen. "How do you even know that?"

"Wait—who's coming? What's going on?"

It takes my brain a second to put together that Vane's mother is standing with us. But I don't have time to worry about her.

"My mother sent me a message," I tell Vane. "They found our trace and they're bearing down on us."

The words knock Vane back a step. I know exactly how he feels.

At least we have time to prepare—though we have precious little of it. Still, it's better than nothing. I have time to strategize. Anticipate. Steer things our way.

We shouldn't try to hide—the chance is too great they'll catch us off guard. The smarter play would be move to a position where we have the advantage and call them to us.

The wind farm.

The gusts are strong there, giving us plenty of ammunition. And we can hide, send our trace in every direction so they won't know which angle to approach from. The pointed blades of the windmills make a wind fight more dangerous—but that will work to our advantage too. I'm sure the Stormers have been ordered to be cautious after what happened with Vane's parents. Raiden needs Vane brought in alive.

"Get changed into something warm," I order Vane. "They're Northerlies, so it'll be an icy storm. And hurry—we need to move fast."

"Absolutely not," his mother interrupts, blocking his path. "You're not going anywhere, Vane. Not until you explain what the hell is going on—and even then. Do you really think I'm just going to ignore that you ran away in the middle of the night?"

Vane runs a hand through his hair. "Mom, you don't understand."

"So enlighten me."

He sighs. "Even if I tried to explain it, you wouldn't believe me. You have to trust me."

"I do trust you. But I don't trust her." She spins toward me, her face much harder than the last time I saw her.

I take a step back.

"Ever since *she* showed up, you haven't been yourself," she tells Vane. "You've been lying, sneaking around, ignoring your friends. I know you like her, but she's not good for you, honey. I don't want you to see her anymore."

The words sting more than they should, and I drop my eyes to the ground. I don't want Vane's mom to hate me. And I hate myself for being wounded by such a petty thing.

"You can't stop me, Mom." Vane's voice is gentle but firm. "I'm going with her—I have to. And I need you to do me a favor." He grabs her shoulders. "Go get Dad and get as far away from here as you can. And if any storm clouds follow you, keep going."

"Storm clouds?" She leans in, staring into his eyes. "Are you on drugs? You can tell me if you are. I just want to help you."

Vane laughs, but there's no humor in it. "I wish this was all some big acid trip—that would be a lot better than the reality. But it isn't. I can't explain it, but you need to listen to me. Please. Have I ever lied to you—about anything important, at least?"

She stares at him for a long time. "You're scaring me, Vane. Please, just tell me what's going on."

Vane looks at me, and I see the question filling his mind.

I shake my head, as hard as I can.

Do. Not. Tell. Her.

I shove at the thought, wishing I could push it into his brain.

Vane's jaw sets, and I know he knows what I'm thinking. The rigid line of his shoulders tells me he's going to ignore it.

"Vane," I warn as he opens his mouth. "Don't."

"She deserves to know."

"She'll never believe you."

"Yes, I will," his mom chimes in. "How dare you tell him what I will or won't do! Tell me, Vane. Please."

Time ticks by, and a soft Easterly streaks past us, singing of the shifting, unsteady world. Vane's shoulders fall. "I'm sorry, Mom. I can't tell you."

I release the breath I've been holding.

"But I can show you," he adds.

Before I can react, he reaches out his hands and whispers the Easterly call, wrapping the draft in front of him into a mini tornado swirling at his feet.

His mom gasps and jumps back, her eyes darting everywhere, like she doesn't know where to look. "How?" she sputters.

"Don't say it," I order him.

Vane looks at me, not her as he answers. "I'm not human, Mom. I'm a Windwalker."

CHAPTER 45

VANE

I don't know what I expected. Disbelief? Fear? Disgust?

All seem like logical reactions.

Instead, my mom says, "You control the wind." Like it's no big deal. Like I just showed her I can pat my head and rub my stomach at the same time.

"Kind of," I say, my mind spinning as fast as the cyclone I've made.

Her not freaking out makes *me* freak out. I mean, doesn't it seem at all strange to her that her son is a *different species*?

"So, what exactly is a Windwalker?" she asks, still mesmerized by the swirling winds.

Seriously—*how* is she taking this so well?

"Vane," Audra warns.

"I'm a sylph," I blurt out, because I've come too far to stop now. "I guess I'm an air elemental or whatever. I can speak to the wind, tell it what I want it to do."

I whisper another command and the wind funnel tightens, stretching high over our heads, spraying us with bits of sand.

My mom gasps, her eyes wide with . . . wonder? Fright? I can't tell.

"So that's how you survived the tornado," she whispers.

Who is this woman, and what has she done with my ever worrying mother?

"Uh . . . yeah. Sort of. But you believe me? Just like that?"

"Well, it's not exactly easy," she says, turning to face me, "but it's hard to ignore the evidence."

She points to the cyclone, which is picking up speed, growing wider every second. I whisper the command to unravel it and the winds streak away, showering us with pebbles and whipping our hair.

My mom wobbles. "Okay, I think I need to sit down."

I grab her shoulders to support her. "Finally—a normal reaction."

"We don't have time for this," Audra practically growls.

"I know. But this is important." I turn back to my mom. "I'm sorry, I know this is a lot to take in. I would've told you sooner—but I figured you'd get kinda weirded out by the whole 'not human' thing. Sure freaked me out when Audra told me."

"Audra," my mom says, frowning as she looks at Audra. "So . . . she's a sylph too?"

"Enough." Audra's voice is more weary than angry. "Do you have any idea how many rules you've just broken, Vane? She's not allowed to know these things."

"Why not? He's my *son*."

"Not biologically."

My mom's eyes flash. "He's my son. How dare you make him keep secrets from me."

Audra's jaw locks.

Uh-oh.

I step between them. "Look, we'll figure all this out later, okay?" I turn back to my mom, who still looks ready to throttle Audra. I take her shoulder, forcing her to look at me. "I need you to go get Dad from work, and the two of you need to get as far away from this valley as you can."

"Why?"

"I can't explain it all, Mom—but the person who killed my parents knows I'm here. He's sent warriors to come get me, and they'll be here tomorrow. So you have to get out of here, because I don't know how big the storm will be and I won't be able to live with myself if you or Dad gets hurt in the crosswinds."

Her eyes get a glazed look as she processes that. Shock must be setting in.

"What about you?" she asks.

"Audra's been training me to fight so we can protect the valley."

"Training? The same training that dragged you home half dead?"

I squirm. "Yes. It's been intense. But it's going to be a hard fight. That's why you have to get out of here."

"Not without you."

I almost want to smile. She's sticking by me—even knowing what I really am.

But that's not important right now.

"They know how to find me—which means it's not safe to be around me."

"Why?"

"It would take too long to explain," Audra answers for me, and I feel my mom tense. "We're running out of time as it is. Just trust me when I say if there were any other option, I would take it."

"And why should I believe you?" my mom snaps. "Do you even know this girl, Vane? How do you know you can trust her? How do you know she's not involved with these—these warriors or whatever?"

I want to tell my mom how paranoid she sounds. But my mind flashes to Audra on the pier, telling me she has a secret about my parents' death—if that's even what her secret was about.

Could she be a traitor?

I glance at the bracelet Audra gave me—the bracelet she hid and protected for *years* after salvaging it from the storm for me. "I trust Audra with my life, Mom."

"But—"

"However you feel about me," Audra cuts in, "I've sworn to protect your son at all costs. I'll protect him with my life."

Her stupid promise makes my heart sink with a thud.

The words have a different effect on my mom. She takes a step back from me, staring at her hands as she wrings them together. "I'm going to hold you to that promise, young lady."

Audra nods.

I want to punch something.

"It's time to go, Mom. Audra and I have a lot to do, and you need to put as much distance between you and this place as you can. Don't think, don't pack, just get somewhere safe."

Tears well in my mom's eyes and she wavers on her feet, like she's not sure which way to go. "You'd better be here when I get back," she tells me.

"I will." I try to sound as confident as she needs me to be, but I hear the fear in my voice.

She wraps me in such a tight hug I wonder if my eyes are going to bulge out of my head. And feeling my mom's tears soak through my shirt makes everything very, very real.

My eyes burn, but I nip that emotion in the bud before any tears form. "Go get Dad and head east. I'll call you when the coast is clear."

She walks to the house in a daze to grab her purse and keys. Just before she closes her car door, she turns to look at me. "I love you, Vane."

"I love you, too. I'll see you soon."

"You'd better." She glares at Audra as she says it.

Then she starts her car and backs down the driveway, never taking her eyes away from mine as she drives away.

It feels like a small part of me leaves with her.

I should call my friends—warn them to get out of town too. But what would I say?

I can't tell them the truth.

I'll just have to fight hard, make sure the storms don't hit the valley floor.

Audra takes my hand.

It's so unexpected, I can't help turning toward her. She doesn't say anything, but her eyes are asking me to trust her.

I squeeze her hand tight. Because I do.

Then I let go and race inside to change into my only pair of jeans. I find it hard to believe it's really going to get cold enough to need a sweatshirt, but I grab one anyway. I look around, wondering if there's anything else I should bring. We have knives in the kitchen, but I doubt they'll do much good. We don't have a gun or a sword. What else do soldiers bring into battle? A first-aid kit?

I dig the kit out from under the bathroom sink and check what's inside. I'm pretty sure any injuries we get won't be patched up with an antiseptic wipe and a Band-Aid, so that's pointless. And there are plenty of painkillers, but it's not like we can take them. Not unless we *want* to make ourselves sick.

My heart stops.

If I need to put Audra out of commission so she can't sacrifice herself, human medicine would do it. I'm not sure how I'll get her to take the pills—but I shove a packet in my pocket so I'll have them if I need them. Then I race back to find Audra.

She looks ready for battle as she paces the grove. Her jacket's tightly buttoned, hair smoothed, windslicer strapped to her waist. I'm usually not a fan of soldier-mode Audra, but right now it's kind of awesome. She looks fierce. Brutal. And freaking sexy.

"Ready?" she asks, offering her hand.

I'm not. But I take her hand anyway, holding tight as she wraps the drafts around us.

Standing under the blue sky, it's hard to believe a storm is bearing down on us. But I feel a change in the winds. They whip with more urgency, their songs clipped and rushed.

They know.

The Stormers are coming.

CHAPTER 46

AUDRA

've never felt so overwhelmed in my life. None of my training taught me how to survive this. But I do the best I can.

I find the ideal defensive point among the windmills, on the second-highest peak, near the shorter, two-bladed turbines. They don't draw attention to themselves, and they all face east, making it easy for Vane to find Easterlies to use. His skills are the strongest in my native tongue. Probably because I triggered his breakthrough personally.

At first light I'll launch a wind flare to lead the Stormers straight to the wind farm. Hopefully, that will keep their storms from spreading to the valley floor before we defeat them.

If we defeat them.

I shake the doubt away. I *will* defeat them. Either with my skill or by my sacrifice.

I'm prepared for either.

I've reviewed everything I taught Vane, made sure he's comfortable with his commands. He can't do much, but he can call the wind, form pipelines, stop himself from falling, and make wind spikes. There's nothing left to do except watch the sunset and listen for some sign the Stormers are near.

I listen to the wind but hear no trace of their trail. If my mother hadn't sent her warning, I'd have been caught completely off guard.

I have no idea what she felt to know they're coming—or how she stalled them what little she did. But clearly she's right. She's far more important to the Gales than I am. No matter how hard I train, how much I push myself, I will never rival her natural talents.

This is how it should be.

Her gift matters.

Vane matters.

I don't.

Twilight settles over the valley, painting the thin clouds with purple and blue. Some would probably call it beautiful, but to me it feels ominous. I close my eyes and concentrate on the Easterlies, listening for some solution or advice. My heritage came through for me once. Maybe it will again.

All I hear is their traditional song of change.

We're on our own.

Vane yelps. I open my eyes to find him flailing as another dove swoops around his head.

I can't help grinning as I rescue the poor creature.

A Windwalker afraid of birds. It has to be a first.

"What's *with* that stupid thing?" Vane grumbles.

"My mother sent her."

I stroke the dove's neck, calming her so she'll let me pull out her wings to check for the message. It's strange to have the dove respond to my touch—stranger still for my mother to send a dove instead of her bitter crow.

I'd figured the first message was carried on whichever bird was closest, since it was so urgent. But this time she could've used any of her birds, and still she sent a dove. Her favorite of all the birds because of their almost worshipful loyalty.

There has to be a reason for the change. And I'm not sure I have the energy to cope with whatever it is.

"See the notches in the plumage?" I explain to Vane, pointing to the dove's wings. "It's a code my mother developed so she could send messages no one would be able to decipher. She uses the birds she's connected with, ordering them not to rest until they deliver the message. Saves the Gales from having to send important secrets on the wind, where Raiden could hear them."

Vane snorts. "You guys have *seen* the cell phone, right?"

"Yes, carrying a chemical-filled radiation machine around in my pocket all day. I can see why you're so attached to that thing."

He shakes his head.

I count the notches on the feathers, triple-checking each one to make sure I'm getting the message right.

"What now?" Vane asks.

"She wants to know if we're ready."

He rolls his eyes. "Tell her some backup would be nice."

I ignore him as I renotch the feathers with my response, finally giving my mother an honest assessment of our predicament. She might as well know what to expect.

Vane hasn't had the fourth breakthrough. When I make the sacrifice, you'll need to come collect him.

Tears blur my eyes as I release the dove and watch her vanish into the dusk.

That's the last time I'll speak to my mother.

I didn't say I loved her. I didn't say goodbye.

I started to notch the words, but I couldn't bring myself to say them. Not when I don't know if they're true anymore. Or if she'd even want to hear them.

I don't know what makes me sadder—not knowing if I love my own mother, or knowing she won't care if I don't.

But it's too late to change my mind. Too late to change anything.

I scrub my tears away and sink to the ground, curling my knees to my chest. Vane sits next to me, wrapping his arm around my shoulders. I should pull away—but I don't have the energy. And there's not much point. In a few hours it'll all be over.

"We're going to get through this," he whispers.

I can't look at him—I'm too close to breaking down to let him see my face. So I feel rather than see him turn his head and press his lips against my temple. Soft as a feather. Gentle as a breeze. Heat explodes under my skin, whipping through me like a flurry.

I hold my breath. Wondering if he'll do more. Wondering what I'll do if he tries.

But he sighs and turns his head away. He's finally learned to respect my boundaries.

Too bad. I'm not sure they're there anymore.

The Gales would banish me for such a treasonous thought—but it's hard to care. I won't be around long enough for them to question my loyalty.

Why not enjoy what little time I have left?

I breathe deeply, soaking up the scent of Vane's skin. Clean and gentle, just like the Westerlies.

"How did it start?" he whispers. "The storm that killed my family. I only remember bits and pieces. I should have some idea what we're in for," he adds when he sees my confusion.

I pull away from him, needing space if I'm going to relive this memory. "It started with a calm. Like all the life and energy were sucked out of the world. I remember standing on our porch, staring at the sky, wondering where the winds went. Then my father grabbed my shoulders and told me to run—as far and fast as possible. Before I could, there was this . . . roar."

Vane squeezes my hand.

"I'd never heard the wind's rage before. It was a beast, come to devour us. I started to cry, but my dad promised everything would be okay. Then he coiled an Easterly around me and launched me out of the storm."

"But you ran back in?" Vane asks.

I fight back a sob. "I still wonder if things would've been different if I'd stayed where he'd sent me. If he hadn't had to help me out of the storm a second time. Maybe he . . ."

I can't say it.

Vane's gentle fingers turn my face toward him. "That's it, isn't it? That's what you're punishing yourself for. You think it was your fault?"

"It *was* my fault."

Everything inside me uncoils as the words leave my lips.

Finally. Finally they're out there.

Tears pour down my face and I don't try to stop them.

Vane wipes them away, his touch warmer than a Southerly. "You couldn't have prevented what happened."

I won't let him let me off the hook like that. I don't deserve it. "It was *my fault*, Vane. All of it. Your parents. My father. Everything. You don't remember. But you will."

I stand and put some space between us, keeping my back to him. "I told you. When you held me in the shreds of the storm, when my father was gone and your parents were dead and the world had ended. We clung to each other and cried, and I told you. I told you what I'd done."

I stop there, needing a breath before I can finish.

"What did you do?" Vane whispers.

I close my eyes as what little is left of my heart crumbles to dust, leaving me cold and empty.

One more deep breath. Then I force the words out of my mouth.

"I killed them, Vane."

CHAPTER 47

VANE

Her words hang in the air: these ridiculous, impossible things that refuse to make sense.

"You didn't kill them," I tell her.

She couldn't have. Wouldn't have.

Would she?

No—she couldn't have.

"Yes, I did."

"So you started the storm that sucked them up and trapped them in the winds? You aimed the gnarled tree at my mom? That was you?"

"It might as well have been." Her lips move a few times, like she's trying to force them to work. "I gave away our location."

She cries so hard then, I want to rush to her side. Wrap my arms around her.

But I need the rest of the story first.

She chokes back a sob. "I had to save Gavin. He was falling and I didn't want him to die, so I called the wind. And then I lied to my parents. I could've warned them—but I was afraid to get in trouble. So I pretended nothing happened. And then the Stormer showed up and it was too late. I tried to help and only made it worse, and now they're all dead and it's my fault."

I run my hands over my face, giving myself a moment to process.

That's a lot of information to get in twenty seconds.

My legs shake as I stand, trying to make sense of the chaos in my head. Each detail swims through my brain, latching to a broken memory and tying them together.

I can remember her now. Standing in the field getting whipped by the winds. Her face streaked with tears and dirt and blood. Telling me the same things she just repeated. Shaking. Sobbing.

I do the same thing I did then.

I close the gap between us, pull her against me, and hold her as tight as I can.

Back then I did it because she was all I had left to hold on to. Ten years later I do it for the right reason.

I slide my hands down her back, trying to calm her heaving sobs. "You can't blame yourself, Audra. You were just a kid."

"It's still my fault." Her voice is hoarse and raw. "I'm so sorry."

My chest hurts for her. For the scared little girl she was. For the hard, broken girl she's become. I can't imagine growing up with that kind of guilt on my shoulders. No wonder she pushes everyone away.

Not anymore.

"Listen," I say, waiting for her to look at me. "I don't blame you for what happened. I will *never* blame you for what happened. The only person who deserves any blame is Raiden—no, don't shake your head. I mean it, Audra. It. Wasn't. Your. Fault. Nobody blames you."

"My mother does." She says it so softly, I'm not sure I hear it at first.

I tighten my grip on her. "Then your mother's an idiot."

I already hate her for denying Audra backup for the battle, and whatever else she said or did to shatter her strong, brave, beautiful daughter. I hope we never meet, because I have a feeling I'll suddenly have no problem getting violent.

I take Audra's face between my hands, cradling it like she's fragile—because she is.

"I mean it, Audra. I'm removing all of your guilt, right now."

"You can't do that."

"Uh—yes I can. They were my parents. I get to blame whoever I want for their deaths—and it'll never be you. *Never*."

Her glassy eyes hold mine, and I want to lean in and kiss all her pain and fear and hurt away. Okay, fine—I also just want to kiss her.

But I won't take advantage like that.

She has to heal first.

I reach up, fingering a strand of her hair that's pulled free and fallen in her face. "Will you do me a favor? Will you please take your hair out of this ridiculous braid?"

I know it's just a hairdo. But it's also this tight, restrictive thing she does to punish herself. And I'm not going to let her do it anymore.

Her hands reach for the knot at the end and I stop them.

"No. Let me."

She doesn't resist.

I help her lower herself to the ground, then sit behind her. In my head, I picture this cool, romantic moment, like something from a movie where violins play in the background and the lighting's all moody and seductive.

In reality, I kinda botch it, tangling her hair about a million different ways and taking three times longer than necessary. But come on, I'm a guy. I don't have a lot of hair-unbraiding experience.

Audra turns to face me when the last strands come free.

My breath catches.

This is Audra. Not the fierce guardian always ready to fight. Just the girl from my dreams. Only now she's right in front of me, and I can reach out and touch her. Grab her. Kiss her.

I sit on my hands and lean back.

I'm not going to force her—even if everything in me is screaming to screw caution and spend what could very well be our last night on earth in a tangle of heat and lips and limbs.

It has to be her choice.

She reaches for me, her soft fingers sliding down my cheek, leaving trails of sparks.

My eyes focus on her mouth as she licks her lips and leans closer.

She's going to do it. *She's going to kiss me.*

I resist the urge to fist pump the sky.

"You're beautiful," I breathe instead.

She leans closer. Our noses touch. I stop myself from closing the distance.

It has to be her.

She sucks in a breath and closes her eyes.

"What are you thinking?" a woman's voice asks. *At. The. Last. Second.*

"Come *on!*" I shout as Audra jumps back like I have the plague.

I turn to glare at the woman.

Her long, dark hair is styled in a tight braid and she's dressed in the same uniform as Audra, but she doesn't wear the jacket. Only the tank underneath. Gavin sits on her shoulder—and I swear he's laughing at me with his beady red-orange eyes.

She lets out a slow, dramatic sigh, letting it rock her whole body as she shakes her head and focuses on Audra—who's busy trying to smooth her hair into some sort of sloppy braid. "No need to put on airs, Audra. I've already seen more than enough. But we'll deal with that later. For the moment, why don't you introduce me?"

Audra closes her eyes and swallows, "Vane, this is my—"

"Yeah, I know," I interrupt—because even if I hadn't seen her in my dreams, the family resemblance is impossible to miss.

Audra's mother arrives at last.

CHAPTER 48

AUDRA

want to claw a hole in the ground and disappear into it for the rest of eternity. But I won't give my mother the pleasure of watching me crumble.

I dust off my pants as I stand. My legs shake and my loose hair blows in my face, making me feel sloppy and weak. But my voice is strong when I ask, "What are you doing here?"

A chilled night wind whips around us and my mother trembles, hugging her arms to her chest and squeezing her eyes shut, like the draft is stinging her skin. Her voice is strained when she finally opens her eyes and asks, "Did you really think I would leave you to take on the Stormers alone?"

Yes.

"Did you really think I wanted my only daughter—my only *child*—to have to sacrifice herself, if there was a way to avoid it?"

Yes.

"Yes." The answer comes from Vane, not me.

My mother straightens up, smoothing the fabric of her tank as she turns to face him. "It sounds like my daughter hasn't given you an accurate picture of me."

"Actually, the fact that you wouldn't call for backup said it all." He sounds colder and harder than I've ever heard him.

Her eyes narrow. "That's because I'd been counting on you to finally become a *real* Westerly. And I was hoping you'd turn out to be less useless than the others."

"Hey," Vane says, the same second Gavin screeches.

"Enough." I rub my temples and hold up my hands to silence everyone. "Then why did you tell me you wouldn't fight with me?" I ask my mother.

She sighs. "I thought if I gave you some extra *motivation*, you'd finally push for the breakthrough the way you should've been doing all along. But I always planned to fight by your side if it didn't work. So here I am. And it appears I arrived in time to spare you from *other things* as well."

My cheeks burn. My whole body burns. But some of that is disappointment—much as I hate to admit it.

My mother clears her throat, snapping me away from a mental image of Vane's lips.

"I'm only going to say this once," she says, putting her hand on her hip, like she's reprimanding a couple of toddlers. "I'm willing to pretend I didn't find you both in such a *compromising* position when I arrived, but only because it's never going to happen again, right?"

I say yes at the same time Vane says no.

"What?" he shouts, making Gavin screech again.

My mother strokes Gavin's feathers and murmurs soft words to calm him. For a second I'm speechless. Gavin's the only bird my mother never reached out to, blaming him as much as she blamed me for what happened. I don't know what to feel when he nuzzles against her fingers, completely swept up in her.

"I'm so sorry, Vane," my mother tells him. "Unfortunately, you're not free to make that decision."

She's using the same soothing tone she used for Gavin, but Vane's not so easily appeased.

"We'll see about that," he snaps back.

He looks at me, pleading for me to say something. But I can only turn away.

With my mother here, I might have a chance to survive this fight. Which means I'll live to face the consequences of my actions if I bond myself to Vane Weston. The shame. The disgrace. Being removed from the Gales, the only thing that gives my life purpose. And that's if they don't banish me for treason.

"So that's it, then? Mommy shows up and I don't matter anymore?"

There's nothing I can say, so I stretch out my arm and Gavin flies to my wrist. I stroke the softer, spotted feathers on his chest, grateful for the distraction.

"I never knew you were such a coward," Vane says, whipping each word at me like a sharp stone.

The words sting—more than he can know. Mainly because they're true. I'm not brave enough to fight the Gales to be with him.

I choke back my tears.

My mother lets out another epic sigh. "When I told you to make him love you, Audra, I didn't mean you should fall for *him*."

"What?" Vane shouts, and I can't help looking at him. "Your mother put you up to this?"

"No. It wasn't—I'm not . . ." I send Gavin to find a perch so I can shove my stupid hair out of my face. The wind keeps blowing it in my eyes. "I'm not up for this conversation."

He snorts. "Right. Enough said. In fact, I'll make this really easy for you."

He stalks away, and when he's vanished into the darkness, my mother approaches me. Her face is painted with sympathy, but I know underneath it she's probably thinking, *Look how Audra screwed things up again.*

"He'll lick his wounds and get over it. No permanent harm done," she tells me, placing a hand on my shoulder.

I shove her arm away. Even if she is sincere, she hasn't earned the right to suddenly act like a loving mother.

And maybe she's right—maybe it's a good thing. But the thought of Vane moving on makes me physically ill. So does knowing he's somewhere in the shadows, thinking I was only pretending to care.

"Been a rough few days?" my mother asks as I sink to the ground, resting my back against the cold base of a windmill.

"You could say that."

"Well, unfortunately, it's only going to get harder." Her hand moves to her golden cuff, rubbing the intricate blackbird. "There's another reason I'm here—I just didn't want to say it in front of Vane. Didn't want to worry him."

Right. Only I get to worry.

I stare her down, refusing to ask a follow-up question. I'm tired of having her control the flow of our conversations.

She closes her eyes and reaches up, waving her hands through the air. "There's something different about these Stormers. Something unnatural in the way they work. So much unrest in the winds."

Pain seeps into her features and she doubles over, hugging her legs as her whole body shakes and a faint groan slips through her lips.

I've *never* seen the winds affect her so strongly, and by the time I realize I should probably try to steady her, shield her—like my father always did—she's already straightened up. But her arms clutch her stomach like she might be sick.

"I don't know what anything I'm feeling means," she gasps through ragged breaths. "But I think it's safe to say we're in for quite a fight."

"Then maybe I should use the emergency call."

"No!" Her sharp tone echoes off the windmills, and her fingers resume rubbing the blackbird on her cuff, like she's trying to calm herself before continuing. "The Gales can't spare any guardians— how many times do I have to tell you? They're spread too thin as it is. You have no idea."

She starts to pace, moving in and out of shadows as she does. "I can't believe Vane didn't have the last breakthrough. You should have pushed him harder."

"Any harder and he'd be dead. I forced three breakthroughs in twenty-four hours—and the winds almost drew him away. I brought him to the west and surrounded him with Westerlies. He even breathed part of one in—but it pulled him so deep into his consciousness he almost disappeared. I had to release his memories to bring him back."

Gavin screeches as she runs over to me and grabs my shoulders. "You released his memories?"

I stare at her thin fingers cutting into my skin. Just like when I told her my father sent me his gift, all those years ago. "Why?"

Her lips part, then freeze. She lets go of me and turns away. "I just . . . always thought that was our last chance. That maybe his parents had taught him *something* that would help him find his heritage. But if you released his memories and he still didn't have the breakthrough . . ."

Her voice fades away.

I rub my shoulders, trying to keep up with my mother's erratically shifting moods. I've never seen her so unstable. She seems almost . . . lost. Fragile.

Gavin's vivid eyes glint at me through the darkness. "Why did you bring him here?"

She turns to face me but doesn't meet my eyes. "When I got your message, I followed your trace, but it led me to your home. I didn't realize you'd been living in such a . . ."

"Hovel?" I finish when she doesn't.

She nods. She looks at me then, and there's something in her expression I've never seen before. Takes me a second to realize it's pity.

Or maybe regret.

"You couldn't find anywhere better?" she asks after a second.

I shrug. Honestly, I didn't look. I didn't need comfort. I needed to do my job.

She wrings her hands. "Well, I saw Gavin there, and . . . I thought maybe it was time to make peace."

I have to lock my jaw to keep it from dropping.

I know the meaning of each and every word she said, but strung together and coming from my mother's lips they might as well be a foreign language.

"Were you really prepared to make the sacrifice?" she whispers.

"I made my oath. I intend to keep it."

She's silent long enough to make me fidget, and her fingers rub so hard at her cuff I'm surprised bits of black don't flake away.

"What?" I finally ask.

"Nothing. Just . . . you really are your father's daughter."

The words feel warm.

That's all I've ever wanted to be.

"You two were always like the clouds and the sky—a perfect pair. Sometimes I didn't know where I belonged in the mix."

I can't read her tone. The words are sad, but she sounds more . . . hurt.

I clear my throat. "The sky would be empty without the birds."

She reaches toward me, like she's trying to feel me out the same way she does with the winds. But she doesn't step closer.

I close my eyes, concentrating on the winds surging across my skin, whipping through my loose hair. They sing of the tiny steps that bring about change. Ripples in a pond.

I'm not sure I'm ready to break the surface.

"We should send Gavin home," I say. "He might get in the way."

My mother drops her arm and nods. "I'll take care of it."

She calls Gavin, and as he flaps at her shoulder I'm surprised to realize that I trust her.

I turn to walk away—then turn back and clear my throat. "Thank you for coming to help."

A few endless seconds pass. Then my mother whispers back, "You're welcome."

It's a small, reluctant step. But maybe with time it will lead us somewhere better.

CHAPTER 49

VANE

We were So. *Freaking*. Close.

One more second and I would've finally known what it feels like to kiss the girl I love.

The red lights of the windmills wink at me through the darkness. Almost like they're mocking me. I want to scream or throw things or . . . I don't know, just *something*.

I kick the nearest windmill.

Pain shoots through my foot, and I force myself to sit down before I get *really* stupid and go confront Audra again.

I lean against the windmill and rub my throbbing foot. My eyes focus on my copper bracelet, remembering the careful way Audra clasped it around my wrist—after saving it for me for ten years.

She couldn't have been pretending. Our connection goes too

deep for that. And I can't believe she would've come so close to kissing me if it was all an act.

But if it's real, why can't she screw her stupid rules and let me in? How can she choose the Gales over me?

Round and round my mind goes, trying to make some sense of the Audra roller coaster I've been riding. I'm not sure how much longer I can deal with the emotional whiplash.

The hours pass and I fight to stay awake through the dark silence. But after so many sleepless nights and endless days, I can't stop myself from sinking into a dream.

I stumble through the storm. Icy flurries make me shiver. Twisting drafts push and pull, trying to knock me down or rip me away. Somehow I know where to step, how to move, how to keep my feet on the uneven ground.

"Mom?" I shout for the millionth time, my throat raw and dry. "Dad?"

The wind carries my pointless calls away. I lean into the gusts and press forward, ignoring the panic that rises in my throat and makes me want to throw up.

I'll find them. Everything will be okay.

Two dim shapes blur through the storm and I race after them as fast as my legs will go. "Mom? Dad?"

I fight my way closer, but I still can't really see them. A wall of wind separates us—a storm within the storm.

I don't know if it's safe to push through, but I have to get to my parents. I charge the winds and fall through an icy waterfall of air into the inner vortex, tumbling across the ground.

I rub the dirt and debris out of my eyes. My heart sinks.

It isn't my parents.

I recognize Audra's mom. But the man is a stranger. I'm about to cry for help when I notice the dark cloud sewn to the sleeve of his gray uniform. A storm cloud.

I cover my mouth to block my scream at the same second he shouts something I don't understand and dark strands of wind tangle around Audra's mom, jerking her off the ground.

"You can't kill me," she yells as she contorts her body and slips one arm free. "Don't you know who I am?"

He laughs. "You're not as powerful as you think."

She starts to shout something, but he wraps a thick draft across her mouth, gagging her with the wind.

"Let's see how powerful you are now." He tightens the drafts and lifts her higher off the ground.

I stumble forward, planning to shove him so he'll get distracted and she can escape. Before I get there, she raises her free arm, bends her fingers into a clawlike grip, and flicks her wrist.

A rush of wind lifts the Stormer and slams him into the ground, breaking his hold on the winds and releasing Audra's mom. She lands with a thud, unable to stop her fall in time.

They both lie still.

Then the Stormer scrambles to his feet, wiping blood off his chin. "That's a neat trick. But I've got a better one." He wraps the drafts around his body, forming a thick shell that covers everything but his face. "Now I'm as indestructible as my storm."

She laughs, a dark, bitter sound that turns everything inside me cold as she pulls herself upright. "You're vulnerable in other ways."

She sweeps her arm and flicks her wrist again.

For a second nothing happens. Then somewhere else in the storm I hear a faint wail of pain.

Another Stormer?

"What have you done?" the Stormer screams, dropping to his knees.

Her features twist with fury. "Raiden has no idea who he's messing with."

She raises her arm again. But that's when she notices me.

Her eyes lock with mine and in her moment of distraction the Stormer tangles her in gusts and launches her high into the full force of the funnel. The winds suck her into the darkness.

The Stormer shouts something at the winds wrapped around him and blasts toward where the other scream came from.

I run the opposite way.

The winds around me rage, making my skin ripple from the force. I claw my way toward the edge of the vortex right as another scream pierces through the storm. A higher-pitched scream.

Audra.

I try to dodge the flying trees and broken pieces of house and rocks as I run, but some of them catch me. Blood oozes down my legs and arms as she screams again and I follow the sound. I finally find her tied to the wall of the tornado, bound by the winds. Stuff flies at her head—branches and rocks and bits of who knows what. She needs help.

But she's too far above me. She doesn't even know I'm there. The winds erase my screams before they reach her. I don't know how to help her.

I wish my parents had taught me something that would save her. A simple command. Anything.

The winds shift. I stumble to my knees as the draft holding Audra rips her higher, until she's barely a speck in the dark sky. Her scream cuts through the roaring storm, making my stomach twist and clench.

The draft drops her like a stone.

"Fly," I scream.

She falls faster.

Some instinct deep inside me takes control. My hands stretch out— but I don't remember telling them to do that—and I hear my voice whisper this crazy-sounding hiss.

I have no idea what I said. But the wind understands.

A gust wraps around Audra and grabs on. It isn't strong enough to catch her, but it slows her fall. She hits the ground hard enough to hurt. Not hard enough to kill.

A man bursts through the wall of wind, and I start to run. Then I realize it's Audra's father. He crouches over her, checking her before he lifts her over his shoulder.

I stumble to his side and he steadies me against the icy wind.

"Thank you," he says. "You saved my daughter's life."

I jolt awake.

The sky is dark—but not nighttime dark.

Storm dark.

Clouds of my breath hang in the air and I stare at them, trying to remember the last time it was cold enough in the desert to see my breath. I reach for my sweatshirt, struggling to get it over my head with shaking hands. The valley is eerily silent. Every windmill still.

The calm before the storm.

"They could be here any minute," Arella announces.

I jump as she steps out of the shadow of a windmill.

"Ugh—watching people sleep is beyond creepy," I grumble.

A half smile curls her lips. "I came over to wake you, but you seemed to be having a nightmare."

More like a memory. "Where's Audra?"

"Why? What do you need?"

She flashes a smile that's probably supposed to make me trust her—but I'm still too ready to punch her for last night. "I need to talk to *Audra*."

She sighs and points to the opposite end of the hill, where I spot Audra pacing among the windmills. I set off toward her.

Arella follows me.

"I can find her on my own," I tell her.

"I'm coming as chaperone."

"Uh, I have more important things to do than try to make a move on your daughter."

"That's not what I hear."

I don't have time for this crap. I do my best to ignore her as she trails right behind me.

Audra's hair's back in the braid—figures—and it's hard not to stare at her mouth, remembering how close it came to pressing against mine.

I shake the flashback away. "I need to talk to you."

"There's not much time. I launched a wind flare about an hour ago. They'll be coming straight here."

I breathe into my cupped hands, trying to stop shivering. "Fine. I just thought you'd want to know that I remembered something in my dream. I spoke Westerly."

Arella gasps and I glare at her. "I wasn't talking to you."

"What do you mean you 'spoke Westerly'?" Audra asks.

"Yes, Vane—what do you mean?" Arella chimes in.

I move toward Audra, keeping my back to her mom. "It wasn't your father who saved you in the storm—at least, not the first time. It was me. I called the wind that caught you."

"But . . . I distinctly remember my father carrying me out of the storm," Audra argues.

"He did. *After* I called a Westerly to slow your fall. Don't you remember how fast you were falling before that?"

She frowns. "I thought my father sent that draft."

"Nope, it was me."

"But—"

"If your father had sent the draft, don't you think it would've cushioned your fall more? You hit the ground hard, right? Because I didn't have enough control."

Arella grabs my shoulders and spins me to face her. "Does that mean you've had the breakthrough?"

Her eyes are bright. Too bright. *Desperate.*

I jerk away. "I can't remember what I said to call the wind. I'm not sure if I even knew back then. It was more like my instincts took over somehow."

Her hands clench into fists as she turns away. "So close."

Tell me about it.

"Something must have triggered those instincts," Audra says.

"Yeah. I didn't want you to die."

Her gaze softens at that, and I have to stop myself from taking her hands. But I step closer, lowering my voice so only she'll hear. "I wanted to save you. I still do."

Pink tinges her cheeks as she stares into my eyes.

She still cares.

Arella clears her throat, ruining the moment.

She's *begging* to be tackled.

"I wasn't try—"

"So if I threatened Audra's life right now," she asks, cutting me off, "would your instincts take over again?"

"Uh . . . probably not—because I'd like to believe you wouldn't actually kill your daughter just to trigger my breakthrough."

"Then you don't understand how much your breakthrough means."

Is this woman psycho? Or are all Windwalkers so caught up in this power struggle, nothing else matters?

I don't know which is worse.

"We need to try," Arella continues. "We need something that will trigger your protective instincts for Audra."

"Don't even *think* about it," I warn when she moves toward Audra. I will pin her arms at her sides if I have to. I remember what she did to the Stormers in my dream.

"It's too late," Audra interrupts. She points to the sky, which now looks like a giant bruise. A thunderous roar echoes off the mountains, drowning out the rest of her words.

The Stormers have arrived.

CHAPTER 50

AUDRA

The last time I heard this sound, my father died.

The roar crawls through my ears, slips through my veins, and plants itself in my feet, rooting me to the ground.

For a second I can't breathe, think, move. Then my training kicks in.

I grab Vane's arm. "Come with me. Now."

"Vane should stay with me," my mother says, grabbing his other arm.

"He's not leaving my sight."

"Which of us is the stronger fighter?" she asks.

"Which one of us is his guardian?" I snap back.

"I'm staying with Audra," Vane says, trying to pull away from my mother. Her grip tightens.

Several seconds pass as we stare each other down. Then she releases her hold. "If he's taken, it's on your head."

"That's not going to happen."

She scrutinizes me as we move toward our position. Then the first winds shift away from us, a mass exodus of Northerlies. Answering the Stormers' call.

My mother reluctantly jogs away, taking her place on the hill right below us. Vane runs with me to the cluster of two-bladed turbines. I point to the center windmill. "Crouch there."

"What about you?"

"I can take care of myself. Please," I add when he starts to argue. "You have to let me be in charge now. This is what I've trained for."

His clenched fists tell me he doesn't want to agree, but he squats in the shadows. "Don't do anything stupid," he orders.

I know what he's referring to, but I can't make that promise. "Keep your hands on the nearest drafts so you can grab them if you need them."

He nods.

The winds whip the windmills into a blur of white, and I let myself believe that keeping Vane surrounded by giant, sharp blades will deter the Stormers from using a vortex attack. But I can feel the winds streaking to the edges of the hills. Forming a wall. Caging us inside.

What are they up to?

I race to the tallest windmill and wipe my sweaty palms on my pants. It would be faster to float to the top, but the Stormers don't know exactly where we are. If I call a draft now, I might as well light a beacon. I have to climb by hand.

My legs burn and my fingers feel raw, but I reach the top and crouch behind the blades. I should be able to see the whole valley from my roost, but the winds blur everything beyond the foothills. I can still make out the two dark funnels plowing across the desert, though. Attacking from the north.

I hope my mother's ready. They'll hit her position before ours.

Sweat streaks down my spine as the funnels unravel on the outer edge of the wind farm, vanishing into clouds of sand and dust. The Stormers' first command licks through the icy air, echoing off the whipping drafts. I've never heard a call so loud. It sounds like bits and pieces of the three languages. Nothing more than gibberish.

But the winds understand.

All around me they change direction, swooping and ducking and diving in unnatural patterns, searching us out.

Probes.

Unlike any probes I've seen. They dip and dart on a whim, almost like they're seeking movement or heat.

Is that possible?

I duck as a probe beelines for me. It misses my head by inches. Another rushes for my legs and I jump to avoid it, barely recovering my balance when I land. I glance at Vane and see he's faring no better. The winds whip and twist around him, making him dive and leap and dance to avoid them.

What kinds of tricks has Raiden taught his warriors?

I dodge another probe and lose my footing, barely catching one end of the platform as I fall. My muscles tear, and I barely suppress my scream as my shoulder dislocates. But I haul myself up and twist into the position the Gales taught me, wrapping my arm around my chest so I can force the bone back into the joint. My hands shake, knowing it will hurt just as much going in as it did tearing out.

Three deep breaths and . . .

The howl of the winds covers my groan as white-hot pain stabs my shoulder like a burning windslicer. When I wipe the tears from my eyes, I can feel my arm working properly again.

Before I can celebrate the small victory, there's another garbled hiss.

The winds disappear. Instantly. Like someone snapped their fingers and made a hundred winds unravel. If I hadn't seen it myself, I wouldn't have believed it.

I crouch again, squinting through the stirred-up sand, waiting for their next move.

One minute. Two minutes. Three minutes.

No attack.

Winds trickle back and my pulse starts to steady. Until I hear their songs.

I can't understand any of the words.

Something is very wrong.

Gavin screeches.

My heart stops when I spot him streaking through the sky. Heading straight for me.

No. *No!* My mother sent him home. Why would he come back?

He circles above my windmill, and I try to transmit a desperate warning: *Go. Away. Now.*

Instead, he screeches again and dives, landing on my shoulder.

My windmill explodes.

The turbine splits in half, the metal peeling like it's made of paper. Gavin flaps away as I fall through a shower of shrapnel, shielding my eyes with one arm and reaching for a draft with the other. Most of the winds feel wrong—broken—and refuse to acknowledge my call. But my fingertips reach a usable Southerly and I command it to catch me.

The ruined drafts scrape against my skin like dull blades as I float a few feet above the ground. I sink deeper into the strands of the Southerly to shield my face.

What are they doing to the winds?

It's hard to see with all the sand swirling through the air, but I catch a glimpse of Vane's blue sweatshirt stumbling toward me, not even attempting to stay out of sight.

"Duck," I shout as another wind spike blasts a windmill directly in front of him, spraying him with metal debris.

The heavy pillar cracks and wobbles, tipping toward Vane.

I scream as he scrambles away seconds before the steel pole crushes the ground. Another windmill explodes next to him, and he dives to the sand and misses most of the shrapnel.

I order my Southerly to drop me near Vane, but another wind spike whooshes toward me and I barely manage to duck. The force spins me into a windmill and stars flash in front of my eyes as my head cracks against the metal. The pain breaks my concentration, and the wind holding me streaks away.

There are no healthy winds to call. My breath is knocked out of me as I crash to the sand.

"Audra!" Vane screams. He sounds far away, and I can't tell if it's because the winds are so loud or because he's been pulled away. Or maybe I've been pulled away. It's hard to think through the pain.

I stumble to my feet, wiping the wetness dripping down my cheek. My hand turns red with blood, but I dry it on my pants and press forward. I feel for a draft—any draft—to call, but find only broken, useless winds.

The Stormers crippled the air.

Crippled *me.*

I unsheathe my windslicer, shredding the eerie winds. But every draft I destroy makes the air thicker, like a fog. It clings to me, stinging like needles as it weighs me down and clouds my path. I press forward anyway. I have to help Vane.

Dozens of wind spikes explode around me, burying me in rubble. I shove myself free of the dirt, rocks, metal, and who knows what else in time to hear Vane scream.

I race toward the sound, wiping blood and dirt from my eyes and slashing the fog with the windslicer. For one second the wall of windy muck parts, and I see two figures dressed in gray drop from the sky. One on each side of Vane.

"No!" I yell, charging forward as they bind him with a thick gray coil of drafts.

A wall of arctic wind slams into me.

I slash at the draft, but it's like stabbing a waterfall. The force overpowers me. I tumble along the rocky ground, barely managing to hold on to my weapon as I drown in the vicious, broken draft.

Vane shouts my name.

I jump to my feet, only to get tossed backward by another icy blast. It pins me to a windmill, tearing my face like the draft's grown chilly thorns.

I hold the windslicer to the airstream and the winds part wide enough to show me Vane. Our eyes lock and he shouts something I can't hear—but it looks like "Don't do it."

Then the Stormers form a pipeline and shoot him out of the storm.

Gone.

A primal sob rocks me as another draft cracks against my chest like a frozen whip. I barely notice the pain.

I won't let them take him.

Everything I've worked for—sworn to—comes down to this.

My sacrifice.

The thought should shake me, but it actually fills me with calm. I wonder if my father felt the same way.

I'm ready.

I shout at the winds, begging all of them to surround me so I can surrender myself to them.

The shattered, ruined drafts won't answer my call.

There's nothing I can do. I can't surrender myself if the winds won't take me.

Tears stream down my face. I want to scream. Crumble. Collapse.

But over the roar of the storm I hear another sound.

Laughter.

I open my eyes and find a Stormer a few feet in front of me. He smooths back his dark hair and grins like a lion stalking his prey.

"Now, now, we can't have you sacrificing yourself. That would ruin everything."

He slams me with a cold, ruined Northerly. Another frozen whip, this time cracking against my face.

He laughs as I wipe blood off my cheek. "We've been chasing your windsong all over the desert, worrying we were up against some all-powerful ghost of a Gale. But you're just a scrawny little girl with the same boring trick up her sleeve as her father. Too bad for you we were ready for that play this time."

He whips me again, pummeling my chest, knocking the wind out of me. He laughs as I hack and wheeze. "Don't worry. If you want to die, that can easily be arranged."

I scream as a burst of strength fills me.

I never *wanted* to die.

I wanted to save Vane.

I *will* save Vane.

My grip tightens on my windslicer.

They can break the winds. But they won't break me.

Time to show these Stormers what kind of guardian they're dealing with.

CHAPTER 51

VANE

I expected to scream, cry—maybe even soil myself—if the Stormers ever caught me. Bravery isn't my thing.

But as the Stormer launches me away from the ground, away from Audra, away from my life, my world, I don't feel afraid.

I feel rage.

This is what they did to my parents. To countless Westerlies.

They won't do it to me.

I'm the last freaking Westerly—I can break some stupid wind bonds.

The streams of cold, semisolid air rush across my wrists and ankles, keeping me tied up and hovering in the gray-blue sky. I strain against them and they tighten. I strain harder and they tighten more. Not my most brilliant moment, but I'm desperate here.

My head's getting fuzzy, my muscles mushy. It feels like the wind bonds are wearing me down, sapping my strength. I don't know if that's possible, but I'm not about to sit around and find out.

An Easterly streaks by and I order it to slam into my bonds. It bounces off like rubber. At least it responds. I must be high enough above those creepy busted winds down in the storm. My skin still remembers the way they scraped against it, like they'd turned rough. Hard.

I guess I should've grabbed a knife before I left. I can move my arms a little—I could've stabbed the Stormer when he gets close.

Metal slicing through flesh. Blood splashing on my skin.

I suck in huge gulps of air, trying to fight the sudden nausea and dizziness.

I'm not going to get out of this with rainbows and sunshine. If it takes violence, I will pull together the guts to use it.

Not that it matters. I wasn't smart enough to grab a knife. All I grabbed was a stupid packet of pain pills.

Pills.

I twist and squirm, straining every muscle in my body trying to reach my pocket.

Dammit—why can't I be more flexible?

I shove all the air out of my lungs and contort myself into arguably the most unnatural position ever—legs up, back arched, arms stretching down. My eyes water from the pain, but my fingers slide into my pocket and feel the edge of the packet of pills.

I pinch the corner between my fingers and pull like my life depends on it—because it does. But the packet doesn't move. I wiggle my hips to loosen it, and it pulls a fraction of an inch, but not enough.

Oh God—this is going to hurt.

And I'm so tired. All I want to do is close my eyes, let my limbs relax . . .

I shake myself awake. Then I hold my breath and strain my back to bend that Last. Little. Bit. I feel something tear—and the scream that slips out of my mouth backs me up on that. But the packet comes free.

It takes more bending and straining—I swear I qualify for yoga master now—to get the packet to my teeth. I tear it open and dump the two smooth pills into my sweaty palm. My fingers close around them before the wind can sweep them away.

Now I just need a way to get the Stormers to swallow them.

I spit out the packet and try not to look as the winds toss it back and forth on its *long* way to the ground.

"I'm not going to fall," I tell myself.

"Oh, we would never let that happen," a deep, hard voice says behind me.

I hate myself for yelping.

Cold hands spin me around and I'm face to face with a Stormer. His wavy blond hair and blue eyes belong on a surfer—not on a heartless warrior in a sleek gray uniform. I never thought the Stormers would look so . . . human.

"If you're plotting escape, you can stop now," he mocks me. "There's nothing you can throw at me that I haven't anticipated."

"Wanna bet?"

"Big words for someone caught in unbreakable bonds."

He shouts something I can't understand and the bonds spread, clamping around my chest. My fist grips my pills as I cough and fight for air.

"Let. Me. Go." I know it's a stupid thing to say, but I'm pretty sure every hostage has to scream it at some point.

"No, I don't think I will."

His bulging muscles and the way he hovers in the air so effortlessly prove he's more powerful than I am. But I'm too angry to be afraid.

"I can't wait to see what Audra does to you when she gets here."

"Is that her name? Wispy thing? Acts all tough with a windslicer?" He leans close enough that his cold breath coats my face. "Not too worried about her. She's bound in a *drainer*."

Everything inside me drops like a stone. "A *drainer*?"

He grins. "Special funnel we make. The hostage can't move. Can't escape. And our hungry winds drain the life right out of them. Kind of like what your bonds are doing to you—but all over her body. She won't last long that way."

"You're lying!"

"I'll send her echo when it's over. Let you feel the loss for yourself. And don't go counting on the other one to rescue you either," he adds as I suck in air to calm my rage. "She took off like a frightened bird the second we found where you guys were hiding. We'll track her down later."

He shoves me then, sending me tumbling through the sky like a useless piece of debris. I barely notice the nausea. My head's already spinning way faster.

Audra's been captured—in a drainer?

Arella abandoned us?

My body finally stops flipping and I breathe through my nose, refusing to let the vertigo overwhelm me. It's all up to me now.

I squeeze the pills so hard they crumble.

Dammit!

Unless . . .

I pulverize what remains of the pills with one hand while my other hand searches the sky, feeling for an Easterly. I'll only get one shot at this, so I have to get it right.

I fight exhaustion as I wait for the winds to surge and let the sound drown out my whispered call. The draft coils around my wrist, and I pray the Stormer won't notice until it's too late.

I don't know the exact command for *Shove this down his freaking throat*, so I'll have to improvise.

I study his breathing, searching for the pattern.

Three.

Two.

One.

I shout, "Rush," and toss the crushed pills into the draft.

The white powder slams him in the face mid-inhale and he sucks it up. Not nearly as much as I'd hoped, but enough to make him gag.

He charges me, gripping my throat. His thick, meaty fingers dig into my skin, strangling me. Then his hands start to shake and I slip from his grasp.

"What did you do to me?" The anger in his voice fades to fear as he chokes. Hard.

Okay, choking is good. And he's scratching at his skin, like he's getting hives. But he's definitely not passing out like I'd been counting on.

Time for Plan B.

I don't know where the strength comes from, but I thrust my body in a half somersault, positioning my feet above my head. I call another Easterly and coil it around my legs.

"Rush!" I scream.

The draft launches me forward, and I strain my legs higher, lining up my aim.

The Stormer notices me a split second too early and tries to twist out of the way. But my legs are long enough to kick him in the head as hard as I can.

I try to ignore the crack-crunch sound of my shoe connecting with his skull, but the nausea still hits me.

Only shock saves me from hurling all over myself as the Stormer's head lolls back, thin lines of red trailing down one side of his face. Then the drafts holding him whisk away, and he drops like dead weight.

Dead.

Don't think about it. Don't think about it. Don't think about it.

Maybe he'll wake up before he hits the ground and stop his fall. Or maybe he'll land in a sand dune and it'll cushion the impact. Or maybe . . .

I start gagging.

I'm thinking about it.

I suck in as much air as I can, focusing on the only thought holding me together.

I had no choice.

Okay, so my guard is gone—but who knows when his evil side-kick will get here, and I'm still tied up with these life-sucking bonds in the middle of a freaking storm. Things could be better.

Deep breaths. Think.

I need a Westerly. It's the only thing I can think of that might break these stupid unbreakable bonds. I have to find a way to call one.

Come on, I know this. I've done it before.

I close my eyes and force myself to imagine Audra bound in a drainer. Feeling the same exhaustion I'm feeling, but a thousand times worse. Every second bringing her closer to death.

I shove past my pain and anger. Past my broken, scattered memories. Deep into my consciousness. My mind buzzes with warm energy and I reach for it, sinking deeper still. Beyond fear. Beyond everything.

Everything except the soft, gentle rush.

A sigh.

A single word.

Peace.

As soon as my mind touches the word, the warmth swells, shoving me up and out. Back to the light.

I open my eyes and inhale as a new voice fills my mind. A hushed, gentle whisper.

A Westerly.

Calling to me. Singing to me.

It's not like the other breakthroughs, where the winds tempted and teased and tricked me away from myself. The west wind *is* me.

And I know how to control it.

"Come to my side. Share your peace. Surge and surround me. Secure my release."

A warm, gentle draft tangles with my bonds, and the icy winds turn warm and unravel.

The celebration lasts about a second. Then I hurtle toward the ground.

The Westerlies calm my panic, whispering a song of peace and security as I call them to me and wrap them around my exhausted body. I beg them to stay—and they obey, sealing me in a warm circle of air.

A wind bubble. Just like my parents used to make.

Tears well in my eyes as I float toward the ground.

My family has never felt closer. Never felt farther away.

I try to absorb as much strength and energy from the winds as I can.

Then my feet touch the ground and the bubble bursts.

I'm back in the thick of the storm.

CHAPTER 52

AUDRA

The Stormers tossed me like a grain of sand.

I couldn't defend myself.

Their broken, useless winds wouldn't answer my call. I slashed as many drafts as I could. But they snared me.

Have they trapped my mother the same way? Or is she with Vane?

It's cold inside the vortex. I can't see. Can't move. Can't hear anything beyond the raging winds. The drafts move in unison, not woven or bound in any way, but still synchronized. Like they're all of one mind.

The funnel swallows every gust that crosses its path, leaving no winds to call for aid. No escape except death. And I feel death approaching. The winds are icy splinters, tearing me apart. Swallowing tiny pieces of me with every sweep across my skin.

Minutes pass. I lose count of how many.

My head turns fuzzy. I try to focus on the songs of the wind, but their melodies are flat. Lifeless. It breaks my heart to hear them. Their very essence has been stripped, leaving nothing but shells of the glorious drafts they once were.

Just like me.

My life never held much joy or warmth or richness—not without my father. But Vane filled my empty world with the thrill of his touch. The soothing peace of his forgiveness.

I should've kissed him when I had the chance.

I should've taken one moment of pure, unadulterated happiness for myself. Pressed my lips against his and let the intoxicating heat erupt between us. Tasted his sweetness. Then pulled him closer till there was nothing separating us but fire and skin.

Audra.

The fantasy feels so real I can almost hear his voice. Almost see the cool blue of his eyes. The warm brown of his hair. Sky and earth blended into one perfect face.

Audra.

His voice sounds louder. Closer. Real.

Have I sunk so deep into the dream I've lost track of reality?

Audra.

I want to open my eyes, but I don't have the strength. I've slipped too far away.

Audra, hold on.

I want to do what he says. But I don't know how. I'm lost to these wicked winds.

A hint of gray rims the edge of the darkness and creeps toward the center, till all the black turns dull. My windsong rings in my ears, ready to be unleashed.

The winds clench and tighten.

White light explodes around me as I feel myself slip too far away. To the end.

CHAPTER 53

VANE

'm new to the whole wind control thing, but I've never seen anything like the funnel Audra's trapped in.

The gray, chalky winds spin horizontally between the blades of
the two tallest windmills, like some possessed hammock/cocoon.
Audra hovers in the center. Pale. Still.

I scream her name. She doesn't move. Doesn't blink.

"Hold on. I'm here."

There's no sign of the other Stormer, but that doesn't mean he's
not nearby. I have to hurry.

Ruined winds fill the air, rubbing my face like sandpaper. But
their gibberish songs are mixed with some healthy drafts that have
broken through the storm. I call a Westerly to me and tangle it
around my legs.

For one second I stare at the sharp, spinning blades of the windmill and wonder if I'm losing my mind. Then I shout, "Rise," and the wind launches me off the ground.

It jerks and flips and knocks me so hard into the pillar of a windmill that I lose my hold and crash to the ground. I dust myself off and call another.

Same thing.

Audra wasn't kidding when she said windwalking takes practice.

I try again and get higher this time. High enough to almost get sliced and diced by the giant blades. I barely release the draft in time and land with a thud, bruising every part of my body.

Okay—new plan!

I grab every healthy wind I can feel and hurtle them at the vortex. They rebound without so much as a dent.

Come on, Westerlies, tell me what to do here.

I let a minute of silence pass before I give up that idea too.

Looks like I'm on my own.

I weave a wind spike and line up my aim. But I know it won't be enough. The winds binding her are ... mutated somehow. I need the power of four. It's supposed to be unstoppable, right?

If only I had any idea how to channel it.

I call a Westerly to my side and coil the draft around the spike. The universe doesn't implode, so that seems like a good sign. But I still have to combine the draft with the others, and I don't know what command to use.

Merge? Combine? Blend?

I have a feeling the difference between success and catastrophe rides on my ability to guess the right one.

Absorb? Meld? Pool? Marry?

I need a bigger vocabulary.

And then it hits me.

Converge.

The word tingles my mind. That has to mean I'm on the right track.

I smooth the Westerly strands along the wind spike, stalling.

Trust your instincts.

I force my lips to whisper the command.

The Westerly sinks into the wind spike, and the drafts spin to a blur. I jump back when the spike shoots into the air, and barely miss getting conked on the head. A crack splits down the center of the spike and I dive for cover, expecting an explosion. But it never goes boom.

It hovers in midair, twisted and blue, with sharp pointed ends. Force and energy flow through it, and when I grab it, it's soft as a feather but somehow solid too. And cold. It conforms to my grip, like it's made for me, and crackles like a lightning bolt.

I love the way it feels, like I hold the power of the wind in the palm of my hand.

Okay—time for the craziest part of the plan.

I point the weapon at one end of the vortex binding Audra and line up my aim.

Don't miss.

Man, I wish I'd practiced more with Audra. If I'm off by even a few inches . . .

And even if it works, there's no telling how the winds will unravel. They could easily fling her into the spinning blades.

My mind flashes to an image of Audra getting tossed through the windmill, shredded and splattered.

The world spins and I grip my knees to send some blood to my brain.

When my head clears, I stare at her pale body, losing life with every second I stall.

I have to do this.

I test my throw three, four, five times.

On the sixth I let it fly.

And.

It's.

Wide.

Maybe the winds knock it. Maybe I suck. But it's going to hit her. *It's going to hit her!*

I thrash my arms at the air, trying to grab it, stop it, change its course.

It has to *divert*.

"Divert," I shout in the Westerly tongue.

And it does.

It arcs left and slams the vortex where it connects to the windmill.

The gusts scream like rabid beasts, and white heat blasts me as the evil gray winds unravel. Audra plummets, and I order a Westerly to catch her, just like when we were kids. And this time I have enough control to set her down gently.

I run to her side and fall to my knees, cradling her face. She doesn't move. Barely breathes.

Her skin is beyond cold, so I wrap her in my arms and let the sparks shoot between us. "Please, Audra. Come back to me."

I crush her to my chest. Kiss the gash on her forehead. The cuts and scrapes on her cheeks. Run my lips along the raw, red scratches on her jaw. I'll make up for every pain, every wound she suffered to protect me.

My hands rub her arms, trying to generate friction.

She's still so cold.

A real kiss might warm her up.

Man—it's tempting. Her lips are right there. Drawing me toward them.

But . . . call me old-fashioned, but I kinda want her to be *conscious* for our first kiss.

I kiss her forehead again. "Please come back to me," I whisper. "I love you."

Nothing happens for a few seconds, and I choke back a sob. Then her eyes flutter.

She moans.

"Where does it hurt? What do you need?"

She twists in my lap, her back arching like she's in pain, and moans again. More of a groan, actually.

"What can I do?" I beg.

She turns back to me and her eyes focus on mine.

Her face crumples. "I thought I'd never see you again."

I pull her against me. "We're safe."

I rock her back and forth, feeling my hope grow as the warmth returns to her skin.

"What about the Stormers?" she asks.

I swallow bile as my mind imagines the blond Stormer's broken, lifeless body somewhere out there.

"I took care of one."

She jerks away from me, wincing like she's just gotten the mother of all head rushes. "Where's the other?"

"I don't know. I haven't seen him since I got free. I'm guessing he's long gone."

"Guess again," a low, vicious voice snarls behind us.

My heart feels ready to explode as I turn to face the gray-clad figure. He has dark hair and light eyes and a jaw so square you could use his chin as a ruler.

He smirks. "Thought I'd sit back and see what the last Westerly can do, in case you clam up like the others when we interrogate you. And I must say, that little toy you have there is quite impressive." He points to the wind spike, which fell a few feet away from me. It didn't explode like the others. It must be too strong.

"Come," I order it in Westerly, and it shoots to my hand. Cool— a voice-controlled weapon. No wonder Raiden wants the power of four.

But he's not getting it.

I point the spike at the Stormer's head.

"Put it down, son, and I'll make this a lot easier for you," he tells me.

"Or . . . ," I say as I stand. Audra tries to stand too, but her legs collapse. I step in front of her, shielding her. "How about you leave now and I won't run you through with this?"

I hold the edge of the spike out so he can see the way it glistens along the edge, like a real sword.

"It's fun to watch you play soldier. But you forget that I know your kind. I've been with Raiden for all the Westerly interrogations. Violence isn't in your blood, boy."

"Your partner might disagree. Or he would if he weren't dead." My voice shakes on the word and my vision dims, but I fight for control.

The Stormer falters. Then he shakes his head. "If that's true, it must've been an accident. You think you have the stones to stab me? Spill my blood all over the ground?"

My arms shake.

He grins. "Typical Westerly. So let's stop pretending there's even the slightest chance you'll do any harm with that toy."

"It's not a toy," I shout, getting seriously pissed. The callous way he talks about the murders he's witnessed—helped with—makes me gag.

"Vane, give me the weapon," Audra orders. She can barely hold out her hand, but I know she means it.

"How cute, your little girlfriend wants to play too. And I'm sure she could at least make good on her threats—if she weren't half dead right now." He winks at Audra. "Don't worry, we'll get you the rest of the way before the day is over."

Some sort of strangled roar erupts from me.

"Ooh, he doesn't like it when I'm mean to his girlfriend." The Stormer moves a step closer and I adjust my aim. Straight at his heart—assuming he even has one.

He rolls his eyes.

Then he grumbles a string of words I can't understand and whips out his arms. A chain of broken gray Northerlies tangle around me like a lasso. I slice them with my spike and they unravel.

He frowns. "Like I said, your toy is quite impressive. Hand it over, come quietly, and I'll let your girlfriend live."

"Don't even think about it, Vane!" Audra shouts.

I ignore her. "How do I know you won't kill her the second I'm restrained?"

"I guess you'll just have to trust me."

"Then I guess you're an idiot."

He growls. Then, with a blur of motion, he grabs the windslicer from his belt and launches it at Audra. I lunge and slash it. The sword explodes, peppering the ground with tiny needles.

"I can do this all day," I warn him, tossing my spike between my hands.

His eyes narrow. "Fine. I give you my word."

"Not good enough. If you want a deal, you'll let me launch her safely out of here in a pipeline and then I'll turn myself in."

"No," Audra shouts. She fumbles, trying to get up. Trying to stop me.

I move away from her. Closer to the Stormer, careful to keep the spike trained on him.

"Do you think you intimidate me?" he asks. "You forget, I've watched your kind let us torture their wives—their kids—and do absolutely nothing to stop us. You're gutless weaklings by nature. Nothing changes that."

He stares me down. Daring me to prove him wrong—knowing

I won't. Can't. It's all a game to him. And I'm tired of playing.

I raise my spike, aiming it between his eyes. "Let. Audra. Go."

My hands shake. My voice shakes. But I mean it.

"I'm done with this!" he yells.

His body's a blur, his next words a mystery, but I know whatever he's doing is going to kill Audra. Break me so I'll have no fight left to resist him.

I watch my arm swing back, almost like it's attached to someone else. It's easier to think of it that way.

It's someone else aiming the weapon at his heart. Someone else letting it fly at just the right point in the toss. Someone else running him through with a revolting squish of flesh and blood.

Someone else.

But it's me who screams. Me who collapses, shaking. Me who can't get the question out of my head—the one I don't want to know the answer to, but have to ask anyway.

What have I done?

CHAPTER 54

AUDRA

I scream as I claw my way to Vane's side. It all happened so fast, I couldn't tell who fell first, or why.

He's not dead. He can't be dead. Please. Be. Alive.

My hands reach him then, and he's still warm. He's curled up on his side, shaking. But he's alive.

Tears fill my eyes as I search his face, his chest—everywhere—for blood, a wound. He's perfect. No injuries.

Then I see the Stormer.

The twisted wind spike sticks out of his chest at a jagged angle. Thick, syrupy blood streams in rivers as parts of the wound disintegrate and float away with the wind. His eyes are glazed. His mouth twisted in a snarl. Cruel even in death.

My stomach heaves.

Vane groans.

It hits me then. *Vane did this.*

A *Westerly* did this.

I pull him closer, whispering, "Shhhhh." Trying to calm him.

He shivers harder, his teeth chattering. I wrap my arms around him and press as much of myself against him as I can to warm him. Fire shoots between us, and his eyes clear enough to meet mine.

He shatters into sobs. Low, deep wails of pain and terror.

I pull his head against my shoulder. Stroke his hair. Cling as tight as I can, afraid if I let go he'll crumble into a million pieces and never put them back together.

The storms slowly calm and the clouds clear, bringing back the sun. Normal winds surround us, singing of hope and relief. But Vane still feels like ice.

How long can he stay like this?

"It's okay," I whisper. "It's okay. You didn't do anything wrong."

He groans into my chest.

"I mean it, Vane. You didn't do anything wrong."

He shakes his head, and the motion rocks his whole body. I squeeze him tighter.

I can't imagine what he must be feeling. I've never killed anyone— and I'm not a Westerly.

I have to say something. Help him. But what magical combination of words will make him okay again? Bring back the funny, obnoxious boy I've grown to love?

Love.

I haven't let myself love anyone—not since my father died.

But I love Vane Weston. And I won't lose him. I can't. I won't be able to survive it.

I try to make him look at me, but his eyes are distant. Lost.

"You saved us, Vane. You made the greatest, most wonderful sacrifice anyone has ever made. You saved me."

My voice leaves me. I'm overwhelmed by what he did for me. By his proximity. By everything.

He doesn't move. His eyes stay glazed.

My stomach knots as I realize what he needs. I'm afraid to say it, but I take his shaking hands and coil our fingers together.

He has to be *Vane* again.

"I love you," I whisper.

Something pulls in my chest as the words leave my lips, but they taste sweet.

True.

"I've tried so hard not to love you that I've driven us both crazy. But I love you. And I don't want to lose you. So please come back to me. Please don't leave me."

My voice hitches and I choke back a sob. "I need you. I've never needed anyone—but I need you."

I stroke his face as my words trail to silence.

Silence.

His sobs have stopped. So has his shaking.

I hold my breath as I meet his eyes, afraid of what I might see.

Vane stares at me. Unsure. Weary.

But it's him again.

My turn to cry.

He reaches up, smoothing my hair. Wiping my tears.

"I really thought I lost you this time," I whisper. "I've lost you so many times, so many different ways. I can't do it again."

"You won't have to," he promises.

Yes, I will.

He puts his finger on my lips, stopping me before I can say it out loud.

"Whatever you're going to say, let me say something first." He takes a ragged breath and sits up on his own, wiping the sand from his face.

He takes my hands. "I'm barely holding it together right now— and the only thing keeping me from losing it all over again is you. So I don't care about laws or oaths or betrothals. I care about you. I *need* you."

We stare at each other, neither daring to move. Holding our breath.

"I won't force you," he tells me.

I know what he's asking me to do—and I want to do it. Oh, how I want to.

But can I? Should I?

I study his hands. His eyes. His mouth.

There are so many things about him I want. But that's it. I want *him*. All of him.

Who has the right to keep us apart? To tell us it's wrong? That we don't belong together, when everything about us proves we do. There's something between us—something deeper than the Gales. Than our laws. Than my oath.

I'm tired of denying it.

So I lean forward. His hands cup my face, soft enough that I can pull away if I want to.

I don't want to.

I close my eyes and take one more breath. Then I press my lips against his.

CHAPTER 55

VANE

All the times I imagined this moment, I never got it right.

Her lips are sweeter and softer, and they fit against mine like we were formed that way. Everything about us matches. Our breathing. Our movements. And the heat. The delicious fire that ripples through my body before it rushes back to hers.

She clings to me as hard as I cling to her, her hands sliding down my back as I grab her waist and press her against me, so there's no space between us. I'll never let anything separate us again.

Now I know why they call it "bonding."

As we burn and connect, parts of her meld to me. Her strength. Her determination. Her honor. They flow to the cracks in my heart and fill them. Heal the places the violence crushed and shattered. Make me whole. I know I'm doing the same for her.

We were two broken, incomplete people.

Now we're one.

No one will ever understand me the way she will.

No one will ever understand her the way I will.

And no one will be able to change that. We've melted together and been reforged into something stronger. Something better.

My hands slide back up to her face, stroking her cheeks before they move to her hair. I want to unravel her stupid braid, let the silky strands fall free so they can tickle my skin. But it's not worth breaking away. I want to stay right here, right now. Holding her against me. Our lips moving together in a perfect rhythm. Never letting go.

Audra's the one who finally pulls away—like I knew it'd have to be.

Her chest heaves as she gasps for breath, and I grin when I see her flushed cheeks. The light in her eyes. Her swollen lips.

I did that.

And God—I want to do it some more.

I cradle her face in my hands and kiss her again, slower this time. Like we have all the time in the world. Because we do. We're safe. The Stormers are gone and . . .

Memories I'm trying not to think about flash before my eyes and everything in me twists upside down and inside out. I break away, holding my head like that could wrangle my thoughts away from the horror show still replaying in my mind.

"What's wrong?" Audra asks, stroking my cheek.

Her touch calms the panic a little. "I can't. Not with . . ."

She frowns for a second, and then I see her put the pieces together. Her eyes dart to the place I'm trying not to look.

Even with the added strength from my bond to Audra, I'm not sure I can see it—him. See his lifeless, broken form. Not without going back to the dark place I sank into.

"Close your eyes," she whispers when I start to shake again.

I don't argue. I squeeze my eyes shut and press my hands against my ears. But I still feel the winds Audra calls to wrap around the body and float it far, far away.

Somewhere out there is the other Stormer I knocked from the sky. I shiver, even though the sky has cleared and the heat's beating down in full force.

I hope we never find him.

I can accept what I've done—sort of. But I know it'll haunt me forever. And I don't ever want to do it again.

Which leaves the bigger question.

I force my eyes open and take Audra's hands. "Now what?"

"I have no idea. I need to speak with my mother. I hope she isn't . . ." She looks away.

I'm glad. She misses the way my face twists with rage.

I haven't forgotten what the Stormer told me about Arella abandoning us during the fight. She made that whole big show, claiming she'd planned to back us up all along. And then she ran. *She has to be the most selfish, pathetic coward I've*—

"I'd better use the emergency call," Audra says, interrupting my venomous thoughts. "That should tell her where we are. It'll alert the Gales, too."

"Whoa—hang on. *There's an emergency call?*"

She won't look at me, and her cheeks flush.

I squeeze the bridge of my nose. "So all this time you could've just made a call to the Gales and asked for help?"

"It isn't that simple. The emergency call broadcasts our precise location for all to see. As long as Raiden didn't know exactly where we were, it would've been too dangerous to use it. But he knows we're here now, after all the turbulence we've caused."

She stands and whispers the call for an Easterly, a Northerly, and a Southerly and twists them in a pattern that feels familiar—even though I've never seen her do it before. Maybe that has something to do with our bond.

She cups her hands around her mouth and blows into the mini cyclone, then whispers, "Launch."

The funnel narrows until it looks like a piece of rope. It streaks into the sky so high I can't see where it ends.

She sits back beside me and I take her hand. "Now we wait."

I can think of a few ways we can pass the time. But I know Audra's worrying her mother won't come back.

And I'm trying to figure out what I'll say when she does.

My blood runs cold when I hear a rush of wind behind us.

"Mother," Audra says, jumping to her feet.

I stand too, grabbing Audra's hand to keep her at my side.

Arella rushes toward us. "I've been so worried."

"Really?" I hold out my free arm to block her from getting too close. "Then where have you been this whole time?"

Arella stops, looking just the right amount of annoyed and

ashamed. "I've been making my way back here. The Stormers bound me in their stripped winds and launched me into the sky. I barely managed to stop my fall, which is the only reason I survived. And they shot me so far into the desert it took me ages to make my way back."

"Ages," I repeat. "You couldn't just fly back?"

"Vane, what's wrong?" Audra asks.

"One of the Stormers told me your mom bailed on us during the fight. Ran away with her tail between her legs and left us to fend for ourselves."

"Well, obviously he lied," Arella insists without so much as blinking.

I'll give her one thing—she's a *much* smoother liar than her daughter. But she's still full of crap.

"Really? 'Cause you don't look like someone who was overpowered and flung into the middle of the desert. You don't have a scratch on you."

Arella tries to hold my gaze, but breaks eye contact first.

Guilty.

"I landed in a soft sand dune," she finally explains.

I snort. "Seriously? That's the best you've got?"

She doesn't have a speck of sand on her.

"You left us?" Audra asks her mother, though she sounds more sad than angry. "When did you leave?"

"I didn't—"

I cut Arella off before she can tell another lie. "The Stormer said she ran off as soon as they found where we were hiding—which was thanks to your stupid bird, by the way. I told you he was evil."

"Gavin's not evil," Audra says quietly, staring into the distance. The winds pick up around her and she closes her eyes.

It's an Easterly, singing of unwanted change.

Audra's eyes snap open. "Why *was* Gavin there?"

When no one answers, she turns to her mother. "You told me you'd send him home—and Gavin would *never* disobey a direct command. So why was he still at the wind farm?"

"How should I know?"

The edge to Arella's voice doesn't match the cool, indifferent stare she's giving us. Neither does the way she's rubbing nervously at the golden bracelet on her wrist.

She's hiding something.

Audra must realize it too, because she pulls her hand away from me, backing up a few steps. "Gavin never would've stayed if you'd sent him home. And he never would've flown to me under those kind of dangerous conditions, not unless . . ."

All the color drains from her face. When she speaks again, her voice is barely louder than the whipping winds. "Did you send him to me?"

"Honestly, Audra—I don't know what you're—"

"Please, Mother!" Audra takes several deep breaths before she speaks again. "You've never forgiven me for what happened to Dad. Admit it!"

Anger flashes in Arella's eyes, but whether she's mad that Audra would think that or furious that Audra figured it out is anyone's guess. "Audra—"

"The whole 'making peace' thing you said last night was just an excuse, wasn't it?" Audra interrupts. "You planned this. You wanted to use Gavin to betray me today—the same way I betrayed you. You wanted me to die, didn't you? *Admit it!*"

Before I can think of something to say to any of that, Arella starts laughing. It's a cold, mocking sound, and I can't decide if I want to tackle her or get Audra the hell away from the crazy woman.

"That's your theory?" Arella shouts. "Then you've officially lost it, Audra. You want to know the truth? Fine—I'll give you the truth. I did what you were too weak to do. I forced Vane's breakthrough. I knew it would never happen unless you were in mortal danger. So I did what had to be done. And it worked—didn't it? You speak Westerly now, don't you?"

"So you gave away our location to the Stormers—without even warning us?" It takes all my willpower not to rip the smug smile off her face. "We almost *died*. And you did it for my *breakthrough*?"

"For the key to defeating the greatest enemy our world's ever known? You bet I did. I'm a guardian, Vane. I did my job—since my daughter didn't have the courage or skill to do it."

"Guardian?" I spit the word. "You're damn lucky I had the breakthrough, because if I hadn't, Audra would be dead now and I'd be Raiden's prisoner. A real guardian would've protected us. You ran because you're weak!"

"You think I'm *weak*?"

She waves her arms, and the winds stir around us without her uttering any commands.

Audra tries to back away, but I hold our ground. I call one of each of the four winds and tangle them around my hand.

Arella gasps.

Yeah—that's right. Let's not forget who's the last freaking Westerly here.

"You may know a few tricks, but *I'm* the most powerful guardian in the Gales," she hisses like a coiled snake ready to strike.

"If you're so powerful, why couldn't you save us during the fight today? And why couldn't you save my family ten years ago?"

Arella laughs again, the sound so harsh it makes both Audra and me jump. "You want to blame someone for your parents' death? Then you'd better blame my daughter. Ask *her* what happened that day."

Audra makes a strangled sound, like she's just been kicked in the gut.

I pull her against my side, supporting her. "She already told me what happened."

Arella steps forward, a glint in her eyes. "Really? So she told you she called the wind to save Gavin after a Southerly knocked him out of the sky? That she branded the draft with her trace and didn't even have the decency to tell us so we could prepare? That she killed her father and your parents? You know all of that?"

Audra starts to shake.

"It wasn't your fault," I remind her. "It *wasn't*."

"I know," she says, surprising me with the conviction in her voice.

She pulls away from me, rounding on Arella. "I never told anyone it was a gust of wind that knocked Gavin out of the sky. And I never knew what type of draft it was. The only way you could know it was a Southerly is if you were there. And if you were there, then you *knew* the Stormer was coming—and you didn't warn Dad. Almost like . . ."

She stares at the sky, like she's watching her words hover over us, not sure what to do with any of them.

That makes two of us.

"You wanted the Stormer to find us, didn't you?" she finally whispers.

Arella hesitates before she answers.

But she knows she's trapped. So she raises a defiant eyebrow at Audra. "Yes."

CHAPTER 56

AUDRA

It wasn't my fault.

The words are so foreign—so impossible—I don't know how to wrap my mind around them. The more they swirl around my head, the more they boil into rage.

Vane tries to hold me steady, but I pull away.

"Why?" I scream at my mother. "You killed Dad. Killed Vane's parents. Let me take the blame—ruined my life! How could you do that? Why would you do that?"

"You think I killed your father?" She reaches under her uniform and pulls out my father's pendant, holding the black cord. "You think I wanted this? I *loved* him. I chose him—out of all the men who wanted me. I bonded to *him*."

She waves her link toward my face, pointing to the worn, tarnished cuff like I don't know what it means.

The winds swell with her anger and she hugs her arms to her chest. Shaking from the pain.

I'm too disgusted to feel sorry for her. "You *let* the Stormer find us. Did you send the Southerly, too? Knock Gavin out of the sky, knowing I'd save him?"

The thought makes my eyes burn and my stomach heave. The birds were *ours*—the one thing we shared. "You know how strong our connection to birds is—you knew I wouldn't be able to resist. You planned the whole thing, didn't you, so I would take the blame?"

Some small part of me wants her to deny it—wants to believe she couldn't possibly be behind all the pain and loss I've suffered for the last ten years.

Instead, she looks away. "All I wanted was my life back. Our lives back. Our beautiful house in the hills, wrapped in Easterlies that soothed instead of distressed." She swipes the skin of her arms like she's trying to sweep the winds aside. "You have no idea what I endure every second, and you don't care. No one does. Everyone only cares what my gift can do for them. Only your father understood—and when we bonded he promised he would shelter me, ease the burden as much as he could. And he did. Until *his* family came along."

She turns on Vane. "They refused to share their language, even after we gave up everything to help them. And they wouldn't fight, either. Claimed the training caused them *pain*." Her eyes darken as she hugs herself, battling another tremor. "They knew nothing of *pain*."

"Pretty sure they felt pain when they were *murdered*!" Vane shouts, holding up the winds he called, ready to hurtle them at her.

I grab his arm to stop him. He studies me for a second, then lets the winds go free.

I take a breath, trying to figure out what to think, what to feel.

The summer sun presses down on us, but my mother shivers as another draft sinks into her skin.

"I couldn't live that way anymore," she whispers. "Out in the hammering winds day and night. I pleaded with your father to give up the assignment. But he was like you. Loyal to the Gales beyond all reason. Put his oath above everything. Above *me*. So I found another solution."

My fingers curl into claws and I want to lunge for her. *"Your solution got everyone killed!"*

"No darling, that was *you*."

The words knock me back and I feel Vane steady me.

"I planned everything carefully," she insists. "I offered Raiden a deal—the Westons in exchange for my family's freedom. Sent the message hidden in a flurry and waited. I felt the moment he received it, and the winds told me he accepted. So I started sending out our location—then I'd warn everyone right before they caught up and we'd run. I wanted to convince your father that we'd always hear them coming, so he'd let his guard down. And I was careful. I found ways to tip Raiden off that couldn't be traced back to me. I knew your father wouldn't understand."

"Because you're a traitor!"

It's like she doesn't even hear me. Her mind's somewhere else as she rubs the bird on her cuff, staring into the void between us. "I did everything I could to keep my family safe. I convinced your father to start eating, so he'd be too weak to fight. I used you to give us away because I knew your father would forgive you. And I thought it would make you more obedient if you thought you were to blame."

"Obedient?" Vane shouts. "You framed your daughter—let her take the blame—"

"She *was* to blame!" My mother's hard eyes focus on me. "When the Stormer came, I'd almost convinced your father to flee—almost convinced him to abandon the Westons because we weren't strong enough to save them. But then you ran back into the storm. That's when it all fell apart. I felt you get caught. Your father went to rescue you, but the storm snared him, too. So I fought my way to the Stormer to demand he release you both and he told me he had orders to kill me."

"Serves you right," Vane spits. "In fact, I think I was there when that happened. I saw you fighting. Right before he beat you and flung you out of the storm like trash."

"He did *not* beat me."

"Really? That's not what it looked like from where I stood. You did some fancy wrist flick thing a few times and pissed him off—but he still launched you out of his way."

"*Because you distracted me!* And I hurt him in ways you can't even imagine."

The chill in my mother's voice turns my blood cold.

She scratches at her skin again, and for the first time I see the pain for what it really is. A poison sinking into her.

I'm afraid to know how far it spread.

"Vane?" I ask, barely able to form the word. "Tell me exactly what you saw."

He frowns, like he's reliving the memory. "I saw the Stormer attack your mom. At first she was losing, but then she flicked her wrist and knocked him over with the wind somehow. Then he made himself an indestructible shell of winds, so she flicked her arm and attacked the other Stormer. That's when he got pissed and launched her away so he could go help his friend."

Spots dance behind my eyes and I don't want to hear any more. But I have to know. "Why did you think there was another Stormer?"

"I heard a guy cry out somewhere in the distance after she flicked her arm. Who else would it be?"

I wobble on my feet, wishing I could drop to the ground and never get up again. Anything to not have to tell Vane the truth.

"There was only one Stormer," I say, forcing myself to look at my mother. She's staring me down, like she knows what I'm thinking and is ordering me not to say it. But she can't hide her secret anymore.

I've always wondered how things went so wrong that day—how two trees could accidentally impale Vane's parents after they'd been captured. The Stormer never would have let anything happen to Raiden's precious cargo.

But with a flick of her wrist my mother could've sent those jagged boughs anywhere she pleased.

"You killed the Westons, didn't you?" I whisper.

Vane sucks in a breath.

My mother doesn't even flinch before she responds. "I betrayed Raiden the same way he betrayed me."

Her words form a storm in my head, twisting and pounding as I fight them, block them—refuse to accept them. But truth always finds a way to sink in.

I search my mother's face for any sign of guilt or regret—or even madness brought on by her poisonous gift.

But she looks . . . blank.

And her voice is unashamed when she adds, "They never would have survived Raiden's interrogation. They were as good as dead anyway."

"That's only because you helped them get captured!" Vane screams.

"They didn't deserve my protection," she snaps back. "They were *weak*—and weak by *choice*. I was done worrying about them. All I wanted was to get my family out of there. And that's what I tried to do. But my husband wouldn't leave *you*. He sacrificed himself to save a worthless little boy." She lunges for Vane.

I yank him out of her reach and shove her back, clawing her skin as I do.

My mother laughs as she stares at the bloody trails I've left on her bare arms.

Laughs.

The cold, empty sound shatters the last of the illusions she's wrapped around herself, showing me who she really is—or has become.

A murderer.

She must see the realization on my face because her eyes narrow and she reaches up, tearing out the knots of her braid and letting her hair fall free. "I guess this means we're done pretending. And I'm done protecting you."

"*Protecting me?* You've done nothing but belittle and ignore—"

"Not you, Audra—you've already gotten more than you deserved when you inhaled your father's gift. But I have been protecting *him.*"

Vane barks a laugh, sounding very close to unraveling. I grip his arm to stop him as he advances toward her.

"Why *did* you protect him?" I ask.

"Raiden wanted me dead. I couldn't risk losing the support of the Gales. Besides, Vane has what Raiden wants. So I erased his memories in case he saw too much and hid him away. Let you watch over him so you'd stay out of my sight—and voted against you being a guardian so you'd push him as hard as possible to prove me wrong. Waited for his Westerly breakthrough. And now it's *finally* happened. I can finally take my revenge against Raiden."

"I'll never help you," Vane growls, reaching for the wind.

"Oh, I think you will," she tells him. "I know how to get through to you."

My mother's a blur of motion as a jagged piece of windmill launches at me, missing my skull by inches.

It takes me about two seconds to process the fact that my mother just tried to kill me. Then I shove Vane out of the way and launch a crusher.

The thick funnel slams into her, squeezing her at the waist—making her eyes bulge. But my mother weaves a wind spike and stabs the winds, breaking free.

She launches the spike at Vane.

I tackle him and the spike streaks over our heads as we crash to the sandy ground. Dirt and debris rain around us.

"You okay?" I ask, scanning him for wounds.

"Yeah. You?"

I hear the next wind spike coming and roll us out of the way. Sand explodes everywhere.

"You're just as hopelessly in love as he is, aren't you?" She blurs again as she launches another spike. Vane barely scrambles away in time. "Maybe *you* should have to feel what it's like to lose what you care about most!"

Vane starts to call the wind to our side, but I place my hand over his lips to silence him.

I don't want him fighting anymore.

Besides—this is my battle.

I jump to my feet, launching another crusher at my mother in the same motion.

She dodges the funnel with unnatural grace and speed.

"What's your plan here, Audra? You can't match me—even with your father's gift. I was always the more powerful one." She flicks both wrists, flinging more windmill debris. I barely manage to dodge in time. "You can't stop me."

She's right. Her gift gives her the upper hand in any fight.

But she's also wrong.

She doesn't know *my* secret.

Vane and I bonded. And when we melded together, he filled my mind with a single word—a word I didn't understand until right now.

Peace.

I know Westerly.

I've never heard of a bond allowing people to share languages. But for us, it did.

So I weave the nearest Westerly into my next vortex and hurtle it at my mother with all the force I can manage. Then another. And another.

One for the Westons.

One for my father.

One for Vane.

She collapses, covering her head, screaming from the pain as the whipping winds tear her clothes, her hair, her skin. Red rivers of blood streak from her face and congeal in the sand. Still I hammer her, unleashing ten years of pent-up rage. I rip my father's pendant from her neck. She doesn't deserve to mourn for him.

This. Ends. Now.

I stare at my mother's dirty, bloody, unconscious face as I weave the four winds into a spike, just like the one Vane made before. It feels cold in my hand.

Deadly.

I raise it over my mother's heart.

CHAPTER 57

VANE

For a second I'm too stunned to move.

Audra speaks Westerly?

Then reality sets in, and I scramble to my feet.

She's hurt and angry and has every right to rage out on her mother. But I throw myself on her, knocking the wind spike free.

I pin her arms as she thrashes for freedom.

"Hey," I breathe. "It's me, okay? It's me."

She slows, just enough to really look at me, and her fury fades.

"There's my girl."

"Let me go, Vane—I have to—"

"Murder your mother? I know she deserves it, but do you really think you could live with yourself? You speak Westerly, Audra. You think you could deal with that?"

"I'm an Easterly."

"But you're part of me now too. So you better think it through very carefully, because you're seconds away from seriously screwing up your life. Which I'd rather you didn't do. I'm kinda looking forward to us being together. Making out all day. Taking a break for dinner. Then making out again all night. But if you want to waste all of that on her—if she's worth that . . . I won't stop you."

I let go of her shoulders.

She looks away. Tears pool in her eyes.

"I know. Believe me—I know. She killed my family too." I punch the ground as I say it, then try to swallow the rage. "It's not worth it. It's not."

I stare at the bracelet on my wrist—all I have left of my parents after Arella stole them from me—and wonder if that's really true. But the arrow on the compass still points west, reminding me of my heritage.

Violence isn't the answer.

Audra rolls to her side and curls her legs into her chest. I pull her against me as she sobs. I stroke her face, her arms. Wipe away the tears, the dust, the dried blood. Try to make her better.

After who knows how long, she finally looks up at me. Her eyes are puffy and red—but she's still gorgeous. "Now what?" she whispers.

I have a feeling that question is going to keep haunting us.

"The Gales are coming here, right?"

She nods.

"Then I think you should leave." I point to her mother's crumpled body. "Do you really want to be the one to tell them what your mother did?"

She glances at Arella—then immediately away, covering her mouth with her hand, like she's feeling sick. "They'll need to question me anyway."

"Why? I can explain everything. Please let me take care of this for you. It won't be easy to testify against your mom. Especially since I'm guessing your army has a pretty serious punishment for murderers."

She cringes at the word, and her voice trembles as she says, "They'll trap her deep in the earth, starve her from the drafts, until her wind form withers and crumbles. I hear it's a pain far worse than death."

I squeeze her hands. "She deserves it."

She doesn't say anything.

I give her a minute to collect herself, but I can't take my eyes off the sky. The Gales could be here any second. "You've been through enough, Audra. Let me handle this."

"But I'm your guardian. If they think I abandoned you—"

"I'll tell them you're looking for the other Stormer. Making sure he's . . ."

I can't say it.

I focus on the winds, letting the Westerlies' peaceful song calm me.

"Are you going to tell them about us?" Audra whispers.

"No."

She sighs with relief, like I've given the right answer. But then she tenses. "My mother knows."

"How? She didn't *see* anything. Besides, would they really believe a criminal over us?"

"No," she admits after a second. She still looks nervous, though.

"We'll figure it out," I promise. "I just need to think through a few things."

I'm still trying to wrap my head around the whole bonding thing, but . . . I have a feeling Audra and I were already connected somehow.

When Audra and I were kids and clung to each other after the storm, something passed between us. A rush of heat. Kind of like what happened today when we kissed—but totally different, too. More like we were drawing strength and support from each other.

Could that be another kind of bond?

It would explain the sparks we feel when we touch, and the way I've been able to see her in my dreams.

And it would mean Audra did nothing wrong today by kissing me. We were already connected, long before the Gales made their little betrothal.

I'm just not sure if that's true. Or possible.

"You should go," I tell her, helping her sit up.

"You're sure you'll be okay?"

"I'll be fine. In fact, I'm looking forward to finally meeting these Gales of yours. I have a few bones to pick with them."

She gives a sad smile. "Don't get yourself exiled."

"Please—I'm the last Westerly. I'm gold."

Her smile fades.

"I'll be fine." I cup her cheek, pulling her face toward me. Ready to kiss her goodbye.

At the last second I shift and kiss her forehead. It's not time to say goodbye. I'll never say goodbye again.

"I'll see you soon," I whisper.

"How will you get home? You won't be able to fly that far."

"I'll have one of the Gales give me a lift. They owe me. Just go. Clean yourself up. No offense—but you kinda need it."

She smiles for real this time, and shoves me. "You're pretty filthy yourself."

"You love that about me."

Her face turns serious. "I do."

My heart swells, and I'm ready to change my mind and kiss her goodbye like she's never been kissed goodbye before. But she calls a group of Easterlies to her side. Our eyes hold as she wraps the drafts around her and floats slowly away.

Audra's mom doesn't stir, but I coil a couple of Westerlies around her hands and feet just to be safe. Then I squat in the shade of a windmill and watch the sky. The winds whip around me, filling the air with songs asking the same question in my head.

What now?

I don't know.

But . . . maybe I don't need to know. I love Audra. She loves me. We survived the storm. We finally know the truth about our pasts.

Isn't that enough?

"Who are you?" a man's voice asks, and I nearly pee my pants.

I turn to face a tall man wearing the same black uniform as Audra.

A Gale.

His dark, shoulder-length hair has an intricate braid running down one side of his narrow, wide-eyed face—but half of his hair remains loose. Maybe that means he's special. Which would be awesome because I have some demands for him.

"Vane Weston," I say, standing and offering a hand to shake. "Maybe you've heard of me?"

His eyes widen, and he turns to Arella's unconscious form. "What happened?"

"Better have a seat. You and I have a *lot* to talk about."

CHAPTER 58

AUDRA

didn't plan to return to my mother's house. I never wanted to see it again. But the winds seemed to steer me here. Like there's something they want me to find.

I stand in the shade of the oak where I swore my oath to the Gales. The oath I've now broken.

What will I do without its rigid structure guiding my life?

What do I have left?

Vane.

I feel like I should add a question mark to the end of his name. Every thought around him is a question.

How can we be together?

How do I let him in?

How do I have anything normal, when my life's been shredded

to bits, turned inside out, painted different colors and reassembled in an order I don't recognize?

How?

The heat starts to suffocate me, so I make my way to the dark, creaky house. My mother's trace hangs so heavily in the air it's like she's here.

A ghost. A shadow. Following my every step.

My hands graze the cold walls as I move down the empty hall. Guiding me to the one thing I have to see.

The wind chimes hang over the table, still and silent. Suffocated.

I reach up and slide them off the hook, my eyes burning as the chimes tinkle from the motion. I run my fingers over the intricate etchings my father made on the graceful blackbird.

This was how he saw my mother.

Beautiful.

Wild.

Perfect.

Sobs choke me as I remove his pendant from my pocket, and my tears drip on the black cord. But it doesn't hurt to let them out. For the first time, I'm glad he's gone. He doesn't have to see her for who she really is.

Or maybe he knew.

Maybe he saw something during the storm. Maybe that's why he sent his gift to me instead of her. He knew I would use it for good.

I'll never know for sure.

But I hope not.

I drape the pendant around the blackbird's neck and knot the cord tight. Let him rest with the version of her he loved.

Now it's time to set him free.

I kick the dust off my feet as I retreat down the hall and cross the threshold. Then I close the door on that chapter of my life and step into the winds.

The air is full of Easterlies, and when I concentrate, I hear one singing the song I always listen for. The song I sometimes believe is my father's windsong.

I raise the chimes to the winds and hook them from the porch's eaves, letting the tinkling melody join in the chorus. The soft, familiar sound fills the air, and I realize I'm asking myself the wrong question.

Not *How?*

When?

I don't know the answer to that, either. But I know it's not now. And that makes all the difference.

I've been caged and silenced for ten years.

It's time for me to sing.

I reach up and unravel my braid, letting my hair fall loose. The wavy strands hurt as I smooth them against my scalp. But the pain only lasts a minute. Then I'm free.

I slip my jacket off my shoulders and run my hands over the thick fabric.

I'm not a guardian anymore. It's time to be *me*—whoever that is.

So I call three Easterlies and give each draft a single word to hold as I coil them around my jacket. I wrap the package tight—then send it to the sky and let the wind carry it away.

Vane will understand.

I hope.

Tears well in my eyes, but I blink them back.

This is my choice. The first choice I've made for me—and only me—in as long as I can remember.

The second comes now.

I call the Easterly laced with my father's song and coil it around me, ready to let it sweep me into the clouds. But it's not what I need anymore.

I send it away and reach for a Westerly.

The smooth, gentle draft rushes across my skin and I open my mind to its unfamiliar song.

It sings of rest. Of hope.

I beg the draft to take me away, humming along to the melody, like when I used to sing with my father.

I don't know where I'm going. But it's time to find my peace.

CHAPTER 59

VANE

My little chat with the guardian ran longer than I planned. He didn't want to accept that his Gales don't get to run my life anymore. But then I showed him a few of my newly discovered tricks and he realized he didn't have the power to control me. Not to mention, the Gales need me—now more than ever. So I got to make a few demands, number one of which was an immediate termination of my betrothal.

I didn't tell him why—and I don't care if he guesses. All that matters is that he agreed.

I also get to stay with my parents.

That one he agreed with right away—said it was important to appear strong. No more running. No more hiding. The Gales will set up base in the dunes nearby to support me. But now that I've had the fourth breakthrough, it's time to make a stand. They expect Raiden to lie low for now, anyway. He'll wait to see what I can do, how powerful I am, before he attacks again.

So I'm safe.

Sorta.

Which is probably the best I'll get, as far as Raiden is concerned. Until he's gone. And the Gales still expect me to be the one to take him down. I don't know what to do with that crazy piece of information, but I've decided it doesn't matter. I'll deal with it when the time comes. Not a second sooner.

The sun has set and the sky glows with oranges and reds when I'm dropped off in my front yard. The house is dark. I need to call my parents and tell them I'm safe—that they can come home. But not until I talk to Audra.

I check inside, half-hoping I'll catch her in the middle of a shower. Or stretched out in my bed. But the rooms are silent. Empty.

I roll my eyes at Audra's stubbornness and take off toward the trees. If she thinks I'm going to let her sleep in a roach-infested pile of dead leaves tonight, she's lost her mind.

The grove is quiet as I run. Too quiet.

I call for her when the pale, broken walls of her house come into view.

She doesn't answer.

I slow to a stop and focus on the winds, reaching for her trace. Our bond makes the connection so strong, I feel a physical tug in my gut, drawing me to her. But it's pulling me two ways. A small, weak part of me is lured toward the burned-down house. The rest of me is drawn away. I can't tell where or why. But it's somewhere west. Far beyond my reach.

"Audra," I call again.

Still no response.

Leaves—or maybe bugs—crunch under my feet as I enter the house, and it's the only sound filling the empty, lifeless space. Until Gavin screeches.

My heart stutters and I curse the stupid bird as he flaps his wings from his perch on the windowsill. His beady orange eyes look almost red as they watch me, and I have no doubt he's wondering the same thing I am.

Where's Audra?

That's when I notice the bubble of winds floating in the corner.

Her trace is laced through every draft, and something dark hovers in the center. My stomach knots.

I step closer, telling myself it isn't what I think it is. But I can see the gold buttons glinting through the rushing air.

Maybe this is some elaborate Windwalker striptease, I try to convince myself as I reach through the winds to grab the jacket. But I can feel everything inside me sink as the winds uncoil and brush my face. They whisper the three words she left me as a message.

Be. Home. Soon.

I know her too well to miss her meaning. Especially since I can still feel her pull in the wind. Slipping farther west with every second.

I fling the jacket across the room.

How could she leave without saying goodbye? Without letting me beg her to stay?

Pain shoots through my hand as I punch the wall, but it's easier to take than the empty ache tearing me apart.

I sink to the floor as Gavin flies to a nearby tree—away from the crazy boy freaking out.

"Why would she leave?" I ask the night, the wind, the stupid bird.

Nobody answers.

Then my eyes wander to the crumpled pile of leaves—the bed she's slept in for ten years. I inhale the sticky, dusty air she's sweat in every day while I relaxed in my air-conditioned bedroom.

She's made nothing but sacrifices for me. Can I blame her for needing a break from it all? Even from me?

I can. But I'll *try* to understand.

Plus, she left me a promise.

Be home soon.

She's coming back. *Soon.*

I touch her trace in the air, drawing comfort from the gentle tugging in the pit of my stomach. She's tethered to me. Permanently connected. It won't be hard to find her if I want to track her down.

But I'll wait.

And hey—at least I'm not the only one she left behind.

I glare at her dumb bird and he glares back at me. At least she ditched him, too. Though, now I'm stuck with her annoying pet.

Gavin flaps and screeches, like he's thinking the same thing.

I roll my eyes.

Then I call a passing Westerly and add my own words to its song. I tie the draft to her trace and send the wind away, letting it reach her at its own pace.

I'll miss you.

I've waited ten years for her.

I'll wait as long as it takes.

I hope she finds what she's looking for. Until she does, I'll be here. Alone, under the calm sky. Waiting for the wind to return.

ACKNOWLEDGMENTS

never planned to write this book—and when I grabbed my laptop at four a.m. and started recording the angsty, sarcastic voices that had been keeping me awake, I never thought I would let anyone read it. This was my secret project, just for fun and just for me, and the only reason that changed was because of the help and support of *many* amazing people.

First and foremost, my wonderful husband, Miles. Thank you for your patience, for eating takeout almost every night, and for not getting (too) freaked out by the fact that I was spending a large amount of time with an imaginary hot boy. Most especially, thank you for always finding a way to make me smile and for all the emergency cupcake deliveries.

I also must thank Mom and Dad for always believing in me, and the rest of my friends and family (you know who you are) for being you, and for bearing with me as I struggle to keep up with my hectic schedule.

To Laura Rennert, my ineffable literary agent, thank you for your incredible guidance and for being there to build me up, answer my questions, or tell me to relax—whichever I need most. I'm not sure the world has enough tea to keep you adequately caffeinated for tackling my abundant e-mails, but I adore you for keeping up with them anyway!

I also must thank Lara Perkins, the rest of the Andrea Brown Literary team, Taryn Fagerness, and Sean Daily for taking care of the many complicated aspects of this business so that I don't have to.

To Liesa Abrams Mignogna, where do I even begin? I could *not* have handled launching two series if you weren't my editor. Thank you for making every deadline, every marathon writing session, even copyedits feel easy and fun (well . . . okay, maybe *not* copyedits . . .) and for helping me shape my stories into what they *should* be. I still can't believe that I get to work with such a talented editor *and* call her my friend. Wonder Twin powers, activate!

I also want to thank everyone—seriously, *everyone*—at my amazing publisher, Simon & Schuster, for their enthusiasm, support, and general awesomeness, especially Katherine Devendorf, Jennifer Klonsky, Bethany Buck, Mara Anastas, Anna McKean, Carolyn Swerdloff, Lucille Rettino, Paul Crichton, Mary Marotta, and the entire sales team. I am so deeply grateful for how hard you all work to bring my books into the world. Tremendous thanks also go to Guillian Helm for her spot-on notes, to Angela Goddard for designing my breathtakingly beautiful cover, to Brian Oldham for his gorgeous photography, and to Brian Oldham and Megan Scalise for bringing Vane and Audra to life.

To Sara McClung and Sarah Wylie, thank you for telling me I wasn't crazy when I finally got brave enough to send you a sample, and for cheering me on as I pushed way beyond my comfort zone to tell this story right. I truly could not ask for better CPs—though it might be nice if one of you changed your name. I don't get nearly enough sleep to keep the whole Sara(h)s thing straight!

To Myra McEntire, thank you for giving me the last nudge I needed to send pages to my agent (and to Myra's children: Sorry about that tardy slip!). I also have to thank C. J. Redwine for insisting that I keep writing through the hard times, Elana Johnson for a lightning-fast critique, Faith Hochhalter for being the perfect cheerleader and a never-ending source of wisdom, and Tashina Falene for helping me create the jewelry pieces described in the book. And to the brilliant Ellen Hopkins, thank you for pushing me to convert the draft to present tense. I may have cursed you as I did it (a *lot*), but you made the book so much stronger.

To Becca Fitzpatrick and Kiersten White, thank you for taking time out of your insanely hectic schedules to read my book. You truly know how to make a girl feel like a rock star. And Karsten Knight, thank you for suffering through our daily title chats and for finally coming up with *the one*. (Also, for everyone who participated in The Great Title Debate of 2011, thank you for not killing me!)

To the amazing ladies of Friday the Thirteeners: Erin Bowman, Elsie Chapman, Brandy Colbert, Renee Collins, Alexandra Duncan, J. R. Johansson, Mindy McGinnis, Ellen Oh, Megan Shepherd, April Tucholke, Kasie West, and Natalie Whipple, thank you for the laughs, the support, and the always entertaining e-mail chains. I also want to thank the Apocalypsies, the Bookanistas, and the WriteOnCon team, as well as my brunch buddies Lisa Cannon, Debra Driza, Kirsten Hubbard, Nikki Katz, Andrea Ortega, and Cindy Pon. Thank you, Dustin Hansen, for being my go-to tech guy; Courtney Stallings-Barr, Matthew MacNish, and Shannon O'Donnell for being such loyal blog followers and friends; and Lisa Mantchev for our endless e-mail chains, most of which make me snort-laugh (and crave baked goods like, whoa!).

I also have to thank 30 Seconds to Mars, Anberlin, Jack's Mannequin, Lifehouse, Linkin Park, Mae, Muse, Paramore, Something Corporate, The Spill Canvas, Trust Company, and Vedera for creating the music that inspired so much of this story. This book truly wouldn't exist without your hauntingly powerful songs.

To everyone at SCIBA, thank you for letting me crash your events for so many years and for being some of my earliest supporters. And thank you Katie Bartow, Alyson Beecher, MG Buehrlen, and Kari Olson for going above and beyond with everything you do to promote my books.

Really, I have such an amazing online support group, I wish I had space to personally thank you all. But alas, these acknowledgements are reaching epic length, so I'll finish with a huge thank you to everyone who follows me on Facebook, Twitter, my blog, or any of the other places I ramble on the Internet. Thank you for laughing at my shenanigans and so generously giving your time to support my books. You all totally blow me away!

(What? I had to make at least *one* wind pun!)

The story continues in . . .

"Charged and romantic—a whirlwind of a love story."
—BECCA FITZPATRICK, *New York Times* bestselling author of
The Hush, Hush Saga, on *Let the Sky Fall*

LET
THE
STORM
BREAK

SHANNON MESSENGER

BOOK TWO IN THE SKY FALL SERIES

CHAPTER 1

VANE

I t sucks to be king.

Maybe it wouldn't be so bad if I got a castle and servants and my face on a bunch of money.

But no, I get to be the king of a scattered race of mythical creatures that no one's ever heard of. And they expect me to swoop in and defeat the evil warlord who's been tormenting them for the last few decades. Oh, and hey, while I'm at it, I can marry their former princess and restore the royal line!

Yeah, thanks, I'll pass.

I already told the Gale Force—my "army" or whatever—what they can do with their "betrothal." And I've been tempted to tell them exactly where they can shove the rest of their little plans for my life.

But . . . it's hard to stay angry when they keep giving me this desperate *you're our only hope* look. And they're all so full of stories about the things Raiden's done to their friends and families, and the horrifying battles they've fought. Risking their lives to protect *me*.

The last Westerly.

The only one capable of harnessing the power of all four winds, twisting them into the ultimate weapon.

Well, they *think* I'm the only one.

Which is the other reason I'm playing along with the whole Your Highness thing.

I have someone to protect too. And I can do that much better as Vane Weston, king of the Windwalkers.

So I'll follow their rules and train for their battles. But as soon as Audra comes back . . .

She left twenty-three days, seven hours, and twenty-one minutes ago—and yes, I've totally been counting. I've felt every second, every mile she's put between us, like our bond has claws and teeth, tearing me apart inside.

And it's been *loads* of fun trying to explain to the Gales why my guardian left me unprotected. Every day that passes makes the excuses I've given seem weaker.

I thought she'd be home by now.

I thought . . .

But it doesn't matter.

Audra promised she'd come home—and I want to give her the time she needs.

So I'll wait for her as long as it takes.

It's the only choice I have.

CHAPTER 2

AUDRA

'm not running.

I'm *chasing*.

Racing the sun across the sky, carried by the whim of the wind.

I have no plan.

No path.

No guide along this journey.

Just the whispered songs floating on the breezes, promising that hope still lingers on the horizon.

The birds circle me as I fly, dipping and diving and begging me to join their game. But they're lost to me now, like everything else. Everything except the one person I *should* be trying to erase.

I can feel him in the air.

In my heart.

In the empty ache from the space between us, mixed with the delicious sparks that still burn in my lips from our kiss.

Our *bond*.

I will not regret forging it.

But I'm not ready to face it either.

Not until I've sorted through the tatters of my life. Swept away the lies and mistakes and found someone who's more than the guardian who broke her oath.

More than the traitor who stole the king.

More than the daughter of a murderer.

The last word turns my stomach, and I'm grateful I've gone back to denying myself food and drink.

I've paid for my mother's sins every day for the last ten years.

I won't pay for them anymore.

But is locking her away enough to erase her influence? Or does it sink deeper, like one of Raiden's wicked winds, breaking me down piece by piece?

I always thought she and I were sunrise and sunset—two opposites that could never meet.

But I have her dark hair and deep blue eyes. Her connection to the birds and her stubborn temper.

I'm more like her than I ever wanted to be.

Maybe I am running.

But not from Vane.

From *me*.

CHAPTER 3

VANE

I really miss sleep.

The clock by my bed says 3:23 a.m., and all I want to do is face-plant on my pillow and close my eyes for about a year.

I drop to the floor and do push-ups instead.

Exercise is the only way to stay awake. And hey, maybe Audra will appreciate how ripped I'm getting from these late-night workouts. Though I'm not sure how much longer I can keep them up.

I haven't slept more than a few hours over the last two weeks—and it was hardly what I'd call restful.

Freaking Raiden and his freaking winds.

The Gales thought he'd wait to see how powerful I am before he made any sort of move—though they assigned me a new guardian and set up a base nearby, just in case. But after a few days Raiden found a better way to torture me.

Creepy, broken drafts keep slipping into the valley, drawn to me like heat-seeking missiles. And if they catch me when I'm asleep, they slip into my dreams and twist everything I care about into a Slideshow of Suck.

Walls and windows can't block them, and no one can find a command to keep them away. So it's either be a Vane-zombie all the time or suffer through the nightmares. I'll take zombie any day.

I've seen my friends and family tortured so brutally it's hard to look them in the eye. And Audra . . .

Watching someone hurt her is like drowning in boiling oil. I wake up screaming and soaked in sweat and it takes forever to convince myself it wasn't real. Especially since I can't hold her or see her to know she's really okay. The pull of our bond tells me she's alive, but it can't tell me if she's safe. For that I have to feel her trace. And that's not easy to do, considering my uptight new guardian, Feng—I call him Fang to annoy him—thinks the only way to protect me is to never let me out of his sight.

He's seriously insane—and I'd probably be going insane too if it weren't for Gus.

I glance at the clock, grinning when I see it's 3:32.

Gus is supposed to take over Fang's *stand outside Vane's window like a stalker* shift every night at three thirty, but I swear he shows up late just to drive Fang crazy.

Tonight he waits until 3:37.

Fang screams at him so loud it scares Gavin—Audra's stupid

pet hawk—out of his tree. But when I glance out my window, Gus is totally unfazed. He winks at me as Fang paces back and forth, waving his burly arms and shaking his head so hard, his dark, scraggly braid keeps whipping him in the cheek. The tirade goes on at least five minutes before Fang switches to the nightly update.

I stop listening.

It's always vague reports from other bases with weird names and weirder army terms, and the few times I've asked anyone to translate, it turned into yet another lecture on Why I Need to Teach Everyone Westerly. It's just not worth the fight.

I switch to sit-ups, trying to keep my energy up, and I've done 314 before Fang finally flies away. Physically, I'm rocking at my training. It's the memorizing a billion and a half wind commands that's killing me. That, and covering for Audra—though hopefully she'll be home soon and I won't have to worry about that part anymore.

If she—

I stop the thought before I can finish it.

She *is* coming back—and when she does, I can think of all kinds of awesome ways to celebrate. In the meantime I settle for making sure she's okay.

I stand and stretch, throw on the first T-shirt I find, and climb quietly out my window.

Well . . . I *try* to climb out quietly.

I can't help yelping when I scrape my arm against the pyracantha, and spend the rest of my sprint across the yard cursing my parents for planting thornbushes outside my bedroom.

"What are you laughing at, Legolas?" I ask when I make it to

Gus. He doesn't get that I'm teasing him about his blond, braided hair, and I've never explained the joke. Probably because he somehow makes the girlie hair work. That, and his biceps are bigger than my head.

"Just wondering when you're going to figure out how to jump *over* the plants, not into them."

"Hey, I'd like to see you do better—on zero sleep," I add when Gus raises an eyebrow.

Gus is, like, Captain Fitness, *and* he has a special Windwalker gift that lets him channel the power of the wind into his muscles. If he weren't such a nice guy, I'd probably hate him. A lot of the other guardians seem to, which is probably why he got stuck covering the late shift watching me. Rumor has it I'm *not* the most popular assignment. Apparently I can be difficult.

"Maybe you should try wearing the Gale uniform," Gus tells me, pulling at the long, stiff sleeves of his black guardian jacket. "It would save you a lot of scrapes."

"Yeah, I'm good."

I'm not wearing thick pants and a coat in the *desert*. Even in the middle of the night, this place feels like living inside a blow dryer.

Plus, I'm not a Gale.

I'll train with them and let them follow me around. But this isn't my life. This is just something I have to deal with.

"Off for another mystery flight?" he asks as I stretch out my hands to feel for nearby winds.

Gus never asks me where I'm going, and he's never tried to stop me.

"Make sure you stay north and west," he warns. "They're running heavy guard patrols in the south. Feng told me the Borderland Base had a disturbance yesterday."

I freeze.

"Disturbance" is the Gales' term for "attack."

"Everyone okay?"

"Three of them survived."

Which means two guardians didn't—unless Borderland is one of the bigger bases, where they keep a crew of seven.

"Don't worry—there's no sign of Stormers in the area. They're picking off all the fringes. Trying to leave us stranded out here."

Yeah, because *that* doesn't make me worry.

My voice shakes as I call three nearby Easterlies to my side, but I feel a little better when I hear their familiar songs. The east wind always sings of change and hope.

"Still don't trust me enough to use Westerly?" Gus asks. "You know I won't understand it."

I do know that.

And I trust Gus way more than I trust anyone else.

But I'm still not risking it.

My parents—and every other Westerly—gave up their lives to protect our secret language. And not just because they were brave enough to stand in the way of Raiden's quest for ultimate power.

Violence goes against our very being.

I'll never forget the agony that hit me when I ended the Stormer who'd been trying to kill Audra. Even though it was self-defense, it felt like my whole body shattered, and if Audra hadn't been there to help me through, I'm not sure I would've pulled myself back together. I can't risk letting the power of my heritage end up under the control of anyone who doesn't understand the *evil* of killing. Anyone who isn't as determined as I am to avoid it at any cost. Anyone who isn't willing to make the kind of sacrifice that might be necessary to prevent it from falling into the wrong hands.

Even the Gales—no matter how much they beg or threaten. And yeah, they've threatened. They've made it pretty dang clear that Audra's "desertion" is considered an especially serious offense right now, when they need her help so much more. But if they had the power of four on their side . . .

I still haven't figured out how to handle any of that—except to add it to my list of Things I Will Worry About Later.

"I'll be back before sunrise," I tell Gus as I wrap the winds around me and order them to *surge*. The cool drafts tangle tighter, stirring up the dusty ground as they launch me into the sky.

It takes me a second to get my bearings, and another after that to really get control. Audra hadn't been kidding when she told me windwalking's one of the hardest skills to master, and I definitely prefer letting her carry me. But it wasn't *quite* the same being carted around by Fang or Gus, and it's hard to sneak around in my noisy car. So I forced myself to learn how to get around on my own.

The first dozen times I tried, the drafts dropped me flat on my face. Then one night I had some sort of breakthrough. It wasn't like the times when Audra opened my mind to the languages of the wind—but I did hear something *new*. A voice *beneath* the voice of the wind, telling me what the gust is about to do so I can give a new command and keep control.

I asked Gus about it once and he looked at me like I was psycho, so I'm pretty sure it's something only *I* hear. Maybe something I picked up from Audra when we bonded, since I hear it best with Easterlies. Whatever it is, I'm grateful for it because it lets me fly faster and farther than even the most experienced Gales.

The lights of the desert cities blur below and I follow the streetlights lining the I-10 freeway, heading up into the mountains. It's a path I've flown dozens of times, but I still feel my insides get all bunched up as I soar over the San Gorgonio Pass Wind Farm. There are gaps in the rows of blinking red lights now. Places where windmills used to be—before Raiden's Stormers destroyed them in the fight.

Every time I relive the attack, I can't help thinking the same thing. *Soon we'll be fighting his whole army.*

The air gets cooler as I fly, and as it sinks into my skin it feels like downing a shot of caffeine. Still, it barely makes a dent in my exhaustion, and my sleep-deprived body stumbles through the landing on San Gorgonio Peak. I sorta half sit, half collapse near the edge of the cliff.

I close my eyes, so tempted to curl up and grab even a few minutes of sleep. But it's not worth the risk. Besides, I came here for something much more important.

I reach out my hands, searching for Audra's trace.

I can't really describe the process. It's like some part of me connects to the wind, following an invisible trail through the sky that somehow always leads me to her. And I know it's *her.*

The rush of heat.

The electricity zinging under my skin.

No girl has ever made me feel like that.

It helps that she's the only connection I have to my past and that I've dreamed about her most of my life—and that she's ridiculously hot. But even if she weren't, Audra's *the one*.

Always has been.

Always will be.

I sink into the warmth, leaning back and letting the sparks shock me with tiny zings. It's almost like she's holding on to me across the sky, promising that she's still out there. Still safe.

Still mine.

And maybe I'm crazy, but the feeling seems stronger tonight.

Much stronger.

So intense it makes my heart race and my head spin. And the dizzier I get, the more I can't help but ask the one question I've been trying not to let myself ask since I found her dusty jacket and her hasty goodbye.

Is she finally on her way home?

I try not to get my hopes up in case I'm wrong. But it doesn't *feel* like I'm wrong. It feels like she's so close I could reach out and—

Vane.

The sound makes my heart freeze.

I hold my breath, starting to think I imagined it when she melts out of the shadows.

She stands over me, her dark hair blowing in the wind, her dark eyes boring into mine. I don't dare blink for fear she'll disappear.

She leans closer, giving me a peek down her tiny black tank top—but I'm more interested in her face. Her lips are twisted into an expression I can't read. Half smile, half—

She tackles me.

I know I should say something—do something—as she wraps her arms around me, but I'm still trying to process the fact that she's actually here, nuzzling her head into the nook between my neck and shoulder. Her hair tickles my cheek and her lips graze my jaw. I tilt her chin up, bringing her mouth up to mine.

She stops me before the kiss but stays close enough that I can feel her smile.

She's teasing me.

She knows it too, because she giggles against my cheek.

Giggles?

Since when does Audra giggle?

Before I can ask, she leans in and kisses me. Everything else drops away.

I've been waiting for this moment for weeks, but it's different than I pictured, and not just because she's lying on top of me—though that is a *welcome* addition.

Everything about her feels cold.

Her hands.

Her breath.

I feel myself shiver as her lips trail down my neck, and even when her skin touches mine, the rush between us feels more like pricks of ice.

I pull her closer, trying to warm her up—but why is she so cold?

I want to make sure she's okay, but she kisses me harder—almost desperate—and I lose myself again, until I'm covered in head-to-toe goose bumps.

Since when does Audra kiss first and talk later?

And since when does she climb on top of me like she's here to fulfill all my fantasies.

The last word feels like a slap to the face.

This is a dream.

But why aren't I waking up? Why is she still pulling me against her, running her hands down my back—

No.

It's not her.

As much as I want it to be, there are no sparks, no heat.

With Audra there's *always* heat.

This is a lie.

A trick.

Another evil trap Raiden's using to punish me.

I try to pull my mind free, but Audra fights back, locking her arms around me and kissing me again and again.

"No!" I shout, pushing her away.

She starts crying then. Telling me she loves me. Needs me. Can't face another second without me. Everything I always wanted Audra to say.

"Not like this," I whisper.

I want my strong, stubborn dream girl back, even if she'd attack me with questions—and probably a few wind tricks—long before she'd ever seduce me.

But that girl suddenly feels very far away.

Too far away. Like my consciousness has been dragged under by whatever wind Raiden sent, and no matter how much I beg my mind to wake up from this sick, twisted nightmare, I can't find the way out.

I can't move.

Can't breathe.

Audra crawls back to me, whispering that everything will be okay. She kisses my neck, my chin, my lips.

I want it to be real so badly.

Maybe if I just pretend . . .

A wicked pain rips through my finger and yanks me back to reality.

I peel open my eyes and find a panicked Gus leaning over me, my pinkie smashed between his teeth.

"You bit me?"

He unclenches his jaw and I stare at the jagged line of punctures in my skin.

"I tried everything else. I even punched you in the stomach. Biting was all I had left."

I'm betting there was still a better option than chewing on my hand, but who knows? I can feel the sore spot on my stomach where he must've hit me—and I didn't feel a thing. Raiden had me pretty good that time.

About the Author

SHANNON MESSENGER grew up among the sandstorms and giant bugs of the desert and was not sad at all when her family finally escaped the heat. She's studied art, screenwriting, and television production, but realized her real passion is writing for kids and teens. She is also the author of the middle-grade series Keeper of the Lost Cities, and she lives in Southern California with her wonderful husband and an embarrassing number of cats. Find her online at shannonmessenger.com.